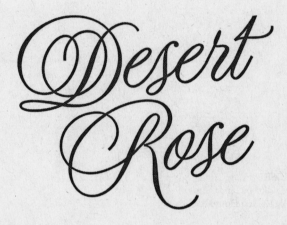

Desert Rose

LINDA CHAIKIN

HARVEST HOUSE™ PUBLISHERS

EUGENE, OREGON

Scripture quotations are taken from the King James Version of the Bible.

Cover by Koechel Peterson & Associates, Inc., Minneapolis, Minnesota

Portions of this book previously published as *Nevada Jade.*

DESERT ROSE
Copyright © 2003 by Linda Chaikin
Published by Harvest House Publishers
Eugene, Oregon 97402
www.harvesthousepublishers.com

Library of Congress Cataloging-in-Publication Data

Chaikin, L. L.
   Desert Rose / Linda Chaikin.
      p. m.
   ISBN 0-7369-1234-7 (pbk.)
   1. Silver mines and mining—Fiction. 2. Fathers and daughters—Fiction.
   3. Women pioneers—Fiction. 4. Nevada—Fiction. I. Title.
   PS3553.H2427D47 2003
   813'.54—dc21

                                                        2002155508

Printed in the United States of America.

03 04 05 06 07 08 09 10 11 / BC-KB / 10 9 8 7 6 5 4 3 2

Linda Chaikin
is an award-winning writer of more
than 20 books, including the popular
A Day to Remember series. Linda and
her husband, Steve, make their
home in California.

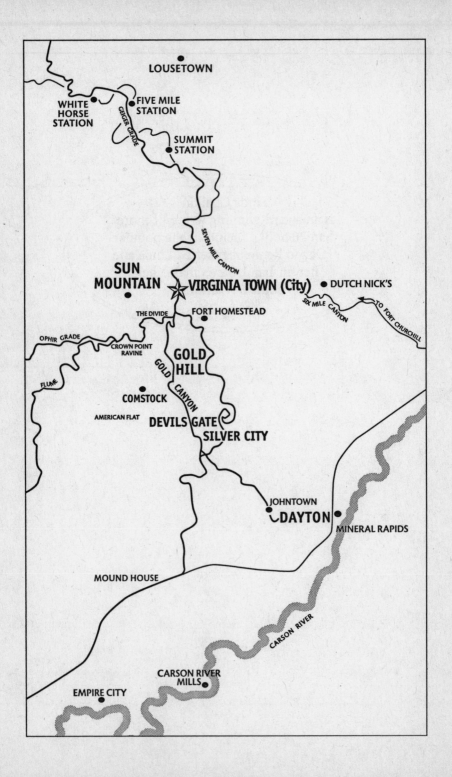

Part One

SACRAMENTO
1858–1859

For thou, O God, hast proved us:
thou hast tried us, as silver is tried.

—PSALM 66:10

One
&

San Francisco, 1858

*A*nnalee hurried down the narrow dark alleyways of San Francisco's notorious Barbary Coast district with the hem of her black cloak floating behind her.

Several times she ducked out of sight between tall wooden shops and narrowly constructed houses near the wharves and warehouses. Although most of the gambling dens, saloons, and theaters were a few streets farther north, even here she could hear boisterous male voices and the shrill foolish laughter of women.

In another hour, with nightfall, the rowdiness would increase. Her mother had spoken about gangs called the "Sydney Ducks" or "Hounds." These merciless ruffians would set fires in order to steal and murder. Large areas of San Francisco had several times before been burned amid looting and loss of life.

A clammy mist clung to her face and throat as though it were drizzling. Odors from barrels of fish destined for the wharf markets satiated the briny air.

Footsteps staggered toward her, echoing on the wooden walkway. Annalee quickly ducked into a small alcove by one of the shops. She hid in the shadows beside steps leading to a door, her breathing loud in her ears. She drew the hood of her damp cloak snuggly around her cheeks, making certain her auburn curls were tucked well out of view.

Annalee knew her mother carried a small .44 derringer in her handbag when she was out alone performing in the theaters, called melodeons. She'd done so since playing the mining camps and "boom towns" of the 1840s and '50s, where gunfights and trouble were usually close at hand. Little had changed in a decade.

7

Law and order had yet to be established in many of the camps of the western Territories.

"A savage land," her mother often said, "without deputy marshals." Miners and businessmen alike often participated in vigilante justice to maintain a level of order.

The footsteps stumbled past her, fading into the fog.

She waited a moment longer before stepping out from the shadows and hurrying on her way.

The fog was thickening with the onset of darkness as she neared the theater where her mother was performing in a melodrama. Piano music rang out from taverns across the street, and someone shot off a pistol.

Vigilant, Annalee kept close to fog-bound buildings. The boisterous voices grew louder. With her heart beating in her throat, she ran alongside the theater toward the entrance. For a horrible moment she heard footsteps chasing her. Whirling, she waited, but the only thing to emerge from the mist was an echo. *Don't be such a coward. If Mother comes here twice a week to play the theater, so can you. It's only right to bring her this good news from Pa!*

"Never take foolish risks, expecting God to deliver you," her mother often warned. "He expects us to be prudent. But when we do find ourselves in danger, we should always call upon Him to rescue us."

It was her mother's custom to gather them all together and pray for their safety before she left the Sacramento farm where they were living with an aunt, Weda. Annalee breathed a prayer of thanks for her safe arrival at the theater.

Inside, the lamps were few and dim. If she was disappointed at its shabbiness, she tried to deny it. She reminded herself that this was not typical of the theaters her mother had performed in during her heyday. The crowds here would shout to one another across the room, even interrupting the actors as they delivered their lines or sang popular songs. Female customers were not permitted in most of these local theaters. But when someone like the rising child star, Lotta Crabtree, came to sing, dance, and mimic, the town firemen, known as the Knickerbocker Hook and Ladder Company, would show up to keep things orderly and respectable.

Would any of the firemen be here tonight when her mother acted in the drama? It was unlikely. It saddened Annalee that her mother had to work in such a place. Her voice and acting ability had once been acclaimed in the Sacramento newspapers. Well, matters would soon change. She smiled, thinking of the letter in her handbag.

At this hour the theater was empty. Annalee stood still for a moment, catching her breath in the cold, silent shadows. The big room reeked of damp wood, stale tobacco, and, of course, liquor. There were always noises in empty buildings, and this one creaked with old timber.

She glanced about. In the dimness she didn't see anyone who might challenge her presence, so she sped down the shadowy aisle to steps that led up to the stage. Her mother, the once-popular Lillian O'Day, would have a room backstage where she could dress and study her lines. It wasn't likely to be much, but Annalee could remember a dressing room with plush red velvet and a chandelier when she was a child. That, however, had been in a theater in one of the gold boom towns around Sacramento.

Annalee climbed the wooden steps onto the stage, but she paused a moment before the musty curtain. She turned slowly and faced the dark rows of empty chairs.

What would it be like to perform here? What if she were singing? Would she have enough poise to step out before a crowd this size and sing her heart and soul?

Her mother had told her, "The Lord has given you an angel's voice, my sweet, but one to be dedicated to the choir at church."

With some effort, Annalee reined in the words that were echoing through her mind and focused her attention on the matter that had brought her to San Francisco.

Her hand shook a little as she removed the envelope from her handbag. She felt the same surge of excitement as when she'd first received the letter from Jack Dawson who was actually Jack Halliday, her father.

The emotional fog they'd been wandering in for months was now lifting at last. Annalee was convinced there was good news in the letter. She smiled down at the envelope. On the back flap her father had humorously sketched a cartoon of an old prospector with a bag of gold slung over his shoulder. It would bring her mother a smile too—and perhaps a great deal of money!

He had struck it rich!

Energized earlier by that expectation, Annalee had rushed into the farmhouse and shown the drawing to her aunt.

"I'd not set too much store on that cartoon, child. Your pa could always draw mighty good. When he was a boy, he wanted to be an artist, but gamblin' and liquor done ruined Jack. He's just showing the flavor of the times in Washoe."

"Maybe, but I'm taking this to Mama anyway. I'm going to San Francisco by stage first thing tomorrow morning."

Weda's forehead had wrinkled. "Do you think you should, child? Are you up to it?"

"I'm well enough now. Don't worry, Aunt Weda. This letter is important. I just know it."

"Well…maybe, but you be mighty careful on the Barbary Coast."

The musty old curtain rubbing against Annalee's arm brought her back to the moment. She imagined the thrill her mother would receive when Annalee produced this long-awaited and much-prayed-for letter. Her pa had been gone for nearly two years.

Jack Halliday was somewhat of a mysterious person to Annalee. He was often away, and when he came home to Sacramento, he had nothing whatever to do with farming. He dressed in black broadcloth and frilled white shirts, and he owned a pair of pistols he kept in well-oiled leather holsters. He wore his guns "tied down," which for some reason caused a few whispers. When Annalee grew older she knew why. Gunslingers tied down their guns for fast and ready use.

The lapses of time between his visits had grown longer the older Annalee became. It was especially hard on her small brother, Jimmy.

Her pa's winsome smile and green eyes won just about everyone to his side, though, and when he did show up at the farmhouse, it was a happy time. He always brought candy, and presents, and a fancy new hat or dress for Lillian. She pretended to be shocked by the gift and asked him where he'd gotten the money to buy such lavish things. And the answer was always the same: He would laugh and say he'd hit "pay dirt."

Annalee had learned that what he really meant was that he'd been lucky at cards.

She believed this because even when he was home he'd go over to the Sacramento River to one of the gambling riverboats and be gone a few days. On one occasion he never came home. She'd heard her uncle tell her aunt that there'd been big trouble and that "Jack had to run."

Behind the theater curtain, Annalee stood in the dimness before a narrow wooden hall that served as a passage to several rooms. At the far end, a door stood half open. Low, urgent voices, one of them belonging to her mother, drifted toward her.

Annalee couldn't say why, but she felt her muscles tensing as she quietly approached. She stopped by the door, peering through the narrow opening between the door and doorjamb.

The room appeared to be a lounge for the entertainers. There was a worn horsehair sofa, a low table, and some chairs.

Lillian O'Day was wearing the one remaining gown she still possessed worthy of the stage. It was a familiar blue taffeta with a princess lace collar and puffed sleeves. The lace was rather limp. Annalee had helped mend the lace just last week after her mother had caught a sleeve on a door frame nail. The crinolines, too, were patched and losing some of their pomp. Even so, it remained a fine dress, and Annalee's younger sister, Callie, had asked to wear it to a church picnic on Saturday.

"You're too young to wear it," Annalee had protested.

"Annalee's right, dear. And it's not the sort of dress to wear to a church picnic."

"I don't know why not," Callie had pouted. "Sally wore a dress off the shoulders to the last barbecue."

"And was brought home early by her grandmother," Annalee had reminded her.

Callie had looked at her crossly. "You're just mean-spirited because you can't wear it."

Memory of the sisterly spat vanished as Annalee watched her mother pace the hardwood floor and shake her head. She looked distraught.

"It can't be true."

Confused, Annalee wondered, *Is she practicing her lines?* Her mother would be playing opposite Harper Browne tonight, an actor who'd also written the play. Her mother had said he was an unknown, but he had talent for creating short melodramas. One day he would work for John Maguire, the power man behind San Francisco theater.

Lillian clasped her hands together, fingers intertwined, and brought them to her chin. "How will I explain this to my children? Oh, tell me it isn't true!"

Annalee was mesmerized. This was the first time she'd actually seen her mother performing. *If Callie could see her now, there'd be no stopping her wish to follow in Mama's footsteps.*

Although Annalee knew "Lillian O'Day" had been a famous stage name a decade ago, it surprised her to see her mother in action. Why, she was a *good* actress. No, she was better than good. Her mother should have been able to perform in New York, not just the theaters of the West's boom towns.

But Annalee's thoughts stumbled when a man came up behind Lillian and spoke gently. One glimpse of the tall broad-shouldered man told her he was not Harper Browne. She had seen Harper in Sacramento when he'd briefly called on her mother about doing the play with him. Harper was a young man with hair redder than her own, a slim man of medium height with a ready smile.

This man was entirely different, yet vaguely familiar…

"I'm sorry, Lillian," came a Louisiana drawl. "I'll do everything I can to help you."

In a flash, Annalee was shaken awake. Why, this man was Macklin Villiers. She'd seen him for the first time in the spring when he'd come by the farmhouse. Her mother had introduced him to her and Callie as their father's cousin from New Orleans.

He was a stalwart man in his thirties with smooth golden ash hair and a carefully trimmed ribbon mustache. A deep cleft in the middle of his chin added to his handsome appearance. Cousin Macklin looked as though he'd come into prosperity recently. He wore a well-tailored chestnut-colored jacket, and his amber-yellow vest was of watered silk. A gold watch chain looped stylishly from his vest pocket and flashed in the light from the lamps.

When Macklin came to the farmhouse, he'd been dressed as a miner in rugged clothing. He'd spent the evening around the supper table filling her little brother's ears with tales about the gold mines. Macklin had gone with their father and Uncle Charlie, their Aunt Weda's husband, to the Fraser River in 1858, when there'd been the huge cry of "gold on the Fraser."

Annalee had heard it said that over eighteen thousand men had sold or abandoned their farms and possessions to make that long, hard trip to British Columbia by sea or by land. Some gold had been found on the sandbars, but for most Californians like her father, cousin, and uncle, there'd been little.

Those forty-niners had straggled back to California broken in health and in spirit to find San Francisco in the throes of a financial depression.

Then new hope revived old broken dreams. A promising new "bonanza" was discovered in the Carson River Valley across the Sierra Mountains down in Nevada at some diggings called Washoe. Her father and all other seekers of gold and silver had answered the siren call once again. All, that is, except Macklin. He'd informed them over supper on that spring night that he was through prospecting. He was going into banking.

Macklin Villiers now stood touching his gold watch chain. "It's natural you'd feel this way, Lilly, but I'm here to tell you it is true. It brings me no pleasure. The law is looking for him now, and if he tried to cross the badlands into Utah, it's likely the Indians got him."

Annalee stood silent, stunned.

"There's some mistake, Macklin. There has to be. Jack had his faults, there's no denying them, but he wouldn't go as far as killing."

Annalee's fingers gripped the envelope containing her father's letter.

"I wish I could tell you otherwise, Lilly, but...there's a witness. A respectable man, a Sacramento lawyer. He swears he saw the whole thing. Jack didn't know he was at the diggings when he shot Frank Harkin in the back."

Annalee nearly gasped aloud.

Her mother walked away to the table, her back toward him, her head lowered.

"I'm sorry," he said again. "I didn't fancy telling you this, but I thought it was better I do it than the law."

"I…I don't want my children to know. If…Jack was killed by Indians, let them think it was for another cause than running from a gunfight."

"Well, they won't learn it from me, but the news is out. Eventually they'll hear about it."

"They'll be older then. More able to handle it. Especially Jimmy."

Annalee's heart was beating like a drum. She stepped back farther into the shadows, aware of sudden weakness.

Her mother was saying, "I can't believe it of him—to shoot a man in the back—" her voice caught on a painful sob.

"It's the way of greed. In this case, for silver. There was a hot argument over who owned the claim. They fought. Harkin won the fight. Jack had had too much liquor. And he'd been gambling. When Harkin mocked him and turned to walk away, Jack picked up his gun and shot him in the back."

Annalee's moan mingled with her mother's.

"No one knows for sure where he is. Until the trouble started, he and Harkin were placer mining near Johntown. Someone saw Jack ride off toward the Forty Mile Desert soon after he killed Harkin. By now he could be in Salt Lake looking for Samuel. Trouble is, Piutes are out that way too. Plenty of 'em. A family coming toward the Humboldt River from Utah in a wagon were butchered this summer by Piutes."

Annalee wanted to run to her mother, to burst into the room and throw her arms around her, but love held her back. It would hurt her mother even more if she knew she'd heard what Macklin had just said.

Annalee's eyes filled with scalding tears. Her shaking fingers latched onto the letter. Whatever good news it had held was now useless, written before Frank Harkin's death.

Macklin's strained voice continued, "I'll be in San Francisco for a few days. I'll do what I can to help you get Jack's financial affairs sorted out. He must have sent you some legal papers."

Her mother was weeping now, unashamedly.

Annalee wept with her in the dimness of the hall. She listened to Macklin's bootsteps walking in her mother's direction. Annalee imagined his solacing hand on her shoulder.

"I'll handle this, Lilly. You don't need to worry about a thing. There's no reason for your son and daughters to know what really happened."

Tears continued to splash down Annalee's cheeks. As she backed away slowly, softly on the wooden planks, Macklin's voice became muffled by the sound of her own heartbeat.

She turned, and in a few more steps was pushing her way back through the curtain onto the stage and then tiptoeing down the stairs into the shadowed theater.

Perhaps her father was dead—would that be for the better?

Fear turned her mouth dry. No. Her pa was not a Christian, and now he'd killed a man. What hope was there for him? The law would have him hanged if he was caught.

Outside the dismal theater, she found the heavy fog settling like a smothering mask. With shaking fingers she pulled the hood of her cloak over her hair as cold wisps of dampness encircled her. The stark, ugly words she had just heard repeated themselves in her mind.

Her pa had shot a man named Harkin—a man working with him on a claim in Washoe—in the back.

Annalee had intended to stay the night in San Francisco with her mother. She had imagined a gala evening after the show; they would celebrate Jack's silver strike. But now the gloom of death and misery wrapped about her like the fog, bringing her down.

Was there even a coach home to Sacramento tonight? Suddenly she realized what a fool she'd been. She rebuked herself for not planning more carefully.

Gilmore School, of course! Callie was attending the girls' school and could take her in—

No, she couldn't do that, either. If Callie saw her now, she'd know something dreadful had happened. And what reason could she give her sister for being in San Francisco without their mother knowing? Callie was not one to take excuses for an answer. She'd force the truth from her some way.

Then I'll just have to get home tonight.

Now feeling weak and fatigued, she paused on the street to catch her breath. There should be a stage. There had to be.

A rig came by, and she stepped out and lifted her hand, hailing it.

She climbed into the back and found her voice weak. "The Overland Stage depot."

As the old horse plodded its way down the bawdy street, she closed her eyes and shivered inside her damp cloak. "Father, strengthen me...please...and my mother. Comfort us and give us both wisdom." The words of Psalm 34:18 came to her mind and brought light into the dark confusion of disappointment and despair. "The LORD is nigh unto them that are of a broken heart; and saveth such as be of a contrite spirit."

Two
※

*A*nnalee's mother arrived home from San Francisco two days later. Macklin Villiers was with her, as was Annalee's sister, Callie. They must have picked her up at Gilmore. Annalee, too, had been attending Gilmore School until her illness.

Annalee had never been strong, but in the last year her health had taken a turn for the worse. For some time she had been suffering from extreme fatigue, weakness, weight loss, night sweats, and a low fever, but now she was coughing. All this so alarmed the school physician, Dr. Harley, that he had called in a second physician to examine her. After getting their heads together, Dr. Harley had come to Annalee with furrowed brows.

"I am afraid I will need to call upon Mrs. Halliday," he said. "You won't be able to stay in school at Gilmore, Miss Annalee. I and my colleague, Dr. Morris, agree that you may have consumption."

The news was devastating. Annalee wept secretly for days before she was able to calm her fears and gather the courage to face her mother and Callie.

As expected, Lillian was extremely upset. "Oh, my poor darling. My poor, poor darling."

"Mama, please don't. I'll be well again soon. You'll see. We'll pray hard, and God will heal me."

Her mother covered her face with her palms and wept unashamedly. All this emotion tore at Annalee's heart far worse than the illness she felt clinging to her like something unclean and hateful. She couldn't control her emotions any longer and wept too. "I'd rather be dead," she cried. "I'd rather be dead, Mama!"

This outburst from Annalee, who was usually the quiet, steady daughter, appeared to shake Lillian to her very soul. She stopped her tears at once and held Annalee in her arms.

"There, there, my baby. It will be all right. You'll see. I'll get you the best physicians in America. Doctors now think warm, dry weather can cure consumption. We'll find such a place. It will take money, but I'll get it somehow. I'll write the governor. Maybe he'll be kind enough to send word to the Fraser River to find your father and your uncle. Until then...I'll go back to the theater."

"Mama, no! Not the melodeons! You said yourself you're too old to play the best theaters. And everyone at church will...will talk. They already look on me and Callie with some suspicion because they say our pa—" she stopped and bit her lip. There was no use in bringing more pain to her mother.

Lillian's face was solemn and determined now. "I'll play the melodeons. I fear nothing. Do you think I don't know what rowdy men are like? And they are not all bad, darling. They may be unmannered, but they respect a real lady when she's around."

"But Mama!" Annalee couldn't continue for the tears running down her cheeks. It was painful to realize she was the cause for her mother acting in the San Francisco melodeons.

Lillian smiled tensely as she took her handkerchief and dried Annalee's cheeks. "We won't talk about it now, love. We'll pray and trust in Jesus."

Annalee tried to convince her that she would be all right with a little rest, that the "problem" would simply go away. She would wake up one sunny morning hearing the meadowlarks, and illness would be a trial of the past.

But though the meadowlarks sang in the fields, Annalee had often been too ill to hear them.

Now, watching her mother arrive with Macklin and Callie, Annalee could see that they hadn't told Callie about Jack, for Callie showed no signs of sadness. Her mother, on the other hand, appeared strained as Macklin helped her down from his carriage and walked her to the front porch. The carriage was elegant, Annalee noted. Macklin's banking business must be doing well.

Annalee had asked her aunt to say nothing to Lillian of the maverick trip Annalee made into San Francisco, though she hadn't explained why. Weda had been curious, but still she promised.

True to her mother's word, when she gathered them all together in the parlor and began telling the latest news about their pa, she mentioned nothing of Harkin's death. She said only that their father had been in Washoe, but had since traveled toward Salt Lake, perhaps to find their Uncle Samuel. There were Indians on the warpath between Nevada and Salt Lake, and there was the possibility that harm could have come to him.

Jimmy ran to her arms at the dreadful news, and she held him tightly.

Callie was pale, but her blue eyes flashed. "Why couldn't Pa just be content to live here on the farm?"

Lillian insisted he was a proud man, too restless to settle down. He was wrong, but he was their father, and they should continue to love and pray for him.

Annalee noticed something the others did not. Her mother continued to speak of him as if he were alive.

Annalee watched her father's cousin with subdued curiosity as he backed up her mother's story.

Macklin troubled Annalee. He was a handsome man, and she didn't like the way he looked at her mother. Lillian, she knew, was a virtuous woman and in love with her husband. She would never be unfaithful, but Annalee felt that Macklin had something on his mind.

"I wouldn't worry too much about those Piutes. Your father knew mighty well how to deal with Indians. There's a strong chance he made it through to Utah."

That was quite different from what he'd told her mother at the theater, but Annalee felt he was modifying the news for Jimmy's sake.

Macklin told Lillian he would be staying in Sacramento for a few weeks, and that he would look into Jack's financial affairs and let her know what she could expect.

"I expect little in the way of money."

At the end of his visit, Lillian walked him to the front door, where he picked up his hat from the table and stood for a moment.

"Did he have stock shares in any mines?"

Her mother's brows lifted. "Well, yes, in the Pelly-Jessup."

"Do you still have them?"

"Yes, somewhere."

"It might be smart to have a lawyer look at them. I've a friend who could help. No charge, of course."

"That's kind of you, Macklin."

He opened the door, stepped out onto the porch, and turned to Lillian.

"In all that travel we did together, Jack never kept much with him in the way of records. I reckon he sent them home to you. They also might be worth letting my lawyer look at."

"If there was anything important, he didn't send it to me. The farm was in Charlie's name, and now it's Weda's, of course. Anyway, the land isn't paid for, and taxes are overdue."

He hesitated, standing in the open doorway, turning his hat brim round and round between his fingers.

"Jack was usually broke, you know that," she said.

"Yes. When you last heard from him, was he in Utah with Samuel?"

"No, it was after Charlie died at the Fraser."

"Ah, yes. Well, Lilly, don't worry, we'll work this out. I'll be in touch with you in a few days." He noticed Annalee standing back near the woodstove. The look he gave her made her blush. Did he think she'd been eavesdropping? But she was nearly twenty-three now! Surely she had a right to hear about her father's affairs.

Macklin put on his hat and tipped it toward Annalee, then Lillian. "Good day, ladies."

When he'd gone down the porch steps to his carriage, waiting under the giant pepper tree, Annalee went to the window and looked after him. The carriage swiftly departed down the dirt road toward town.

Annalee fingered the lace curtain. "I don't trust him."

Lillian turned toward her with a small intake of breath. "Annalee!"

She looked at her mother. "I'm sorry, Mama, but I have never liked him much. He doesn't smile, and his eyes have no warmth."

"That's silly talk. Shame on you. He's your blood cousin, don't forget that. We need every friend we can get, and so far Macklin's showed himself a gentleman and a friend. We'll treat him that way till he proves otherwise. And," she said, turning away to leave the room, "I don't expect that hour to come."

Rebuked, Annalee kept silent and watched her mother walk briskly down the hall. The door to Charlie's old cubbyhole study shut behind her with a sharp click.

Annalee's brows nipped together. She walked quietly to the stove and held her hands out to warm them. If her mother was determined to cooperate with Macklin Villiers, there was little she could do about it. But now that he seemed to have won her mother over, Annalee was more uneasy than ever.

Stocks…important papers…just what was on his mind? Or was she being unfair to him? Her mother knew Macklin far better than she did. Annalee sighed. Then she went to the kitchen where her aunt was baking up biscuits.

Weda glanced up from the big kitchen table. She was a small, frail lady of barely a hundred pounds, with curly white hair and clear gray eyes. She was quite dedicated to her baking, cooking, and sewing.

"There's coffee."

Annalee took down a tin mug from the long pine shelf above the stove and filled it with the hot, black brew.

"Aunt Weda?" she said thoughtfully.

"Hmm?"

Annalee turned from the stove and watched her roll and cut the bed of floured dough in front of her with familiar expertise.

"Did Uncle Charlie send you anything from the Fraser?"

Weda looked up, tilting her head to one side as she studied her. "Now why would you go asking me that?"

Annalee sipped the scalding coffee. She loathed it when it was so hot it could burn the tip of her tongue. She removed the pot from the coals and set it back.

"I'm just wondering."

"There's got to be a reason for wondering."

Annalee set her cup down. "Macklin was asking Mama about shares Pa may have had in mining claims. He was interested in any records too. He said he wants to help us financially."

Weda thought it over while she set the biscuits on a flour sack to rise.

"He thinks Jack might have had mining shares worth something?"

"That's the impression I received. Why else would he be asking her about such a thing?"

"Can't think of no reason, lest he's just nosy. Never did set a big store by Macklin Villiers. Charlie didn't, either. He did, however, send a box of his things home from the Fraser, but there was nothing in it belonging to your pa." Weda stopped rolling dough and gazed a moment out the kitchen window. A reminiscing expression covered her lined brown face. She lifted a hand and pushed back a swath of hair that came undone from the hard knot at the back of her scrawny neck.

"I just thought Pa might have sent something to us. He may have thought it best to use Uncle Charlie's box."

Quick, shrewd eyes fixed on her. "What are you thinking, child? That your pa had something valuable he didn't want Macklin to get hold of?"

Annalee felt her face turn warm at her aunt's directness. "I'm not accusing Cousin Macklin of anything wrong. It was just a thought."

"Don't blame you at all. Macklin has a sorry reputation in Louisiana. When he was younger, he was run out of New Orleans. Charlie said Macklin had himself a riverboat. That young nephew of Macklin's just as bad."

Curious, Annalee looked at her. "Who is that?"

"Rody Villiers. He's a gunslinging gambler. Macklin and Rody both had quick tempers with a gun—like your pa."

"Mama may not know that Macklin wore a gun—"

"She knows. She knows plenty about them old days. If anything, she's convinced he's changed, that's all. Me? I don't think so. A leopard don't change his spots. Macklin's a fancy banker now, so it seems. And doing well with money."

Annalee felt her own suspicions were perhaps going a bit too far and on the verge of becoming ugly. She said quickly, "Oh well, Mama thinks he's trying to help us out financially. After all, Macklin is the only man left in the family except Uncle Samuel, and he's not here." *Oh, that he was.* "Naturally, Macklin would think it gentlemanly to concern himself with two widows and Mama's children."

Weda considered that, but she offered no comment either way. Then, "What happened to your pa's letter? You gave it to Lilly, didn't you?"

Annalee turned to the sink, rinsed her cup, and set it aside. The letter. What had she done with it? She'd been so upset when she hurried out of the theater and ran that she'd all but forgotten it. She remembered the rig she'd hailed to the Overland Stage depot. She must have stuffed it inside her handbag. When she reached home ill, she'd gone straight to the loft to her bed. Weda had come up to help her out of her damp clothing and get settled with warm blankets, a water bottle, and steaming tea with eucalyptus—a horrible brew that was enough to make one feel worse. Ugh... She remembered awakening next morning to find her black cloak hanging up to dry, along with her shoes and stockings. Her handbag was in the loft where she always kept it, undisturbed. The letter must still be in it. Unless—perish the thought—she'd dropped it or left it somewhere along the way in her haste and grief. There were parts of her journey home that she scarcely remembered, she'd felt so bad. Thankfully, no one else had been in that late-evening stage to Sacramento.

Annalee looked at her aunt. "You've not told Mama I went to San Francisco?"

"You asked me not to, didn't you?" she said a little defensively.

Annalee smiled. "I did. Thanks, Auntie. I'd better tell her myself. Pa's letter is likely to make her feel moody, hearing from him after—"

"Now, now, Jack's a canny fellow. If anyone can outsmart them Piutes, it's your pa. He's probably still alive and looking for Samuel."

Escaping the Indians and looking for Samuel in the Salt Lake area wasn't on Annalee's mind when she'd halted her explanation.

She and her mother alone knew the news Macklin had brought about Frank Harkin.

Weda's words of encouragement about her father being alive were, however, appreciated. Weda and Charlie, Jack's eldest brother, had raised Jack and Samuel. Samuel had worked hard on the farm and gone off to seminary training, but Jack, always restless and wild, had left home at the age of sixteen to strike out on his own. Since then he'd been in and out of every sort of scrap.

Even so, Jack had kept in contact with Charlie, and they'd gone together in search of gold on the Fraser River. Charlie had been in debt and was hanging on to the farmland by a thread when Jack had spoken glowingly of gold in British Columbia. Charlie told Weda he was going north with Jack and Macklin, and he left her in charge of the farm.

"I'll talk to Mama soon about Pa's letter," Annalee said, walking from the warm kitchen. "She's not in a very good mood right now. I upset her when I said I didn't trust Macklin."

Weda frowned. "That worries me. She knew him mighty well at Sutter's Mill before she met Jack."

Annalee, too, was uneasy. "Is that a reason to defend him?"

Weda used her rolling pin with renewed energy. "You'll have to ask Lilly about that."

So Weda had also noticed Macklin's interest in her mother. "Mama's never been a woman tricked by flattery. She's mighty careful."

Weda made a throaty sound. "She is. But she upped and married your smooth-talking pa, didn't she? That boy was always a rascal. Lilly's human like the rest of us, girl. When a woman's lonely and in need, a handsome man with strength and money can be mighty tempting. You watch yourself too."

Annalee looked at her aunt, shocked. "Me!"

"I'm thinking that Gordon what's-his-name has been hanging around more lately. You're gaining your looks back, and he's got eyes in his head. But when you was mighty sick, where was his interest in your looks then, eh?"

Annalee stared at her, taken aback. Her words stung, but there was truth in them too.

"Gordon *Barkly* has one thing on his mind right now. He wants to start his own newspaper, and that takes finances. That's all he's thinking about."

"What about that new gal who moved in to Sacramento a year ago? Her family has money."

Annalee kept her features from revealing the turmoil boiling around in her heart. Louise was terribly pretty too.

"I'm sure I'm not worried about it," said Annalee as she turned and walked from the kitchen.

But she was worried. She was worried about a lot of things.

She climbed the short wooden steps to her loft. It was warm up here, and the sunshine poured in through the low window framed with blue plaid curtains. She took her handbag down from its hook on the wall and, holding her breath, reached inside for the envelope.

Yes, it was there! She let out her breath while looking at the letter again. The old miner with the sack of gold slung over his shoulder brought a lump to her throat.

Oh Pa, how could you shoot a man in the back?

The lure of finding gold and silver was powerful! It was the glittering mirage of men and women alike. But had her father and the man named Harkin actually discovered some rich ore and fought over it? Why else would the partnership have ended so tragically?

She stared at the envelope. More than ever she was anxious to know what he'd written to her mother.

Turning suddenly, she climbed down the steps and walked to the little cubbyhole study in the back. She wouldn't wait. It could be important. She would need to face her mother in her unpleasant mood and get it over.

Annalee tapped on the door. "Mama? Can I talk to you?"

There was no answer.

"Mama?"

Still no reply. Was she praying and choosing not to respond?

Annalee reached for the doorknob and hesitated. Then she silently turned it and opened the door a crack to see if her mother was on her knees.

The room was empty. She glanced toward the hook where her mother's cloak usually hung and saw that it was missing. She must have gone for a walk, wishing to be alone.

Annalee sighed and looked down at the envelope again. Straightening her shoulders, she entered the little study and went behind the desk. She sat down in the scarred chair and picked up a pen and a piece of paper.

> *Mother, this letter from Pa arrived a few days ago. I confess I was so happy I took a stage to San Francisco to bring it to you at once. I was at the melodeon the afternoon Cousin Macklin told you about Pa and Frank Harkin. At the time I wanted to keep my presence a secret, but I now apologize. I meant no harm, and hope you will understand and not be disappointed or angry with me. I'll be up in the loft resting should you wish to speak with me.*
>
> *I love you, Mama*
> *Annalee*

A few minutes later she left the room as silently as she'd entered and went up to her bed to rest.

❧ ❧

At supper Lillian made no mention of Annalee's visit to San Francisco. Annalee glanced at her several times from the corner of her eye, but Lillian displayed no unusual behavior. Maybe she hadn't found the note and letter yet.

After supper Annalee slipped into the small study and saw that both items were gone. Then her mother had simply decided not to bring it up. Of course she wouldn't have said anything at the table with Callie, Jimmy, and Weda present.

Annalee turned when she heard the door click shut.

Lillian stood inside the study. She smiled sadly. "Yes, I found them, darling." She went around the desk, drew out the chair, and sat down. "I'm sorry you heard the dark news, but you were wise not to say anything to the others. Macklin could be wrong."

"We can only hope so. How did he hear about it?"

"He's been in Washoe. He's bought into the Pelly-Jessup, a mine next to the claim staked by your father and Mr. Harkin. Your father told me about it in the letter."

"That's why he drew the prospector on the envelope?"

"Yes, but don't make too much of that. I doubt they found anything. And it's better not to mention this to anyone else right now."

"And the witness who saw Pa shoot Harkin?"

Lillian turned her head, her greenish eyes grave. "A respected man. Will Colefax, a lawyer in Sacramento. He's moved to Washoe, thinking he's found a gold mine of clients in the months and years ahead. Disputes and claim jumping are common. I saw it happen in Coloma."

Her mother always called the town that had sprung up around Sutter's Mill by its given name, Coloma.

"I still can't believe Pa would do such a thing," Annalee said, sinking onto a footstool.

Lillian stood and began to move restlessly about the small room.

"Your father was a lot of things: restless, selfish, and irresponsible at times. He also took pride in his skill with his gun. Unless this man Harkin was even more skillful, Jack would have faced him head on. And yet," she paused, lifting a hand to her forehead, "even I can't be certain."

The silence in the study became suffocating.

After a few moments, though, Lillian looked down at Annalee with new determination in her features. "But I intend to find out."

Annalee lifted her head, alarmed. "How, Mama? What do you mean?"

"You heard Macklin yesterday. Your father's no tenderfoot. He knows how to avoid the Indians. If, as Macklin seems to think, he left Washoe and crossed the badlands into Utah, then he would know how to travel to avoid them. He's still alive. I'm sure of it."

Annalee didn't know whether to contest the notion. Was she deceiving herself to ease her pain?

"I'm going to find him. I want the truth about Harkin and the mine."

How could she find him? Was she dreaming?

"Besides, your health changes everything, Annalee. I want the best doctor in the States for you."

Annalee didn't see what her health had to do with finding her pa, even if he was alive. Her mother must have more on her mind than she was willing to explain.

"Besides his own claim, your father has some shares in the Pelly-Jessup. He sent the share certificates to me months ago. Macklin said he knows someone willing to buy them from me for a good price. He's arranging everything."

"Mama, I know you don't want to hear this, and I don't mean to sound disrespectful, but is that wise? It seems to me Macklin's taking over the family." She stood and moved a little closer to Lillian.

Her mother sighed. "You really don't like him, do you? Why not?"

Annalee straightened the items on the old desk. "I don't know."

"His 'cold' eyes?" Lillian wore a rueful smile. "His 'unsmiling' face?"

"You make it sound foolish."

Lillian took her by the shoulders and brushed an auburn curl from the side of Annalee's face. "I've known him longer than I knew your father. He was a friend then, and he's one now. You'll need to get used to him, my sweet. He's going to open a theater in Nevada near the Comstock Lode, and I'm going to work there, not as a performer, but as a partner. We're going into business together. And Macklin's going to help me hire a man to locate your father."

Annalee forced the unpleasant words from her heart, "What if the law finds him first?"

Lillian's mouth tightened. "Then we'll hire the best lawyer around to defend him against false charges."

Annalee saw that her mother's eyes were gleaming with determination.

"You're serious," Annalee spoke softly. "About the theater, finding Pa—about everything."

Lillian's brows lifted. "Absolutely."

Annalee turned slowly away and sank into a chair.

She had never dreamed it would come to this. Her mother and Macklin Villiers, partners in establishing a theater on the Comstock.

"If Callie finds out, she'll want to go with you. She'll want to act on the stage. You know how she feels."

"Callie's going to continue with her schooling at Gilmore. Going into business with Macklin won't change my plans for either of you or Jimmy."

Callie wouldn't see it that way. When she learned their mother owned part of a theater in a boom town, she would be determined to began a theatrical career.

"Then you're going to Nevada?"

"Yes."

She waited, her heart on edge. She wanted to cry out, "Don't go back there, Mama. Pa is dead!" But she had neither the strength nor the wish to hurt her.

Annalee paused. "When?"

"Soon. The melodeons don't pay enough. Besides doctor bills and Callie's schooling, Weda can't possibly pay taxes on the farm. They've gone up since Charlie died."

"If Pa's alive, how will he feel when he learns you've gone into business with Macklin?"

Her mother appeared to be surprised at the question.

"Why, he'll be pleased. There's no trouble between Jack and Macklin that I'm aware of. If there'd been any dislike or jealousy, they'd have parted before the trouble at the Fraser. After all, Cousin Macklin is family."

Annalee hadn't forgotten that Macklin thought her father was dead, even if her mother refused to deal with it.

"But what if he's right about Pa?" she said gently. "What if the Indians did find him?"

Lillian's features stiffened. "Your father is alive. I feel it in my soul. And I'll be there waiting for him when he returns from Utah. I believe he went there looking for Samuel. Perhaps they'll return together." Her eyes softened. "It would be wonderful to see Samuel again. His faith in God has a great stabilizing effect in the lives of those around him."

Unexpected tears filled Annalee's eyes. "I'd love to see him too."

Her mother smiled, encouragingly. "Knowing your uncle, the first thing he'll do is start a church. When he does, I'll be one of his most loyal members." She cupped Annalee's face between her palms. "So stop worrying, darling. You're too young to be carrying burdens meant for your parents' shoulders. All I want of you is for you to get well and strong again." She straightened and walked to the desk. "And when you are, we'll talk seriously about that art school in New York."

Annalee had developed a love for painting, especially sketching and watercolors. She had dreamed of attending an art university in New York before she became ill.

Knowing how her mother looked at things, Annalee gave in to a haunting sense of helplessness. What if Macklin was right about her father? What if he had been killed by Indians when crossing the Utah badlands?

Lillian appeared to take it all calmly enough. She was convinced she was doing the right thing. Perhaps it was the only thing she could do.

Annalee gave in and said nothing more to cast shadows on the path her mother was about to travel.

Three

The news she'd overheard at the melodeon three weeks ago remained a secret between Annalee and her mother. Had Lillian told Macklin that Annalee was aware of the situation? Annalee didn't think so. Macklin hadn't mentioned it to her on any of his frequent visits to the farmhouse during Lillian's preparation for the trip.

Weda tried, but even she couldn't change Lillian's mind about leaving to find Jack. "It's a cryin' shame, that's what it is. A fine lady like Lilly going to the Comstock. I know all about boom towns, mind you, girls. Godless miners, gamblers, hurdy-gurdy houses, that's what."

Callie wrinkled her nose and looked at her aunt.

"Hurdy-gurdy houses? What on earth?"

Weda lifted her brows. "Nothing good, I can tell you that. And your mama traveling alone across the Sierras. It ain't ladylike. Why, there was a stage robbery just this summer. I read about it in the paper. There may have been more since."

Annalee was also worried about her mother's journey across the mountains, but Callie's fair face was pink with excitement, and her blue eyes glowed.

"Now, Aunt Weda, there's not a thing to worry about, you'll see. Mama knows how to take care of herself. You've seen that little derringer she has."

At the mention of the gun, Weda breathed in deeply. "My land! What is this wicked world coming to when a lady needs to carry a gun in her handbag?"

Nothing surprised Annalee now that she'd maneuvered her way through the Barbary Coast and heard Macklin say her father killed a man.

"Mama's sure she's doing the right thing," Callie continued.

Weda waved her hanky as if to repel mettlesome gnats. "By chasing off to Washoe with nothing more than a portmanteau and a promise?"

"There's more to it than that. Why, Cousin Macklin's staking Mama in business. Just think! A theater on the Comstock! It couldn't be better." Callie must have understood the expression on Weda's face, for she added swiftly, "And more importantly, he's promised to help her find Pa." She looked over at Annalee, her blue eyes plainly asking for help to convince their aunt. "Isn't that right, Annalee?"

"Yes, that's what Macklin told Mama."

Callie folded her arms. "You needn't sound so doubtful about it. We should thank God we've someone like Macklin around."

Annalee still believed there was something odd about Macklin Villiers regardless of Callie's swooning over him or her mother's amusement about her description of his eyes. She often caught him looking at her without blinking. He had icy gray eyes, like a deep river without a bottom.

There was a wistfulness in her sister's tone that caused Annalee to look toward her. "I wish I were going with them."

Callie was primping before a small mirror on the pine door. In one hand she held a drawing of a young lady of high fashion she'd clipped from a magazine. With her other hand she pulled a strand of her dark hair from the bun at the back of her neck. She arranged a fancy curl on the side of her temple according to the drawing, then preened, evidently pleased with what she saw.

Callie was certainly pretty and talented enough for the stage. Her dark hair and deep blue eyes attracted plenty of male attention, as did Annalee's auburn hair and green eyes.

Where had she gotten the pattern, seeing that they didn't have even pennies to spend on personal luxuries?

"If the stage is held up, Macklin's got a gun too. I saw it," Callie said.

"Don't surprise me none. I always said there was something not quite right about him," Weda said, lowering her head to jab fiercely at her embroidery.

"That's a strange thing to say, Aunt Weda," said Callie. "You're sure you don't feel that way just because you don't want Mama leaving us?"

"Child, your Uncle Charlie wrote to me from the Fraser River. Said Macklin was mighty fast with that pistol of his. That he'd run from something in Louisiana. Something a might unpleasant."

Annalee glanced at Callie. Her sister frowned. "Then we'd better mention this to Mama."

"I done told her. She said talk's cheap."

Callie looked relieved. "Well, if she's not worried, there's no need for us to be. You know yourself, Aunt Weda, what a big talker Uncle Charlie was. All those hunting tales. And you know he never liked the Villiers family. I heard him tell you so more than once."

Weda rested her hands in her lap and looked off toward the window. "True enough. But he weren't telling stories in his letter. He was sick and a mite worried about us all."

"Well, Macklin's now a respected banker. He's even got friends in the stock market in San Francisco. That settles things for me. The past is dead." Callie smiled at them as though everything was going to be all right and left the room.

Annalee walked over to her aunt, drew up a footstool, and sat down.

"Was the letter you mentioned in the box of things from the Fraser?"

"It was. Nothing else important, though. I looked careful. Just Charlie's personal things. Nothing belonging to your Pa. Nothing Macklin would be interested with. Seems to me he's asking questions about mine shares and important papers being sent to Lilly on account of his plans. He knew he was going to ask her to go with him to the Comstock. To become partners with him."

Annalee had to agree. Perhaps they were being a little unfair with Macklin. "Mama told me Pa owned shares in a mine. She's planning on selling out now to buy into Macklin's theater."

"Them shares must've been the meaning of that cartoon he drawed on the letter."

"Mother's said nothing else about it, so it might be."

The sound of a carriage came from out front. Annalee stood, looking toward the window. "Macklin's here now to take Mama to the stage depot."

Annalee knew change was coming. There was nothing any of them could do to stop it.

⚜ ⚜

Lillian stood on the front porch and promised she would write them just as soon as she was settled.

She kissed Annalee goodbye. "I'll send you money soon. It won't be long. A few months and I'll be back for a visit. Maybe your father will be with me. Then we'll take you to a good doctor in New York."

"We'll all be together soon," Annalee said a little too brightly. With an attempt to show trust and faith, she returned her mother's tense smile. She didn't want to add to Lillian's troubles.

"Oh, Mama, I wish you'd change your mind and let me come with you," Callie cried, hugging her goodbye.

Macklin laughed. "Here's another star on the rise, Lilly. And a very pretty one." He tweaked Callie's dimpled chin, and she smiled up at him with her best theater smile.

Her mother bent down and held Jimmy for a long minute, and Annalee could see they were both crying. Then Lillian glanced Annalee's way. Taking the hint, Annalee came up beside Jimmy and put her arms around his neck, drawing him back against her skirts as their mother turned away.

They stood watching Macklin as he helped Lillian board the carriage that would take them to Sacramento. He climbed in beside her and picked up the horse's reins, then tipped his hat.

"Goodbye, ladies. So long, Jimmy boy. You be a man and take good care of your sisters and aunt. We'll see you soon."

Weda called out, "Take care, Lilly!" as Lillian turned on the seat, smiled, and lifted a gloved hand to wave.

Annalee waved back. She swallowed hard. It was a time to show courage for Jimmy's sake.

After their departure Annalee prayed often that whatever the future held in store for them all, they would be overshadowed by the guiding hand of God.

It had been late October when Lillian and Macklin left Sacramento on the Overland Stage for Placerville, which was the last stop before one attempted the difficult climb over the Sierras and then went down toward the great Carson Valley and the Comstock Lode.

During the cold season, mail was transported over the Sierras by "Snowshoe" Thompson. Thompson, a Norwegian farmer living in Putah Creek, California, had heard that settlers in Carson Valley, and placer miners at Gold Canyon, were without mail and supplies during the winter and would pay well for such a service. In the fall of 1856, he fashioned a pair of skis such as were used in his native land, and he became Santa Claus to the few people on the east side of the range. Until Snowshoe arrived by ski, there was no mail during the deep winter season, and settlers waited eagerly for their first letter in months.

Thirty days later Weda, who had taken to her bed because of a heart condition, received papers threatening foreclosure after the first of the year unless back taxes were paid promptly.

"Ol' Joe Lehi wants my land, that's what," Weda complained. "If he has his way, he'll get it. I'm too tired to keep up the fight. Everything's on his side. It was different when Charlie was here to head him off. Charlie had spunk enough for both of us."

Joe Lehi was becoming one of the largest ranchers in the Sacramento region, and he wanted the pasture and creek Weda was trying to pay off.

Annalee didn't want to believe that power and greed owned the day. Lehi was a political contributor and friend to Tom Davis, who was running for the senate. Lehi was hoping for favors.

Annalee was expecting some of the money Lillian was to receive when she sold the few shares Jack owned in the Pelly-Jessup mine, but would it arrive in time?

One day in December, Macklin's lawyer friend came to call on them. He insisted no funds from a stock sale had arrived.

"You're sure?" Weda prodded.

"Quite certain, Mrs. Halliday." He bit off the end of his cigar and lit it expertly. "There's been a blizzard on the Sierras, closing off the mountain passes to the Comstock. Nothing is getting through, not even Snowshoe."

"Then I need a loan. The bank's foreclosing in January."

"I am afraid you won't be able to get a loan against those shares, Mrs. Halliday. It's said the Pelly-Jessup mine has run its course. Shares are selling for less than a dollar on the stock exchange. The owners are dumping their stocks. I'm afraid the few shares Miss Lillian owns are worth very little now."

"But that can't be!" Annalee cried.

He looked at her over a cloud of smoke. "I'm afraid it's already happened. Happens all the time. Once the rich ore is hauled out, a boom can go bust overnight."

"I don't believe this," Callie stated, hands on hips. "Do you have any proof of this, mister?"

"Callie—" Annalee began.

"Just take a look at the stock market, Miss Callie. Pelly-Jessup shares are down from a hundred dollars to one dollar."

"Then somebody is buying up cheap," Annalee said quietly, watching him.

He shrugged his thick shoulders. "It's a free country, Miss Annalee. If you want me to buy some shares for you at this low price, I'll try and do that."

Annalee sat down. "We haven't money for that." He knew it as well as she. She didn't think he was as sympathetic as he pretended to be.

He puffed his cigar and shook his head sadly.

"Well, there's nothing to be done then, girls," Weda said tiredly. "Looks like lack of news from Lilly and Macklin has allowed Mr. Lehi the opportunity to buy my land."

"Yes, very convenient," Callie said dryly.

"Now, now, miss, it's not a matter of convenience. It's just a routine business matter to sell out when you run into difficult—"

Weda interrupted. "What do you suggest I do, Mr. Wilcox?"

Annalee exchanged glances with Callie. Weda was just giving up. Charlie's death had sapped her of the will to fight on against the winds of change.

"It so happens I've heard from Joe Lehi. Being a gentleman, he's offered to let you stay on until summer. That will give you more time to come up with what you owe."

Weda brightened. She looked over at Annalee and Callie.

"We're sure to hear from Mother before summer," Annalee said encouragingly.

But what then, if the mining shares were nearly worthless? There wouldn't be enough to buy into the theater Macklin wanted to open and accomplish the other plans so bright on Lillian's mind when she'd left.

"I'll raise the money somehow," Weda said.

When Mr. Wilcox left, Callie stormed her frustration. "We're worse off than when we started! What will we do come summer? You need to let me go to work in a melodeon."

Annalee turned on her. "Don't even talk that way, Callie Halliday. Mother wouldn't hear of it!"

"Do you have any better ideas, Miss Know-it-all?"

"Aunt Weda's right. We'll get the money. Somehow."

"Fiddlesticks! Why—"

"You'd never make money enough at a melodeon to pay off the taxes," Weda broke in. "Why do you think Lilly headed for the Comstock? Now, stop your quibbling. Both of you. I've still got the farm animals. I'll sell 'em to Ol' Lehi for a sum. That should see to our wants for another year. By then, Lilly will know what to do." She raised a hand to rub her forehead. "I'm too old to be worryin' about such things. If only dear Charlie were here. Callie, get me some coffee to warm up my bones."

News arrived from the Comstock before summer. It was said Snowshoe made it through to Placerville, but still there was no letter from Lillian. However, a letter of a far different kind arrived at the farmhouse one Monday afternoon, from the authorities at Placerville.

There'd been an accident on the Sierras back in October during a blizzard. The travelers, injured and without medical aid, had run out of food and apparently froze to death before help could arrive. The remains of two passengers had been identified in February. Lillian Halliday, once known as the beautiful stage actress Lillian O'Day, was one of the "unfortunates." There were believed to be two survivors, Macklin Villiers and the driver. Mr. Villiers, a banker in Virginia Town, had gone for help and had arrived in Carson weak and delirious. The driver was still missing.

Annalee was dazed, but her love for Jimmy rallied her to a show of faith and courage.

A second letter followed in May, not from Macklin as they had expected, but from Samuel.

"Uncle Samuel's in Virginia Town," Annalee cried happily. "He's working with the miners and the Indians."

"Uncle Samuel!" Jimmy cried. "Is he coming?"

Annalee read the comforting letter aloud as Callie and Weda gathered around her.

> *Jack—your pa—had a little gold dust set aside. I've seen Macklin. He's opened a bank here. I've happy news. Your pa is alive. Soon as I find out what's going on, I'll contact you.*
>
> *Love,*
> *Uncle Samuel*
>
> *P.S. The law of thy mouth is better unto me than thousands of gold and silver. Psalm 119:72*

Annalee looked at the others, amazed.

"Pa, alive?" Callie breathed.

Jimmy threw his arms around Annalee. "Pa's alive! And he's got gold. Oh, let's go to Virginny Town and find Pa and Uncle Samuel!"

The news swirled around in Annalee's mind. Then her mother had been right. She'd suspected he was alive, and she had been right. Jimmy's cry echoed in her heart. She must go to Virginia Town.

Yes, why not? There was nothing here in Sacramento now. And if Macklin still held her mother's mining shares, and her father had some gold dust, then she could get the money to pay off Weda's taxes and forget about that wily Joe Lehi.

While the others rejoiced over the news, Annalee felt the muscles tighten in her jaw. She had questions to ask Macklin. She wanted the details of her mother's death. And she had plenty of questions about those mining shares. Had they been sold before the price dropped? Did they still own them? If her father were alive, it changed everything. She longed to see Uncle Samuel and discuss her concerns with him.

Samuel's letter had brought hope. They were not alone. The God who held the universe together also cared for the common sparrow, and He would certainly care for His own children.

Annalee wrote Samuel that she would go to Virginia Town. She would attempt to find their father. She also planned to learn all she could from her uncle and take an interest in his missionary work.

Convincing Jimmy and Callie would be easy, so she thought, and Weda might go along with the idea in order to save her land. But her roots were in Sacramento, and she was not likely to leave the farmhouse Charlie had built for her. Her age, too, would cause such a trip to be a drain upon her.

Annalee's own lack of health and strength was a consideration, but she was determined to overcome any obstacle. She believed there was a divine cause behind the inward restlessness that pressed her onward to follow her mother's steps to search for her father.

Annalee wanted also to visit their mother's grave in Carson, where Samuel said she'd been laid to rest. Her mother had been convinced that Jack was alive, and Samuel had pushed the door of hope wide open.

Part Two

VIRGINIA TOWN
1859–1860

Receive my instruction, and not silver;
and knowledge rather than choice gold.

—PROVERBS 8:10

Four
꙳

*A*nnalee, hurry! We'll miss our ride."

It was Callie's voice. Annalee had seen the rig arrive out front to take them to the Overland Stage depot. She called down from her loft, "I'll be there in a minute. Where's Jimmy? Have you seen him?"

"He's searching for his cat. I told him he's got to leave it here. It can catch field mice."

"Going without her will break his heart."

"You don't really want to bring a kitten all the way to Virginia Town?"

"Go hunt Jimmy down, will you?"

"Oh, all right."

A moment later the front door banged shut behind Callie.

Annalee smiled. Callie usually let her feelings show, but she wasn't nearly as rebellious as she pretended to be.

Annalee hurried back to her mother's wooden keepsake box. Inside, Lillian had stored precious letters and mementos from her early years as Lillian O'Day. Annalee couldn't bear to leave it behind. There were other treasures too, letters from Lillian's mother in Louisiana. Annalee's grandmother had been gone for many years. She'd never had a chance to meet her, so she wanted those letters dating from the late 1830s. There were also some small packets of papers and letters from her father written to Lillian during the early years of their marriage. Annalee placed her own letter from Gordon inside, and then, using the key that dangled from the end of a piece of faded blue ribbon, she locked the chest. *Just the way I'm locking up my heart.*

The keepsake box was too precious to carry, so she packed it carefully inside her small trunk. Then she placed the little key in the lace envelope she kept in her Bible.

She put on her green bonnet and tied the ribbon under her chin. She tilted her head for a scrutinizing look. The color matched her eyes. It was the prettiest hat she owned, and it matched her one nice dress, an apple green velvet with black embroidery. She thought sadly of Gordon Barkly. Her relationship with him had ended. The sooner she accepted that fact, the more at peace she would be.

She turned away from the little mirror and looked about the loft for the last time. There, mewing plaintively on her mattress pad, was Jimmy's amber-colored cat.

"How did you get up here? Don't you know Jimmy's searching for you?"

Annalee scooped her up in her arms and stroked her soft fur. "Oh, whatever will become of any of us? And how can I leave you?"

The morning sun streamed through the little triangular window onto the floor. The smell of autumn was in the breeze that drifted up from the yard. She held the kitten to her chest, her emotions about Gordon, and about leaving Sacramento, swirling in her heart. She had already given those conflicting desires to the Lord, but how quickly they raised their heads again to demand their own way. Sometimes it seemed that her heart was a constant battleground.

Gordon...how could he do this to her? Yet she knew the answer. Why mull it over again? She had placed his last letter in the chest to be preserved with the other items because she could not bring herself to leave it. Her mind was picking up certain of his words, remembering again the pain they had brought to her when she'd first read them.

Gordon. It had always been Gordon Barkly from the time she'd first met him at church. They would eventually marry, or so it had seemed. Then came the scandal about Jack Halliday, her mother's death, and the back taxes. Also, there was her unexpected illness.

"Unexpected…" Wasn't serious illness always unexpected? It had sapped her strength, even threatened her life, and the long months she'd spent in bed watching the seasons come and go had been resented. How often she had cried out to the Lord as she watched all her plans slip away, and Gordon with them. *Why, Lord?*

Her health had improved. And Gordon came to call again in person instead of writing. It seemed for a time that things would remain unchanged between them. But over the summer months Annalee had to face the fact that she had somehow lost him to Louise. Her fears proved genuine when his letter arrived three weeks ago. "Louise and I will become engaged in the spring…"

Annalee couldn't sort her feelings out right now. Her life was beginning to resemble one of her aunt's so-called "crazy quilts" that were sewn from scraps of odd materials. Nothing appeared to harmonize. But that's where her trust in the Lord must prevail. Her life might seem confusing, but that was because she couldn't see beyond today. Annalee preferred to pretend that Gordon's rejection didn't have anything to do with his mother. Mrs. Barkly had been shocked by the illness, as though it were a judgment of God for some personal shortcoming. Callie had heard that Mrs. Barkly warned Gordon that someday Annalee could die early and leave him with motherless children, or even pass her illness onto helpless babies.

Gordon had obviously succumbed to family pressures. Or perhaps the fact that Louise's family had wealth and prestige had more to do with it than Annalee's health. There was a rumor that a loan would be given to Gordon to start his own newspaper. In any event, she no longer could look forward to a life with him.

But Someone stronger than herself was holding her up, enabling her to face her losses without self-pity. Suddenly her prospects in faraway Virginia Town bloomed with hope. She would see her father and Samuel again. And the opportunities for painting seemed unbridled. Indians! And there would be miners, silver mines, and mule trains winding up the rugged mountain passes. Like an eagle set free from a cage, Annalee felt anxious to be on her way. Yes, she was certain she was strong and well enough for such a trip. She wanted to go, and she was not a bit afraid of the future.

"Annalee! Annalee!" came a nervous shout from Jimmy below in the driveway. She thought she knew what was troubling him.

She hurried to the open window where the trellis wound around the garden posts. The October sky was a pale, cloudless blue. Leaves on the maple trees were yellow and burnt red.

She poked her head out the window, and the breeze played with her auburn hair.

Jimmy stood shading his eyes, looking up at her window. Dark-haired, small, as serious of face as a young man twice his age, he had seen much sorrow for his eight years, and his heart was sensitive, his eyes a cinnamon brown. Then he saw Keeper, and he brightened.

"There she is! I couldn't find her."

The cat saw the boy, and as though on cue, she sprang from Annalee's arms into the vine and quickly scrambled downward.

His small shoulders went back and his chin lifted with relief. He ran up to the trellis with outstretched arms. "Here, Keeper. Come, girl. It's all right. Come on, Keep, come…"

Annalee placed the small leather Bible Samuel had given her years ago inside her handbag. It would be a long trip to Placerville by stagecoach.

There were so many things she had wanted to take but couldn't—just like having a Christmas wish list with too many presents to buy and not enough money. One thing she was taking was her painting satchel and sketches.

She called down to Jimmy, asking him to let the rig driver know her trunk was ready. A few moments later she climbed down the loft steps, a stuffed satchel in each hand. She smiled at her aunt. The straight-backed little woman was waiting. Her black dress contrasted beautifully with her white hair and sparkling gray eyes.

"Girl, you're positively too pleased with this new adventure."

Annalee laughed. "The most difficult part is leaving you behind, Aunt Weda."

"Horsefeathers," she sniffed. "I'm too old for that sort of thing. Probably bust my leg on the way. Besides," she said with hope in her voice, "you'll come back soon as you find Jack and Samuel."

Annalee bent to kiss her wrinkled cheek. "Indeed I will. We're going to pay off the farm, that's what. Just as soon as I find out from Macklin about those mining shares. And Uncle Samuel says there's a little gold too."

Weda flushed with pleasure, but as usual, pretended she was thick-skinned. "I don't think Samuel should fill your ears with too much talk of silver and gold or your pa being alive. Jimmy's sure of it, an' just as sure Jack has a silver mine. I can't see as how any of this can work out, but, well—" she drew in a breath. "Well, girl, you best be on your way. The rig's waiting."

They walked out the door and stopped on the wooden porch.

"We'll all be together again in a far better country," Annalee told her, thinking of more than a Sacramento reunion.

Weda nodded. They went down the porch steps together and walked to the rig. Jimmy came behind the man carrying Annalee's trunk. The driver tipped his hat and helped load the luggage along with the sacks of Weda's sandwiches and hot coffee they were taking on the stage.

"All aboard, ladies."

Callie embraced her aunt, and for a moment Jimmy clung to her. "I'll be back, Auntie."

"You better," she said, smiling even as she wiped tears from her cheeks.

"Bye, Aunt Weda. You take care now," Callie said. "Remember, we love you."

Annalee gave her a last farewell embrace, and then she allowed the driver to help her step up into the rig.

The driver flicked the reins, and they headed on down the road. They looked back at Weda standing alone in the yard until they went around a corner and the farmhouse was no longer in sight.

For a time they were quiet. Then as the excitement of what lay ahead took hold, Jimmy cried, "We're going to find Pa! Then we're going to dig for silver!"

His little voice rattled on, describing the wonderful adventures that lay before them all.

"I'm going to have my very own horse. I want him to have white spots. Then I'm going to ride with Uncle Samuel to visit the Indians. I'm going to claim me my own silver mine too. What will you do with all your silver, Callie?"

"Oh, lots of things," Callie said, playing along.

"Like what?"

"I'm going to have lots and lots of beautiful frocks and silk stockings."

"Well, I'll put silver on my boots, silver on my belt, and make coins and put holes in them so I can hang 'em around my neck with a leather strap. Maybe I'll make Keeper a silver collar. Then when I ride my spotted horse in the Nevada sun, we'll glitter like a Christmas tree. Maybe I'll call myself 'Silver.' Silver Jim Halliday!"

"Suppose you get robbed?" Annalee teased.

"Then I'll just draw my pistol like this—bang!"

"Jesus won't like that."

He sobered. "It wouldn't do to displease Jesus. Then...guess I'll just pray first. Maybe an angel will come, and I won't have to pull the trigger."

Annalee saw two small amber ears poking out from beneath his jacket where he'd hidden Keeper. She smothered a smile and glanced at Callie. Her sister hadn't noticed. Soon it would be too late to turn the cat loose. Not that Annalee would allow it to happen. She didn't think Callie really would either.

"When we reach Placerville, will Uncle Samuel be there to meet us?" Jimmy asked.

Annalee was deliberately quiet and fussed with her bonnet.

"No, at Strawberry Flat on the Sierras," Callie said. "He promised to meet us there, didn't he, Annalee?"

"He didn't promise. But I'm sure he'll be there."

Callie gave her a sharp look. Annalee looked out toward the Sacramento hills. She didn't dare tell them that Samuel hadn't answered her letter yet. Until now they'd all assumed he had, and that he had wanted them to come to the Comstock. With winter approaching, there'd been no time to wait. There was no choice but to leave Sacramento.

"Straw'bry Flat, that's where all the new prospectors wait to go down the mountain into Nevada," Jimmy told Callie. "Uncle Samuel will bring a mule and a wagon." He looked at Annalee suddenly. "Suppose Uncle Samuel doesn't show up?"

Annalee turned to look at him. Whatever possessed him to say that? The boy looked unexpectedly insecure, and Annalee offered a brave smile.

"Of course he'll come to Strawberry Flat."

Five

The small family traveled without incident from Sacramento to the Placerville depot, which was known as the last chance to load up on everything necessary for the difficult trip ahead. The stage now swayed and pitched its way up the narrow wintry pass on the high Sierra-Nevada mountain range. Their destination was Strawberry Flat, the midway rest stop between Placerville and Virginia Town.

Jimmy and Annalee sat on one side of the coach, and on the other Callie sat next to a bulky older man in a dusty brown jacket that was too tight in the shoulders and across his barrel chest. His deep eyes were brown and sleepy, and the smell of whiskey was on his wheezy breath.

A dapper, well-dressed young man sat on the other side of him. His eyes were quick and cautious. His fingers seemed always to be moving. Annalee, whose artistic mind studied appearances, noticed his restless, slim fingers and well-manicured nails. His untanned skin told her he hadn't been in the western Territories for long. He leaned over to peer out the window, causing his russet jacket to open a little. The movement revealed his gun belt.

His swift gaze indicated he was aware that she watched him, and she looked away, but not before feeling his eyes move over her without deference. There were other young men riding on top of the stage—how many she hadn't counted when they boarded at Placerville. There were no women except the two of them, a fact not lost on the men. They all appeared to be curious, but she and Callie knew not to engage in any long conversations with them.

"A bunch of snakes," Weda had warned before Annalee and Callie left the farmhouse. "Wouldn't trust a one of 'em alone. I could be wishing you had Lilly's derringer about now."

Annalee, who had prayed for safety before they embarked, nevertheless agreed. Here, amid so much danger and with all the folks packing pistols and carrying Winchesters, a man or woman was taking a mighty big chance in depending on mere civility for protection.

Trying to ignore the young man seated opposite her, Annalee focused her attention on the scenery beyond the confines of the stagecoach. On either side of the trail, tall gray-green pine bunched together. Clouds thick as San Francisco Bay fog smothered the high chaparral, fast hedging them in. The fall air grew cooler the higher they climbed. She could feel the chill on the windows, turning the stage into a cold box. Her feet were aching inside her high-button leather shoes. She now wished she'd worn an extra pair of woolen stockings. She tried not to shiver and pulled her hooded cape snugly about her. She made sure Jimmy's cap was down over his ears.

A drizzling rain lasted into the dismal afternoon. The coach groaned and creaked beneath its heavy load, now and then bumping over rough places in the narrow road—if it could be called a road. But far worse than just a dreary downfall was the threat of sleet or snow in the gray-white clouds ahead.

The burly man with the tight jacket broke the silence by commenting on this fact to whoever would listen.

"About this time a year ago we had ourselves a blizzard. Some folks in a stage like this one plum froze to death after it lost a wheel."

Annalee refused the pain she felt in her heart. She wouldn't dwell on what had happened to their mother on this very pass. A glance her sister's way informed her that Callie was remembering. She was staring tensely out the window, her mittened hands clasped on her lap. The younger man with the quick eyes kept glancing her way too. If Callie was aware, she didn't show it.

"Seems someone could have tried to get help from Placerville, instead of Virginia Town. Placerville's so much closer," Annalee found herself saying.

"That's greenhorn thinkin'. Anyone who's been around the Territories knows you stay together and hole up somewhere's till it blows over. *Then* somebody treks into Placerville."

Macklin was no city boy. He'd traveled to many of the mining camps and to the Fraser River. Why then had he struck out for Virginia Town instead?

"There was a stage driver too. What became of him?" asked Annalee. As far as she'd been able to find out from the authorities in Placerville, his body had never been found.

"Don't want to upset you, miss, but wolves probably got him." *But they recovered the other bodies.*

Was it Annalee's nerves, or did the younger man suddenly come alert?

"Where'd this happen?" he asked the burly man.

"Around the American River, not far from Straw'bry Flat."

"The man who went for help. Know his name?"

"Villiers, wasn't it?"

Callie sighed deeply and turned her head. "Yes, Macklin Villiers. He's a cousin of ours. We're on our way to see him in Virginia Town."

Now Annalee was certain about the young man's attention. *Why doesn't Callie keep quiet?*

"My mother was on that stage. She...she died there," Callie continued.

"Well, if that don't take the cake," the burly man said, shaking his head sadly. "Ugly. Mighty ugly."

Annalee caught Callie's eye, but she lifted her chin.

The stage rumbled over the wet road, slowing at times for a puddled dip or when it became steep.

"Miss Lilly was your mother?" asked the younger man.

"Yes. How'd you know her name?"

His lips smiled a little. "Well, isn't this something." He leaned forward and held out his hand. "Meet another of your cousins. Must be a heap of us. The name's Rody. Rody Villiers. Macklin's my uncle. I'm from New Orleans, Louisiana." He pronounced it "Lu-zi-ann."

Annalee and Callie stared at him. Jimmy was looking straight at the pistol that was visible as Rody leaned forward and proffered his hand to each of them. "How do, cousins!"

"What a surprise!" Callie said.

Annalee briefly clasped his cool, damp hand. "I'm Annalee. This is our brother, Jimmy."

"Callie Halliday," said Callie, smiling prettily. "So you're the one Aunt Weda spoke about. She said your mother sent her and Uncle Charlie a letter when you were born."

"Ma and Pa are both dead. Long time ago. I've been on my own for years."

"Following the gold rush?" Callie asked, interested.

He smiled thinly. "No, Cousin Callie. Riverboats. Had a run from Natchez to St. Louis."

"You're mighty young to be a captain of a riverboat," Annalee said.

Rody kept his cool smile, but his eyes, so much like Macklin's, glittered icily.

"I've been workin' at things since I was fourteen, cousin."

Working at things. What kind of things?

Annalee remained silent, aware that his eyes kept straying to her.

"What brings you here?" Callie asked in a friendly voice.

"Uncle Macklin. He has a job for me. Sent me a wire this summer from Sacramento."

"But Macklin's a banker," Annalee said.

He smiled as though he didn't understand the meaning of her words. Obviously if Rody spent his life on the river, he wouldn't know about the inner workings of finances. So why would Macklin send for him?

"Uncle Macklin aims on being the only banker."

Whatever the young man intimidated by this, no one else appeared to catch it except Annalee. Cautious, she lapsed into silence, wondering about him and trying to recall anything Weda might have said about him.

"Can you shoot with that, Cousin Rody?"

Rody looked at Jimmy, who was pointing at his gun belt. Annalee pulled his arm down. "Don't point. It's rude."

A confident grin spread across Rody's thin, triangular face. He wasn't what Annalee would think handsome, but he certainly was attractive.

"Why, kid, I can drill a penny at fifty yards."

"Our pa is good too. I saw him practicing once."

"Jimmy!" Callie scolded, flushing.

"Jack Halliday needs to be mighty slick to come up one quicker than Rody Villiers." He looked at Callie. "Heard he rode to Salt Lake City."

The bulky man watching him seemed to have decided *he* was a bit too slick, for he turned his head to the window, looking uncomfortable.

"They say the Indians got him, but Uncle Samuel thinks not," Callie said.

"Samuel's in Virginny Town?"

"Yes. But we're meeting him at Strawberry Flat."

Annalee thought an unpleasant look showed in his cool eyes. He asked no more questions, and the silence grew as nothing was heard but the creaking stage.

Annalee exchanged glances with Callie. Callie lifted a brow, showing she, too, was curious about what Rody Villiers was up to, and then she turned her head to look out the window.

Rody leaned back and closed his eyes as though going to sleep.

Annalee smiled down at Jimmy, hoping to convince him all was well. She prayed Samuel would be at Strawberry Flat, waiting for their stage to arrive.

There were some things to be thankful for. The news that Samuel was in the Comstock had come to them as an unexpected blessing from God. She wondered if he knew anything about Rody. Rody had seemed uneasy at the prospect of his being in Virginia Town. For that matter, what did Macklin know about him, and why had he offered his nephew work to lure him there?

Lure. Was that a fair word to use? Maybe she was jumping to conclusions. Rody was Macklin's nephew, closer to him by blood than she. Why shouldn't he want his nephew in Virginia Town? Still, she couldn't help but feel that something was wrong about the situation.

She looked below to where the steep embankment met the American River. The stage accident may have happened somewhere near here. The road was steep and narrow at this sharp bend. She could see how a blizzard would add to the danger.

Accidents were not that unusual. There'd been talk in Placerville of other mishaps, but mainly covered wagons overturning. One had slipped off the trail and gone over an embankment. The covered wagon had, by the grace of God, caught in a huge pine, and all the passengers escaped by climbing down the tree. It had not turned out so well for her mother.

The thought of the drop below made Annalee's spine crawl. She listened to the wheels creaking as they struggled through well-worn mud ruts.

"Yee-aay-ee!" The whip cracked above the heads of the horses.

"What's the matter with that driver!"

Callie must have been thinking much the same as Annalee, for she opened the window and poked her head out, her ebony hair unraveling from beneath her hat as she shouted up against the wind.

"Hey, mister! Please slow down! You'll get us all killed."

"Hang on. Ol' Harry will have ya at Berry's 'n time for beef 'n' beans!"

Callie slammed the window closed with a toss of her head. She pushed her hair back in place. "Beef and beans!"

Rody was amused with her and laughed to himself, his eyes taking her in with a spark of interest.

"It's whiskey he wants," Callie said.

The bulky man beside her moved uneasily.

Annalee's long illness had left her with little appetite. Her stomach turned queasy at the thought of such heavy food. She pulled Jimmy back from the window.

"Don't look, Jimmy. It will be all right soon." She was pleased her teeth didn't chatter. Within, she felt tense and worried.

The stage hit a sharp bump, and Annalee bounced on the seat and struggled to keep from landing on Callie's lap.

"Are you sure Uncle Samuel is meeting us?"

Annalee glanced at Rody, but his eyes were closed again, and he didn't appear to be listening. Callie's constant interrogation reminded Annalee of a blue jay that had made its nest by her window in the loft. For the entire summer Annalee had been bedridden, that sparky little jay had quarreled with the other birds, defending its territory. Annalee ignored her question while straightening her skewed bonnet.

Callie lowered her voice. "If he's not there, we'll be in trouble. Is there a stage from Strawberry to Carson?"

Annalee had been too busy while in Placerville to find out. She'd left Jimmy with Callie and gone to see the deputy to gather all the information she could about her mother's death. She'd also stopped at the mail post to see if Samuel had sent a letter that hadn't reached Sacramento yet. By the time she'd returned to the stage depot, the passengers had boarded and were waiting for her.

"I thought you might have checked about a stage from Strawberry," Annalee said defensively.

"You're the one who bought the tickets in Sacramento. Didn't you find out then?"

"Stop worrying. Of course there's a stage from Strawberry."

But Annalee, too, was worried. What if there wasn't? All she could do for the moment was to maintain a confident demeanor.

Her thoughts turned to Weda. Joe Lehi was anxious to tear the farmhouse down and turn the property into pastureland. The one hope to save the farm was in locating Macklin in Virginia Town and obtaining whatever money there was from the sale of the mining shares.

Weda's farm animals had sold for less than they'd hoped. After the bills for groceries, medical expenses, and the stage tickets, there was two hundred dollars left. Weda, generous soul that she was, had kept fifty dollars and entrusted the rest to Annalee to be used in Virginia Town.

"If things go wrong, I want the two of you to start a business of sorts."

Other than the one hundred and fifty dollars in gold pieces Annalee had stored in her satchel, their spending money for food and travel had already dwindled to the coins left in her handbag. Callie also had a little money stuffed in her stocking, but she wouldn't say where she'd gotten it.

"It'll be toward evening by the time we reach Strawberry. You saw them hordes of miners at Placerville? I'll wager Berry's will be packed with them. What are we going to do? Eat and sleep in the same common room with gamblers and gunslingers?"

"Stop it, Callie, you'll frighten Jimmy."

At the mention of being frightened, Jimmy managed a brave smile.

"I'm not scared, Annalee."

She knew he was trying to encourage her.

"Neither is Keeper."

Annalee saw him holding tightly to the bit of tense amber fur hidden under his coat. The cat was obviously frightened. Jimmy kept a rope tied to her collar so she couldn't dart off. Annalee understood what the cat meant to him. The night before she'd overheard him praying words that still tugged at her heart. "Please, Lord Jesus, take care of Keeper. Mama's with you, and Keeper's all I got left to hold tight to. Help me be a man, help us find Uncle Samuel—but especially help us find our pa. Amen."

The stage continued to twist up the forest trail. Then she saw a roughly hewn wood-and-canvas structure with a weather-worn sign carved from pine, swaying in the wind.

Strawberry.

The stage rumbled to a halt at the landing platform, and a few moments later they disembarked. "I'll look for you in Virginny Town," Rody told them as he drifted away.

"Isn't he going inside Berry's Flat?" Jimmy asked, a shade of disappointment in his voice.

Annalee watched Rody walking toward the woods. A second man came riding into view leading another horse. Rody mounted and the two men rode off. She wondered aloud if they were headed toward Carson.

"Doesn't look as if he is. It's just as well."

"Why do you say that?" Callie wanted to know.

Annalee's legs were weak from illness, but she tried to keep that fact hidden as she stood looking about with her hand on Jimmy's shoulder. A blast of bitter wind blew right through her, causing her hair to come undone. Long auburn strands whipped across her face. She pushed them impatiently away with a gloved hand.

"What about Cousin Rody?" Jimmy asked curiously.

She looked down at him. He held Keeper in one arm with the rope dangling, and he wore a grave but determined smile. With the snow clouds on the Sierras as a background and the miners and mules sprawled behind him on sections of yellowing grass, she thought her small brother would have made a perfect subject for a sketch in an Eastern newspaper. Unfortunately, there was no time for sketching.

"I think we should avoid him if we can. I remember now something Aunt Weda said last year. She said Rody had a quick temper with a gun."

❧ ❧

There was a covering of thick white on the higher elevations above forest green.

"Look, snow!" Jimmy said, his eyes glowing with enthusiasm.

"Ooh—that wind." Annalee looked around for shelter. Except for Berry's, there was nothing. The wood structure offered little in the way of cheer, although a hot cup of coffee and a rest was a welcome thought. Berry's also offered grub, a stable with feed for mules and horses, and a common sleeping room.

Callie turned her back toward the wind and drew her arms around her.

"I think that man in Placerville was right. He said we shouldn't come this late in the year."

Annalee scanned the darkened clouds. There was a threat of an early and perhaps severe winter in the stinging wind blowing down the mountain pass. She could feel it coming in the way the freezing autumn leaves crunched and crumbled beneath her shoes.

"Look at all those campfires!"

Annalee followed Jimmy's stare out among the pines to where small fires glowed in the shadows. Certainly the news of the great silver discovery of the Ophir mine had spread like a wildfire. Men were everywhere, riding horses and mules or walking with packs on their backs, all headed for one location—the Comstock Lode. Closer at hand, horses and mules were tied or corralled. Men sat hunched before their fires eating from tin plates. She was amazed to see so many for October. She'd have guessed three hundred, maybe more. Things had changed here since the accident last year. There was no longer the isolation the area had known then.

Ahead, Berry's Flat was packed with men, who were two and three deep at the makeshift counter. They had stopped for the night to eat and camp before traveling on in the morning. Some were awaiting the arrival of mule trains from Carson to take them down over the mountain.

Where is Uncle Samuel?

"This is a nest of fleas if ever I saw one," Callie remarked. "I don't see any ladies, either. And where's Uncle Samuel?"

"We'd hardly recognize him. It's been years since we've last seen him."

"It's not too late to go back to Placerville and wait to hear from him," Callie suggested.

"And spend our money on a hotel room before we even get to the Comstock? We can't afford it." That hundred and fifty dollars must be kept secure.

"What's your vote, Jimmy?" Callie asked.

Jimmy glanced from Callie to Annalee, and then he pulled his hat lower over his eyes. He looked at his black boots and kicked at a stone. "Aw, c'mon, Callie. You'd better get used to miners if you're gonna be an actress."

Annalee smiled at Callie. Maybe she'd quickly change her mind about her theater dreams once she saw what she was up against.

"There's bankers and lawyers in Virginia Town too. Plenty own feet in the Ophir mine."

"Well, it's too late in the day to go back now." Annalee dug into her handbag. "All we can spare is fifty cents to buy supper. Uncle Samuel will have a wagon, so we'll have privacy. And look! Women—over there."

Callie squinted. "They're wearing men's trousers."

"Not all. See that lady?"

"Oh, Annalee! You're so gullible." Callie's tone was scornful and worldly-wise. "Don't you know what she is? Look at her face—she's painted like a firehouse."

"Shh." Annalee glanced at Jimmy, but he was staring toward a man in a buckskin coat and coon cap. The tall man carried a long rifle and strode toward the shack.

"I have to admit her dress is mighty fine, though." Callie sighed her discontentment and ran her mittened hands over her plain cotton skirt. "Mama used to say her aunt wore silk dresses. She has a fine house too. Wouldn't shock me none if it weren't a mansion with cotton growing tall—"

"Mama's Aunt Lorena wouldn't have a thing to do with her after she married Jack Halliday. And with all the talk of war, do you think she'd have anything to do with us now?"

"I suppose not...but I'm not sure if I'm Union or Confederate."

Annalee thought Callie might switch to either side depending on what suited her best at the moment.

"Anyway, Aunt Lorena has never laid eyes on us. You know Aunt Weda sent her a letter about Mama's death. Aunt Lorena wouldn't even send condolences. If there was any hope from that end of the family, we could've turned there by now." Annalee straightened Jimmy's hat, giving him a reassuring smile. "Honestly, Callie, we couldn't simply show up on the front porch of total strangers with our baggage. That wouldn't go over well, would it?"

"And don't forget Keeper," Jimmy hastened, tightening his hold on his cat. "She'll need to be fed at least her supper. Maybe our Mama's aunt wouldn't give her any, even if Keeper's a Reb. Besides, I want to see Uncle Samuel and some Indians."

Callie didn't appear to listen. "Mama said Aunt Lorena's house was grand. And when she was a girl she had her own bedroom. Think what it would be like, Annalee," she crooned. "A whole closet all to yourself, just stuffed with beautiful ball dresses."

Annalee didn't want to think about it. Right now, she had two dresses to her name.

"Mama turned her back on all that when she went against Aunt Lorena's will and became an actress."

"Here it's going to be awful. They say the alkali dust gets in your mouth and ears and seeps through your skin. With you getting sick all the time, and never knowing when you'll need a doctor—"

Annalee turned quickly away, setting her jaw. "I don't want to hear it. I'm not ill. Not anymore. I'll be all right."

"You're not all right," Callie's voice was cranky. "There are smudges beneath your eyes. That always happens before you get really ill. You're wearing yourself out, and I'm worried, and why shouldn't I be?"

Annalee turned to her more kindly. "Don't worry so. I won't let you down."

"Oh, I didn't mean it that way, sis, it's just—" Callie stopped helplessly, frustration in her sigh.

"Never mind. It's all right. I'll make it. We all will. Won't we, Jimmy?"

Jimmy kept his head down and ran his small fingers through Keeper's silky fur. "Keeper's heart's pounding." With his other hand he checked the rope tied to his belt. "Got to be sure it doesn't come loose. If she darts off into the pine trees, I won't be able to find her. Some bear might get her."

Annalee knew that Jimmy was loyal to her. Of his two sisters, she was his favorite at the moment because she understood his childish fears. She was also compassionate about his cat, whereas Callie had been practical about the difficulty in bringing her.

"Keeper likes you too much to run off," she soothed gently. "Just don't let her get spooked, and she'll be all right."

"Keeper's sleeping under my coat tonight. I won't let her get spooked none." He sighed and looked up at his sister. "It was awful for you to have to spend all them months in bed, Annalee. What would I do all that time? Even Keeper would get bored and go out the window. I think Annalee's brave to come to Washoe, don't you think so, Callie?" His voice pleaded, as though he wanted them to get along. Annalee was aware that bickering made him feel insecure.

Callie's blue eyes scanned Annalee worriedly. "Oh, sure she is. But you heard Dr. Kelsey, Annalee. Before we left he made it clear that the sickness can come back anytime. We've got to be careful. Plenty careful."

"That man with the beard is looking at us," Annalee whispered.

Could he be Uncle Samuel?

"They all have beards—and guns," Callie warned.

Annalee had never seen a more rugged looking group of men, ranging in age from youths to those with gray mustaches. After seeing gentlemen from the civilized business districts of Sacramento, the sight prompted her to stare. Some were seasoned placer miners from the California gold rush of '49. Others appeared to be pilgrims who expected to strike it rich by easy diggings in Washoe. Still others spoke with the accents of England and Ireland. They all looked similar. Their hair dusted their collars, and their rugged faces were bronzed from the sun.

They wore every conceivable style hat she could imagine, from Tennessee coonskin caps to sombreros, evidence that men in search of financial success came from all parts of the country as well as abroad.

Even as Callie had noticed, each man appeared to own a number of weapons: a rifle, a pistol, or both, and likely a knife somewhere too. Nevada was part of Utah Territory, and there was little law governing the Comstock Lode except what the miners had decided upon. The lure of easy riches and the ability to enforce a man's own pioneer justice had awakened the appetite of more than the honest, hardworking miner; it also lured the unscrupulous and the dangerous.

The prospector who'd left his farm or his job to cultivate dreams of striking a silver bonanza knew he must be ready at any moment to defend his life, should he hit "pay dirt," for no one else would do it for him.

Suddenly Annalee felt isolated and a bit foolish in her apple green velvet dress and bonnet.

"If Pa is alive," Callie whispered, with a cautious eye toward Jimmy, "do you think he'll want us here? I have my doubts."

Jimmy lowered his head as though he hadn't heard and fussed with Keeper. Annalee nudged Callie's foot with the toe of her shoe.

It wasn't likely their father would want them in the Comstock. Macklin had suggested that he was a drinker, a gambler, even a gunfighter, but Annalee refused to believe the worst. But she could take comfort that Samuel was there. If the Lord had sent him to Virginia Town to preach, then why wouldn't it be right for her to come and help him? And Jimmy desperately needed a good man to look up to.

"I'm sure there will be ways we can help Uncle Samuel and earn our bread and butter."

"If Pa's alive, I'll bet he struck silver," Jimmy said.

"We won't count on it," Callie said. "We'll have to work, both me and Annalee. At a theater, like 'Lillian O'Day.' I may even take the name. 'Callie O'Day.' Sounds about right, don't you think?"

Annalee refused to be drawn into an argument now. Her lungs were beginning to feel familiar twinges of discomfort. The cold wind bit into her flesh.

She became aware of Jimmy's hand clutching her arm. She was now all the mother he had. She could no longer be a little girl who sought comfort; she needed to be a source of strength and courage.

She brought Jimmy against her in a hug. "It's going to be all right. I'm not going to get sick again."

And to herself Annalee thought, *I won't be a burden in Virginia Town. Somehow, with God's help, I'll make it. I must.*

She teased lightly, "The reason Callie wants to act at the theater is so she can find a rich husband who owns a silver mine."

Jimmy smiled, and so did Callie, ruefully.

"Make fun if you want. I just may do that. But he doesn't need to own a mine. A lawyer or a banker will do very nicely, thank you."

Annalee again glanced around her as they stood undecided on the wooden platform. While she disliked admitting it, Callie could be right. If Samuel hadn't yet received her letter, he wouldn't be expecting them, and he wouldn't be here to meet the stage. He might even be off among the Indians somewhere.

Then again, she had better go look for him. He might be inside preaching and had simply overlooked the arrival of the stage. Whatever would she do stranded here in Strawberry with Callie, Jimmy, and the cat?

Well, she couldn't just stand here till nightfall, expecting things to happen. As much as she disliked taking to the tavern for help, it must be done. Maybe she could locate the proprietor named Berry and ask about Samuel. Perhaps he'd sent a message.

Annalee stared down her first obstacle.

Don't panic like a frightened goose, Annalee, she told herself. *You knew what you were getting yourself into when you came here. Now it's up to you.*

She touched the stylish bonnet that set off her green eyes. No more beds for Annalee Halliday. No more being a burden. She would be a blessing. She would serve others! She would make it. She would not be weak, but strong. Gordon had been wrong...she was *just* as capable as Louise.

She reached into her carrying bag. "Here, divide this between you."

She handed them the last gingerbread cake and a small jug of milk that had grown a little sour since leaving Placerville. The peace offering was enough to humor Jimmy, but not Callie.

"Now what?" Callie demanded.

"I'm going inside to see if Uncle Samuel sent a message. He may even be there now."

"I'd better go with you."

Annalee ignored Callie's concerned frown. "Please stay with Jimmy. Besides, all those men in there can't be thieves and fools."

"Don't say I didn't tell you so when some old goat makes a remark."

"I can take care of myself." With that Annalee gathered her velvet skirt and eased her way down the platform steps in the direction of Berry's, cautiously avoiding the crowd of men.

The commotion grew louder as she neared the structure. Within she heard the plucking of a banjo and many voices rising and falling. The place was packed to the door.

Near the freight platform she saw heavily loaded mule trains. Precious commodities of flour, coffee, side bacon, beans, and blankets would be hauled over the Sierras before the winter snows closed the pass and isolated the mining camps until spring.

Boisterous men were hollering back and forth, as they worked, but all Annalee could make out were the words "silver," "blue stuff," "veins," and "rich ore."

Her eyes fell on sweating men hoisting crates and barrels. Others were leading mules and horses. A few of the men turned to gape, as if seeing a blossom in the broiling sun. Some went so far as to tip their hats.

"Evening, miss."

"You watch them chug holes, miss."

From the women she felt only resentment. It was her fine dress, of course, and her fair appearance. Most of these women had given up the feminine things so prized by ladies in order to be with their husbands in the California mining camps—if they were married. Life in harsh elements was hard to cope with. They lived with few comforts in shanties or wickiups.

Her eyes drifted to a mule-drawn wagon that was close by. A young woman sat on the buckboard, holding the reins. There was a hard, unpleasant expression on her tawny brown face, and her mouth was firm and unsmiling. Her heavy dark hair fell across her straight shoulders in two pigtails, and she wore blue Indian beads across her forehead.

Was she full Indian? She looked as though one of her parents might have been European. A rifle lay across her knees. Silently, the girl picked the weapon up and caressed it. Her midnight eyes shot arrows at Annalee as instant dislike caused them to become as cold as ice.

Annalee was startled by this open resentment, and she could almost feel the woman's sullen stare fix like hungry flies on her pretty dress. "You won't last a winter in Washoe," the woman seemed to warn.

Annalee turned her head away, unaccustomed to such hostility.

The sign that hung out over the yard on timber aged by the seasons read: Berry's Flat.

Dare she venture inside? If she was to find help, she must.

Six

A bitter wind shook the stained canvas siding of Berry's tavern. A striking young man wearing a black winter duster and a black flat-crowned hat entered and glanced about. Beneath his coat his thick leather belt housed a stash of bullets and two ivory-handled guns.

At a makeshift counter stretching across some old beer barrels, men crowded shoulder to shoulder eating from tin plates and talking Comstock silver, State's rights, and secession from the Union.

Three men stood off to themselves in a corner, watchful and silent. The younger man's wavy brown hair just touched the faded Mexican poncho covering his shoulders. His eyes held no more warmth than a bottomless pit as they measured the man who'd come through the door and stood scanning the crowd.

"Him in the black duster. Seen him around before, Hoadly?"

Hoadly's long bony face looked as if its skin were pulled back, tightened, and then left to dry like leather in the desert sun. He looked up from his shot of whiskey, his wiry movements giving the impression of a man of nervous energy, as though he were walking a precipice. When he saw the man in black, his eyes shrunk away. He quickly tossed down his drink.

"Stay away from him, Delance. He's poison. We want no messin' with him, not yet."

The younger man named Delance, from Apache country in Arizona, stared at the man by the door. He noticed his pistols were tied down, his gun belt well oiled.

"Yeah? Who is he?"

"Brett Wilder. Got a chip on his shoulder a mile wide. Like to hang us all and stand 'round and watch."

"Who does he work for?"

Hoadly sloshed himself another drink, leaving the third man to reply.

"Hisself," the big man named Roc answered. Roc spoke with a hoarse whisper. A few years back in the boxing arena, his wind pipe had been injured. His bulldog jaw tightened, the muscles working. "Wilder's a lawman."

Delance's gaze sharpened on Roc, whose barrel chest and bulging shoulders identified him as a brute few would tangle with. He'd been teamed up with Hoadly for the last four years. Delance didn't like Roc. Didn't trust him to keep a cool head. He was easily riled. Like a bull seeing red, he'd charge too fast. If anybody could mess up the job they'd come to do in Virginia Town, it would be Roc.

"Wilder's got no authority here," Hoadly said. "He can bluff, is all. But it takes iron nerves to put up with his bluffin'."

"I'm itching to put a bullet in his belly or crack his skull," Roc said. His hand doubled into a huge fist and gently smacked his other palm. His mouth widened to a grin.

Delance looked at him. "You sure got your venom riled. What's he got on you?"

"Said I killed a man in the ring on purpose." He gestured his bald head toward Hoadly. "Blames him for a shootin' he didn't do. Took place years ago when Wilder were nuthin' but his pa's cub."

"Shut up, Roc. You talk too much," Hoadly said.

Delance raised his beer and watched Hoadly throw down another swig of hard stuff. "Take it short if you want to make it over the mountain tonight."

"Don't worry yourself. There's not a miner 'round here who knows this territory better'n me except Ol' Snowshoe."

"If Wilder came from Utah, he'll have all the jurisdiction he needs. You'd better tell me who wants to hire me. I'm not keen on killing a lawman," Delance said. He was liking this job less and less. He usually worked alone.

Hoadly filled his glass with more whiskey. He shook his head. "You'll meet the chief when he decides. He calls the shots. Wilder makes me nervous, is all. Too calm." He looked at Delance. "Come to think of it, you and Wilder both is too calm."

Delance glanced back at Brett Wilder. "Mighty young to be a lawman. You sure about him?"

"Couldn't be more sure. He proved himself as a bounty hunter before he took the badge. I told you, didn't I? That he'd enjoy seein' us hang?"

Delance stroked his chin. Wilder, for all his fancy duds, suggested a hard man.

"Anyhow, Wilder didn't come from Utah. He's from Frisco."

"What if Downey's sworn him in? I hear the governor of California does what he pleases. I don't like this, Hoadly. I didn't figure on courtin' a hanging when I agreed to hear what your boss has to say. This job had better be worth a bundle."

"It's worth a bundle, all right. And no lawman's comin' in to lay a trap. So take it easy."

"I say I take him now," Roc breathed.

"Don't be a fool," Hoadly said. "You can't outdraw Wilder."

Roc leered. "I weren't thinkin' of usin' a gun."

"You're not thinking at all. You heard the orders. No trouble. Not yet. You can't rile him. He won't bluff. He talks calm. Saw him take Clint in Sacramento."

Delance pursed his lips. "Fast, huh?"

"As cool as you please. Unsettles a man, when he acts that way."

Delance's eyes flickered. "All this chatter is making me curious. I've a reputation to defend. Him taking Clint raises the stakes. Clint was a friend of mine."

~ ❧ ~

Brett Wilder stood near the door inside Berry's tavern. His gaze scanned the faces of the crowd, missing little. He really didn't think his quarry would be here in the open. Jack Halliday, whatever else he was, was no fool. He'd worn a beard when Brett last trailed him through Sacramento into Nevada.

It only took a moment for Brett to become aware of the three men in the corner. He recognized Hoadly and Roc from the trouble in Sacramento. Hoadly was a cheap gunfighter, and Roc was a brute, a sadistic killer with his fists. The younger, good-looking man wearing a poncho was Rick Delance, one of the fastest guns around Tucson and Yuma. That he was here, and apparently with Hoadly, didn't make things any easier. Not if the three of them had ridden in to join up with Jack Halliday. But not even Halliday could stomach a man like Roc. Had someone else hired them?

As Brett looked at Hoadly, the tall wiry man turned his back and stared at his whiskey.

Brett's gaze then met Rick Delance's over the men seated by the barrels. Delance took that moment to lean one elbow back against the counter so his gun belt showed. His meaning was clear.

Brett looked back evenly. From what he'd heard about him, Delance played it fair. But Brett wouldn't play any game now. It was Hoadly he wanted. Roc the boxer was just evil and one day would come to his natural end.

The lawman let his attention circle the room again. It was as hot inside as it was cold outside. Berry kept a strong fire blazing with logs five feet long stretching across the andirons. Men stood as far from it as they could.

"Hey, Strawberry—you tryin' to roast us alive?" a man joked.

"That's to keep you guys from standin' so close to the fire that you block the heat," Berry snapped good-naturedly.

Brett smiled to himself. He knew Berry disliked the recent crowds converging on his tavern and wanted them to keep moving on. Many had caused trouble. Berry looked over, saw Brett by the door, and gestured a greeting. Going behind the counter, he tossed Brett a tin mug. Brett walked up, ignoring the three men at the other end.

"Say, Wilder, what brings you this way? Gonna get yourself a claim on the Comstock?"

Brett held out the tin cup. "I've a mind to try. Don't know how long I'll be staying, though. Right now I'll settle for some of that coffee."

Berry filled the cup with the steaming brew.

"How's things?"

Berry shook his head wearily. "Busiest crowd I've ever done come up against. Been this way since summer." He shook his head again. "Every last one of 'em thinks he'll hit a bonanza. Most won't stay more'n a month or two before they drift off to another camp. Can't tell 'em that, though. Dreams are sky high."

"You can't blame them. Berry, you make the best coffee on the Sierras."

Berry chuckled. "Comin' from a San Franciscan, I'm right pleased." Berry glanced about at the throng. "Looking for someone, I 'spect."

"Ever heard of Jack Halliday?"

Berry paused with a scowl, blackened coffeepot in hand, and rubbed his beard. "There's a cantankerous parson workin' among the placer miners in Virginny Town. Name's Halliday, Samuel Halliday. Never heard of Jack."

"Anyone passing through recently mention Halliday?"

"I must've fed a good ten thousand since the news of silver this June. Names come in one ear and out the other. Some real sidewinders come through here." He lowered his voice. "There's a few fellers over there now. The hombre in the poncho is Rick Delance. Other fella is called Hoadly, and the big grizzly is Roc the Jawbuster. Hoadly's been setting up fights for him in the mining camps. You best watch that young'un, Delance. He's been sizing you up ever since you stepped in."

"I noticed."

Did Rick Delance know who he was? Hoadly recognized him, of course. So did Roc. They'd had a run-in at Sacramento awhile back. They would have told Delance.

"Heard of their plans?"

"Talk's cheap, but for what it's worth, Hoadly was approached in Virginny Town after he set up one of Roc's boxing matches. Someone hired Hoadly for a job."

"Any idea what it's about?"

"Not a word. Rick Delance showed up here first. He came in on a horse from Placerville yesterday. Kept to himself, a real loner, that one. Didn't bother nobody. Then Hoadly and Roc and another fella come in this mornin' from Virginny. Hoadly's been hashin' things over with Delance for hours, waiting for the stage. Looked nervous to see you come walking in."

"You said three men rode in from Virginia Town to meet Rick Delance. Where's the other one?"

"He was waiting in the trees in the camp area last time I seen him. I been busy and lost sight of him."

"You say they waited for the stage?"

"They asked when it was due."

Brett drank his coffee and turned, looking across at Hoadly. Delance pushed his mug aside. He dropped some coins on the counter and straightened, turning as if to leave.

Brett had walked over. "Heard you're working the Comstock now, Hoadly."

Delance paused. Though Brett was looking into Hoadly's unfriendly eyes, his senses were attuned to any movement from Delance's hand. But Delance folded his arms. There was something of a smile on his face, as though Brett's little visit to Hoadly amused him.

Hoadly scowled down at his cigar. Slowly, careful not to move his hands quickly, he picked up a nearby candle and lit the end.

"Your badge don't give you any authority here. Virginny Town's wide open."

"You're right about Virginia Town. I hear the law is left to vigilantes. One warning, and then a rope. Impatient, aren't they? But you're an honest man, right, Hoadly? You don't need to worry about being hanged."

"Hanged—"

"A brave, upstanding citizen such as yourself would never shoot a man in the back. Would you, Hoadly?"

The tense silence held between them. Out of the corner of his eye Brett saw Rick Delance standing perfectly still, arms still folded.

"What are you getting at, Wilder?" Hoadly demanded.

"Not an unarmed man, anyway, right?"

Hoadly licked his lips. "No—of course I wouldn't. What are you trying to say?"

"Suppose I say you're lying."

Hoadly froze.

Delance's cool dark eyes measured Brett.

Roc stepped from the barrel counter. "Sounds like a threat. Don't you think it sounds like a threat, Hoadly? It's a threat. Say it's a threat!"

Hoadly fingered his empty whiskey glass. He remained silent.

"Hoadly doesn't think so," Brett said smoothly. "Do you, Hoadly?"

Hoadly threw his stubby cigar onto the floor. "This don't concern you, Roc. I'll meet you in the stable. Get our horses ready to ride."

Roc started to say something, but Brett smiled.

"Better listen to him, Roc. Hoadly's right. One of these days your temper's going to get you into more trouble than even your fists can handle. Maybe you should have stayed in Salt Lake."

Roc's mouth twitched. He stood with his big shoulders slightly hunched forward, his breathing coming hard. He looked like a bull ready to charge.

"You heard me, Roc," Hoadly gritted.

Roc's fists slowly released, his thick arms hanging at his sides. He swallowed hard, looking as if he tasted gall, and then he turned and strode across the room to the door.

"One of these days you'll push Roc too hard," Hoadly warned. "Even I won't be able to rein him in. He'll kill you with those iron fists."

"Where's Jack Halliday?" was all Brett's response.

Hoadly looked across to Delance. "You heard of Jack Halliday?"

"Never heard of him."

Hoadly shrugged. "Sorry we can't oblige you none, Lawman. We ain't never heard of him."

Brett knew he was lying. He wasn't as sure about Delance.

Suddenly Hoadly cracked a smile. He looked at Delance. "The lawman here thinks we're out for trouble. You know anything about trouble in Virginny Town, Delance?"

Delance watched Brett.

"We're miners, Wilder," Hoadly said. "Out to stake us a good claim on the Comstock Lode. That's all."

"It was an ugly night on the Sacramento River. Remember, Hoadly? You were on that riverboat five years ago."

Hoadly shot him a startled look. His eyes narrowed thoughtfully. "I got no cause to remember. No cause at all."

"I'm sure you remember. Just think about it. The *Golden Queen*, it was called."

Delance glanced from Brett to Hoadly. A curious glint showed in his eyes.

"An innocent man was shot that night. Shot deliberately." Brett leaned his elbow on the counter. "Sure you haven't seen Jack Halliday?"

"I said I ain't seen him. You aiming to push me into a fight? Is that it? Just keep it up, Lawman, and even me an' my good temper is likely to snap."

"If I were you, Hoadly, I'd pack up your two-man circus with Roc the bull and ride back to Tucson. Virginia Town's going to get a little crowded. Me? I don't like crowds."

Rick Delance's eyes narrowed. He looked at Hoadly. "Something going on I don't know about?"

"No, nothin'," Hoadly snapped. "This don't concern you none."

"Because I don't like to be surprised," Delance warned softly. "Surprises make me jumpy."

"I tell you he's just ranting. Hinting 'bout things I had nothin' to do with. He's got no proof. If he had any, he'd have arrested me by now. He's trying to spook me into drawing. He wants to kill me, using a badge to hide behind so he won't hang. He's been trackin' me for years." He wiped beads of sweat from his forehead with the back of an arm. "He's crazy I tell you, plain outta his mind." He sloshed himself another drink and emptied the glass.

Rick Delance took a step back from the counter. "I've never been in Sacramento, Wilder, not even in the gold rush. I'm from Tombstone Territory. I don't know what's eating you, but if you think you're going to lay this riverboat business on me—"

Brett turned to him for the first time. He'd heard things about Rick Delance that set him apart from a gunfighter like Hoadly.

Brett had heard Delance came from an honorable family, with roots back in Texas. Brett had no idea what had altered his life and caused him to pick up a gun, but he had no row with Delance. He wanted to keep it that way. Brett had enough enemies flowing into Virginia Town.

Hoadly was a different man. He'd been slithering on his belly in the dust all his life. He wasn't likely to change now, especially if someone behind the scenes was paying him. Did Delance know this? He'd implied he didn't. Was it just a cover?

"You're a long way from Tombstone, Rick."

"It's a free country."

"My business with the likes of Hoadly isn't your concern. I'd like to keep it that way. If Hoadly hired you for business in Virginia Town, you'd be wise to step out of it now. Ride back down the mountain to Placerville."

"I don't work for Hoadly," Rick said flatly. "I work for myself."

"I've had enough of this lousy tavern, and your tongue, Wilder. I'm leavin'," Hoadly said. "I'll meet you in the stable, Delance."

Hoadly brushed past Brett. Delance hesitated and then started to follow.

"Wait a minute, Rick."

The young man turned slowly as though he expected to see a gun aimed at him. Brett kept his hands away from his belt to ease the tension. Rick was fast and deadly. Just how fast, Brett didn't know, but he was sure of one thing. If it happened between them, it would be decided by a fraction of a second. He had the feeling Rick understood this as well. He, too, was a careful man.

"I can tell you what Hoadly's keeping from you."

Rick's dark eyes flashed. "I'm listening."

"Jack Halliday is expected to ride in soon from Utah."

"I told you, never heard of him."

"You will before this is over. I'm looking into his and Harkin's claim in Gold Canyon."

That got his attention. His head lifted. "Frank Harkin?"

"I heard you were a friend of Frank's. He was shot. In the back."

Rick's mouth tightened. "Halliday?"

"There's a witness. A man named Colefax. He's a lawyer in Virginia Town. Frank Harkin has a younger brother named Dylan."

"I know Dylan. Met him in Tombstone."

"He's not going to take Frank getting shot in the back kindly. He'll be riding in if I know him."

Rick Delance gave him a measuring glance.

"It's going to get messy," Rick murmured. "That's what you meant about Virginia Town getting too crowded."

"Dylan's just the beginning. Winter's coming. Snow will close down the pass soon. That will slow things up from this direction. But a man can still cross from Salt Lake.

"Come spring, though, there's likely to be ten thousand going to Virginia Town from Placerville. Many of them will be the regulars who follow every mining boom from here to Colorado. Most don't cause serious trouble. But like flies, the cry of silver will lure the worst."

Rick smiled. "That's fine preaching, Wilder, but what's that got to do with me?"

"I've an idea Hoadly's hiring guns. Plenty of them. Not for himself, but for someone else who hired him and offered good pay. Someone who wants to stay in the shadows. I could think it's Halliday, but there's something about that idea that worries me. For one thing, if he killed Frank Harkin, he'd be a fool to come back now and face Dylan, and he knows it. If Halliday's riding in, it's because something else has drawn him back here from his safe place in Utah. It could be the claim he shared with Frank Harkin. Maybe not. Seems a shame you'd join up with the likes of Hoadly to buck Dylan Harkin."

Delance considered, but he remained silent.

"There was another killing some years back in the Sacramento gold fields. Took place near Sutter's Mill. Halliday was there then too. So was Hoadly. An old miner was shot for his claim. Again, in the back. There was a witness, but he disappeared."

"I've never shot a man who didn't draw on me first."

"Others aren't as thoughtful. Frank may have struck something big. Dylan's going to want his brother's claim."

"You'll need more than hunches. Like Hoadly said, you've no jurisdiction on the Comstock."

Brett didn't respond to that. Instead he asked, "Who wants to hire your gun, Rick? Who's Hoadly's boss?"

Harmonica and banjo music rang out over the voices.

Rick's earthy dark eyes flashed. "What makes you think I'd side with a lawman?"

"I've heard about you. A man doesn't turn his back on what he grew up believing. Not without it hovering just below the surface. Yancey's my brother. He has a cattle spread in Texas. He mentioned you to me once. Said you came from a good family."

Rick's easy smile vanished. "Don't dig around in my past, Wilder. I don't look kindly on it."

Brett shrugged.

Rick reached a hand toward his poncho, stopped, and glanced at Brett's gun hand.

"I'm hankering for a smoke," Delance explained.

Brett watched him roll the makings of a cigarette and light it from one of the grease candles on the barrel nearby.

"Hoadly doesn't know who's chief in Virginia Town," Delance said a minute later.

"Somebody pays him."

"Somebody does. But it's not the chief—whoever the chief is. It's someone else. A go-between."

Now this Brett hadn't expected. Someone wanted to stay in the shadows pretty badly. That might mean it was Jack Halliday. Then again, it might mean someone with bigger plans.

"What's the middleman's name?"

"Don't know yet. Hoadly doesn't like to talk much. I've been offered high pay just to come and hang around. That's all."

"That won't be all."

"Don't suppose so. But until the chief decides to contact me through Hoadly and let me know what the job is, I thought I'd go along with it and pick up some easy money. Just may want to see about getting a claim for myself and maybe settling down south of Tombstone. The notion of my own ranch sort of interests me."

"Settling down is a fine notion. But if you side with Hoadly and whoever's paying him, that will end your chances. Think about it, Delance."

The lack of information was disappointing. So even Hoadly didn't know who was calling the shots. Unless he was lying.

But the more he thought about it, the more sense it made for someone important not to risk his identity to a lowdown gunfighter like Hoadly. It was just possible that Jack Halliday was not behind this. There was someone else manipulating the strings. Someone known for clean hands and respectability? Perhaps.

"Hoadly was wrong about me, though."

Delance looked at him, dark brows lifting. "About what?"

"I'm under authority from Governor Downey. I've a commission as a deputy marshal."

Delance became still.

"I'm to bring Jack Halliday back to Sacramento for trial. That innocent man who was shot on the riverboat was a friend of the governor's, a good friend. He was my friend too. He was my father."

Delance stared at him for so long his cigarette started burning his fingertips. He dropped it quickly and ground it out.

"Well, now. That changes things a mite, doesn't it," he stated.

"For me, yes."

"You're riding into a heap of trouble, Wilder. One man with a gun and a badge will find himself circled by hungry wolves. It won't be easy."

"No. It won't be easy."

"I figure you're a man to know that. It's you against maybe five or six others."

"Are you going to be one of them?" Brett asked quietly.

Rick seemed not to hear. "All of them have reputations for being fast. Even Hoadly isn't too bad when he's laid off the liquor for a day or two. He's drinking too much. It's making him shake. He's nervous. I don't like nervous men. They make mistakes."

"You've given me advice, Wilder. I'll give you some. Don't take them without a friend. Two, if you can get them. And watch that boxer. He aims to kill you."

"Don't intend to take them all on alone—just one at a time."

Rick settled his hat. "See you in Virginia Town."

Brett thought that Hoadly must be pacing the stables by now waiting for Delance. Would Rick tell Hoadly what he'd said? If he did, it would accomplish what he intended. The news would draw them out of the shadows. Hoadly would arrive in Virginia Town ahead of Brett. By the time Brett arrived, the news would find its way to their chief. It was dangerous to play it this way, but he had to smoke the man out and get him to step into the sunshine.

A discussion about States' rights had broken out into an argument between a South Carolinian and a man from Illinois.

Berry set his pot down and shouldered his way through the crowd, intending to boot both men out before they got into a fistfight.

The heat and odor in the main room was unbearable. Brett took his tin cup, refilled it himself, and stepped out into the cold wind.

There was the feel of snow in the blowing gusts sweeping down from the Sierras. He lifted the cup to drink but paused when he saw a girl. Quite a beautiful girl, in fact, with lush auburn hair and a look of class. She reminded him of someone...who?

Brett watched her approach, noticing the tension in her face as she glanced at the men milling about. What was she doing here? He couldn't help thinking of a young doe among snarling wolves. He studied the expression on her face. Every blink of her dark lashes spoke her caution, but it was the determination in the set of her pretty jawline that caught his interest. Now here was a woman with something she had to prove. Was it to herself or someone else?

She was obviously unprepared for what she saw. She appeared to have just escaped her mother's parlor for the first time.

All at once there were shouts from within Berry's.

Brett stepped calmly aside, steadying his tin mug of coffee.

Some men ran out. "Durned Yankee!" Someone else raised a Rebel yell. The fight was on.

Seven

༚

The raucous sounds coming from inside Berry's tavern were followed by shouts and splintering wood, as though a chair had been smashed in a scuffle.

Annalee halted her approach toward the entrance. She stepped back when someone came hurtling backward through the door, landing in the dirt.

She stared down at the man wearing patched trousers and a mustard yellow coat. His battered old hat followed his ungraceful exit from Berry's and was thrown with contempt by a rugged man wearing a coonskin cap.

"We'll end up teaching you self-righteous Yankees a thing or two."

A rifle click of disagreement drew the Southerner's attention. The girl who had been sitting in the wagon had her rifle aimed toward him.

"You help my pa to his feet and apologize, mister, or you'll taste some Union buckshot."

There was laughter from the men. "Looks like you've bitten off more'n you can chew, Johnny Reb."

But the Southerner wasn't amused. "Now lookee here, you half-breed squaw—"

A deadly cracking sound from the girl's rifle splintered the plank near his footing, sending the Southerner ducking and running inside Berry's. There was more laughter. "Thata girl!" someone shouted.

Berry came storming outside, fit to be tied. Annalee had never seen such a soiled apron. From the looks of the man's scowl, he wasn't above whacking the girl.

"Della, you ornery thing! You get your pa outta here and don't come back, hear? I've had me enough of the both of you! I'll serve Garth no more whiskey on my premises."

Della appeared neither apologetic nor timid. She tossed the mule reins aside and slid down from the wagon, landing confidently on her booted feet while still holding the rifle. The trousers she wore only partially masked her feminine form.

Annalee couldn't help but stare. It was the first time she'd seen a woman in men's clothing. Della appeared oblivious to fashion.

The young woman sauntered up to where her pa lay sprawled. She didn't seem appalled by his stupor. In fact, she looked as if she expected him to be drunk, as though it were routine.

She snatched up his hat, knocked off the dust, and placed it solidly on his grimy-looking locks. She glanced up toward Berry's and paused. Then her sultry dark eyes brightened beneath her lashes.

What had suddenly altered her feisty demeanor into an expression Annalee felt she'd seen a bit too often on Callie's face?

Annalee turned her head, seeking the subject of Della's attention. Her gaze discovered a tall, ruggedly built young man with broad shoulders and slim hips. He held a tin mug and was drinking from it as though he were in pleasant, peaceful surroundings. He was not looking at Della—but her.

His gaze held hers in recognition of her attractive appearance, yet he did not remove his dark hat, nor did he smile. They stood, measuring one another.

He wore a black duster, hat, and a gun belt with two pistols. He impressed her as a stranger to the silver ambitions around him, as though some other purpose was on his mind. He radiated a different spirit than the miners. Because her faltering health made her aware of her frailty, she was attracted to his strength.

Annalee was embarrassed by her thoughts.

Her lashes narrowed with an abrupt decision to dislike what she saw. Too masculine. Too reckless. Too attractive. He must be rejected at once. No man who looked like that could be of any spiritual consequence. No doubt he was a gunslinger, maybe even a gambler. Yes, both of those descriptions would fit him.

Still, Annalee felt flattered that she'd attracted such a man, yet—she quickly turned her head away.

Della was sending dagger looks in her direction again, as if she'd noticed the stranger's interest in her. Then she dropped to her knees and shook the man sprawled in the dirt.

"Oh, Pa, wake up. You're stewed again. Wake up!" She continued to shake his shoulders until his hat tipped precariously over his eyes.

"N-no g-good secesh," he stammered with a thick tongue.

Annalee had no trouble surmising that a "secesh" was a Southerner who threatened to secede from the Union. She'd heard talk in Placerville that certain sympathizers to the "Southern cause" were intending to take control of the Comstock Lode and declare it a free territory for the Confederacy.

Della struggled to get the flask away from her father.

"Throw that tarantula juice away, Pa. It'll kill you. You won't need to fight Rebs."

The girl's anguish kindled feelings of sympathy in Annalee. She thought of her own pa. Both of their hard-drinking fathers needed more to set them free than frustrated lectures from their daughters.

Annalee knew of nothing but faith in the only Savior of mankind who rejoiced to set men free from all kinds of bondage. *Oh, Pa, where are you? Is Uncle Samuel right? Are you even alive?*

Della finally got Garth to his feet and into the back of the wagon.

Annalee picked up her skirts and walked between some wagons that were beginning to block her path toward Berry's tavern. A driver's shout halted her.

"Ho! Miss! Easy there! You'll get yerself run over and kilt!"

She found herself blocked by a sad-eyed mule that brayed, refusing to move. The mule's ribs showed, and Annalee knew a sudden burst of anger. Why didn't the old miner feed it?

She turned and looked straight up at the bewhiskered old fellow holding the reins.

"That poor mule is hungry, sir."

"Hungry?" he gave her a blank look, squinting one eye.

"Yes. You ought to feed it better. Look at that huge load it has to carry for miles and miles."

"We're all hungry, miss. Me an' a whole lot of others on our way to Washoe. I ain't 'et since yesterday mornin'." He pushed his hat back and scratched his gray, limp locks. He grinned, showing he was toothless. "You aimin' to feed us both?"

She thought of the few cents in her handbag, and the heat came to her cheeks.

"I'd like to help. I'm afraid I'm unable."

"Same problem as me. Ol' Jenny understands. Her an' me been together for many a year."

"Yes…I'm sorry," she murmured. Ducking her head, she squeezed past the mule and wagon.

She bit her lip. She'd made a fool of herself.

She walked up to the tavern door, hearing banjo music in the background, and a harmony of male voices talking. Dishes clattered.

"How now, missy! You're a right pretty one, to be sure. Gotta minute?"

Annalee turned to face the unpleasant voice. She looked up at a big strapping man she'd noticed earlier watching her and Callie when they left the stage. At first she had thought he could be their uncle, but from the leer in his eyes she knew otherwise.

"I've no minute to spare you." She stepped aside, but he cut in front of her. He leaned closer. She recoiled from his sour breath and the tobacco juice stains at the corners of his mouth.

"You and the other one—the gal with the black witches' locks—you alone? I didn't see none with you 'cept that kid with the cat."

Her lips tightened and her heart beat faster. "You're in my way, sir. Please let me by."

"Wanna get rich? I got an offer to make you and the other one. I'll buy you a drink. Come inside and we can talk private like."

"I don't care to hear about it. Please—"

"You'll sing a different tune, little canary, once you start collectin' silver and gold nuggets. We can go into business together. You go get that other one—she your friend? I'll buy her a drink too. Between the three of us, we'll make more money than those who own feet on the richest claim on the Comstock."

Her skin crawled at the evil gleam in his eyes. "I find your suggestions disgusting! Get out of my way." She tried to brush past him.

"Going into business fer yourself, eh? I'll warn you now it ain't done that way on the Barbary Coast in Virginny Town. My boss runs the Chinatown there, see?"

She tried again to get past him, the heat of outrage flaring in her cheeks.

His big hand locked like an iron vise around her arm. "Hold on now, Miss High 'n' Mighty—"

"You heard her. She's not interested," came a toneless voice.

Annalee glanced quickly aside, seeing the stranger in the black duster.

Irritated, the big man sputtered angrily, "You tellin' me what to do?"

"I am. Keep your grubby paws to yourself and let her pass."

The leering man turned back to Annalee. His lips flared back against stained teeth. "You ain't heard the last of me, Canary. You'll be wishin' you showed me some ra'spect before this here is over."

The stranger grabbed the front of his dirty vest and pulled him forward.

Annalee was shocked to see the strapping man come so easily.

"You bother her again," he gritted, "and you'll be wishing otherwise." He gave a shove, and the big man stumbled backward, falling clumsily into a table. The miners there grabbed up their tin plates, still eating as they moved away.

The man's eyes were cautious now, but they still spat fireworks. He straightened his jacket and wiped his mouth with the back of his hand. With a menacing look, he strode outside.

Shaky, she turned at once in appreciation, but before she could speak to the stranger, the proprietor had elbowed his way through the crowd, scowling.

"Ho, it's you, Wilder." He gestured his head toward the door where the big man went out. "Things under control?"

"They are now."

"Dangerous man. Calls himself Big Burt; others call him Birdie. Works for Jang Li out in Chinatown. Hangs around here sometimes seeing what he can pick up for his boss. You've got another enemy now, Wilder. Jang is a knife expert."

"You're disturbing the lady, Berry."

Berry glanced at her as though he'd forgotten she stood there. "Sorry, miss—hey!" he called over toward two men arguing about something. Berry, heavy black iron pan in hand, charged over to stop them.

Annalee turned to the man Berry had called Wilder.

"Looks like Berry has his hands full," he said with a faint smile.

Under his duster he wore good quality clothes: a buckskin shirt and well-fitted trousers.

It was as she had expected. Up close she couldn't find anything about his appearance she didn't like.

His hair was dark. There was a scar on his throat that looked to be years old, but it only added to his masculine appeal. His eyes were an unusual light gray, very clear and vibrant under dark lashes, as though something exciting stirred just beneath their surface.

Those interesting eyes were studying her just as carefully, as though wondering why she was alone in such a place. Although this was a stage stop, women were few.

"I appreciate your gallantry just now, Mr. Wilder. Thank you very much. That man was revolting."

"Where he comes from, they don't much notice."

Was that a mild warning? Undoubtedly.

He gestured around the room. "But most of these men are decent and hardworking. Any number of them would have come to your aid if they'd noticed what was happening. Especially for a decent woman. You may run into Big Burt again if you move around the mining camps."

Another warning.

"The lure of gold and silver can attract all kinds. Unfortunately, the worst are like vultures. You can count on it."

She tried to place his accent. It wasn't quite Southern, but neither did it have an Eastern twang. She believed his warning about the mining camps was simply his way of finding out why she was here.

"My mother once traveled the mining camps of California as a member of Henry Valentine's Song and Dance Troupe," she said, wanting to make it clear she knew what she was getting into. "So I'm aware of the dangers, Mr. Wilder. In fact, I was born in a mining camp. Coloma, to be exact."

His eyes were keenly aware.

"I've seen men like Big Burt before in certain sections of San Francisco. My mother told me stories of the boom town days. In fact, I'm on way to Virginia Town now."

"You're in the theater?"

"No…I've come on some other business." She was reluctant to tell a stranger too much. He may have helped her with that odious man, but she must still remain cautious.

He studied her more carefully. She glanced about the throng with a confidence she did not feel but wanted him to think she did.

"Is someone meeting you?"

"How did you know that?"

Faint amusement sparkled in his eyes. "Just a lucky guess."

"I suppose I do look out of place here," she added quickly.

"Something like that. If you're on your way to Virginia Town, the trail over the mountain is tricky this time of year. It won't be easy getting there, even by mule."

Her gaze swerved to his. Had she heard him correctly? Oh, no…

"You mean there's no stage that runs from Strawberry to Carson?"

"Maybe by next spring."

"Next spring!"

He regarded her. "Even in June the only way in or out of Virginia Town is by horse or mule, unless a man wants to hike in. A few do. Now in October we'll be lucky to make it down the mountain without meeting a fair-sized snowstorm."

Annalee knew her dismay was showing, but she couldn't help it. No stage! How was she going to explain this dilemma to Callie?

"I see you expected a stage. I'm surprised your mother didn't explain before she sent for you."

Her wish to trust him was strong, and she began to doubt that he was a gambler. His manner suggested he was sensible. Yet first impressions were often misleading. She knew nothing of this stranger, and yet...she must trust someone, especially now. If Samuel wasn't here, and she didn't see him anywhere about, then Callie and Jimmy were in a difficult situation also.

Had the Lord sent him?

She glanced around, sensing there wasn't anyone in the room she'd feel more comfortable trusting, for the men all looked like a rough bunch of miners. Polite, perhaps, and a decent sort, but with more than enough problems of their own.

"You look as if you could use a cup of coffee and a few minutes to think. Why don't we sit down at that table over there?"

She hesitated. She smiled briefly. She could use some advice on traveling. "All right. Thank you."

He walked her across a floor of wood chips and pine branches toward a roughly hewn table in a corner in the back of the room. The two men seated there saw her, looked at her escort, and then politely yielded the table.

While he went in search of coffee, Annalee worried over Callie and Jimmy, who were waiting in the cold wind at the freight platform. She mustn't be gone long, yet it wouldn't do them much good to rush back without a solution to their growing problem.

She looked about her for the proprietor named Berry. There was a possibility that Samuel had sent his response here to Strawberry.

Wilder returned with two cups of coffee and set one of them in front of her. "I can vouch for Berry's coffee, but not much else."

She smiled. "I could drink anything right now."

He sat down opposite her. She noticed he kept his coat open. Was it for easy access to his gun belt? Was he normally cautious, or did he have some present concern? Surely it wasn't the miners. He'd told her most were of the decent sort.

She warmed her palms on the tin mug as she tasted the coffee. He was right. It was quite good, but stronger than she preferred.

"I'm Brett Wilder."

"Annalee O'Day."

Upon leaving Sacramento, she and Callie had decided to adopt their mother's maiden name. If their father was alive and in trouble, it was best not to use "Halliday" until they met with Samuel and learned what was happening in Virginia Town.

"I thought you reminded me of someone. Lillian O'Day was your mother?"

Was. Then he knew about her death.

"Yes, she...she was my mother. Then you've read about the stage accident last year? I suppose everyone has. I understand it took place not far from here."

She'd given herself away. She might as well continue

"She left San Francisco in the fall of last year with a cousin to open a theater in Virginia Town." She held back about her father, the main reason her mother had been going there.

"I'm sorry. Losing both your mother and a cousin is hard to take. What brings you to Virginia Town now?"

"Actually, my father's cousin is alive. He managed to reach Carson for help, but by the time they formed a rescue party and got here, it was too late."

Brett Wilder appeared to notice the change in her voice, for he regarded her with sudden interest.

"Your cousin is Macklin Villiers, the banker?"

She supposed he knew his name from the newspaper account of the accident.

"Yes. I hardly know him. He's more a stranger than kin. I'm going to the Comstock to meet my uncle. It's a matter of some mining shares that belonged to my mother. Cousin Macklin was to help her sell them and then reinvest the money in building the theater."

For a moment he didn't speak. "The Pelly-Jessup, by any chance?"

"Why, yes. Unfortunately the stock price fell to practically nothing after she left for Virginia Town, so the shares are almost worthless, but I still intend to have them. Macklin or his lawyer, Mr. Colefax, must have them in safekeeping."

"Those mining shares, she bought them on her own in San Francisco?"

Why was he asking that? Perhaps she was telling too much...

"No. My father bought them and sent them to her."

Why did she think his manner had changed to one of heightened interest?

Uneasily she set the cup down.

"My mother also went to the Comstock in search of my father. We hadn't heard from him, and there was talk about the Indians. My father...travels a good deal. That's another reason I'm here. To find him."

The tension between them seemed to be unusually high. She couldn't understand why. In order to break the mood, she looked around toward the counter. "It's likely Berry is holding a message for me now. I'll need to inquire about any mail."

"A letter from your father?"

The voice held no emotion. Her eyes swerved back to his. Whatever friendliness he had shown was gone, or was something else bothering him?

"No. A letter from my uncle."

She hoped she sounded confident. Did she really believe a letter would be here?

"We'll ask him." Brett Wilder gestured, Berry walked over to their table.

"More coffee?"

"Berry, this is Miss O'Day. She's expecting a letter from Virginia Town. Have you got anything?"

"Might have. Billy brought the mail in just yesterday. If there's anything from Virginny, it'll be there." He nodded toward Annalee. "Be right with you. Take me a while. I ain't sorted through the bag yet."

Annalee turned to Brett after Berry left.

"You've seen my mother perform?"

"No. I think I would have enjoyed it."

"That was silly of me. You're too young to have seen her at the heyday of the California gold rush. She left the theater when my sister and I were children, execpt for a short time in San Francisco. I'm just surprised you'd think I reminded you of her."

He smiled, his vibrant gaze flickering over her.

"I saw one of the early advertisements at Sutter's. There was a picture of Lillian O'Day."

She flushed under his steady gaze, for her mother was known to have been a beautiful woman. To think this man might think she was as well was pleasing, yet also disturbing.

"She was right about opening a theater at Virginia Town. By this spring the mining camp will open up into a fair-sized community. I'm sorry it didn't work out for both of you. An actress who was as talented as your mother could end up a wealthy woman if the miners liked her. From her past success, there's little doubt they would have." He studied her. "Does this mean you're going into acting?"

She flushed. "Not if I can help it. I've no talent for the stage. That belongs to my sister. I sing—and play the banjo. But I'm not inclined to perform. I'd rather sketch and paint."

"Sounds like you're a woman of many talents." He smiled.

Annalee picked up her cup.

"I'd heard your mother was back on stage when I was in San Francisco. I wasn't able to attend her show, though."

So then he did know about her performances at the melodeons. Annalee tried to keep herself from displaying embarrassment. But did that mean that he was from San Francisco? Maybe he'd just been passing through.

She also noted he hadn't called it "Frisco." No true San Franciscan ever insulted their city by doing so. She was as curious about him as he appeared to be about her, although for what reasons she didn't know. It was disconcerting that she hadn't been able to ask any questions about who he was and what he did. Perhaps that was best. It wasn't wise to show much interest in a too-handsome stranger.

He set his cup down. "Here comes Berry."

"Not a bloomin' thing, ma'am. Maybe tomorrow."

Annalee bit her lip, remembering. Brett Wilder had told Berry her name was O'Day. But Samuel wouldn't have sent a letter using that name, but Halliday.

She glanced sideways at her companion. Now what?

"Is Flint Harper's mule train due tomorrow?" Brett asked Berry.

"Yep, if the weather holds. Any mail from thereabouts, and he'll be bringing it up with him from Carson when he picks up supplies."

Annalee remained silent. She'd need to go to Berry when Brett Wilder wasn't there to ask about mail for Halliday.

But why make more trouble for yourself? she considered. *Why not just come out with the facts? There is no harm in going by Mother's maiden name.*

She knew why. Mentioning the Halliday name might open a door to a nest of scorpions.

"When did you send the letter from Sacramento?" Wilder was asking her.

"Three weeks ago."

"Then he should have received it. The Pony goes through here now. Maybe Berry's got it right. Tomorrow on the mule train."

Her brows knitted. "Pony?"

"That's what they call the riders with the Pony Express. A letter can travel from San Francisco to Missouri in nine days. That's two thousand miles through Indian territory. Since mail arrives down in Dayton once a week, your uncle should have gotten your letter."

"Are the riders ever attacked by Indians?"

"You can be sure no timid gentleman would seek the job. One Pony rider came into Dry Creek shot through with a dozen arrows."

Unease shivered through her.

"I noticed you said 'we' earlier. Someone else is with you, perhaps a guardian?"

She felt the muscles in her jaw tighten. "No, I'm in charge, Mr. Wilder. My younger sister and brother are with me." She rose to her feet, pulling her cloak about her. "And I'm remiss in getting back to them. They're waiting at the freight depot now. The news that our uncle isn't here won't go over well with my sister."

He stood and leveled a hard look at her. "Wait a minute, please."

She did, meeting his gaze reluctantly.

"Correct me if I'm wrong. Your mother is dead, you don't know where your father is, and your uncle hasn't shown up to meet you here at Berry's. Evening's coming on, and you've got a younger sister and brother with you—and you don't look much older than eighteen yourself." A crooked smile lifted his mouth. "Do I have it right, Miss O'Day?"

Now the warmth in her face was from more than embarrassment. Her temper kindled, yet she managed to retain a dignified demeanor.

"You have it nearly right, Mr. Wilder. I happen to be twenty-two."

"A grave error." He bowed his head.

Annalee, with what she imagined to be flair and unintimidated spunk for having faced a man who could be as dangerous in his own unique way as Big Birdie, turned with a rustle of skirt and made her way through the crowd of men with her head held high. It was to the men's credit that they moved back to clear a path for her exit.

She swept though the door and outside, nearly losing her breath from a chill blast of mountain air.

The door opened from behind her; Brett had followed. Their gazes locked. Just then a voice shouted, and they turned in its direction.

"Annalee!"

Jimmy ran up, breathless. Excitement and cold left two bright spots on his cheeks. His expressive brown eyes, tender under a shock of dark brown hair, were wide as they stared up at Mr. Wilder.

"Hi, mister, I'm Jimmy. That man over there—" he turned and pointed back toward the old man Annalee had met earlier on the wagon pulled by Jenny the mule. "That man says he knows you and that you're a lawman! Can I see your badge?"

Annalee gaped, astonished. Lawman?

Brett obliged him by removing something shiny from beneath his duster and displaying it against his palm for the boy to see.

Annalee turned slowly and faced Brett Wilder.

Eight

A lawman!

She wondered if she looked as foolish as she felt. Even so, her knees were shaky with relief. A lawman could certainly be trusted to help them through the dilemma facing them now, unless—she didn't dare think of that. She cast him a side glance.

She was nearly as awed as Jimmy, who'd been permitted to hold Brett's badge. His small fingers gently stroked the shiny metal that represented respect and authority.

"You could have told me who you were, Mr. Wilder," Annalee said when their gaze locked above Jimmy's head.

"Beyond the few who already **know**, I'd prefer to keep quiet about it for now."

Did he have enemies? Thinking back to that horrid confrontation with Big Birdie, she realized the man hadn't known who Brett was. There would be others as well.

"I suppose you took me for a gunfighter?"

"A gambler, actually. I suppose they go together." She lifted her chin a little and tried to look grave. "My apologies, Mr. Wilder."

A hint of amusement flickered in his eyes.

"Think nothing more about it, Miss O'Day."

"You're a lawman in Virginia Town?"

"Sacramento, until two years ago. I left law enforcement to start a ranch in Grass Valley."

Why, she might have run into him recently on several occasions, and yet they'd met here at a small stage stop on the Sierras, a most unlikely spot. She was impressed anew with the sovereignty of God. Life-changing events could happen when least expected during everyday situations.

Sacramento. Well, that accounted for the manners just beneath his rugged demeanor, and for the quality of his clothes, though the black duster and buckskin proved Brett Wilder was at home on the frontier.

While Brett was looking at Jimmy and commenting on his cat, she studied him. He was young for a lawman, but coming from Sacramento meant he would have earned that distinction. Just how often did he actually use a gun?

"What made you decide to take up your badge again?"

He didn't answer at once. She'd began to wonder if she'd asked the wrong question.

"I've been temporarily deputized by the California governor," was all he would say. She understood he might be holding back because Jimmy's eyes were round and his ears were wide open.

The term "gunfighter" reached out and caught her childhood memory in its painful grip. She could remember hearing loud explosions—at least they had seemed like explosions to a small child. She'd peered out the front window to see her father practice drawing his gun from its holster and shooting into cans. He would sometimes shoot for what had seemed like hours to her. Her mother had appeared tense during those seasons of their life, even afraid, although she'd been strong too.

"Daddy's just practicing—like playing a game," she would say with her acting smile. "He's seeing if he can hit the tin cans."

"Me too, Mama, me too," Jimmy would say in his baby talk. "Me play like Daddy..."

As the memory faded, Annalee drew her cloak about her. She realized suddenly how cold and forlorn she felt. She caught Brett's eye. He'd been watching her, and he seemed curious. She wanted to ask him why his work had brought him here, and was that the reason he'd left his ranch in Grass Valley.

"Are you all right?"

His quiet concern brought a small flush. She wished she wouldn't find her emotions responding so easily to the drawl of his voice, or notice the wind moving his dark hair and duster.

It's because we're vulnerable. Because he's strong and protective, and we—I— feel weak and ill....

"Yes. I'm fine. Thank you."

She hadn't meant for her tone to sound so dismissive. She saw a muscle flex in his jaw. He couldn't know her defensive armor was simply a safeguard against the effect he had upon her. Sometimes she found that her defenses put her at odds with the real Annalee, and certainly with someone like Brett Wilder.

A shiver of caution went through her on a gust of mountain air as his duster moved and the Colt .45 showed.

"There you are!" came Callie's breathless, scolding voice as she hurried up. "I've been looking all over for you—"

Callie halted when she saw Brett Wilder.

Annalee experienced an unreasonable irritation with the way her sister stared at him. Had Callie been within reach, Annalee would have given her a sharp nudge with her elbow.

Callie's lips closed as she came toward them, dimples showing. Annalee knew her every response all too well: the lift of her head, the straightening of her shoulders, the smile. The wind favored Callie too. It tossed her ebony hair in an attractive way and added color to her cheeks. Even her blue eyes appeared to sparkle in the nip of chill, like turquoise.

Drat! Annalee wanted to stamp her foot.

Instead, she said in a crisp voice, "This is my sister, Callie. Callie, Mr. Wilder. He's a deputy marshal from Sacramento."

Callie went through her typical metamorphosis and emerged the sweet, submissive butterfly. Her demeanor took on added maturity, and she was now the older sister with unselfish thoughts.

"Hello, Mr. Wilder. Thank goodness you rescued my sister from inside that tavern." Callie showed her dimples—again. "I'm afraid Annalee is, well, just a *little* impulsive." She turned to Annalee with furrowed brows.

"Dear, it's dreadful the way you ran off like that. You too, Jimmy. You both worry me so. You might get lost. With your frail health the way it is," she directed her look back toward Annalee, "why, anything could happen to you in this weather. You keep in mind what Dr. Harley said before we left Sacramento."

Annalee had an almost irresistible urge to box her sister's ears. Callie was deliberately putting her in a bad light.

"Don't be silly. I'm not going to curl up and die in the snow. I'm all right, as you well know."

Annalee then wanted to bite her tongue—her tone must have sounded peevish and unreasonable to Mr. Wilder. And Callie! It wasn't that she lacked character, but she definitely put on a performance when a good-looking man was around! And Brett Wilder was without a doubt the most desirable male they'd ever laid eyes on.

Again, Callie displayed superior wisdom in not responding to Annalee, as she surely would have done if Brett wasn't listening—and watching. A glance his way showed his vibrant gaze was attached to Callie.

"Jimmy, honey, you mustn't make a nuisance of yourself with Mr. Wilder." Callie looked at Brett. "I'm sure your duties keep you busy."

Butter wouldn't melt in her mouth, Annalee thought dryly.

The past year of illness had seen Callie plump out in the appropriate places, even as Annalee had grown thinner. She'd been forced to use a needle and thread on her best traveling frock before it fit her waistline. It was with a prick that she recalled Brett thinking she was eighteen.

Annalee glanced at him again to try and judge how he was reacting to her sister. Guessing him to be still in his twenties, Callie's age would not escape his range of interest. He was watching her, but at least his expression didn't betray his thoughts—whatever they were.

Annalee was nettled more than she had a right to be. Why, she hardly knew the man! Suddenly, she was amused. As far as either of them knew, Brett Wilder could be married with eight children waiting back at his ranch. Annalee was still smiling a moment later as she lifted the hood of her cloak over her thick auburn hair. Brett noticed and a brow lifted. Annalee arched her own brow in return. His mouth turned slightly.

"Has Uncle arrived?" Callie asked her.

Uh-oh, now it's coming.

Jimmy was talking to Brett about his cat again. Annalee used the moment to draw Callie aside.

"Stop flirting," she whispered. "Mother would be ashamed of you."

"Tsk, tsk, so Miss Tattletale rides again. Do I detect a sliver of jealousy?"

Annalee ignored that. "Listen. We've more important things to concern us now than Brett Wilder."

"We do?" Callie's eyes sparkled mischievously.

Again Annalee had to resist the urge to stamp her foot. "Uncle Samuel isn't here. And I've found out there's no stage to Carson. We need—"

Callie caught her arm. "Didn't I warn you this could happen?" she hissed.

"Shh! He'll hear us. Listen. There's a mule train coming in the morning with the mail. The proprietor thinks we'll likely get a letter from Uncle Samuel."

"I wouldn't put much faith in what that old grizzly told you. There's no way of knowing." She folded her arms. "I just knew we were headed for trouble. I could feel it coming on just like a case of winter's grippe."

Annalee couldn't keep from smiling. "You and your 'feelings.' You wanted to come as much as I. We all did."

Callie glanced around, drawing her cloak tighter. "So I did. I'll admit it, but not to get trapped here." She glanced about nervously. "Those clouds spell trouble."

She was right. Annalee had to find an answer to their problem. If they spent their remaining few cents in her purse on supper and a night's lodging, she would still need to think about transportation in the morning.

"Didn't I say don't fret? The Lord hasn't forsaken us, has He?"

"Of course not, but He expects us to use the good sense He gave us."

"Well, that's just what I'm going to do," Annalee said, miffed. "Mr. Wilder is on his way to Virginia Town, isn't he?"

Callie looked toward Brett Wilder. "Is he? I hope so."

"He also thinks our letter reached Uncle Samuel by now."

"What if he's off doing a little placer mining?"

Annalee remembered that her mother had said he sometimes did mining for his upkeep. "He'd still be close around the mining camp at Gold Hill. We'll find him—once we get there."

"We'll have to find him before we try to find Pa. In the meantime, where do we stay tonight?"

Annalee thought of the campground where all the miners were bedded down, but blankets were needed in this cold, and worse, the clouds threatened rain.

How would she get them to Virginia Town in the morning? Hitch a ride in someone's wagon? She thought of the old gentleman with the mule named Jenny.

Mules or horses, Brett had said. That would cost them a pretty penny. Reluctantly she thought of the one hundred and fifty dollars in her satchel. Even Callie didn't know where she'd hidden it. Annalee had said nothing, but she had feared a stage holdup on the bumpy, narrow road into the Sierras. So she had stashed the money inside the lining and sewn it back up. She'd added some of her prized books to obscure the bag's heaviness.

Jimmy was saying to the lawman, "Keeper sure could use a little milk."

Annalee's spirits sank lower.

"He's turning us into beggars," she murmured to Callie.

Embarrassed, Annalee hurriedly stepped forward to silence Jimmy. He merely looked hopeful on seeing her.

"And that ginger cake sure didn't help me much neither, Annalee."

Annalee forced a bright smile. "Well, we'll have supper a little later, Jimmy."

He didn't appear to hear. His eyes wandered toward the tavern where the smell of food wafted to them. It broke her heart to see him like this, grasping his kitten for comfort. She'd need to use one of the gold pieces, that's all there was to it. She couldn't do it in front of crowds of men, though.

Jimmy was standing on tiptoe and trying to peer inside the tavern.

She glanced at Brett, unaware that he'd been watching her, not Jimmy. How much of the truth had he discerned? Probably too much. She took hold of her little brother's small arm.

"Come along, Jimmy."

"Where we going, Annalee? Did you find Uncle—"

"We're going to hold a little powwow with Callie."

Before they could move away, however, Brett directed a question not to Annalee but to Jimmy.

"You sound as hungry as I am. What do you say we go inside and see what we can find?"

"Thank you, no—" began Annalee, casting a warning glance toward Jimmy, but he was all eyes for the deputy marshal.

"Yes, sir! I'm mighty hungry. And so's Keeper."

"I think it's time we all had something to eat. Come on."

Annalee tried to protest, but it seemed ungrateful to argue. She had the idea Brett understood her dilemma and intended to pay. The thought embarrassed her, but he'd already commandeered the situation, and quite smoothly too. She'd lost control of Jimmy. The boy was in a state of hero worship. *His attention has been arrested—by a lawman,* she told herself.

She could hardly expect anything different from the boy. He'd been without their father for so long, and it had only been a year since their mother's tragedy. Considering the losses, Jimmy was doing well.

Annalee watched them enter the tavern. Brett knew she'd have no choice but to join them. Callie followed. Of course—*she* would!

I'll pay him back when we find work, Annalee insisted to herself, silencing her pride. *As soon as I invest the money in a business of sorts.*

For another moment she stood in the cold wind, thinking. She'd reminded Callie to pray and trust in God's protection and guidance, but what of her own faith during these troubling times? How easy it was to talk of confidence in God, but living that out was difficult when all around there was a mist too thick to understand what lay ahead.

The sun was setting early in the wintry weather. She turned and glanced off towards the darkening trees. Above the climbing ridge of ponderosa pine, the clouds that had threatened all day had settled in, shrouding the Sierras.

She hunched her shoulders. Callie was right about rain. It might even snow. It certainly was cold enough.

The fragrance of a hundred campfires drifted to her on the wind. She was a fool to stand here debating because of pride when food and warmth waited inside. Why was she reluctant to accept help from Brett Wilder? She'd trusted him earlier, before she'd known he was a lawman. She had more reason to trust him now.

She squared her shoulders and went into Berry's to join them.

Nine

As Annalee reentered the hot, stuffy tavern, a sudden weariness swept over her. She was becoming aware of how exhausted she actually was. She'd taxed herself beyond what Dr. Harley warned in her condition, but she must keep going forward, keeping her eye on the goal, confident that God was fully in control, and that He would see her through.

"My flesh and my heart faileth: but God is the strength of my heart, and my portion forever." She repeated the psalmist's words as she'd been doing since leaving Sacramento. She believed God had given her that promise, and she clung to it and embraced it.

Once they were settled in Virginia Town things would be different.

Annalee forced a bright smile as she walked over to Callie and Jimmy. She brushed Jimmy's wavy hair from his forehead.

"You should wash first, but the river's too far."

"And too cold," Callie chimed in. "I'll just wager it snows before we reach Washoe."

"Real snow," Jimmy breathed with excitement. "It never snows in Sacramento. It's good Keeper has lots of fur."

Brett was at the counter of wooden barrels where the proprietor was ladling food onto a tall man's tin plate.

Berry looked over at the forlorn little family.

"Looks like you got your hands full, Wilder. What'll ya have?"

"Whatever you've got."

"Beans and beef."

"I'll take it. Add some of that pan bread too. Any butter or honey?"

"Sure. Plenty."

Jimmy came up beside the marshal. "Can you make that fifth bowl with cream, sir?" he asked Berry.

Berry looked down at him and smiled. "Cream?"

"Yes, sir."

Brett grinned at Berry, reached over, and opened the boy's coat. The cat's two big golden eyes stared back.

"Mee-yeow?"

Berry shook his head. "Sorry, lad. I ain't got no cream, an' no milk, neither. All used up till milkin' time in the morning. How's a saucer of gravy sound for Whiskers?"

"That will do fine, sir. Her name's Keeper. She was a stray kitten, you see. But Annalee—that's my sister there, the prettiest one—" he pointed at Annalee, "she told Callie—that's my other sister, the one with the black hair—" more pointing, "'Oh, let him keep her.' So I decided to call my cat Keeper. Get it?"

Berry grinned. "Got it, son."

"Anyway, Keeper likes gravy, especially chicken gravy."

"She'll need to settle for beef," Berry said with a wink toward Brett.

Brett gestured inquiringly toward the kitchen.

"Sure, it'll be quieter there. Take 'em on back. I'll bring the grub in a minute."

From where she stood waiting with Callie, Annalee noticed Berry frowning unexpectedly, and then he leaned towards Brett. She listened through the din and caught a few words.

"...fella you asked about...into Placerville. Overheard Big Birdie...and Hoadly...mebbe won't need...Virginny Town after all."

Who was Brett looking for, a stage robber? It sounded as though the man he'd asked Berry about earlier had ridden to Placerville.

Brett came back to Annalee and Callie and walked them into the kitchen area that appeared to be a part of Berry's personal quarters. There was more privacy here, and a sheet-metal stove glowed where the fire heated its sides. There was a wooden table and rough pine chairs covered with canvas seating.

No sooner had Annalee sat down than the last of her strength ebbed. Even her thick auburn hair, which she'd pulled into a cascade of wind-blown curls at the nape of her neck, felt heavy. For a moment the sawdust floor dipped and swayed beneath her. She clutched the edge of the table.

She became aware that Brett was watching her. She avoided his eyes. She didn't want him to guess that Callie's words about her were close to the truth.

Even so, she sensed his alert gaze and felt unmasked. The thought that he suspected brought a tight feeling of vulnerability, even fear. No one must know, especially Brett. She was ashamed of her illness. Besides that, he already appeared to disapprove of their venture into Virginia Town.

He left them seated and went for coffee. As soon as he was out of hearing, Callie leaned toward her across the table. Her blue eyes narrowed.

"I kept saying back at Placerville our plans were like a rusty bucket. Here we are with no Uncle Samuel and dependent on the mercy of strangers."

Jimmy was fussing with Keeper, tying the rope to the leg of the chair and coaxing her toward the beef gravy.

"We won't worry about Uncle Samuel now. I'm sure we'll find him in Virginia Town," Annalee said wearily.

Jimmy didn't look worried. His eyes shone.

"We can sleep outdoors tonight like the miners. Have us a campfire too. Maybe we'll see us a bear! Say, Keeper, you'd better stay close to me tonight."

"Outdoors? Fiddlesticks! It's going to rain," Callie protested. "It may even snow before morning."

"I'll bet Pa and Cousin Macklin sleep under pine trees all the time," he wheedled.

"Well, Macklin doesn't sleep that way anymore," Callie said dryly. "Not since he got into the banking business."

"Maybe the deputy sleeps under the pine trees." Jimmy's eyes widened. "I know what, Callie. If we could sleep near the deputy marshall, it wouldn't be so bad—"

"No," Annalee said.

"We'll buy a tent from the proprietor. Where's the hundred and fifty dollars, Annalee?"

"Hush, Callie! There could be thieves about."

"If there's thieves, the deputy'll get 'em," Jimmy said confidently.

Callie cupped her ear toward the side flap of the kitchen. "I knew it. Rain." She let out a deep sigh.

"I'm thinking the proprietor may have a tent we can rent for the night, instead of buy," Annalee said. "It shouldn't cost much. Mr. Wilder said many of these miners are hardworking men with families back home. I'll wager more than one would help us set it up."

"Bet Deputy Wilder will do it for us," Jimmy said. "I'll watch how he does it. Next time I'll know how."

Brett returned with hot coffee. Callie smiled up at him sweetly.

"You're mighty kind, Mr. Wilder," she drawled.

Annalee winced.

"The least I can do, Miss Callie." Brett returned her smile, a flicker of amusement in his eyes.

Berry came in carrying tin plates of spicy beans and beef chunks and set them down.

Annalee took one whiff and wanted to gag. Her illness gave her a poor appetite. The Mexican chili looked red-hot. She wouldn't be able to swallow the stuff, no matter how good a cook Berry was or how kind Brett had been.

"I don't suppose there's a stage through to Carson tonight?" Callie asked Berry dubiously.

"Stage? Ain't no stage, ma'am." He set the pan bread on the table beside tins of butter and honey.

The bread at least looked eatable. Annalee took a small piece and spread some wild honey on it.

"From here to Virginny Town it's all by mule," Berry continued.

"Mule?" Callie grimaced.

"Mule!" Jimmy grinned. "Hear that, Keeper? Whoa!"

"Um, where do we get mules?" Annalee asked Berry, refusing to meet Callie's level stare.

Berry rubbed his whiskered chin. He glanced toward Brett, who was eying his coffee silently. "Usually folks buy mule tickets in Placerville, ma'am."

"Oh, I see." Annalee studiously kept her dismay from affecting her voice. She was embarrassed she hadn't even heard of the mule passage from Strawberry Flat, much less tickets.

"When do the mules leave?" Callie asked.

"Soon as Harper rests 'em a spell. Then after he loads supplies for Dayton."

"Harper? The man who brings the mail?" Annalee asked.

"Same fella. Flint Harper runs mule trains in and out of Carson. Mighty good with 'em too."

"Then we can rent mules to ride from Mr. Harper," Annalee's voice revealed her relief.

"Mebbe. If'n he's got spares. Depends on how many rode the stage from Placerville."

At that Annalee recalled Macklin's nephew, Rody Villiers. Whom had he ridden away with?

"There were six others besides us," Jimmy spoke up. "I counted 'em at Placerville. Two inside and four on top. One of 'em won't be taking a mule, though. He had a friend waiting with a horse when the stage stopped out front."

Brett looked up, alert.

Annalee noticed. "Yes, we were surprised to discover Rody Villiers on the stage. Macklin Villiers is Rody's uncle. He said Macklin sent for him from New Orleans to work for him in Virginia Town."

"He carried six shooters too. I saw 'em. Big ones." Jimmy looked over at Brett, but his gun belt was discreetly covered up by his jacket. "I recognized 'em. Pa has guns like that. 'Member, Annalee? Pa said they was mighty good—"

"Eat your supper before it gets cold, Jimmy," Annalee said quietly but firmly, her cheeks warm with embarrassment. Leave it to her little brother to tell the world their pa was fast with a gun. She glanced at Brett. He wore a sober, thoughtful look on his handsome face as he stared at the piece of bread in his hand.

"Then Harper might have an extra mule or two," Berry told Brett.

"Where did you say Rody got his horse, Jimmy?" Brett asked casually.

"A man was waiting for him in the pine trees. Rody was mighty fine with a horse too. He got in that saddle as smooth as you'd like. Say, Annalee, can I have me a pony in Virginny Town?"

"More like an old mule," Callie said dryly.

"Before Rody left, he told Annalee he'd see her in Virginny Town," Jimmy told Brett.

Annalee thought Brett's eyes flickered, and he wore no smile.

Does any of this mean anything? Annalee wondered, uneasily. *Is it possible Brett is looking for Rody Villiers?*

The plate of beans and chunks of beef stared up at her. Out of politeness she pretended to eat, fussing with her fork and knife and taking tiny swallows that lumped in her throat. The spices made her eyes water. Several times she nearly sneezed. She glanced at Callie to see how she was handling it. Callie was eating the beef and leaving the hot beans. Jimmy was enjoying both. Brett was just eating the bread, she noticed.

He stood from the table. "You'll need to camp here tonight, ladies. I'll ask Berry to keep an eye on you until Harper arrives in the morning with the mules."

Did that mean he was not going to Virginia Town? Annalee recalled the little she'd heard Berry tell him about a rider and Placerville. The rider couldn't be Rody, though, because he'd gone on to the Comstock. Who, then?

She was grateful to Jimmy when he called out, "But, Wilder! I mean, Marshal. Aren't you coming too?"

It seemed to Annalee that Brett refused to look in her direction. She looked down at the cold food on her plate.

"I need to return to Placerville."

"When will you come back?"

"Soon," he promised.

"Are you looking for a gunslinger?"

"Don't ask so many questions, Jimmy, it isn't polite," Callie said.

When Brett didn't respond, Annalee glanced up.

His gaze captured hers. "Sure you won't change your mind and go back to Sacramento? I can arrange for horses to be sent up from Placerville. They'll arrive tomorrow. I'll look for your uncle when I ride into Virginia Town."

For a moment it seemed his clear gray eyes could fill her entire world. Quickly she lowered her head and picked up her fork.

"Thank you, Mr. Wilder, but we're going on to the Comstock."

Callie's foot nudged her beneath the table. Annalee refused to cooperate.

"And…thank you also for supper and for your concern, Marshal."

He hesitated, his poise unabating.

"All right." He bowed his head in their direction. "Then I'll see you in Virginia Town."

When he'd gone, Annalee pushed away her supper plate. The table was silent, and she sensed a strange emptiness already setting in.

Callie sighed. "Well, we're on our own again." She scooped up her tin cup and stood. "I need some water. How about you, Jimmy? Annalee?"

"Is there any sarsaparilla?" Jimmy asked hopefully.

"You'll need to drink water." Callie walked into the tavern to find Berry.

A glimpse at Jimmy told Annalee he was disappointed Brett had left.

She pushed his plate closer to him. "Finish up," she encouraged quietly. "We won't eat again soon." She offered a smile of sympathy. Trying to cheer him, she said, "Maybe tomorrow we'll see Uncle Samuel." She added with a whisper, "I'll get you a sarsaparilla."

～∗～

There is something else in her face beside youthful innocence and weariness from travel, Brett thought as he left the kitchen. What was it? The faint darkness under her eyes was more than lack of sleep; it was the look of a young woman who'd been quite ill recently…or still was?

Brett had seen too much illness growing up not to recognize it now. As he left the tavern he spied Berry.

He pressed a gold piece into Berry's hand. "This is for your trouble. Keep an eye on them, will you? Can you arrange for them to sleep indoors tonight?"

"Sure. I'll give 'em that back room. Got extra quilts an' all."

"Tell Harper to get them safely to Carson or he'll have me to reckon with." He smiled, touching his brow in a two-fingered salute. "I'll be in touch, Berry."

The gusts of wind were turning icy. He pulled his hat lower. Between the clouds stars glistened like crystals, but in the east heavier clouds heralded a storm. Rough weather ahead. He made sure his long-legged zebra dun was well fed for the journey. He saddled it and then led it from the stable out across the yard toward the trail.

Brett frowned and lifted the collar of his coat, hesitating before riding out. He looked across from Berry's Flat to the ridge of thick ponderosa pine darkly silhouetted against the horizon. Pinpricks of red and gold from campfires glowed in the darkness.

His eyes narrowed with his thoughts. There was something wrong about all this, but he couldn't put his finger on it. He thought again about Macklin Villiers, recalling what he'd heard about him from time to time.

Villiers had traveled from one boom camp to another. Although connected with trouble, Macklin always managed to stay just on the outskirts while others took the blame. Now Macklin was a banker in Virginia Town. Respectable? He wondered.

He knew more about Rody. He was a cheap gambler who'd been in and out of gun trouble since he was sixteen. He'd killed a man, claiming the man had cheated at cards. There'd been enough paid witnesses to get him off. As far as Brett was concerned, there was only one reason for Macklin to send for his nephew, and that was because he needed another gun—probably because Macklin either expected trouble coming his way, or he intended to make trouble of his own.

Brett leaned his arm against his saddle, musing, looking off toward the campfires and breathing the aroma of pine-scented woodsmoke.

What if Hoadly took his orders from Macklin Villiers? Why not? Villiers could be the man in the shadows, the respectable banker portraying himself the honest citizen while becoming powerful thorough underhanded means. He wouldn't want Hoadly to know for fear he or others could use extortion against him in the future.

Something else bothered Brett. Hoadly and Big Birdie had passed information to Berry that Jack Halliday had ridden into Placerville. This was only after he'd let it be known he was looking for Halliday. This smelled like a quick setup to him. Something Hoadly might try out of desperation.

Brett looked toward the road. He'd be an easy target on the trail down the mountain to Placerville. One crack of a rifle was all it would take.

That gave him something to ponder. Did he want to risk it?

Macklin came to mind again. So he'd survived that stage accident last year. The one man to do so. The driver had yet to be found. More than likely he was dead.

Why had Macklin survived? If there was something ugly about it, what reason did he have for wanting the others on the stage dead? How had he managed the stage accident? The driver wasn't around to talk—that only helped Macklin. Again, no witnesses. Nothing could be proven.

If there was a reason to risk the ride to Placerville, it was to learn more about that stage accident. Who else had been on that doomed stage besides Lillian O'Day?

He was ready to mount when someone came running. The light footsteps told him it was a girl. He turned, still holding the reins.

"Mr. Wilder?"

Callie O'Day hurried up, breathless. She was a striking young woman. If he'd seen her before Annalee, he could have gone for her. But there was something about Annalee that had nabbed his attention from the moment he saw her. Maybe he was partial to auburn-haired beauties with unusual green eyes.

"I was wondering if I could impose on you a little further?" she said, looking embarrassed for the first time since he'd met her. He covered a smile.

"You're not imposing at all, Miss Callie. What can I do for you?"

"Well, our mother, when she was alive, had an aunt in New Orleans I'd like very much to contact."

He listened, saying nothing.

"But, well, Annalee won't hear of it. She's determined to go to Virginia Town. She'll be mighty steamed up if she learns I wrote Aunt Lorena asking if we might go to New Orleans. If someone else notified our aunt of our situation here, and she responded kindly—which I'm mighty certain she will—then maybe I could change Annalee's mind about going there."

"Mind telling me why Annalee's so determined to go to the Comstock? She mentioned your uncle being there, but there seems to be another reason."

"Macklin convinced Mother she could sell some mining shares and then use part of the money to partner with him in opening a theater in Virginia Town. It all sounded worthwhile, but none of us knew at the time that the price of stock in the mine was dropping fast. An attorney came to see us last year. He told us the shares are nearly worthless now. But Annalee wants to talk to our uncle about them. Perhaps the mine will pick up again."

So that was it. It was all beginning to tie together.

"Your sister said those shares were in the Pelly-Jessup."

"That's right. At least, I think so. I never paid much mind to it. Pa bought them when he worked there, and then signed them over to Mother."

"You mean Macklin Villiers never sent the money for those shares to you in Sacramento?"

"Well, his lawyer friend said they were worthless. Macklin himself has never contacted us, not even to send condolences about the accident. Annalee suspects the shares are still with him, or his lawyer, Mr. Colefax. We realize Cousin Macklin was injured in the accident. Maybe that's why we've not heard, but Annalee doesn't trust him."

"I see." He nearly smiled. Smart woman.

She had good reason not to trust Macklin Villiers. That went for Rody too. Brett didn't like the idea that Rody told Annalee he'd see her in Virginia Town.

"I'd also like to know what's wrong with Annalee. She's not well, is she."

Callie glanced over her shoulder. "She'd be mad as a hornet if I said anything about it."

He wanted the truth, and he wouldn't take no for an answer. "What's wrong with her, Callie?" he insisted quietly.

Callie glanced back at him, scanning him thoughtfully as if she wondered why he was so interested. He kept his expression unreadable to those pretty blue eyes.

Callie's voice came so quietly he could hardly catch her words. He decided this girl was loyal to her sister, though the competition between them sometimes bordered on cat fights.

"Dr. Harley diagnosed consumption."

He was shocked to silence. He had not expected that.

"She almost died a few years back. She's stronger now, but she's not well. It can come back if she doesn't take care of her health. I'm worried. I don't think things will be all that easy for her at the Comstock."

"They won't. There's nothing there but dugouts and tent taverns. How long has she had it?"

"Annalee's spent a good part of her life in bed. That's where she learned to sketch and paint. Dr. Harley doesn't think she'll ever get well. It comes and goes, and—"

"I understand tuberculosis. My father's a physician."

Callie looked surprised but pleased.

"So she's come here? To the worst possible place?" He had a difficult time keeping frustration from his voice. Why he should care so much he couldn't say, but the fact was, he did. "Does she know what the winters are like here? And the alkali dust is enough to clog a man's nostrils and parch his lungs."

"She knows. We've told her. But she has a mind of her own."

He listened as Callie explained about their Aunt Weda and the farmhouse in Sacramento, and then about an engagement to Gordon Barkly that had fallen through.

"Annalee has something to prove to herself. What it is, I don't know exactly, but she refuses to accept her weakness. We came because we only had two choices. We either find money in Virginia Town to pay off Aunt Weda's taxes, or I work in one of the

San Francisco melodeons. Annalee could do the same, she can sing mighty fine. And maybe we'll do theater in the Comstock, but she's not keen on that. She wants to help our uncle in his Christian work with the Indians and do some painting. She hopes to sell her artwork to an Eastern newspaper or magazine."

Annalee interested him more and more. "How long was she engaged to Gordon Barkly?" Was she in love with him? Maybe risking her health in a trip over the mountains had something to do with losing the man she loved to another woman.

"She and Gordon had more of an understanding than an actual engagement, but they were friends for years. He only decided to marry Louise because her family has money. Gordon wants to start his own newspaper, and her pa will set him up."

"I see. Is she still in love with him?"

Callie tilted her head and looked at him from the corner of her eye. A smile loitered. She shrugged. "With Annalee it's hard to tell. Now I think she's more in love with the idea of being a missionary to the Indians than she ever was with Gordon. He was sort of strange too. Sort of, well," Callie paused and smoothed her hair while looking at him through her lashes, "he wasn't true to her, if you know what I mean."

"I know what you mean." No doubt the pretty and sassy Callie had made headway with Gordon Barkly.

"I'll be pleased to send a wire to your great-aunt in New Orleans. Do you have her address?"

"I've got it right here." She handed him a folded piece of paper. "How can I thank you, Marshal?"

"No need to thank me. I'll have your aunt write your father. What's his name?"

"Jack Halliday."

Brett stopped. He looked at her with what must have been blank astonishment, for Callie, too, looked unnerved at his response. She stepped back.

"Is…is something wrong?" she asked, fingering the collar on her cloak.

He said nothing. He couldn't have spoken had he wanted to. He felt his jaw clench. Jack Halliday! It couldn't be.

Callie glanced in the direction of the tavern.

"Well…I'd better get back. Thank you for your help, Mr. Wilder."

He couldn't let her leave yet. Not until he had the answers he wanted.

"Just a minute, please."

He noticed her reluctance, as though she'd become uncertain about him. Brett was still holding the horse's reins, and his hat was low.

"Your father's from Louisiana?"

"Yes, he was from there originally. He met our mother at Sutter's Mill when she was doing theater with a traveling group. We've been in California ever since, though he drifted from one mining camp to another. He always said he'd strike it rich one day."

"Was he up at the Fraser in '58?"

"Yes. So was Macklin. They were with Aunt Weda's husband, our Uncle Charlie. Charlie died there. That's why we're about to lose the farm in Sacramento."

His hopes sank. It was the same man. Why hadn't he put it together? "Seen your father lately?"

"No, not for several years now." Her voice grew a little bitter. "He didn't even show for Mama's funeral. I shouldn't hold it against him, though. We thought he was dead too. It was our uncle who wrote us recently saying Pa was alive."

"Samuel Halliday is your uncle?"

"Yes. He was supposed to meet us here at Strawberry—according to Annalee. I've my doubts about that."

So Annalee was using the O'Day name instead of Halliday. Then she couldn't be all that in the dark about her father. When she'd learned he was a deputy marshal, she'd held back. No wonder Berry hadn't found Samuel's letter—if he'd even sent one.

Brett smiled a little and shook his head. Annalee was probably asking Berry right now if there was any mail for "Annalee Halliday." That would send a jolt through Berry.

"Why did you think your father was dead?"

"Because Macklin came to see our mother in San Francisco with the news. He told her that my father had been killed by the Piutes crossing the Forty Mile Desert into Salt Lake."

Macklin again. He had lied to Lillian Halliday. Why? To lure her to Virginia Town? To get his hands on those mining shares? What was it about those Pelly-Jessup shares that had Macklin Villiers scheming? Or was there something more?

Yes, it was beginning to make some sense. Lillian had gone with her husband's trusted cousin Macklin to set up a theater on the Comstock. All she had to do was sell those mining shares. And Macklin's lawyer, Colefax, would take care of everything. Then the stage accident... Strange, too, how Colefax was also the witness to Harkin's death.

"Who owns those shares now, Callie? Do you know?"

"Why—" she looked surprised, as though she hadn't thought about it before. "We do, I think. Me, Annalee, and Jimmy. Mother would have left them to us. Probably to Annalee, since she's older. She trusted Annalee to care for Jimmy."

"They wouldn't belong to your father?"

She frowned. "You know, Mr. Wilder, I'm not actually sure. Maybe Annalee would know that. She knows more about all this than I do. But I've the impression our pa doesn't own the mining shares. Of course, Cousin Macklin may have already sold them. It was Mother's wish to sell. That's why Annalee thinks his lawyer is holding either the shares or whatever money there is for us. But he's sure taking his sweet time contacting us."

"If your uncle is there, I've heard good things about him. He's most likely looking into it as well."

Brett didn't want Callie becoming too suspicious about Macklin yet. He could be a dangerous man when someone stood between him and what he wanted. He may have arranged for Lillian's death. If Annalee was next in line to own those shares to the Pelly-Jessup—

Brett frowned and looked again toward the trail to Placerville. He wanted to look into all this for himself first. There was even the possibility that Jack Halliday had returned to Virginia Town to retrieve those mining shares and look into his claim with Harkin. Did Frank Harkin's death have anything to do with any of this? Just where was the Halliday-Harkin claim located? If it was near the Pelly-Jessup, the two mines might be on the same silver lode.

Brett said nothing of his thoughts to Callie. He needed proof. But he didn't want them in Virginia Town. He had to convince Annalee to return to Placerville, or even Sacramento, and let him handle this.

He said goodnight and watched Callie walk quickly back to Berry's.

Several minutes passed, and still Brett remained, mulling over the details of their conversation in his mind.

❧ ❧

Annalee returned to the table after asking the proprietor if there was a letter for Annalee Halliday. There wasn't, but he'd certainly eyed her curiously. She didn't blame him. For some reason she thought he'd heard that name before. He'd also told her it was arranged for them to sleep in the back room.

"That's mighty kind of you," she had said.

"You can thank Wilder, miss. He seen to it 'fer he left for Placerville."

"The marshal?" she had said, surprised and flattered.

"Wilder's a man you can trust when the bottom's out, ma'am. None like him. None faster with a gun, either. Has himself a ranch in Grass Valley. Cattle, horses. Nice place, I hear."

"He's not married, I take it?"

Berry grinned knowingly.

"Had plenty of opportunity, but he's mighty careful. Knows what he wants. Won't take less."

Annalee was seated at the table again thinking about Brett Wilder when Callie came indoors, her cheeks flushed with cold. Annalee noticed her blue eyes were excited. All of a sudden she grew suspicious—and nettled.

"Callie, did you go running after Brett Wilder?"

Her sister's delicate dark brows lifted. "What if I did? He's the only friend we have."

"What did you tell him!"

"What is this, an inquisition?"

"Don't be silly. I just don't want you filling his ears with tales about me, is all. Did you talk about me?"

"What if I did? Oh, Annalee, don't be so touchy. Why is it such a big secret? You act as if being sick were criminal."

"It's a personal matter, Callie. Can't you understand that? It's not something I want shouted about to just anybody."

"Brett Wilder isn't just anybody. And I didn't shout it. I'd never have told him except that he asked."

"He...asked?" her voice was small. Now why had he done that? "You told him about what Dr. Harley said, didn't you? And I'll wager you even told him about Gordon Barkly." When her sister didn't deny it, Annalee jumped to her feet. "Callie, how *could* you! It's humiliating."

Callie looked miserable. "Honestly, Annalee, so what? He wanted to know. He kept asking. I had a notion he'd force it from me. He's quite a man, actually. Not one to toy with. He's very different from Gordon."

Annalee flushed. The idea that he'd asked about her brought a certain pleasure, but the information Callie had given him was mortifying. Drat Callie.

"What did he say when you told him I had the illness?"

Callie met her gaze without apology. "The same thing I've been telling you ever since we left Aunt Weda's. Did you know his father's a doctor?"

That startled her. Annalee considered cautiously. Then Brett wasn't likely to be timid about illness. Not that she could imagine him being timid about anything. It also meant, like Gordon, that he'd come from a fine family.

"He was concerned about you." Callie smiled at her. "You sure have his interest."

Annalee looked away. *Do I?*

Callie wrinkled her brow. "Odd, though. He sure did behave strangely when I mentioned Pa."

"You told him our name was Halliday?"

"It...slipped out."

Callie looked uncomfortable, as though she might be hiding something more from her.

"What did he say?"

"He asked more questions, is all. But when I said Pa's name, he looked as if, well, almost as if I'd slapped him."

Their eyes met. A horrid thought came to Annalee. Suppose…suppose being a lawman, Brett Wilder wasn't looking for Rody or someone else, but Jack Halliday?

She shuddered. There was no proof to warrant her fears. It had been a trying day. It was easy to allow her imagination to stray as wildly as the wind.

At least she could tell Callie the good news about sleeping in the back room—again, thanks to Brett Wilder.

Ten

Before retiring for the night, Annalee spread the rest of the pan bread with butter and honey and wrapped it up in a kitchen cloth. She picked up the plate of food she'd hardly touched, slipped into her cloak, and went out the back door.

The cold wind whipped against her. She headed off toward the wagons and stable where she'd seen the old miner and his mule Jenny bedded down for the night. She found him there huddled in the back of his wagon with a thin blanket over him.

When he saw her his mouth dropped open. "Well, I'll be plum snookered. That fer me?"

"It sure is. I'm Annalee—Halliday. It isn't much, but it's something."

He crawled nimbly out of his wagon and tipped his battered hat. "Name's Elmo. Ain't got no last name. Least none I remember. Thankee much, miss. That looks durn good. Ain't had me no Mexican chili since I were in Santa Fe way." He whiffed the aroma. His shaggy brows wiggled with appreciation.

"I brought a little something for Jenny too."

"A bag o' corn! Say, miss, that must a cost ya' a mite. Jenny'll be mighty 'preciative. Don't know how to thankee."

"Jenny's got to get you over that mountain," she said with a smile. "A faithful old mule like that is worth the nickel I paid for the corn. Besides, the marshal paid for our supper."

"Well, yer mighty kind. Won't forget it. You going on to Virginny Town?"

"In the morning. We're waiting for Flint Harper's mule train."

"Flint's a right nice fella. You can trust him. That marshal too. I knows 'em both from way back. Say—if you need me or Jenny fer anything in Virginny Town, you come a callin'."

"Thank you, Elmo. Goodnight."

"Bless you, miss. Goodnight. Say goodnight, Jenny."

The old mule flicked her long ears and turned her head to cast an eye at her.

Annalee was still smiling when she walked through the field back toward Berry's.

She stopped. A tall broad-shouldered figure stood in her way. His hat was low and his knee-length coat blew in the wind. He held the reins of what looked to her like a fine, strong horse. She was surprised when she recognized the resonant voice of Brett Wilder. "What were you doing in the wagons just now?"

She folded her arms, holding her ground.

"Did you think I was sneaking off to see my father?"

"If I'm fool enough to believe Big Burt and Hoadly, Halliday's ridden to Placerville."

Her excitement climbed. Then her father was alive and may even be looking for them! But why hadn't he stopped here at Strawberry Flat?

She didn't know who Hoadly was, but any association with Big Birdie shed light on his character.

"That horrid man knows my father?"

"I doubt it. More likely, it's a trap."

"For my father?" she felt alarmed.

"No, for me. It's pretty lonesome on the trail this time of night."

She tried to piece together the meager facts at her disposal. Was someone out gunning for Brett Wilder? Her dismay was swift and fierce.

"You can't be suggesting that my father would be setting an ambush for you on that trail! He may be a gambler, Mr. Wilder, but he's not a cold-blooded killer. And I resent your—"

"Take it easy. I haven't suggested anything except that I didn't trust Hoadly and his boys."

She breathed deeply. "I don't know who Hoadly is, and from the sound of him, I hope it stays that way."

"I think it's wise I give you a word of advice, Miss Halliday."

She lifted her chin. "I'm listening, Mr. Wilder." She tried to maintain her poise, for she suspected what was coming.

He came a little closer. She looked at him, but in the darkness she couldn't see his face well enough to read his expression.

"There's nothing in Virginia Town for a girl like you. The town, if you want to call it that, is mostly tent-shelter saloons. Soon it will attract the worst sort of gamblers and gunslingers out to get rich. I've seen men throw away a fortune in one night. I've seen others kill over a card game. It's a man's town. Not even Samuel will be able to keep you out of trouble."

So he knew Samuel. At least his good reputation cast them in a favorable light.

"It can't be as savage as all that. My mother intended to go into business there, and Macklin's a banker. Anyway, I must go there. I've business to see to that won't wait."

"Yes, Callie told me about those shares in the Pelly-Jessup. Does Macklin have them?"

It looked as though Callie told him everything. She wasn't sure how she felt about it. Maybe it was for the best.

"He must, because my mother's trunk was never sent back to Sacramento. That's another reason I want to see him. I've questions about her death I want answered."

She could see he watched her carefully. Did he guess her suspicions? He, too, was cautious, as though uncertain what to tell her.

"Let me look into all this for you. I'll speak to Samuel soon as I get there. He may have already collected those shares from Macklin. Do you mind telling me who owns them now that your mother's gone?"

"I do," she said quietly.

He looked displeased. She wondered why.

"Not your father?"

She shook her head, shivering. The wind blew in cold, breathtaking gusts, shaking the pines and bending the field grasses to the ground.

"No. Mother told me not long before she left Sacramento that the shares were in her name and that I was listed as her beneficiary.

That's why I want to speak to Macklin for myself. You might as well know, Mr. Wilder, that I don't trust or even particularly like Macklin Villiers. I believe he was out to take unfair advantage of my mother. The fact that neither he nor Colefax has contacted me convinces me all the more."

He smiled a little. "You and I agree at least on that much. I don't trust Villiers either. That's why you need to let Samuel and me handle this. Look, I'll make you a deal."

"A deal?"

"Yes. Let me take you, your sister, and brother back to Sacramento to your aunt's farm. I'll loan her money to pay off the taxes. That should keep the wolf away from the back door for a time. Time enough to handle trouble in Virginia Town."

She was stunned. "You mean you'd loan us money?"

"Why not? The risk is small. You can either pay me back when matters are settled with Macklin or I'll simply end up with some more land."

"I…we couldn't do that, Mr. Wilder. I…we hardly know you."

He smiled wryly. "I don't suspect you know the bankers in Sacramento any better, but you'd still take a loan from them, wouldn't you?"

"But I would not even be able to pay you interest?"

He slapped the horse's reins against his palm, watching her. "We can talk about that later."

They stood gazing at one another. She felt herself drawn to him and quickly looked away. She stepped back and turned toward Berry's Flat.

"I'll need to think about it, Mr. Wilder, but thank you very much for the kind offer. I'd better get back or Callie will start worrying."

"Then you won't go back with me tonight?"

"No. My mind's made up. If my father's in Virginia Town, then I want to see him. Jimmy, too, needs him. And he needs Uncle Samuel, a man of God. We all need Samuel."

"That much I'll agree with. But I also must warn you. There's going to be real trouble on the Comstock before this is over. I'd hate to see you mixed up in it."

She turned and faced him, trying to hide her fear.

"What kind of trouble?"

He considered. Then seemed to make up his mind.

"Several dangerous renegades are reported to be in Virginia Town just now. The lure of silver is just too much for them. And there's one man in particular I'm to find and bring in."

Annalee shivered. She feared to inquire any further, afraid of what she might hear.

He reached over and took her arm.

"I've kept you too long. Better go inside."

She responded to the quiet concern in his voice.

"What about you? You're not going to ride the trail to Placerville? Not when you expect a trap?"

"I need to do some research in town. A trap is only good when it's kept secret. I'll see you again."

She watched him mount, rein his horse around, and ride off into the wind-swept night. Her prayer came swiftly for God's protection. Did Brett Wilder have faith in the one and only Christ? She must be sure of it before allowing her emotions to go any further. And to think she'd met him just that afternoon. How quickly a heart could be captured, and how easily lost, in the maelstrom of physical attraction. She must be very careful.

❧ ❧

Brett rode his zebra dun slowly along the trail. The wind was stronger now, rushing through the tops of the pines. The starlight, once glistening, was now hidden by clouds, giving him more confidence. He would make a poor target should anyone be waiting for him beside the mountain trail. No one in his right mind would try for it now. Even so, he'd drawn his Winchester and rested it across his saddle, the muzzle pointed toward the road.

Then his horse, wily creature that it was, drew up a little and lifted its ears, not liking something ahead.

"That's what I thought," he told it quietly. "Easy now."

He walked the horse to the side of the trail, drew in among the trees out of sight, and waited.

The noise of the wind was to his advantage. He was also downwind of anyone approaching his position. He sat, his rifle almost casually laid across his saddle, his hand near the trigger.

He didn't need to wait long. He could just make out the sound of horse hooves, more than one. In another minute two dark forms on horseback rode along the trail in the direction of Strawberry.

"Wilder's canny. Knew he weren't no fool. Only a fool's going to fall for that tale about Halliday at Placerville. Told Hoadly as much. Can't see more'n a yard ahead in this darkness. Most likely Wilder's sound asleep under his blanket. It's black as aces out here!"

"Most likely get soaked 'fer we get back too," the second rider said. "I don't like getting wet. Should'a stayed in Tucson."

Brett couldn't see their faces, and he didn't recognize their voices. He was glad one of them wasn't Rick Delance. But Rick was from Tucson. Would he know the second renegade?

These were two unknowns. The renegades were moving in toward Virginia Town just as the governor had told him. He wondered how many there would be.

The two gunfighters rode on by. Brett relaxed a little, listening for any further sounds, but the wind smothered everything except his own heartbeat thumping steadily in his ears.

A cold splash of rain fell on his face. Then a second and a third. Soon it was pouring. He drew his slicker from his saddlebag and slipped it on. One thing he shared in common with one of the renegades was that he didn't like being rained on either. He'd rather be under a warm blanket. Only duty would force him on his way down the long, steep mountain trail back to Placerville. Duty, and something more; a growing interest in Annalee Halliday. He wanted to know more about that stage accident and Macklin Villiers, who survived it.

Eleven

The morning dawned windy and cold with pine trees etched darkly against the golden fleece of morning clouds. Callie took Jimmy with her to await the arrival of the mule train. She'd left Annalee down at the cold creek washing her face.

Callie heard the musical tinkle of bells and hooves clattering on the frozen trail. A few moments later her eyes fell on a young man riding a strong mule around the mountain bend, leading a long train of saddled mules and pack animals. So this was Flint Harper. He was more impressive looking than she'd expected.

"Higher part of the trail's full of ice," Harper called over to a skinny man from Texas. "Took me an extra two hours."

"Howdy, Flint." The Texan walked over to him. "Ain't seen you since California."

"You're a sight for sore eyes. Thought them Injuns got you scalped back in Oklahoma."

"Me? No Injun's takin' my hair. Heard them Piutes is on the warpath, though. Say, how's the diggins' at Washoe?"

"Better'n the Fraser, I can tell you that. You come at a good time, Stoke. By this spring the place will be crawlin' with folk. Now's your chance to get yourself a claim on Gold Hill or maybe down Six Mile Canyon."

"Look at them mules, Callie." Jimmy's eyes widened at the sight, and he surged toward them, anxious for adventure.

Callie was in a cross mood. She hadn't slept well, and she wasn't looking with anticipation on the long travel ordeal ahead of them. Annalee's cheerfulness had also pricked her conscience. Her sister was up an hour earlier reading her Bible. Her dedication come rain or shine made Callie feel both guilty and out of sorts. Annalee battled both sickness and the loss of Gordon Barkly, yet she handled her pain and disappointments with grace. Under the same trials Callie knew she'd be angry and questioning God's purposes.

She studied the mule driver, trying to find something she didn't like about him besides his job. His looks were dynamic. He wore an old coonskin cap, a fringed buckskin jacket, leather chaps over his pants, and a pair of leather boots. He was broad at the shoulders and tanned by the desert sun. His hair was sandy colored and wavy, and it contrasted nicely with his amber eyes.

She stood staring at the mules. She walked up and down the long train with knitted brows. *This is going to be a very long, very uncomfortable ride.* She sighed.

Flint Harper saw her. He removed his cap and ran his fingers through his thick hair.

"Say, now. Where'd you come from?"

She tossed him a superior glance. *I am not interested in mule drivers,* she told herself. *I am going to become famous on the stage and go to New York. Maybe I'll even marry a Yankee.*

"Sacramento," she stated briefly.

Flint didn't appear the least put off by her coolness.

"It shows. Don't tell me you're coming to Washoe?"

Callie had no intention of answering.

"Are we supposed to ride these creatures all the way to Virginia Town?"

At her disdainful voice he put his coon cap back on. "The name's Flint Harper."

"Callie Halliday," she said reluctantly.

"You intending to ride with me to Carson?"

"I'm intending to ride to Carson, yes."

His eyes squinted. "Where's your pa?"

"In Virginia Town."

He pushed his hat back and scanned her curiously. He looked over at Jimmy, who was engrossed in counting the mules aloud. "That your youngster?"

"My brother. I also have a sister who will be here shortly."

"What's your pa's name? I know most folks in Virginia Town."

Callie felt a flush tint her cheeks, and she became speechless. It was one of the few times she wished Annalee were with her to help the conversation.

She remembered the marshal's reaction last night when she'd mentioned Jack Halliday and didn't want the same response. But...she might as well get it over with. She drew in a breath. "His name's Jack Halliday. Do you know him?"

He flashed another grin. "No, ma'am. Never heard of him."

"That's a relief," she murmured to herself.

"You was saying, Miss Callie?"

She cleared her throat. "Nothing, Mr. Harper."

"Call me Flint, ma'am, everybody does. I've heard of Samuel Halliday. Any relation?"

"Yes, if he's a preacher."

Flint grinned. "Samuel's a preacher all right, and a brave man to survive at Sun Mountain all these years. I take it he's expecting you and your sister?"

"My sister insists that he is." Callie looked warily at the mules. "We're friends of Marshal Brett Wilder, so I was hoping you'd give me a tame mule."

"Wilder! Why, I'll be! He's a marshal again? Who's runnin' his ranch for him?"

"He didn't say."

"Nice place, Wilder Ranch. Got about a thousand head of beef and some fancy Virginia horses. I wonder what worried him back into a badge?"

Callie had no idea, of course, but she was struck by the news that Brett Wilder owned a ranch. She wondered where it was located.

"I envy him that ranch," Flint was commenting in thoughtful good-naturedness. "That's my ambition too. Only I want horses. Down around Santa Barbara."

Callie had no notion where Santa Barbara was until he'd told her it was about three hundred miles south of San Francisco. She supposed he was working the mule train to save money for the land.

"So Wilder's here?" Flint asked, looking about.

"He was last night. He went back down the mountain to Placerville on business."

Jimmy, who'd come up beside Callie, spoke in a low, mysterious voice. "He's after a bad man."

Flint looked down at the boy with amusement. "Unfortunately, there's a lot of 'em around. And who might you be?"

"Jimmy Halliday. This here's Keeper."

"A mighty fine cat, son. Better keep her tied, though, or you'll lose her over the pass."

"Oh, I keep her good and tied, sir!"

"Well, ma'am, any friends of Brett deserve the best. How about this mule right here? This is Lady Jane. 'Course, you're twice the lady she is."

Callie saw the imp dancing in his eyes.

She gave a little curtsy. "You're mighty grand with your compliments, Mr.Harper."

He grinned. "Now, why don't you ride Lady Jane here right next to me and Jimmy, and I'll fill your ears all the way to Carson with fancy compliments."

Callie surveyed the mule. "You're sure she won't throw me?"

"Lady Jane? Why, she has the manners of a queen."

"Hey, Flint!" Berry called over from the front of the tavern. "Got one more mule to rent? We got us a passenger from Frisco."

"Sure. Send him over."

The man coming toward them took Callie by shock.

"Gordon! What on earth are you doing here?"

Gordon Barkly smiled and came up to her, taking her hand and bending over it as though he were a British lord and she Lady Halliday of Buckingham Palace.

"Looks like I just made it in time. I'm coming with you and Annalee. I'm going to try my hand at publishing in Virginia Town."

Wait till Annalee finds out.

Callie searched his face for quick, simple answers, and Gordon seemed to read her questioning gaze. "I got a loan to start my newspaper. Louise and I, well, we decided it was too soon to know how we truly felt about one another. We've agreed on a year's separation."

"Oh!"

Gordon glanced quickly around, ignoring Flint, who studied him in silence. "Where's Annalee?"

"Down at the river. She'll be here soon."

"I think I'll walk down and meet her." He turned to Flint. "How much to ride the mule?" His voice was blunt and his gaze unfriendly.

Flint sized him up and then gestured his head toward Berry's. "You can pay inside." He turned and walked off.

Gordon looked after him. "Unpleasant fellow."

Callie remained silent. Gordon looked dashing. She was happy he was here. But how was she to keep him from Annalee?

Gordon smiled down at Jimmy and tousled his hair. "Come on, let's go find your sister."

❦ ❦

The damp earth, slick with wet pine needles, smelled fresh in the crisp morning air. The crows cawed and a squirrel darted behind a tree trunk at Annalee's movements along the creek bank.

The rain had passed over during the wee morning hours, leaving the forest smelling clean. But clouds still lingered, and there was the feel of more bad weather to come.

The icy creek water was so cold it stung. Annalee patted her face and throat dry and added some of her mother's fragrant oil to protect her skin from the elements. With her long hair drawn back and coiled on top of her head, she was ready for the day's mule ride. She wore her woodsy green riding habit and boots.

Suddenly her senses tingled. Was that someone behind the trees? Her spine stiffened. A large shadow she could just see made her think of Big Birdie. Her heart leapt. She stood quickly. He'd been watching her.

Was it her imagination or a shadow of forest foliage moving in a gust of wind? Reason tried to tell her that awful man wouldn't dare bother her again after Brett Wilder's confrontation.

But Brett had ridden to Placerville and Big Birdie might know that. Where had he gone after Brett warned him away from her?

Big Birdie must have been waiting for the mule train to Virginia Town the same as several others at the rest stop. He may have seen Brett leave.

She backed away from the creek, glancing over her shoulder toward the tavern. It wasn't far, but she'd better get back at once.

Wait! Her satchel—where was it?

She looked around frantically. She'd left it only a few feet away sitting on that boulder. Her hand went to her forehead in despair.

She searched around the gray rock, keeping an eye on the trees where'd she seen something.

She looked up toward the line of ponderosa pine. Weda's hundred and fifty dollars in gold pieces were in there!

But how had the thief known?

She started to run into the trees after him until better sense overruled her emotions. If it was Big Birdie, he was dangerous.

As much as it pained her, she decided to go back to Berry's Flat and report the theft.

She climbed the creek bank and started toward the tavern and eatery.

She hadn't gone far when she saw Jimmy running toward her with a man following. Brett Wilder? But he wasn't as tall and—

Annalee stopped...Gordon! But that was impossible.

Jimmy ran up breathless, anxious to be the bearer of exciting news.

"Guess what, Annalee? Gordon's going with us to the Comstock!"

Annalee was still staring, speechless, when Gordon came toward her. He paused, looking at her uncertainly before coming on swiftly.

"Annalee!"

"You're going with *us?* But how? I mean, what about your newspaper and—" she stopped before saying "Louise."

His lean strong hands took hold of her shoulders, and he smiled ruefully.

"Father has friends in the banking business. He managed to get me a loan. I'm going to start my newspaper writing fresh on the scene from the silver-crazed Comstock. I feel I can make it there, Annalee. And...I'll be able to see you."

She didn't know what to say as she looked up at him. She smiled suddenly.

"I'm glad, Gordon. I'm glad things have worked out for you." She hesitated to ask, but she must know…and of course he would expect her to be curious.

"But what about Louise?"

His smile slowly disappeared and his eyes studied her carefully.

"We decided to call off our engagement. I want to get my newspaper started first and get the loan paid off. Louise agrees it's best this way. We parted friends."

Annalee remained silent. What would all this mean to her, to Gordon, even to Callie? Her sister had a crush on Gordon. But then, Callie had feelings for more than one!

Her immediate situation rushed back to the forefront of her attention. "My satchel! Gordon, there was a man down there by the creek who stole it. Everything we have of value is in that bag."

He looked quickly toward the creek. "Which direction?"

She pointed to the thick stand of ponderosa pine. "Over there. But be careful, please. He may have a gun."

"So do I. Wait here. Both of you."

Annalee watched him run toward the creek, but she had little hope of recovering her satchel. By now the thief could be anywhere, even back at Berry's ready to mount a mule. But he couldn't take her satchel with him. There was no place he could hide it.

"Did you see who the thief was?" Jimmy asked. " 'Cause if you did, you can tell Marshal Wilder when he comes back. He can find him and arrest him. Is there a jail in Washoe?"

"I'm sure there's a place somewhere," she said absently, straining her eyes to see off toward the trees.

"That's the mule bells, Annalee!" Jimmy pointed back toward Berry's. "We've got to go. That's Mr. Harper telling folks to hurry up."

"You run along. Find Callie and tell her what happened. Tell her we'll be there in a few minutes. Tell Mr. Harper too!"

Jimmy ran off, but he'd only been gone a few minutes before Gordon reappeared. He waved at her, beckoning. "Over here!"

Could he have caught the thief? Annalee ran toward him, but she'd not gone far before she began to feel fatigued and slowed down.

"Here's your satchel," Gordon called. "He dropped it in these shrubs. He must have searched quickly—is there anything missing?"

She took her satchel and stooped down to rearrange her clothing items, and handful of books. She didn't tell him about the gold pieces. As she drew her hand away she touched the inside lining. Yes, it was still sewn shut. The thief, in a hurry, had overlooked her hiding place.

She knew her heavenly Father was sovereign over her affairs. She believed it wasn't just negligence that had kept the thief from discovering the money, but that God had protected it for them. She closed her eyes and thanked Him for His watchful care.

When they walked up to the mule train, a few minutes later, Callie was waiting for her with their baggage.

"I suppose you ladies want those small bags with you on the mules," Flint said. He and the other men were loading the pack mules with blankets, foodstuffs, and other store-bought goods for Virginia Town. "This canvas trunk yours?"

"No…" began Callie hesitantly. "Oh, I think…it is. That's Aunt Weda's trunk, isn't it, Annalee?"

"Yes, she gave it to me."

"It'll need to go on the baggage mules," Flint said. "Anything you need from it on the way over the mountain?"

"No, it just contains extra clothes and some books and papers that belonged to my mother."

❧ ❧

The pilgrims were getting into their saddles, and most of them seemed to know exactly what they were doing. Callie was a little nervous.

"Now don't you worry about a thing, ma'am," Flint told her. "You just mount Lady Jane nice and easy like—that's it. See? Nothing to it." He flashed a smile.

Jimmy had insisted he ride up near Flint Harper with Callie. Callie turned in her saddle and looked toward the back. She saw Annalee and Gordon and waved.

Flint had mounted and given the signal to move out.

Jimmy looked across at Flint and then grinned excitedly at Callie.

"This is a fine mule, Mr. Harper," Callie grudgingly admitted when she'd begun to relax.

"Well, ma'am, any friend of Brett Wilder is my friend too. I owe him my life. Wilder's a fair man."

Jimmy perked up at once. "Did he save you from the Piutes?" He was riding the older tan mule Flint had chosen for him.

Flint grinned down at him. "He saved me from far worse than a war party of Piutes."

"What could be worse than Indians?" Callie asked, shuddering. She looked about the distant ranges as though she expected to see smoke signals.

"Many things. I was a placer miner, sometimes a trapper, but I lost most of what I earned gambling. I used to hang out all night with Ol' Virginny and a man named Comstock, drinking tarantula juice. I don't suppose Miss Callie would want you to know what that is, Jimmy. Then Wilder came, and for a while he joined us at Sun Mountain. But looking back, I'm sure it wasn't silver he was expecting to find."

"What then, gold?" Jimmy asked. He made sure Keeper was covered inside his jacket. Callie smiled to herself as she caught a glimpse of Keeper's ears.

"Gold?" Flint repeated. "Not Wilder. He makes good money ranching. He pulled out his little black Book every night and did nothing but read. He didn't preach, mind you. He just read the words long and deep and slow like until Ol' Virginny couldn't stand it. Comstock huffed off looking back over his shoulder with a suspicious scowl. Somehow I just sat there."

Jimmy stared up at him intently. "Then what?"

"After a few weeks of those good words, something inside of me began to change."

"Like what, Mr. Harper?"

"Like I understood I was a drinker and a gambler, and if I kept on turning my back to who Jesus was and what He did for me, I'd have to pay the full debt of my sin."

"That's a mighty big debt to pay, Mr. Harper."

"You're right. And not all the silver in the Comstock Lode could pay that debt. It took something much more precious than silver and gold. It took the death of God's Son, Jesus.

"So you see, I owe Wilder. He's the best friend I got. If it weren't for him coming to me and staying around that summer, I'd still be drinking tarantula juice with Ol' Virginny and Pancake Comstock."

Jimmy smiled up at him and laughed at the names. "I get it about tarantula juice and gambling, but who are Ol' Virginny and Pancake Comstock?"

"Well, Ol' Virginny's the miner who named the settlement under Sun Mountain Virginia Town."

"After himself?"

"Humble, wasn't he? But he's a fine miner when he's sober. Knows more about mining than all the rest put together. And Pancake, well, he falsely claimed that all the diggings on Sun Mountain belonged to him."

"Why?"

"Greed, and because he was there first, or so he said. He fooled a lot of people, that one. Got a tricky tongue. But he's all right. I feel sorry for him."

"So that's how the silver find was named the Comstock Lode?" Callie asked from behind them.

"The name seems to stick."

"Are Comstock and Ol' Virginny rich now?" Jimmy asked.

"Nope. They sold out before the rich ore in the Ophir diggings was ever located. Ol' Virginny's mostly drunk, poor fellow, and Comstock's too lazy to bake his bread, so he fries his flour into pancakes. That's why folks call him Pancake.'"

Jimmy laughed. "Hear that, Callie?"

Callie glanced toward Flint. "Seems that Mr. Harper isn't a bad one for spinning tales himself."

Twelve

❧

*T*oward afternoon, as the mules pressed on to the summit, the weather turned colder. Snow blanketed the mountain ridges and the wind brought dark clouds. The mules seemed to sense a warning in the brisk wind. They hurried forward, knowing the trail so well that Annalee simply relaxed the reins.

Riding along hour after hour, she became aware of little else except weariness, and she tried to keep her teeth from chattering. She looked back over her shoulder at the other passengers. She tensed. A familiar man rode far back on the last mule, his shoulders hunched forward against the wind, his hat slouched over his forehead, partially concealing his bulldog face…Big Birdie.

Then she'd been right. He was here. Was it Birdie back at the creek? If so, why hadn't he taken anything? What had he wanted? Or had he just been trying to intimidate her?

She turned away, looking ahead at Flint Harper. Jimmy rode beside him, and just behind him, Callie. Gordon had told Flint about the incident back at the creek, and the two of them had made the rounds of the passengers asking questions, but no one appeared to know anything about it. Flint had spoken to Big Birdie, who had denied being down by the water. "She has it in for me," he had said. "Her, and that two-bit gunfighter from Frisco."

"If you intend to ride with us, you'd better watch your manners. Otherwise you can find a mule somewhere else. That 'two-bit gunfighter' happens to be a deputy marshal. You keep that in mind."

Annalee had enjoyed seeing the anger in Big Birdie's face turn to bewilderment and wariness upon learning who Brett Wilder was.

The road was little more than a crude, well-rutted trail. The mules, however, knew the way and trudged ahead with determination. Annalee's mule seemed to know exactly where it was going and was set on getting there so it could eat and rest at day's end.

Gordon rode beside her, but his enthusiasm appeared to dwindle as the hours marched on. "I wonder if this mule train driver ever takes into consideration that he has people aboard?"

Annalee had already noticed that Gordon didn't appreciate Flint Harper.

"I suppose he does this so often he's as determined as the mules," she suggested. "He must know the trail like the back of his hand."

Several times they came upon deep ravines beside the trail caused by mountain run-off water which had since frozen.

"Gullies full of ice," Gordon warned. "Looks like a frozen maze."

Does the mule know where to step? Annalee worried. *I certainly wouldn't!*

But the mules plodded through the rocklike ridges apparently knowing every section to avoid. She reached over and patted her mount's neck. "Smart animal. I bet you don't get half the appreciation you should. I wouldn't trade you for a Virginia horse right now."

Gordon laughed and then looked curious. "Who was the deputy marshal Harper talked about to Big Birdie?"

She glanced away toward the front of the mule train.

"Mr. Wilder? He was at Strawberry Flat. He's out to arrest some renegades."

"Is that why he went back to Placerville?"

"I believe he heard that someone he wanted had gone there." Remembering what Brett had said about a possible trap, she worried. But at least Big Birdie didn't lie in wait on the trail.

"Wilder? Brett Wilder?"

At the surprise in his voice, she looked over at him. "You've heard of him?"

"Most people have heard of the Wilder family. He owns cattle, lots of them. Has a brother in Texas named Yancey who owns another big spread. His father's a physician with a respected name.

I wonder what got Wilder interested in accepting a commission from the governor? Did he say whom he was after?"

Uneasily, Annalee brought her hood up, bracing against the wind. "No."

She noticed Gordon glanced sideways at her. He looked a little out of sorts talking about Brett.

"Wilder's getting engaged to the daughter of a leading citizen in Grass Valley. The Munroe family."

Annalee kept her expression poised. "Oh?"

He must have read disinterest in her tone, for he smiled and looked more at peace with himself. He began to whistle "Shenandoah."

Getting engaged. To the daughter of a leading—and undoubtedly wealthy—citizen of Grass Valley. Well, why was she surprised? Any man like Brett Wilder would be the number one target of a great many classy young ladies.

Annalee lapsed into silence. She refused to dwell on him. He had come in a night and gone in a night.

Would they ever stop? Would they ever reach their camping area?

Like a winding snake, the train of mules continued to move slowly along the trail. They caught up with other seekers heading for Washoe who had left Berry's Flat before them. Annalee saw wagons and horses surging forward. None of them wanted to stop or even rest out of fear that others would get ahead and claim the best sites on Sun Mountain.

It was a harsh road, with men and mules needing to climb over rocks, the men sometimes losing their balance on icy patches.

Farther up the ridge they came upon melting snowdrifts, dirty with slush, and rock and mud slides. Flint Harper maneuvered the mule train around the trouble spots with expertise. *These are a special breed of men,* Annalee thought. *Far different than the well-dressed bankers and shopkeepers in Sacramento.*

At last they struggled their way up to the narrow trail's crest. The scene was breathtaking. They saw miles of ponderosa green pine, purple-and-tan mountain ridges blanketed with white, and, despite the overcast sky, a clear blue lake.

Flint Harper turned the mule train aside and led them into the trees. It wasn't long before they came to a flat area that looked as though it had been used many times.

Annalee sat wearily on her mule, her eyes resting on the blue water.

"Lake Tahoe," Harper announced. "The Jewel Lady, I call her. We'll camp here for the night."

Annalee was too tired to comment or even enjoy the beauty. Stiff and sore, she allowed Gordon to help her down from the mule. When her boots touched solid ground, she tried not to sway as a dizzy spell struck her.

"Here, sit on this tree stump," Gordon said.

"I'll be all right now."

Despite her exhaustion, Annalee forced herself to help the others gather branches and pinecones for the fire. All she could think of was her bedroll, warmth, and sleep.

Flint showed Callie how to gather pine boughs and dried brush to spread under her bedroll for the night. Callie came to show Annalee.

"I've never been so sore," Callie complained. "How about you, Annalee? Are you still okay?"

"Exhausted. Coffee and supper are going to taste mighty good tonight."

"You'll get no complaints from me." Callie glanced over at Gordon, who was helping to set up camp. Her sly glance came back to her sister.

"Looks like Virginia Town will be more interesting than we thought."

"I can't get over his decision."

"Don't think Louise has surrendered him yet. I know her kind. It wouldn't shock me if she showed up here, too, before long."

"Her parents wouldn't allow it. She's too accustomed to fine parlors and sweet dresses." Annalee looked down at her boots. They had mud on them.

"Never underestimate a girl who wants a particular man," Callie said. "I know Louise. If she had to, she'd talk her pa into coming just so she could get here."

"I'm not worried about Louise. I've no claim on Gordon now. He called off our relationship, and I'm in no hurry to reclaim it."

Callie's lips turned ruefully. "Especially after meeting the deputy marshal?"

Annalee turned away, gathering more pine boughs. "Don't be silly. Anyway, from what Gordon says, Brett Wilder already has a girl. He moves in fine circles, I understand. The Munroe family are leading folks in town."

And Brett had money if he owned a ranch with a huge cattle spread. He wouldn't be interested in the Hallidays, whose father was a gambler and a heavy drinker.

Annalee's feet were heavy as she carried pine boughs and grass to put under her bedroll.

Later that evening, the fragrant smell of smoke from the campfire hung in the air. Flint was cooking up a side of bacon, and the coffee aroma was delicious. Annalee glanced around but didn't see Big Birdie anywhere.

But when she went to her bedroll, she saw that her other bag had been rifled. This time anger surged through her instead of fear. The big galoot! What was he trying to do? She'd half a mind to go tell him what she thought of his hideous sense of humor. What was he searching for? Was it even Big Birdie?

She sank to her knees on her bedroll and gathered her scattered clothes, stuffing them back into her clothing bag, too weary to fold them again neatly. She'd do it in the morning. She needed sleep.

A few minutes later, Callie and Jimmy tumbled into their bedrolls beside her. Callie yawned widely.

Slowly Annalee's anger ebbed. "Let's pray together first. Jimmy—where's Keeper?"

"Right here. I've got the rope tied to my belt."

Annalee smiled. After they'd prayed together and were snuggled down under the blankets, Annalee stared up at the sky and wished for bright stars, but the clouds were their roof tonight. Annalee could hardly keep her eyes open…the cares of the day were fading and drifting away.

❧ ❧

At dawn the light was cold, bleak, and gray. Someone had already built a fire, and the crackling of wood and the aroma of coffee caused Annalee to stir. Her eyes fluttered open at the sound of horse hooves approaching camp. A horse whinnied, and a mule brayed in greeting.

"Hey, Flint!" the Texan's voice shouted across the camp. "Wilder's just rode in! Look's like you got yourself a lawman to ride with us the rest of the way."

"You sure it's Wilder?" Flint called.

"I'd know that hombre anywheres. It's him, all right."

"None better."

Annalee's heart quickened. She was wide awake now. He'd come back. Her reaction to the news disturbed her, bringing a self-inflicted frown.

Don't be silly, Annalee. He didn't come back because of you. He hardly knows you. Remember, he's engaged—or as good as—to a woman in Grass Valley.

Quickly she awoke her siblings as she pulled on her boots. Grabbing her brush from her bag, she smoothed her hair and tied it back with a ribbon.

"Hear you're looking for a man. Maybe I've heard of him, what's his name?"

Silence followed. Brett's voice dropped, and Annalee couldn't make out what he was saying. Had he deliberately lowered his voice? She glanced the distance to where some men stood around the fire. Brett was pouring himself coffee.

A strange bubble of suspicion rose in her heart. That wanted man *couldn't* be her father, he just couldn't! Her eyes fastened themselves on the marshal.

He turned his head and glanced in her direction. She looked away and finished rolling up her blankets.

Jimmy and Callie walked over to him, and he spoke quietly.

Annalee buckled her satchel and tried not to listen to snatches of their conversation. She picked up the words "New Orleans" and "Lorena." Could Callie have told him about Lorena?

"Good morning," came the smooth voice.

Annalee glanced up. Brett stood a few feet away, the wind moving his dark jacket. The sight brought a quickening of her pulse.

"Good morning, Marshal." She hoped her expression didn't give her thoughts away. "This is unexpected. I thought you'd stay in Placerville."

Did she detect a flicker of amusement at her feigned surprise?

"I was able to get the information I needed."

She remained hesitant to ask directly about her father.

"So now you'll go on hunting the men you're after. You still think they're in and around Virginia Town?"

"I'm almost certain." He changed the subject. "I see you've survived your first night on the trail. Had enough yet?"

So he was still set against her decision to go to Virginia Town, and he wasn't going to offer much information on the man he was seeking.

He squinted up at the sky. Dark clouds were rolling with the wind. "Looks like snow. There's rough weather ahead if you go on with Harper. I was hoping you'd reconsider after a good night's rest."

She glanced at him. He smiled.

"It will take more than a night under the pine trees to change my decision about going on, Marshal."

"Brett."

She stooped to pick up her satchel, but he caught it up first. The satchel jogged her memory, and she looked at him, the smile leaving her face.

"My bags have been searched—twice. Once at Strawberry and again last night. With no attempt at secrecy." She explained what happened at the creek and walked toward the fire. "I think it was Big Birdie, but I can't be sure."

"He's gone. Flint told me he lit out on his own late last night. That would have been after he searched your bag. Anything missing?"

"That's what's curious. Nothing. Not even the hundred and fifty dollars Aunt Weda gave us to invest in a business at Virginia Town. It's sewn inside the lining, but any thief could have found it if he'd searched carefully. You think he was just trying to harass me?"

"If I didn't have a few notions of my own I'd probably think so, but I've found out he's friendly with a gunfighter named Hoadly. Hoadly was at Berry's when the stage you were riding came in. I was right about that trap waiting for me on the trail. Two men were riding this way. They mentioned Hoadly."

"But why search my bags?"

"I've reasons to think Macklin Villiers may be involved."

"Macklin," she said, surprised, "whatever for?"

"That's what I'm hoping you could tell me. What do you know about the Pelly-Jessup and your father's claim?"

"Not much about either. Mother had a few shares in the Pelly-Jessup. I've told you about them and her intentions to sell. My father's claim is near the Jessup mine, but Mother said not to think too much of it."

"That's interesting. That narrows Macklin's interest. He came to her about those shares in San Francisco. Did he offer to buy them from her before suggesting a business partnership in a theater?"

Surprised, she wondered. "Why...I don't know. She never said. They did have a few dinners together. She insisted it was all about business, but she never talked about it. Just that she was going to Virginia Town to make money to care for us, and to look for my father. She believed he was alive, even though Macklin was sure he'd been killed by Indians."

He looked thoughtful. "We'll look into those shares when we get to Virginia Town."

She was relieved for his help. With Brett on her side, she was no longer alone.

"But I don't see how that ties in with my bags being searched."

"Maybe it doesn't, but I aim to find out. Just as soon as I get to Virginia Town. You think about it. If anything comes to mind, let me know."

"Ho!" Flint shouted from the campfire. "If you two want anything to eat before we take off, you'd best line up."

Brett smiled down at her. "I think that was a command."

She tensed slightly when Gordon walked into camp from the direction of the lake. When he saw her and Brett standing together, visible tension showed on his face.

Brett apparently noticed as well. "Know him?"

She hesitated, aware that Callie had told him about her long friendship with Gordon and how he'd broken it off recently to become engaged to Louise.

"Yes, he's Gordon Barkly. He's decided to go to Virginia Town and open his newspaper."

Brett was as smooth as silk as Gordon walked up. She saw Gordon's eyes measuring him.

"I'm Gordon Barkly, Sacramento."

"Brett Wilder."

"You've a ranch out at Grass Valley. I hear it's the biggest spread this side of Texas."

Brett sized him up calmly. "My ranch grows bigger every time I hear about it."

Annalee moved uneasily. She glanced from one man to the other. What was Gordon trying to do?

"There's talk about that land. Talk that says some decent people were bought out cheap, or maybe forced out. As a journalist I intend to dig up the truth and bring it before the people of California."

Gordon looked like a peacock spreading its tail and blustering.

Annalee held her breath. Her cheeks turned warm.

Brett smiled. "You do that." He turned and nodded to Annalee, before walking over to the campfire.

Gordon was stiff as he looked after him. Annalee had never seen him like this before.

"That was uncalled for, Gordon. What are you trying to do, make trouble for no reason?"

"The Wilder brothers are too big for their own boots. It's time a journalist took them both on, and I intend to be the one."

"That's unwise. He's got a commission from Governor Downey to arrest dangerous men heading for Virginia Town. I'm sure you're wrong about his land."

His eyes turned cool. "I'm not wrong, and I'll prove it before this is over. The governor's a friend of his father. He helped the Wilders get that land at the expense of homesteaders. Wilder and his brother ran them off. I've witnesses."

She was speechless as he continued. "Right on this mule train. Just happened to talk with one this morning down at the lake. He saw Wilder ride in. He told me his story, and it isn't a pretty one. If you're wise, Annalee, you won't believe a word he tells you. He has more than one reason for going to Virginia Town. He's not just hunting a gunfighter. Wilder's out to get a claim on the Comstock, and he knows how to buy out an honest man cheap and dirty."

Annalee turned away sharply and walked over to where Callie and Jimmy were eating a breakfast of bacon and bread.

Callie looked at her and her brows lifted.

"You look as upset as a wet hen. Something wrong?"

Annalee shook her head and remained mute. She took her tin cup to line up for coffee. Gordon watched her defensively, but she chose to ignore him. She stole a glance at Brett. He stood alone by one of the pines, eating from a tin plate. In the dark duster, hat, and gun belt, he looked anything but tame. Could there be any truth to what Gordon said? Even his badge was out of sight. Could a cold streak run through his blood?

"You hol' yer cup steady, Miss Annalee, lest you get burnt. This be mighty hot coffee."

"Why, it's you! Hello, Elmo."

The old miner she'd met at Strawberry was wearing a soiled cook's apron.

"You're the cook?"

"Just hired on last night." He chuckled. "Ain't had me so much fun since I rode as chief cookie for cattle drives. Ain't no place I ain't been. Worked Abilene, Santa Fe, El Paso."

She held her mug steady while he poured. The steam curled in the cold air. Elmo piled bacon and grits on her plate.

"I can't eat all that," she said with a laugh. "Take some back."

"You'd best eat, Miss Annalee. You'll blow away in a Washoe zephyr if'n you don't put some meat on."

She laughed and walked over to Callie. Jimmy was going back for seconds. Keeper, tied to a stump, was licking up bacon pieces and purring.

Her thoughts returned to Gordon. Did Brett realize that someone on the mule train was claiming to be a witness to his taking homesteader land?

Flint was anxious to be on the trail. As quickly as possible, everyone headed for their mules. A few, including Brett, had horses. Annalee was standing beside her mule and contemplating the thought of another long, tiring day on its back when Brett came up beside her.

"You might be more comfortable if you rode with me."

She avoided his gaze and was furious that he had such an effect on her.

"Thank you, but I don't think it would be wise."

"Concerned about the newspaper man with a chip on his shoulder?"

"I don't know what got into him. I've never seen Gordon act that way before. He was always so…well, casual and friendly."

"For a man who turned his back and walked away when you needed him, he's had a drastic change of mind."

"He didn't turn his back on me," she said shortly. "It was a mutual decision."

"Then I heard wrong."

"If you're talking about what you heard from my sister, she had no right to discuss my private business."

He pushed his hat back. "Looks like I touched a raw spot talking about Barkly."

She fussed quietly with the reins. As the silence grew between them, she felt her face turn hot.

"Here—like this—you mount with your left foot."

"I know how to mount a mule!" She looked at him. The flicker in his clear gray eyes sent a spark between them. She tore her gaze away.

If his father was a physician, as Callie had said, then he would know something about illness. How much did he suspect from what her sister had told him?

"Annalee?"

This was the first time he'd spoken her name.

"Are you sure you want to go through with this? Take my word for it, you need to be under a doctor's care."

The quiet remark brought another confused moment. She was prepared to resist, but the veiled sympathy in his gaze silenced a retort. She didn't know how to answer him. Unlike Gordon, who didn't want to talk about her illness, Brett wasn't going to let her pretend everything was normal.

"Callie had no right to tell you," she choked.

"I'm glad she did. I know what you're trying to do now. I understand perfectly, as a matter of fact. There's more driving you than getting things cleared up with Macklin or even locating your father."

"I don't know what you mean," she said stiffly.

"Have it your way. I know illness when I see it. I strongly disagree with the risk you're taking. It could do you real harm."

She gripped the leather reins. "I've been well for over a year. I can handle it. There's no reason to think I'll get sick again. You've been listening to Callie. She worries too much."

"I don't need your sister to tell me. I can see for myself. There's more than one kind of trouble waiting for you if you go on with this venture. And helping your uncle with his missionary work won't stave off the inevitable."

"She told about that too?"

"I'm not questioning your devotion. Truth is, for such a frail young thing, I find your courage commendable."

Frail young thing!

"There are many ways to serve God without deliberately risking your life, though."

She turned and faced him. "Do you always lecture like an overbearing guardian, Mr. Wilder?"

He smiled, undisturbed, his voice as smooth as honey. "Granted, you're a determined young lady who finds a contrary opinion irksome. But in this instance, I think you may need a guardian. If you force yourself to go on like this, you could end up fainting in your saddle, and that could be dangerous."

She sucked in her breath, hands on hips.

"Let me tell you something about pack mules. They don't stop for anybody," he said easily. "They press ahead, and pity anything that gets in their way."

"I'm sure you know more about mules than I do, but as I have already explained, I'm a grown woman now. On my own. I've no need for a guardian."

"Just someone to protect you from snakes like Big Birdie?"

He had her there. She might insist all she wanted to that she could take care of herself, but that wasn't entirely accurate and they both knew it. There was the matter of her bags being searched, and perhaps trouble with Macklin if Brett's suspicions, as well as her own, turned out to be true.

"At least you needn't worry about me fainting."

Silence hemmed them in. His eyes grew slate colored. He pulled his hat lower and scanned her.

"You know," he breathed, "you've got a stubborn streak a mile wide."

Surprised by this bold assertion, she held her hood up to keep it from being blown back, and studied his face to see if he was serious. He was. His expression was set. He wasn't about to apologize.

"I'm learning a few things about you as well. And about your ranch," she said meaningfully.

His handsome jaw set and his eyes narrowed.

Now why had she said that?

Suddenly he laughed his dismissal, convincing her he wasn't afraid of Gordon and his newspaper story or of her challenge. His eyes held a challenge of their own.

Not waiting to reply, she placed her boot firmly in the stirrup and mounted easily. She couldn't help looking at him with an "I told you so" expression on her pretty face.

He laughed again and stepped back.

❧ ❧

Flint Harper was tightening the cinches on his lead mule when Brett walked up. Flint nodded his head over in Annalee's direction. "Fine girl. Mighty good lookin' too. But I get the notion she's gritting her way through this."

"There's iron under that silken exterior. It would help if you'd pull over and rest a time or two today."

"She's in poor health, is she?"

"She won't admit it."

Brett hadn't told Annalee, but in Placerville he'd visited Dr. Perkins, a friend of his father. He'd been able to get medication Brett had seen his father use on cases like hers; not that it cured anything, but it was better than nothing. Brett thought it wise to bring it along, because he didn't know the doctor in Virginia Town. Neither had Doc Perkins. "For all I know, he could be a horse doctor," he'd said dryly. "Here, better take this tonic too—helps the patient's appetite."

"What's she planning for in Virginia Town?" Flint was asking.

Brett looked at him with a slanted brow. "To convert Winnemuca."

Flint chuckled. Winnemuca was chief of the Piute Indians. "Say, now," he breathed, with a twinkle in his eyes. "Looks to me, Wilder, like you got your hands full this time. Word's out you're looking for someone in Virginia Town. Big trouble?"

"The usual amount."

"Maybe I've heard of him. What's his name?"

Brett glanced at Callie and Jimmy nearby.

"Jack Halliday."

Flint Harper followed his gaze. "Their pa?"

"Afraid so."

Flint shook his head sadly. "Do they know you're looking for him?"

"No."

"Are you going to tell them?"

"Not yet. I want to see them safe with Samuel Halliday first."

"It's going to be rough on them. That boy's looking up to you now."

Brett knew that, and it worried him. He thought Annalee might suspect something, but she wasn't sure and she was reluctant to ask him flat out—he hoped she wouldn't. How would he tell her without bringing the kind of pain and disillusionment she didn't need right now? That went for Jimmy and Callie too. But that wasn't the half of his problem. If he was right about Macklin Villiers, he would need to go after him and his nephew Rody as cold-blooded killers. Brett had questions about last year's incident on the stage from Placerville to Strawberry. He now thought Lillian O'Day was an intended victim, and that the Pelly-Jessup had something to do with it. Brett had looked into it at Placerville, but he had no proof to bring Macklin in, and no motive, for Macklin had gained nothing by her death.

He mounted his zebra dun and rode back farther along the mule train to where Annalee was. Gordon was mounted beside her and looked sullen when he saw him. Brett deliberately smiled at Annalee as he rode past, ignoring Barkly.

Flint, in the lead, had wasted no time getting them on the trail. It was a little after sunrise when he headed them out. He grinned as he heard Jimmy behind him talking to his cat.

"Let's go see Ol' Virginny and Pancake, Keeper. Giddyap, mule! Ho! On to Washoe!"

Thirteen

*Though the sun was hidden, it seemed as though they had been riding for hours past high noon. The trail wound its way through magnificent country, but it held no sympathy for the weak. As the day wore on, a biting blast of wind stung Annalee's face. A few drops of rain fell and then stopped. High above the granite rocks, dotted with pine, she watched an eagle soaring effortlessly. If only her heavenly Father would make her strong so that she could soar on spiritual wings.

Gordon had ridden ahead to talk to Callie. Brett rode up beside Annalee.

"Wondrous sight, isn't it?"

"If I could only capture the *feel* of its flight with my sketches!"

"I'd like to see your work sometime."

"You shouldn't have said that. You'll be doomed for hours."

Annalee tried not to shiver as the wind blew against her. With gloved hands she gripped the reins.

"Tired?" he asked softly.

"A little."

With him beside her, she tried to rally her faith and sit up a little straighter in the saddle. Even so, she was aware he was not fooled by her brave front. He said nothing more, however, and neither did she. She was content to have him riding with her. His mere presence imparted strength.

The trail had grown icy, but the brave mules pulled doggedly ahead. Brett's horse, too, appeared surefooted. Brett rode smoothly, she noticed, as though he was long accustomed to the saddle. What had interested him in cattle ranching when his father was a doctor? Interesting, also, that his brother was a rancher in Texas.

Her curiosity, however, began to wane as she became aware of little except her weariness. Every jolt of the mule throbbed in her temples.

Brett's dark brows slanted downward. "I'll tell Harper to stop for the night."

"No, please don't. He has his schedule. I don't want us quitting early just for me."

The bone-chilling wind whipped about them, billowing her hooded cloak.

He smiled, undisturbed. "We've come far enough today."

She turned her head away.

He cut away from the line, rode ahead to Flint, and spoke to him. Harper glanced back at her over his shoulder. Annalee fumed. Perhaps she was being too defensive. Why did she need to appear so unthankful for his concern?

Brett rode back to her. "We'll be stopping for the night soon."

"Thank you," she said quietly.

They rode on for another ten minutes and then the lead mule turned toward a clearing.

Brett twisted in his saddle and his clear voice rang out.

"Make your own way, gentlemen. Harper has given the signal to stop for the night."

Behind them she heard a few men grumbling. "Every hour we stop means somebody else is laying claim to Washoe."

Coming up the trail in the other direction, disconsolate pilgrims had passed them, heading back to the gold country of Sacramento.

"You're all makin' a mistake," one grizzled old miner shouted as he led his three mules. "There ain't nuthin' in Washoe. Nuthin' but zephyrs and alkali dust."

A little farther on they had met another man, gaunt and beaten. "Rich country in silver, best I ever seen, but what miner can hold his claim? If you ain't aimin' to draw your rifle, you folk had better turn back while the gettin's good."

"That bad?" asked Stoke the Texan.

"You bet. No disputin' claims on Sun Mountain. Fastest draw owns the richest vein."

Three or four men were pressing forward past Flint. Hearing the returnee's words, they exchanged smiles. That sounded good enough to them; they were plenty fast. They spurred their mules to trot on toward the Washoe silver a little faster.

❧ ❧

They made camp a good hour before sundown. Brett located a spot sheltered from the wind and possible rain, and he advised her to use it. "How is it you know so much about the wilderness?"

"My father was busy in his medical career while I was growing up, so my older brother, Yancey, and I did a lot of adventuring during the summers when we were home from the university."

"Yancey owns a cattle ranch in Texas?"

"Around Fort Worth. He's a better cattleman than I am."

"That's hard to believe. Is your brother married?"

He looked at her. His clear gray eyes flickered with energy.

"No. He should be though. He's fourteen months older than I. We were as close as twins, but Yancey's the ornery one." He winked at her.

She flushed and turned to Jimmy. "We'd better look for pinecones." Out of the corner of her eye she saw Brett's smile.

Annalee forced herself to aid in the hunting of dry branches and pinecones, even though all she could think of was lying down someplace where it was warm and falling asleep. Her feet felt like lead as she walked, keeping an eye on Jimmy. He was bursting with energy, and he had his eyes on a small creek below some boulders.

Annalee's courage, which had once refused to blink at the thought of entering the untamed West, now wavered. Maybe she *had* made a mistake. She hadn't been this fatigued since leaving Sacramento. Occasionally she felt a chest pain, and the fear of what it could mean increased her anxiety.

Under the blighting winds of uncertainty, the dim remembrance of past days of illness replayed their tragedy in her memory.

She'd walked out of sight from the others now, and she tiredly sank to an old fallen log. Alone, she didn't need to pretend, and she dropped her head into her hands.

Jimmy was whistling in the distance. She lifted her head. "Don't go far, Jimmy. Stay in sight."

To herself she thought, *I must rest for a little while...just a moment will do.*

Through blurred vision she watched Jimmy picking up pinecones. As always, Keeper was with him. Jimmy tied the kitten's rope quickly to a shrub and called, "There's a whole bunch of cones down here, Annalee."

He slipped on some ice in the shadows and slid laughing to the bottom, unhurt.

"Are you all right?" she called, standing.

"That was fun!"

She sat back down, shivering, too tired to either walk back to camp or ahead to the slope where Jimmy was. The girl with the rifle came to mind. She appeared to be both strong and independent. For a moment Annalee envied her, although the Indian girl had also looked tough and insensitive to others.

Annalee squared her shoulders, as though by determination alone she could conquer the troubling road ahead. There was no turning back. She would make it here, or she would die.

And yet...as the wind rustled her auburn hair, she could feel her weariness in her face, and knew it must show itself to anyone who looked at her with a thoughtful eye.

She had felt so well until arriving in Placerville. Could Dr. Harley be right? A relapse could happen?

Annalee pushed the thought from her mind. The possibility of facing new battles with her illness was nearly unbearable.

Don't panic. The LORD *is my light and my salvation; whom shall I fear? the* LORD *is the strength of my life...*

Growing unaware through fatigue, her eyelids grew heavy and drooped. Her head nodded. She almost drifted off sitting on the log...

She started awake, sitting straighter. A snap of twigs drew her gaze toward the trees.

Brett stood there, rugged and silent, his clothes dark against the white background. He walked up. "You'll freeze out here, Annalee," he said gently, and taking hold of her forearms, he helped her to her feet. She swayed a little but fought against it. He steadied her so she would not fall.

The feel of his strong, caring hands clasping her seemed to complement her weakness. Hardly aware of what she was doing, she gave in to the comfort of his strength, her cheek against his buckskin shirt.

Annalee's eyes flickered as she stood in the shelter of his arms. For a brief moment, she was unable to think of anything else. He did not say a word. As awareness crept over her, she stepped back, fumbling to smooth her cascade of auburn curls.

But his voice was casual, as though he'd been unaware of her. Was he?

"Where's Jimmy?"

Feeling as though she'd failed, she pointed down the slope.

"There's a steep drop further down that slope. It's dangerous. Wait here. I'll look for him."

But she didn't wait and tried to hurry after him, ignoring her fatigue.

They paused near the cat, who was alone, frightened, and straining at her rope. "Nice Keeper," she said in a soothing voice. The cat relaxed a little and then meowed plaintively.

Jimmy had ceased gathering pinecones and was wandering in a direction away from the clearing.

"Jimmy!"

The boy heard Brett's commanding voice and looked up. Seeing Brett, he came running.

"Be careful, son. Stay clear of that area. And next time you'll need to tie your cat better. Another minute or two and she would have gotten loose."

The thought of losing Keeper brought a look of fear to Jimmy's brown eyes. He scooped up his cat and hugged her. Keeper snuggled closely.

❈ ❈

Back at camp the fire was inviting. The mules, free of gear, were led to water. Brett watched Annalee and Callie carrying pine boughs and grass to make their own beds in the spot he'd recommended to Annalee. She'd refused to let him help.

"It's going to be like salt on a raw wound when they find out what brings you to Virginia Town," Flint said quietly. "The boy dotes on you, and I don't think Annalee will look you square in the face again if you arrest her pa."

Brett's expression showed the frustration he felt.

He shook his dark head while sitting on his boot heels before the fire. "I represent the law, Flint. Jack Halliday killed a man in Sacramento on that riverboat. I admit meeting Annalee is making this a whole lot more difficult for me. But I'm sworn to uphold the law."

"That's rough," Flint agreed, looking at the coffee in his tin cup. "Learn anything in Placerville about Macklin Villiers?"

"Enough to convince me he's either working hand in hand with his cousin Jack or against him. It's not clear yet what's going on between those two. But it has something to do with the Pelly-Jessup. I aim to learn more from Samuel."

"Samuel's a good man. You'll find him an ally. He loves Jack's kids, though. Won't like it if you bring them any grief."

"That's the last thing I want to do, Flint. You should know that. If I had my way, I'd send all three of them back to Placerville until this trouble is cleared up. Their presence in Virginia Town is going to make things harder for me."

"I see what you mean."

"It's getting complicated. If Halliday and Harkin were partners in a claim near the Pelly-Jessup, that mine may be on another part of the same lode that's running through the Pelly-Jessup claim."

Flint gave a low whistle. "So that's it. Whoever owns them shares may end up rich. Told the girls yet?"

Brett glanced toward them. "I want to make certain first. They've had enough disappointments."

The wind was roaring through the tree branches and light snow was falling. Brett glanced over at Annalee, who was asleep under extra blankets he'd bought her and Callie from Flint's pack supplies.

A fine place for a woman! Especially Annalee. He brought his collar up around his neck and went to attend his horse. The horse, too, looked unhappy.

"Missing your oats, are you?"

The horse rolled an eye and snorted.

"Spoiled hombre."

❧ ❧

Later in the evening Jimmy crawled up to Annalee's blanket. "Annalee?" he whispered.

"Don't you think it's time for bed?" she asked him with a smile.

"Mr. Harper's going to tell some stories about the Piutes and the old emigrant trail from Carson to Salt Lake."

"Well, I hope it doesn't frighten you into having nightmares." He was truly enjoying himself in the company of fine men like Brett Wilder and Flint Harper. She thought of Gordon.

"Why don't you sit next to Gordon? He was your good friend in Sacramento, remember?"

Jimmy's smile slowly left. "Gordon took out on his own to Virginia Town."

"He *what?* Jimmy, are you sure about this?"

He nodded. "He don't like the marshal none. I heard him say angry things to him while you was asleep. Gordon told him to stay away from you."

Of all the silly attitudes—

"What did the marshal say?"

"He said he wasn't taking orders from Gordon. That Gordon was behaving like a 'spoiled little boy.' Gordon tried to hit the marshal with his fist."

"Oh, no, Jimmy! This is awful. Why, it's downright ridiculous."

Jimmy grinned. "But he didn't hit him. Flint—I mean, Mr. Harper stopped him. Then Gordon paid for a mule and left. He told me to tell you he'd see you in Virginia Town."

What a dreadful situation. What had gotten into Gordon? He'd never shown a jealous bone in his body in all the years she'd known him. He'd even broken off their relationship to become engaged to Louise. Now, suddenly, he was unreasonably jealous.

Jimmy's large eyes shone in the firelight. "I'm going to go hear 'bout them Indians. But first, Marshal Wilder's going to read to us from the Bible. Would you like to come?"

Her heart warmed. *Brett—reading the Scriptures. What a delectable thought.*

"I can hear fine from here."

Jimmy stared down at her for a moment, sudden fear evident in his face.

"You'll be okay, won't you, Annalee? You...won't die like Mama, will you?"

She reached up and fondled his hair.

"Where's your trust in the Lord Jesus? He never makes a mistake, does He?"

He shook his head firmly. "Never. He's got no sin. He's the Son of God."

"And He's our Shepherd, isn't He?"

He nodded again firmly.

"Then there's nothing to fear. Whatever happens, we can trust Him."

"Yes, but I don't want Him to take you to heaven yet."

She smiled. "Not tonight, anyway. Now go and sit by Marshal Wilder and listen with respect when he reads the Scriptures. No wiggling around."

Jimmy scampered back to the fire. Annalee was still smiling to herself when she noticed Brett sitting on his heels by the fire, drinking coffee from a tin cup. He'd been looking in their direction and probably guessed that some small counseling session was going on. He smiled at her, a pleasant smile that was completely disarming, and she couldn't help but smile back.

As Brett read the Scriptures, the words seemed to bring a spark of warmth and life to the cold darkness. Annalee felt a comforting sense of God's nearness as her eyes grew heavy. Soon Brett's voice became distant. She was tired, very tired...

Annalee awoke to Callie shaking her shoulder.

"Sis, wake up. You've got to eat something."

"No, Callie, I'll eat it in the morning," she mumbled.

"You can't do that. It'll be frozen. It's snowing. Look!"

Annalee poked her head out from under her blanket. Even in the darkness she could see the swirling white flakes. She raised herself to an elbow and took the plate of hot food.

"What is it?"

"Fried potatoes and onions. They're good. I helped Flint and Elmo make them."

"You and Flint Harper are getting on mighty well." Annalee smiled. "How long's it been snowing?"

"An hour or more. Flint's worried about crossing the mountain in the morning."

When Annalee had eaten and gone back to sleep, she awoke feeling a little stronger and then drifted off to sleep again.

Now Jimmy's hand gripped her shoulder and shook it anxiously. "Annalee! Annalee!" he whispered. "Wake up!"

Her mind struggled to consciousness. What time was it? It was still dark. Dark and cold with the earth covered in a blanket of white.

She raised herself to her elbow. The camp was quiet, and she didn't see anyone. Jimmy bent over her, his eyes wide and full of fear in the faint glow of the campfire.

Annalee came fast awake. "What is it, honey?"

"I...I can't find Keeper."

She groaned. "Oh Jimmy, didn't you tie her to the tree?"

"I did tie her good, but something must've scared her, because she got her head out from her collar." A sudden splash of tear ran down his cheek, and he wiped it quickly.

Annalee crawled out of the warm, snug bedroll, reaching for her boots. "We'll find her," she whispered, and then she reached for her woolen cloak.

He pointed toward a cluster of dark trees. "She's in there, I know she is. I think she's caught on a shrub. If we don't find her soon, it'll be too late. Keeper will freeze, or a bear—"

"What is it now?" Callie poked her head out from under her blanket.

"Keeper's missing. Get up and help me look for her."

Callie moaned as she tried to move. "Oooh—every muscle in my body hurts. Two miserable days on a mule and two nights lying on the ground! And you want me to get up in the snow? Go wake one of the men to help you."

Annalee wasn't about to go sneaking through the campground full of strange men in search of Brett or Flint. She had no idea where either was sleeping.

"Hurry, Annalee, hurry," Jimmy begged.

Annalee scrambled into the darkness toward the stand of trees.

The clouds were heavy and strong gusts of wind whined through overhead branches. Her boots sank into almost a foot of snow, leaving footsteps in the dim smooth white.

"Keep the glow of the wood coals in sight, Jimmy."

His cry of desperation urged her onward. If anything happened to his cat… Ignoring her weariness she grabbed his hand, and they trudged together in the direction he pointed.

"Would Keeper go this far in the snow, Jimmy?"

"I…I think she's been gone a long time, maybe before it got so deep. This way, Annalee!"

A few flakes fell as they moved through the shrubs. Jimmy was pulling her. "Hurry!"

Ahead there was a steep embankment and thicker forest. Jimmy pulled his hand free and surged impatiently ahead. "I think I heard her, Annalee!"

"Careful! It's too dark to see anything."

"She's up here. I just heard her again! Keeper! Here kitty, kitty."

"You'll frighten her. Move slowly. Don't sound alarmed."

With the wind rushing through the trees, Annalee wondered how he could hear anything. She paused to listen. Jimmy's voice echoed to her, sounding farther away.

"Be careful where you walk Jimmy! Wait—"

She scrambled to the base of an embankment, feeling the soft snow give way in a little avalanche beneath her. She grabbed hold of a pine shrub to help herself up.

Short of breath in the thin air, her heart pounded as she struggled upward. The wind caught her hood and blew it back from her head, its cold fingers whipping her hair free from the pins.

She reached the top on hands and knees, trying to catch her breath. Her throat felt dry as she listened in the dark.

"Jimmy!" The wind hurled her voice back into her face. She pushed herself up onto her feet and edged forward, her toe fumbling over a protruding rock half buried in snow.

Jimmy's cry came with a distant echo. She stopped, uncertain, trying to decide which way to go.

"Keeper." His voice was far off. "Keeper, where are you?"

She strained her eyes to see in the dark. The incline continued into thick silhouettes of pine. She turned and looked back over her shoulder. "Stay within sight of the campfire," she had told him. A faint reddish glow could be seen among the trees. She cupped her hands to her mouth. "Jimmy, do you hear me?"

The wind crooned mournfully through the branches and snowflakes were coming down faster. She continued forward in the deep darkness. She hadn't gone far when his distant cry reached her ears. "Annalee! I found her!" A grateful sigh escaped her lips, but then she heard a crack as though a branch had snapped. His frightened call stabbed the darkness: "Annalee!"

He's fallen. Lord, help him! She struggled forward, her boots alternately slipping on smooth rocks and sticking in the snow, her numb fingers brushing branches and shrubs. It was difficult to hurry when her body wouldn't keep up. *I've got to reach Jimmy.*

"Jimmy! I'm coming! Hang on!" Her voice barely penetrated the wind.

Her weakness and the fear of failure increased. "Lord, keep him from falling—"

She struggled onward in the direction she'd heard his voice, her boots getting heavier and heavier with snow.

"Annalee—I'm falling—"

Panic seized her. Her strength was ebbing quickly. A sickening dizzy spell enveloped her brain as she struggled onward. How far it seemed when it wasn't far at all. Jimmy's voice was calling in desperation, and she could not reach him quickly enough. Overwhelmed with faintness she crouched down against a pine tree, exhausted.

"Jesus! Help me!"

Sullen thunder rumbled, followed by a flash of intense white. Instantly the trees and boulders glistened into view.

"Over here, Annalee!"

She'd collapsed, unable to breathe. Her lungs swelled painfully with convulsing spasms.

"Annalee!" he sobbed, "—it's breaking—"

She crawled across the snow, her hands numb, using every ounce of strength. She was going to faint...

Her brave armor, so carefully in place when she left Sacramento, disintegrated. She gave a lurching cough that tore at her insides. *No! Not now!* Her breathing came in gasps, her heart pounding and sending each beat pulsating dizzily in her eyes.

She lay there gasping, waiting, lungs burning, praying that it wouldn't happen, and then, it came. That which she feared the most. The terrible seizure of coughing that wouldn't cease, exacting all will to live.

Retching miserably, her face slumped on the snow, the coughing spell wouldn't stop. When she thought she could stand it no longer, it continued, tearing at her lungs. The earth was moving beneath her.

At last it eased...she barely felt the snow against her cheek. Despite the icy cold her flesh was wet with perspiration. She began to shake.

Let me die...if You love me, let me die...

"Annalee—" Jimmy's terrified voice echoed in the space of her mind hovering between unconsciousness and wakefulness.

Whispered voices of despair drowned out his call. *Give up. God doesn't care about you—He doesn't love you. See? Look at you!*

Her numb fingers slowly clenched. *No.*

There was a distant, sullen rumble of thunder, and then another intense flash of white lit up the eastern sky, momentarily outlining dark pine trees and boulders. The rain followed in a swift downpour, drenching her.

Defeat claimed her at last. She had failed to save Jimmy. She was worthless! Frustration filled her vision with hot, angry tears, and she despised herself for all she did not want to be but could not escape.

Yet her mind wandered feebly into paths of comforting faintness. Words moved within her soul, pulsating with energy. *I AM with thee...I AM with thee...My grace is sufficient...*

Was it her own mind searching the dimness for hope, or was it Him?

"Father..." The thought penetrated her soul. *He neither slumbers nor sleeps. He knows our sitting down and our rising up. He encompasses our paths...He's acquainted with all our ways...neither is there darkness with Him...*

"Father..."

⤞ ⤝

Annalee lay curled up in her crumpled cloak, understanding that she had not run away from what she had feared. The illness would yet steal strength from her body. Virginia City, looming with energy and life, could not hide her masquerade. She was still the same Annalee, forced to bear her humiliation. And now she was here. It was October. The snows of winter were around her, and Jimmy—she had lost him in her fruitless quest for significance.

"Annalee. Annalee." A distant voice was calling. Then again— "Annalee! Jimmy! Where are you?"

Her eyes blinked open. She was still alive. She couldn't move, but someone was shouting her name. Too feeble to reply, she lay silent as a half dozen men from camp came searching for them. Help was coming—but Jimmy! Was he still alive?

Brett Wilder and Flint Harper approached and knelt beside her.

"Annalee—" Brett took hold of her, turning her over and lifting her out of the snow. He held her close in his strong, comforting arms.

She tried to focus on his face. "Jimmy," came her feeble whisper. "Ledge—"

Brett looked at Flint. Harper was up the mound in a sprint. "Hold on, boy!"

"I failed him," Annalee murmured. "Jimmy and the Lord, I failed—"

"Hush," Brett said softly, his voice comforting. "You're a brave young woman. Flint's helping Jimmy."

His confidence calmed her. Annalee wanted to stay in his warm arms forever, protected, cherished, and with her cheek against his chest near the beating of his heart.

He was carrying her back toward camp. She yielded to the warm solacing thought of rest and sleep, and the sweet, sustaining presence of God's nearness embracing her soul. Just where He had always been. Right there with her in the midst of suffering and fear.

❧ ❧

Flint had arrived at the rocky ledge. Callie followed close behind. There was Jimmy just below, clutching a pine bush with one arm and holding Keeper in the other.

Jimmy could feel loosened pebbles and earth shifting beneath his elbow and chest. He had fallen in a washout of mud and rock and had slid down into darkness. "Jesus," he had called, the tears running down his face, "I'm scared!"

The pine shrub held as he closed his eyes and rested against the earth. Some hail fell, and sullen rolls of thunder still threatened like a terrible growl, but there was a garrison about his mind and heart.

Then he heard voices shouting down above him.

"Oh, thank God! He's still there! Hang on, Jimmy!" Callie cried, dropping to her knees in the snow by the ledge as Flint handed her a lantern.

"Nice 'n' easy, son. I'll have you up in a minute."

Jimmy felt the wet earth moving up beneath him as he held Keeper and strained to grip the bush. His hand felt numb. If the mud and rocks fell—

He heard Callie's voice. "Hurry, Flint." Jimmy's toe found a small rock. He saw Flint leaning over the ledge and forming a loop in the end of a rope. He tossed it down past Jimmy's boots. Jimmy listened as Flint spoke. "As I raise the rope, put your boots in the loop."

In the dim lantern light Jimmy tried not to think of the deep scary fall down into darkness. He carefully put one boot at a time into the loop as Flint raised it around his legs. Jimmy caught on, raising his waist off the gravel and letting the loop slide up to finally cinch around his chest. Keeper crawled higher under his chin. He felt the rope tighten and press into his flesh.

"Let go of the bush, son, and keep your elbows against your sides."

His numb fingers slowly let go, and then he felt himself moving upward. The faces of Flint and Callie came closer. Flint reached out a muscled arm toward him. In another moment he was lifted over the ledge with Keeper yowling in his ear.

Flint loosened the rope as Callie's arms wrapped tightly about her little brother. Jimmy clung to her, crying and shaking, and Callie hugged him back tightly, Keeper and all.

"It's all right, honey. Everything's all right now."

Fourteen

ℰ

*I*t was dawn. The sky was iron gray, and there were still snow flurries. Brett poured coffee and looked toward the mules to see Flint facing down a group of riled miners and prospectors.

Brett thought he understood. He'd carried Annalee back to camp last night and warmed her by the fire until Callie came back with Flint and the boy. He'd taken Jimmy and left Annalee in Callie's care. He also told Flint that Annalee wouldn't be able to travel for several days, perhaps a week.

Brett walked up to where the men were confronting Harper. "Trouble, Flint?"

Flint scowled. "Depends. The men here are worried we're considering laying over a week."

"That's right." The spokesman for the group stepped forward. He was a lanky man with deep eyes and a Midwestern accent. "We were telling Harper here that we won't stand for sittin' 'round. That girl might not improve in a week. It might take longer." He looked back at Flint. "We paid good money to ride your mules. We ain't camping here for days on end. You got a schedule to meet too, Flint. Look at those clouds. The weather's worsening by the hour. We need to move an' move now."

Flint looked at Brett. "He's right. Some of those supplies are needed in Carson. An' if the weather holds, I'm contracted to bring a load of ore down to Placerville to be packed over to Frisco. You see how it is. I'm obliged to go on."

"Fair enough. Take Callie and Jimmy with you. We'll join them soon as Annalee can travel."

"Where you thinking of takin' her?" Flint looked worried.

164 ~≤ Linda Chaikin

"My first thought was to head back to Berry's, but it's too far. You're right about this storm. It's just the beginning."

"Remember that trapper we met up north? He's got a cabin not more'n a few miles from here."

"Harry Thompson?"

"Seems the safest bet."

"The only recourse, perhaps. How far?"

"Not far. Maybe three miles. Got himself a squaw now. Calls her Anastasia."

"I'll explain my plans to Callie," Brett told him.

"She'll want to stay with Annalee. So will Jimmy."

"It's best if they go on with you. The cabin is probably small. Even the two of us will be imposing on Thompson."

"I'm agreeing. I'll see they get to Carson. I can bring 'em to Ma Higgins. She'll like the company of a young girl from Sacramento."

≈≈ ≈≈

Two days after the snowstorm, Flint Harper's mule train came down from the Sierra pass into Nevada on a morning wild with desert winds.

"*Diabolis*," Flint told Callie. "Mexican cowboys call 'em devil winds."

"There are Mexican cowboys here?" she asked, surprised.

"They come through now and again, driving strings of wild mustangs."

Callie didn't see any wild mustangs, but she did notice a few Chinese men working placer mines along the Carson River at Johntown. They'd been railroad workers who were brought over to lay track. They were now on their own, and like the rest, were seeking "El Dorado."

The mule train passengers from Strawberry went on to Virginia Town while Flint, with Callie and Jimmy, went to Dayton. He'd delivered the mules to two old codgers working for him who led them to pasture and a well-deserved rest. Much of the freight would be sold on the Comstock and was stashed for safekeeping in a storage cabin.

Callie noted a man by the cabin with a rifle. "You need to have a guard?"

"You betcha. Come this winter when the folks run out of goods, that haul will be worth a good bundle. There's more'n one way to make money on the Comstock besides getting lucky on a claim. You, for instance. Why, you could make more money opening a store or a cafe than you'd ever make in Sacramento."

"I have plans, Flint. I want to perform just the way my mother did in California. She was going to open a theater with Macklin Villiers. I may want to do the same."

Flint doesn't look none too pleased, she thought, glancing at him, but it didn't matter. Her mind was made up. Half the money from Weda belonged to her. It wasn't fair that Annalee should arbitrarily decide what to do with it.

"Well," he said after a minute, "if you can act, Callie, then it's sure as shootin' you'll get yourself a paying audience in these parts."

"I think I'm a good actress. Not as good as Lillian O'Day was, but I intend to be one day."

"If your heart's set on it, then it's something you'll have to try. If you don't, you wouldn't be a woman a man could live with and enjoy a moment's peace."

Her head turned sharply. Her dark brow arched. Then he flashed a smile and she smiled too, making sure her dimples showed.

"Why, Flint Harper, I don't think you're half as ornery as you like to make out."

He settled his hat and looked ahead.

They came to the mouth of what Flint told her was called Gold Canyon. Here, since the 1850s, placer miners had panned for small quantities of gold long before Ol' Virginny had discovered silver farther up the mountain.

They rode on to a narrow rocky pass between two greater boulders.

"They call it Devil's Gate," Flint told them.

With wide eyes Jimmy read the sign stretching across the narrow dirt trail that passed between the boulders.

"Devil's Gate Toll Road—50 cents. Pass on and up."

Flint brought Callie and Jimmy to what was called by the miners "a grub-and-boarding station."

"This belongs to ol' Ma Higgins. Once I deliver a load of silver ore to Placerville, I'll be back this way," he told her. "By then your sister will be up to travelin', and Wilder will bring her down the mountain to join you and Jimmy. I don't know what your future plans are besides finding Samuel and, er, your pa, but till Wilder gets here, I'd feel better if you stayed with Ma."

"She's your mother?"

He grinned and pushed his hat back from his wheat-colored hair.

"Not exactly. My folks died soon after we crossed the Forty Mile from Utah. She's the only ma I remember. She's never married, far as I know, so she looks on me as her boy. But she's been a mother to many of us miners. I think you'll like her. She's not what you'd call a 'Sacramento,' lady," he said with a grin, "but she's a decent woman.

"I staked her on this second grub house just a month ago. I know it's not much of an offer for a girl like you, with her heart set on the stage, but, well, I'd like you to think about coming into business with me, Callie. I'd like to open another place in Virginia Town."

Callie had no desire to own a cafe. She was still thinking of New Orleans and the wire she'd asked Brett to send to Lorena. Brett had told her he'd done so while in Placerville. And there was still her dream of the stage. "Callie O'Day."

What she didn't want to reckon with was the amber eyes gazing down at her and the rugged sun-bronzed face of Flint Harper.

She frowned. "I'm not much of a cook, Flint...I never was. I probably would be a failure at running a cafe. I just never went in for the usual things a lady does. Annalee's always put me to shame with her sweet manners and ways. She can bake the best biscuits a man ever tasted."

"Don't need to be the best cook around here. Men like myself aren't very fancy. Anyway, Ma can teach you everything you need to know about running a place."

She smiled. Flint was handsome and he was good to be around. But he wasn't the kind of man she had set her mind on falling in love with and marrying someday. She wanted someone in the theater or a gentleman from a fine family in New Orleans. And besides that, Gordon Barkly would be in Virginia Town. She couldn't get Gordon out of her mind. He would be starting his own newspaper, and he dressed well and had fancy manners—that is, when he wasn't scowling at Brett Wilder. That situation between Gordon and Brett at camp over Annalee still nettled her. Gordon had wanted to fight Brett over her sister! Callie felt a stab of jealousy.

"I don't know, Flint. I'll think about it."

"That's all I ask for now." He smiled.

"I'll help Ma Higgins out until Mr. Wilder brings Annalee in. But with Annalee in poor health, well—I just don't see how we can stay in the Comstock. The marshal doesn't think so either. I'm expecting a letter from my mother's aunt in New Orleans. If she wants us, I think I should take my sister there. She'll get good doctor's care, and Jimmy can be put in school." And she would be able to think about the theater. But she didn't say that to Flint.

"Better make up your mind before mid-November. Once the pass gets snowed in for good, no one will get across to Placerville till spring. You'll be forced to stay in Washoe."

That's what she was afraid of.

"I'll take you to Ma now," he said.

Jimmy tugged at Callie's skirt. "When's Annalee and the marshal going to come back?"

"Just as soon as she can travel. Then we'll find Uncle Samuel. Come, let's go meet Ma. That looks like her coming now."

✣ ✣

Annalee's last memory of that frightening night on the trail was of Brett. How strong and comforting he'd shown himself on her behalf.

In the days following, Annalee hovered somewhere between dreams and reality. There always seemed to be something hot to drink, but it didn't always taste good. When she feebly protested, realizing that it was Brett who was feeding her, she was smoothly assured that everything was under control.

At last awaking from what she guessed was a very long sleep, she found herself in a small wooden cabin. The cold wind was howling around the little building, seeping in through cracks in the logs and rattling the door like a bear wanting to come in out of the cold.

Annalee realized she was resting on bedded straw close to a fire that sputtered and hissed in a stone hearth. As consciousness returned, so did the details of that last night in the snow.

"Jimmy—"

"He's safe. Flint took your brother and sister on to Dayton. They're probably there by now. We'll join them when you can ride."

"But…but where am I?"

"Harry's old cabin," he said easily.

"But…"

"Relax. If you'll look over in the corner, you'll see we've got a stalwart chaperon."

Annalee managed to turn her head and squinted a little to bring things into focus. Every movement was uncomfortable, and she tried not to wince. She saw a bronzed statue dressed in buckskin with two long snakelike pigtails. Only when it moved to pour something hot and steamy into a bowl did Annalee realize that the statue was a woman, an Indian.

"Harry's wife," Brett said. "Feeling better now? You must be. You've got some healthy color at last. Here, drink this."

Annalee cringed. "I can't."

"Drink it. I'm a stubborn man. If you don't, I'll have Anastasia see that you do. She knows a good wrestling hold."

Annalee smiled in spite of herself. "You don't give up easily, do you?"

"I'm a man of my word."

"Anastasia?"

"That's what Harry calls her. I don't know what she calls him. Since he can't speak her language, he probably doesn't know either." His smile was so charming that she was afraid to look at him for long.

He sees me as a "poor sick little girl." He's just being kind and unselfish because of his faith, because without him I wouldn't have much of a chance.

She wondered how awful she looked—until she touched her hair and understood. Anastasia must have brushed her hair until it shone and braided it.

She looked over again at the woman. "How can I thank her, and you?"

"Don't try right now. We both want you stronger."

"I'm all right now. I think I can get up—and ride."

The arch of his dark brow countered her optimism.

"Determined to the end, aren't you, Miss Halliday? There's snow falling right now. We'll need to wait."

"How long?"

"Probably a few more days. By then there should be a break in the weather and you'll be up to handling a mule."

"I hate to be a burden like this. I've interfered with your work in Virginia Town."

Brett immediately seemed to catch her vain attempt to try to cover up her condition—as though she could ever do that now. He'd seen her at her worst.

He was about to say something, but then he apparently decided it wasn't the time for a confrontation. He looked into the fire for a moment and then said quietly, "Annalee, do me a favor?"

Startled, she studied his face. What possible favor could she do in her condition? "Yes, if I can."

"The favor is this. Stop apologizing for your frailty."

Stunned by hearing the last thing she'd expected, Annalee stammered, "W-what?"

"Stop implying that your company isn't worth much because you're not as strong as Anastasia."

"I didn't realize…" She managed to rise to her elbow, but then a wave of dizziness swept over her. The Indian woman moved from her place by the fire to push Annalee down against her pillow. She muttered something in a language beyond Annalee's comprehension, but she understood the meaning very well. "Stay put."

Annalee went back against the pillow like a rag doll.

"You see?" Brett's eyes sparked with restrained humor. "Better behave yourself."

A glance toward Anastasia convinced her he was right.

"I'm serious about your apologizing for yourself, Annalee. You seem convinced that your worth depends on how well you can forge through desert sands to win the entire Piute tribe to Christianity."

She was taken aback by his bluntness, smoothed as it was by his calm, resonant voice. She didn't know how to take him.

"Do you think you mean less to God because you've been placed in this trial of illness?"

"My health isn't so bad," she insisted. "I simply got lost—"

"You don't need to play games with me. I know sickness when I see it. And you're a very sick young woman. Your exertion has weakened you to the point of a relapse. Tuberculosis demands bed rest and good meals."

Annalee recoiled at the words she hated, and even more now that someone like Brett Wilder spoke of her affliction.

"You...sound like a doctor," she murmured.

"I've always been interested in medicine. I attended medical school for a few years before I made a final decision to leave."

"You!" She didn't know why she should feel so shocked. It was because he wore a gun belt, she supposed, because she knew without being told that he would be fast and deadly should he need to be.

"When did you get involved in upholding the law?"

He didn't answer at once. She didn't think he would, that something was unexpectedly bothering him about her question.

"Over three years ago," he said at last.

But she felt compelled to know more. "What made you leave medical school?"

His eyes held hers. "I'd rather not discuss that now." He changed the subject. "What do you think of this verse? 'But Zion said, The LORD hath forsaken me, and my LORD hath forgotten me. Can a woman forget her sucking child, that she should not have compassion on the son of her womb? yea, they may forget, yet will I not forget thee. Behold I have graven thee upon the palms of my hands.'"

"Isaiah, chapter 49," she whispered.

"If you're anything like me, you find it easy to sing hymns about trusting the Lord when the sun's shining. It's when I'm in dark shadows that trusting Him is tough. And that's where most of life is lived."

She smiled a little.

"It's when we don't have the answers, and the trial goes on, and we don't understand why He's permitting things we can't make sense of, that faith is proven genuine and precious to God. We trust and rest. Not because we always understand, but because we know His character and Word are infallible."

She looked at him, not knowing what to say, not sure he even wanted her to answer.

He smiled and stood, looking down at her.

"Enough sermon for one day."

"I didn't know a lawman could be a preacher."

"There are many ways to serve the Lord. We're not all called to pastor churches or serve as missionaries. A few of the finest saints I've met gave silent sermons from beds of pain. I doubt if even one of them could serve Christ out on the Forty Mile Desert. Instead, they served Him where they were, with what gifts He put in their hands. Maybe you, too, should reconsider. Think instead about your painting."

"I thought you were through preaching at me."

He smiled and walked to the door.

She raised herself to an elbow. This time she felt a little better. "Brett?"

He turned at her quiet voice, his hand on the door latch.

"Don't think I haven't appreciated what you said."

She wondered why her words had apparently sobered him.

"Annalee, I intend to be completely honest with you. Soon I'll have something unpleasant to tell you, but it can wait till I take you to Samuel."

The same suspicion she'd felt at Strawberry Flat reawakened in her heart.

"Now," he warned with a pseudo frown, "if I hear you fretting and fussing around in here, anxious to be up and busy, I'll use my seniority to settle you down. As for helping Samuel as a missionary among the Piutes, here's one fine Indian woman you can witness to while you lie in bed. She's not a Piute, but she'll do. Isn't that right, Anastasia?" he turned to the great woman.

"Right," Anastasia said. "You tell me about the Son."

"Yes, Anastasia, the Son. God's Son."

"The Mighty Son."

Annalee watched Brett shoulder into his coat, settle his hat, and reach for his Winchester.

Gordon had told her Brett was about to become engaged to a girl back in Grass Valley. She wanted to ask him, but it would seem too obvious.

"Where are you going?"

At her tense inquiry he looked back at her. "To hunt up a steak for supper."

"A steak!" she laughed. "Out here?"

"Well, if you insist on accuracy, a venison steak. Anastasia? Look after Miss Annalee."

"Right."

Fifteen

Ten days later Brett and Annalee left the cabin to ride to Carson and then on toward Gold Hill, which was about a mile from Virginia Town.

In the crimson dawn of early morning, Sun Mountain arose from the desert plain stark and bleak against the light. It was the loftiest pinnacle on the Washoe range. It was here that the "Ophir diggings" were discovered. The terrible "blue stuff" the placer miners were mucking out of the sluices and throwing away in their search for gold had been assayed, and it turned out to have far more value in silver content than in gold.

Annalee viewed her new surroundings through the eyes of her paints and brushes. Wild, harsh, majestic, almost untouched by man, the mountains stood etched against the horizon in artistic shades of purple and black, monuments to the greatness of their Creator. The words of Psalm 121 came to her mind. "I will lift mine eyes unto the hills, from whence cometh my help. My help cometh from the LORD, which made heaven and earth."

"When the first silver was made into bars and placed on display at the bank in San Francisco," Brett told her, "people stood at the window, dazed, just staring. Then the frenzied rush was on. Miners and pilgrims from the four winds descended on Sun Mountain. Honesty means nothing where many of them are concerned."

"You mean claim jumping?"

"Claims overlap other claims, and men are short on patience. Mines are springing up everywhere, some of them producing nothing except fraudulent mining stocks sold in San Francisco.

Others, like the Gould and Curry and the Savage, are producing millions of dollars in silver."

He stopped and waited until she tied a bandanna across her nose and mouth; the soil churned by the horse's hooves was fine and dusty. Annalee rode with Brett on his horse, and a pack mule came behind carrying their baggage.

The distant Sierras were behind them now, capped with white, and the desert mountains about the canyon were little more than barren ridges dotted with rock. She saw little vegetation on the high desert except for scrubby pinion pine and artemesia sage. When it was crushed, the odor was strong and at times disagreeable. Sometimes a clump of bunch grass shot up.

Gold Canyon was windy and dusty too. The handkerchief helped to shield her lungs from the alkali, but she could still feel the grit between her teeth.

The barren hills were now rising toward Sun Mountain, and at the mouth of the canyon she saw a narrow rocky pass between two great rocks: "Devil's Gate."

"Someone's devised how to get rich the easy way," Brett commented. An old man lounged in a rough hewn chair collecting user fees. "A question of title, mister."

"So I see." He dropped the coins in the cup. The miner lifted his tattered, dirty hat. "Much obliged." He let the hat drop back comfortably on his head and settled back on his chair.

They rode forward as the gusts struck them with sudden furious bursts.

"There's a hotel in Gold Hill. We'll stop there," Brett told her.

Gold Hill. The words conjured up visions of rich yellow splendor. Annalee didn't know what she really expected to see, but when they arrived there were no golden streets, nor golden hills gleaming in the sunlight. There weren't even silver streets!

They rode in and stopped near a mining settlement.

"This…is Gold Hill?"

Brett's eyes glinted with amusement as he swung her down from his horse.

"This is it, my dear Miss Halliday. Welcome to Washoe."

"But where's the town?"

Brett kept a straight face. "You're looking at it."

"Where!"

"There."

She stood staring off at—what?—cabins? Not even that. They were soiled lean-tos made of canvas. A few were built with pinion pine, but the rest were mere blankets and shirts flapping precariously in the wind.

"I warned you," Brett said softly.

She knew he thought he'd won.

"Ready to go back?"

She could smile now, undaunted again. She was feeling much stronger, and her hopes were high for locating both her uncle and her father.

"I'm fine." The only thing that worried her was how she was going to pay him back for his expenses.

There was one hotel in Gold Hill called the Vesey. They'd seen Flint Harper at Dayton, and Flint had said he'd bring Callie and Jimmy over to join her at the hotel tomorrow.

Her gaze swept two adjoining sections of the hotel. After almost two weeks of living outdoors and in the Thompson cabin, it looked luxurious. One was a three-story wooden structure; the other a two-story building constructed of rubble stone with a covered wooden walk. "I'm sure a room here will be expensive."

"You can count on it," he retorted with a smile. "By spring this area will be packed with people. Businesses and hotels will go up quickly, some overnight. There's money to be made here, and now's the time to invest. You might think about loaning your aunt's money to someone opening a store or even another hotel."

She noticed he still assumed she would not be staying and opening a business herself with Callie. "I wouldn't know who to loan it to."

"I know a few men you can trust. And there's a good lawyer around named Bill Stewart."

He had omitted Macklin's friend and associate, Mr. Colefax.

Men were playing monte when she entered the Vesey with Brett. Eyes drifted in her direction and then to her escort. One look at Brett, who stared back at them evenly, and they turned their backs toward Annalee.

"I'll get you settled here, and then I'll see what I can learn about Samuel."

How Brett ended up getting her a room of her own, she wasn't sure. She only knew that without him she would never have made it this far. How did she ever think she could have managed on her own? Looking about at the rugged men, the gamblers, the steely-eyed loners, she realized she could not easily have found her father or uncle. Surely the Lord had sent Brett Wilder. She smiled to herself. He must never know that she considered him her guardian angel, not after all the fuss she'd put up to maintain her independence.

The room had a double bed, a rug on the wood floor, and a dresser with a mirror.

"Oooh, it's gorgeous. And a bath!"

But she already owed him for their meals, the mules from Strawberry to Dayton, and now the hotel room.

She glanced at him sideways. "I'll pay you back as soon as I sell some of my sketches."

"You can pay me back by having dinner with me tonight here in the hotel."

She smiled. "You're impossible. I don't understand you."

"Strange, I thought I was being transparent." He glanced around the room and then back down at her. "You'll be fine here. I've been assured the owner will keep an eye on you. But I want you to promise me something."

She had a feeling he was going to make her say she wouldn't go out alone.

"Stay out of trouble until I get back from Virginia Town tonight."

She was still mulling over what he might have meant about being transparent. "Why, Mr. Wilder," she said innocently, "what possible trouble could I get into here?"

His brow slanted. "No comment. Take your lunch up here and keep your door locked. Have you any idea where Samuel is camped?"

"I believe he has a dugout in Sun Mountain, but there's a cabin at Gold Canyon. The cabin belonged to my father and a partner—" she hesitated, wondering how much he knew about

Mr. Harkin's death. If he knew, why hadn't he spoken to her about it? Was she fooling herself? A lawman would have to know about the charge that Jack Halliday had shot his mining partner. Yet Brett had said nothing.

"Better stay away from that cabin until I know more about it," he said. "The safest place for you is here in the hotel or with Samuel."

She couldn't afford to stay in the Vesey for long. "I intend to fix the cabin up and move there with Callie and Jimmy."

"Annalee, this is no time to play games with me. I want the truth. Does your father go by another name besides Jack Halliday?"

She tensed. Now it was coming. The awful truth.

His eyes measured her response.

"Any information you can give me will make it easier to locate him," he said.

Was that all there was to it? His manner was casual, but could she believe it?

A battle began to wage in her heart. How much to tell him? What about loyalty to her father?

"As a matter of fact, he did use another name. Before my mother died, he wrote her a letter. He used an alias more than once when corresponding with her."

Now why had she told him that when she wasn't sure of his intentions? Did he merely desire to assist her in locating her father, or was he looking for Jack Halliday as a deputy marshal?

But he'd tell her if he was. Surely Brett wouldn't play her along, trying to get information to use against her father, and not be straightforward about the reason.

"What alias?"

She turned away and walked across the room fingering the green drapery at the window. "Jack Dawson."

"And the letter came from Virginia Town?"

"Johntown."

"Do you still have the letter?"

"If Mother kept it. She had an old keepsake chest for letters and mementos from the gold rush days. I brought it with me, but…"

"You're unsure? Do you think she put the letter in the chest?"

"I don't know." She turned and faced him, thinking, and her thoughts worried her. "The last letter from Jack Dawson arrived just before Macklin came to see her with news of his death."

He considered, and he didn't look pleased. "Wouldn't she have kept the letter? It being what she thought was his last letter at the time?"

"Mother was sentimental about things like that. Maybe, yes, it could be in the chest. I didn't take the time to sort through its contents before we left Aunt Weda's. I just knew I wanted that little chest because it meant so much to her."

He glanced toward her bag and satchel still sitting on the floor. "Can we have a look?"

"I don't have the keepsake chest with me. It's in the larger trunk, the one Flint packed on one of the baggage mules. But Callie will have the trunk with her tomorrow."

She saw a flicker of uncertainty in his eyes. He was debating something in his mind that bothered him. Was it her or the letter?

Her eyes fell to his buckskin shirt, but he kept his badge out of sight. He was leaning his shoulder against the doorjamb, watching her. She wondered at his slight frown.

"Jack Dawson," he repeated thoughtfully. "Seems I've heard that name before in Sacramento, but it was another Dawson, one from Texas. I wonder…"

"I can't tell you why he chose Dawson, but an alias isn't surprising. He gambles," she confessed. "Mother once admitted he had a quick temper, and was…rather fast with a gun. He has enemies."

A chill went through her when Brett's eyes became hard as granite. He remained silent. The awkward moment continued. She hastened, "I believe I explained my father isn't a Christian. Even Uncle Samuel's been trying to reach his heart for years. It was Samuel who turned my mother to the Lord."

He straightened, and put on his hat. "I'll see if I can find Samuel at Sun Mountain."

Annalee left the window and walked toward him. She was somewhat baffled. Was that all he was going to ask?

"I'll be as quick about this as I can. Hopefully I'll have Samuel with me when I return. In the meantime, get all the rest you can. Our trip back to Sacramento won't be easy. The snow in the mountains is increasing every day."

What trip? Her lashes narrowed. "You seem to think my father will want me to go with you."

His gaze became remote. "I'm sure Samuel will. As for your father, Annalee, I hope he cooperates, for your sake."

Something in his voice caused her to search his face. It was unreadable. Then he smiled. "You'll feel better when Callie and Jimmy get here tomorrow. I'll see you tonight."

He paused in the open doorway to look down at her. A heady feeling enveloped her when his fingers lightly lifted her chin.

"I don't want to keep harping on this, but remember to stay in your room. I don't like the way things are adding up." His hand slowly dropped. He shut the door behind him, and Annalee slid the bolt into place.

She crossed the room to the window again. It looked down on the dirt street. She saw a couple of miners going by with mules and ore wagons.

There was a man standing across the street near the livery stable, a lone man who was staring toward the entrance of the hotel. Something about his manner caught her attention. A minute later he stepped backward out of sight. Then she saw Brett. He'd just come out of the hotel and was walking across the dirt street. He was heading straight toward the livery stable where he'd left his horse.

Something about the scene she was witnessing was not right. That man had been waiting—and he hadn't wanted Brett to see him when he'd stepped back. Why? Why didn't he want Brett to see him? And what was he doing now—

Sudden fear squeezed her heart. The trail to Placerville...a trap, he'd said—

Blindly she struggled to open the window with the hope there'd be time to shout a warning. She dare not pound with her fists to get his attention. Even if he heard, he'd only turn to look up, and then his back would be toward the livery stable—

The window was stuck. She shoved! Pushed! Gasping, she leaned forward against the pane staring below. It was already too late.

Brett!

❦ ❦

Brett walked unknowingly straight into danger. His mind was not on his surroundings as it would normally be if it weren't for Annalee. That girl had a devastating effect on him. She'd changed everything from the moment he'd laid eyes on her outside Berry's tavern, and—

With a loud crack, a bullet passed overhead. Brett crouched low, gun pointed toward the livery as he darted for cover, throwing himself to the side of the wooden building.

A man lunged from the doorway of the livery, his pistol pointed toward Brett, firing once as he skidded to a stop in the dirt street, his bullet splintering wood in Brett's face.

Brett squeezed off a careful shot that caught the gunman through the chest.

Then, silence fell on the street.

Brett waited a moment and then broke from his cover for the livery stable. He kept to one side, his back pressed hard against the building. He edged closer along the wall until he was just beside the entry. He heard hesitant footsteps inside. An older voice shouted, "Don't shoot, Wilder! Ain't no more snakes in 'ere! It's me, Elmo—and ol' Jenny!"

Brett held the barrel of his Colt pointed up.

"All right, Elmo, come out nice and easy."

A moment later the grizzled old miner appeared leading Jenny.

"No one else is in there. Can vouch for it. Durned well woulda killed you, that rabid varmint!" He gestured his head toward the gunfighter lying dead in the street. A small group of men, and a woman from the saloon, began to gather in the street to see who he was.

Elmo patted the mule. "Was takin' a nap with Jenny in one' o' them stalls while the hostler was away when in comes this feller.

Never seen him before. He didn't see me, but I seen him sneak in. When I guessed what he was about aimin' that gun of his, I lifted my Winchester over the stall and fired one right over his head. Well, he done split outta there like he were afire, running to the street." Elmo rubbed his whiskers and looked at Brett's Colt. "That was good shootin', Marshal. Be one less fer you to worry about now. But there be more in Virginny Town, I'm thinkin'."

Brett walked over to the dead man, stooped, and looked at his face. He recognized him from the "Wanted" posters. It was Coyle Hardy, a hired gun from Utah.

How many more?

❧ ❧

From the window in her room at the Vesey Hotel, Annalee stared below. Her heart was still hammering, and her hands were sweaty and cold. She'd witnessed it all, and she wouldn't soon forget. Her gaze swerved back to Brett. That gun had come out of its holster faster than her eye could see it happening.

She thought of her father, and her fingers tightened on the drapery.

A few minutes later, she watched him mount his horse and ride out without looking up in her direction.

From the public rooms below came the sounds of music and loud laughter. She turned away, shaking, and opening her handbag she took out her Bible. She held it to her cheek, and the cool leather felt good. She blinked hard and sank to the bed. The mattress felt like a cloud of feathers after sleeping on the ground. Seeking refuge and strength, she read for only a few minutes before her eyes grew heavy and the frailty of her body demanded sleep again.

"Father God," she whispered just before drifting off "bring Brett back to me…and if it's possible, if he's part of Your plan for my life, I would be deeply thankful…"

Sixteen

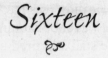

Brett rode into Virginia Town knowing what to expect. Beneath Sun Mountain a mining town was emerging. Wherever he looked he saw men digging or throwing buildings together. For every hut there seemed a dozen noisy saloons full of gambling. In one night men lost fortunes and gained others, only to risk and lose them again.

He walked into the Bucket of Blood saloon. *What a name,* he thought.

"What d'ya have?" the man behind the counter spoke with a Welsh accent.

"Coffee."

The man's beady eyes whipped over him. "We got us another preacher comin' to Virginny Town?"

"No. Looks like you could use a few, though."

The man fell silent. He poured the cup with steaming dark stuff and set it down. The brew looked like mud and tasted worse.

"Ever heard of Jack Dawson?"

The man glanced slyly toward the corner of the room, but he shook his head no and went about his business.

Brett picked up his cup and turned around. Leaning against the counter, he surveyed the customers. He looked over at a man with a wide mustache and a hawk nose—the object of the bartender's glance. The man was watching him.

Trouble, Brett thought. Slowly he set his cup down and casually moved his black coat behind his holster.

The skinny young man sauntered up to the counter. He flicked his fingers at the bartender. The bartender knew what he wanted and set down a bottle of whiskey. The man slowly poured a drink and then turned to survey Brett with his deep-set black eyes.

"What'd you want with Dawson?"

"My business."

He slugged down the whiskey, wiping his mustache dry with the back of a browned hand. He licked his lips, his eyes like rock. "My business too."

"Friend of yours?" Brett asked.

"He wouldn't think so, but I'm looking for him. And when I find Dawson again, he'll be buried out on Boot Hill."

Brett pulled back his coat and the small badge stared up from his chest. "Let me handle Dawson."

"You'd be too generous, Wilder."

Brett tried to place the lean gunfighter. "You must be Dylan, Frank Harkin's brother."

"News is out you're here lookin' for Dawson."

Brett thought of his meeting with Hoadly at Strawberry. Did Dylan Harkin know Jack Dawson was really Jack Halliday? It was safer for Annalee and her siblings if no one knew, but that was probably too much to hope for.

"News travels fast," Brett said. "Coyle Hardy a friend of yours?"

The black eyes were wary. "No, can't say so. Why?"

"He's dead."

Harkin's stare was unblinking. "You killed him?"

"He tried to kill me first. He was waiting, in hiding like a rat."

Dylan took another drink. "Anyone who gets hurt does so 'cause he got in my way."

Brett knew why Dylan was after Annalee's father, but he was hoping he'd let something slip. "Why do you want Dawson?"

"He's a cheat and a killer. He stole my brother's half o' the claim out at Gold Canyon. They was working together. Partners. Dawson shot him in the back."

"Who told you how it happened?" Brett asked.

"Macklin Villiers. He has a witness. Lawyer named Colefax."

Brett hadn't forgotten Villiers. How much of this was true? "Let me handle this, Dylan. If you take matters into your hands, Jack won't be the only gunfighter buried on Boot Hill."

Dylan's thin mouth hardened. "You threatening me, Marshal?"

"If you want to call it that, yes. You'd be wise to ride out of here today. If half that silver claim belongs to Frank, the law will see that you get it fairly."

Dylan stared coldly, refusing to back down. "I'm stayin'." He whipped around and walked out.

Brett looked after him. If he didn't find Jack Halliday soon, he wouldn't live long enough to stand trial in Sacramento.

First, though, he wanted to see Samuel.

He turned back to the bartender. "Who else hangs around with Dylan Harkin?"

He shook his head. "Just rode in last night. A loner. Deadly as a rattler. So you're a deputy marshal?"

Obviously he'd been listening.

"Right. I've a commission from Governor Downey. Seen a man named Hoadly around?"

"He comes in all the time. Him and that crazy boxer. Boxer's a bully. Hoadly's fixing up a fight now over in Lousetown. There's some horse racing too. If you're a marshal, maybe you ought to straighten that out."

"I wasn't sent here to stop horse racing or boxing but to bring in Jack Dawson. I'd appreciate it if you'd help spread the word."

"You're asking for trouble, ain't you? They'll all come gunning for you."

"Where can I find Samuel Halliday?"

"The preacher? He's got a place in the mountain. Ask around, you'll find him. He's been gone for a week—least, I've missed his preachin' at me 'bout that long. Been nice havin' him out of my conscience."

Brett smiled at him. "I'll tell him to keep up the good work."

"He doesn't need encouragement."

As Brett turned to leave, a voice farther down the counter spoke.

"Samuel's back," said a man with a slow Arkansas drawl. "He rode in last night, was told, with an arrow in him."

"Wretched Piutes," the bartender said. "They come 'round humble like and then put a knife in you."

"Trouble?" Brett asked.

"Usual amount. Braves resent the white man pouring into Washoe. Claim we're ruining their hunting ground. Chopping down all the pine trees for burning and building. They depend on the cones for food in the winter."

"Sounds like trouble in the future."

"More'n likely. But if they come, we'll be ready. Ain't no Indian chasin' us out of Virginny with a silver bonanza in the working. We'll chase them from here to the Forty Mile."

Brett walked outside, feeling the chilly blast. A moment later Arkansas came out. "If you're lookin' for Samuel, I can show you where his dugout is."

"Appreciate it. Name's Brett Wilder, and you?"

"They jes' call me Arkie."

They walked together toward the slope of Sun Mountain, Brett leading his horse by the reins. The sun shone across the rocky soil.

The town was sprawling up the lap of the mountain like children climbing up into her arms. Brett walked uphill to where Arkansas told him he and his two brothers and three cousins were starting a shaft. They had dug about six feet or so. Brett watched them from under his hat until a lanky redheaded man squinted up at him.

"You a marshal?"

Brett smiled. "Yes, but some folks around here don't think so." He gestured to the shaft they were working on. "What do you think? Look promising?"

"Too soon to tell," drawled the redhead. "It don't look like Sutter's to me." He hiked up his trousers and spat. "Why, in '49 in California, we was picking up gold nuggets."

"Listen to him. Why you was a toddler danglin' on Mama's knee back then."

"Well, I ain't no toddler now, Tom!"

Brett smiled a little. "Seen Samuel Halliday?"

Arkansas pointed farther up. "He's got himself a regular church inside the mountain."

"Inside?"

"A dugout. Go have a see. He's nursin' an Injun wound."

"Thanks, I will."

There was a cold wind coming off Sun Mountain. What he thought was bound to become a booming town in the coming year was now a cluster of stone huts and dugouts. What he'd told Annalee outside the Vesey Hotel at Gold Hill was true. This was opportunity just waiting for the right minds to take over. Soon, there wouldn't be an empty spot on the mountain to lay a claim. If he intended to stake his own claim somewhere, he'd better do it before spring. He'd want to beat the rush of new people who would cross the Sierras. He'd keep an eye out for something that interested him.

Leaving his horse with his helpful new acquaintances, Brett walked uphill. The Halliday-Harkin claim was located at Gold Canyon near the Pelly-Jessup. Macklin Villiers knew something.

Samuel's dugout was midway up the mountain and actually built back into it. There was a makeshift pine wood door and a sign posted: Samuel Halliday, Preacher.

A rugged man, broad shouldered and wearing a worn black frock coat reaching to his knees, stepped outside and met Brett at eye level. Heavy boots covered his muscled calves.

"Who be you, lad?"

It was a long time since he'd been called a lad. Brett almost smiled. "Name's Brett Wilder. I've a commission from Governor Downey as a temporary deputy marshal."

The greenish eyes gleamed as they measured Brett. "Well...I've been expecting something like this for a long spell. A deputy marshal, huh? From Frisco?"

"Sacramento."

"Temporary, you say. Why not permanent?"

"I've a ranch to run in Grass Valley. I'm a cattleman."

"That's better than most around here. Even so, you aiming to reach heaven by showing God your badge?"

Brett hesitated. So this was Samuel. He smiled.

"I don't think He would be impressed."

"You show good wisdom."

"Besides being a lawman, I also carry this." He took out his small black leather Bible.

A smile spread across the bronzed face. "Now you're talking my language, lad. Come in, come in. Don't just stand there!"

Samuel's rugged features still bore a handsomeness for his fifty-odd years. The eyes were set wide apart below bushy arched brows that were as black as a raven. His thin hawk nose flared into wide nostrils over a flowing mustache, which drooped downward and disappeared into his short beard. His coarse dark hair was cut to the nape of the neck and held in place across his forehead with a braided headband, tied at the back of his head.

Brett saw little resemblance to Annalee except for the shade of green to his penetrating eyes. Knowing she had an uncle like Samuel Halliday was a consolation.

As they entered the small dugout, Brett's eyes fell to Samuel's shoulder. He wore a sling.

"Piutes?" Brett inquired easily, sitting down on a barrel chair.

Samuel's brows came together, and he winced as he reached to touch the back of his shoulder. "So that's what they're saying. Blame everything on them Piutes. No, it's a bullet wound! Rascal's still in there too."

Brett looked at him sharply. "Any notion who it was?"

"Too dark. But it wasn't an Indian. No reason they'd want me dead. I've powwowed with Winnemuca. No, this was one of Jack's enemies. They must think I pose 'em some trouble on account of that claim at Gold Canyon."

"Better let me get that bullet out."

"Obliged if you would, lad. I got the water boiling now." He produced a sharp-looking knife. "Know what you're doin'?"

"My father's a doctor."

"Make it quick then. I got no time to be held up in here. I've got to cross the Humboldt again into Salt Lake."

Brett sterilized the knife in the boiling water and soaked some cloths Samuel had sitting ready.

Samuel squinted at him. "Say you're a lawman?"

Brett worked smoothly and efficiently. "I'm bound by truth to hold nothing back. I'm here to arrest a man, but I'm not looking forward to it. It's keeping me awake nights."

Samuel grimaced but otherwise made no complaint as Brett worked. "I'm suspecting the worst news. Go ahead. I'm listening."

"I've come for Jack Halliday, alias Jack Dawson."

"Ah…" sighed Samuel.

"He's wanted for the death of one man and the wounding of another in Sacramento and on suspicion of killing Frank Harkin here in Virginia Town. The first shooting took place several years ago on board the *Golden Queen,* a riverboat. The card dealer is dead. The man injured was a doctor trying to help the dying man."

"Jack said the dealer was cheating."

"Others at the table refute that. Jack was losing badly. He lost his temper."

"He's got a bad temper, that's so, always did, since we were boys. Ouch—easy, lad!"

"The doctor is alive, but his right arm is crippled because of that bullet. He used to be one of the greatest surgeons in the country."

Samuel shook his head and moaned, but it was unclear to Brett if it was because of the pain or the news about Jack. Brett continued calmly, "His gift was stolen from him. He's unable to do surgery. The physician is James Wilder, my father."

After another muffled groan from Samuel, Brett held up the bullet.

"What do you have to pour on the wound?"

Samuel focused burning eyes. "That ornery tarantula juice isn't permitted in my abode. Not even for medical purposes. Seen it kill and maim. And it will kill Ol' Virginny the way he's going. Use water, lad."

"Water won't do."

"This kind will," he said dryly. "It's enough to make a man sick. Many *are* sick. It comes from the mountain and has arsenic in it. Mule died the other day…poor creature drank too much of it. Be sure you go easy on it yourself." He shook his head. "About Jack, are you sure you've got the right man?"

"On the Sacramento shooting, yes. I'm not sure about Harkin. I haven't met Macklin Villiers yet, but I'm not sure about him either."

"Ah…you're a smart man, Wilder. Do you good not to buy into everything Mac tells you."

"I understand Rody Villiers has come to Virginia Town."

"You'll have to watch out for that one. Rody's a gunfighter. Fast too. Haven't seen anyone faster."

"Macklin sent for him."

"So I heard. Macklin's had a reputation with a gun too. He tries to hide the fact around here, wanting to make himself into a new man. He's a banker now, by the way."

"Where'd he get money to open a bank?"

"Good question. Says he has Frisco partners. A few big names. Same gents who made a million in the California gold rush. He owns most of the Pelly-Jessup too."

"Interesting they'd back Macklin. Wonder if the lawyer Colefax had anything to do with it?"

Samuel cocked a brow toward him. "Never thought much about it, but you're probably right. Colefax is the lawyer for the Pelly-Jessup. Represents the finance gents in Frisco."

"Then Colefax would be privy to inside information, the financial books, and all that."

Samuel nodded slowly. "See where you're headed…yes, he sure would. Look, I'll say it again—watch yourself. These could be a couple of mean fellers. I happen to know Cousin Mac was carrying a gambler's gun up his coat sleeve when I saw him at the Fraser. Don't have any reason to think he's slacked off since."

This was just as Brett had suspected about Macklin. The man was no less a gunfighter than Jack Halliday, but he was trying to climb the ladder of respectability into a new society. At heart, he'd do anything to get rich, but now he must do his dirty work behind the scenes.

That brought his mind back to the man in the shadows, the man that Hoadly was working for. More and more it looked as though it was Macklin Villiers.

"Know anything about a gunfighter named Hoadly?"

"Seen him around with Rody recently."

Brett finished bandaging his arm. "Know if he works for Macklin?"

Samuel put his shirt on. "I've not seen them together. Why? You think he does?"

"It would fit what I have in mind. Hoadly's working for someone who wants to remain anonymous. Someone who had Hoadly hire a crew of fast guns. One of them is Rick Delance out of Tucson."

Samuel frowned as he put on his frock coat. "Heard of Delance. He passed through Salt Lake when I was there. A loner. Doesn't seem to go out of his way to look for trouble, though."

"He doesn't. I'm hoping when the chips are down he'll come over on my side, but I can't count on it. If Macklin's the one paying, he has money enough to try and buy Delance."

Samuel's room was built back into the mountain, carved from rock. He poured himself and Brett a hot broth from a kettle.

Brett sniffed the strong aroma. "Sage?"

"Sage 'n' mule root tea. Nothing like it. Cures everything, even keeps fleas away. Beats that poison they call coffee to all get out. I gather my leaves and mule root on my travels. Dry the leaves and root in the sun. Stores as good as iron soda biscuits."

It was bitter and poignant. Brett coughed a little. Samuel grinned broadly, pleased. "Good for nasal passages too." His smile faded. "Okay, lad, better tell me about my little brother. It hurts me to no end knowing Jack shot your God-fearing father. How'd it happen?"

"My dad doesn't think it was deliberate, although Jack warned him not to treat the dying man. It may have been a warning shot gone awry. There was a little confusion at the time. Maybe it was unintentional, but when selfish men demand their own way, someone else is usually hurt. Often someone who had nothing to do with it."

Samuel gave him a searching look that probed his soul. "So Downey authorized you to bring him in for trial. Any root of bitterness, lad?"

Brett met his piercing eyes evenly. His voice was calm. "Yes—at first." Brett looked at his hands. He flexed his fingers. "I've practiced shooting consistently for one reason, to hunt down the man who destroyed my father's hand and turned him into being just a good doctor instead of the finest surgeon."

Samuel was silent.

"I was twenty then. I've changed. I'm not bitter anymore. For the last three years I've been free of that poison. It took awhile, but the Lord handled it. I've been into ranching at Grass Valley for two years now." He looked steadily at Samuel. "After meeting Jack's family, I know why the Lord had me settle it before I got here."

"I'm pleased to hear that. And I believe you, son. It's written in your eyes, your style. It's good that your gun is devoted to the law. No reason a smart young man like yourself would want to be slower than them rattlers Hoadly's called into town, not when you're risking your life for justice."

"My father's hand is crippled, but if we believe the wisdom of God is behind the incidents of life, then there's purpose behind even this bitter cup. Retribution is left to God. He knows the other man better than I do."

Samuel's eyes narrowed as he took the rugged young man in from head to boot, seeming to measure his character as well as his strength.

"You're a refreshing drink of cool water, Brett Wilder. Somehow I believe you're not just trying to hoodwink me. I don't think you're on a quest for vengeance. If you were hunting Jack out of personal hate, you wouldn't of stopped till you got him."

Brett tasted again the odious sage "tea."

Samuel held his hands toward the small stove. "Jack's got to be stopped before he kills someone else. Harkin?" He shook his head. "Not sure he did it. He and Harkin were close. They wouldn't have gone into a claim together if they didn't get on." He looked over at Brett. "You heard about the witness?"

"A lawyer named Colefax."

"Right. Mac's lawyer. An odd one, Colefax. No more emotion than an icicle, but smart in the way of the law. Smart to turn and twist what's good into something he can use to break the law, if you know what I mean. Crooked lawyers and judges—the Bible has plenty to say about that."

Colefax and Macklin. Had they made a pact together to frame Jack Halliday for his partner's murder?

"What can you tell me about Jack?"

Samuel leaned back, getting comfortable, a reminiscing look on his leathery face. There was wistfulness too, and a sad longing for a relationship long gone awry...

Seventeen

ॐ

Brett listened as Samuel Halliday spoke of his younger brother, Jack.

"Jack Halliday—alias Jack Dawson. He used Dawson because of Lilly. Didn't want her name ruined. Jack was the youngest of three boys. Charlie, the eldest, Weda's husband, is dead. Charlie claimed to be a Christian, but only God knows. I surely don't. Jack was the wild one. He never wanted much to do with me after I took to preaching Christ. Unlike Charlie, Jack's never claimed faith. He's addicted to alcohol, gambling, wandering, and guns. Shoots fast too. Whenever he needs money or is in trouble he comes to me. I preach and pray and he listens. That's as far as it goes. When I'm done, he goes right back to his cards.

"I've always loved Jack. Somehow, in spite of his badness, he's always meant the most to my heart. I've spent more time on my face before God for Jack than I ever did for anyone else. And still he's as wrong as can be!"

Brett liked Samuel. "Sometimes it works that way. His own will is involved. No one can decide for him."

Samuel heaved a sigh. "You're right. He's grown meaner with the passing years. He left Lilly and the children in Sacramento with Charlie and Weda while he went off to the gold fields. And you've never seen a finer lot, especially my lovely Annalee. Jimmy's a great kid. Callie's a beauty too, but she's not learned yet to walk with the Lord."

So Samuel didn't know they were coming to Virginia Town.

"Better prepare yourself, Samuel," Brett said with a smile. "Annalee's at the Vesey in Gold Hill. Callie and Jimmy are staying with Ma Higgins in Dayton. They'll be joining Annalee tomorrow."

Samuel leaned forward. "Here in Virginny Town? This is no place for Annalee. My niece has bad lungs! Why, it'll kill her."

"I tried to convince her to turn back at Strawberry Flat. She won't be convinced. She's definitely got some of your spirit, Samuel. She's determined to help you in your Christian work. She's also determined to find out from Macklin what happend to those mining shares in the Pelly-Jessup. And you're right. Annalee's a very ill young woman. On the way over the mountains I had to bring her to a cabin belonging to a trapper friend until she recovered from a spell. She's better now, but she needs to be under a doctor's care."

Samuel groaned. "The relapse came then? I've been praying night and day it wouldn't."

"I've put her up in a room until you can impress upon her the wisdom of seeking medical help. I haven't mentioned this to her yet, but my dad's opening a sanitarium in the desert. He's studying tuberculosis. If she'd allow it, he'd take her in for no cost."

Samuel stared at him. "Your father's studying lungs now?"

"When he got over his depression about losing the use of his hand, he began reading about the disease. I watched his interest grow, and now he's determined to open a sanitarium."

Samuel just shook his head as if he were hearing news too welcome to be true.

"Praise God!" he said with unashamed zeal. "She'll go to see your father, all right. I'll insist upon it. I'll go to Gold Hill tonight."

"Samuel, she doesn't know I'm here to bring her father in for trial."

Samuel shook his head. "I know, lad. This is rough business, especially with the girls and Jimmy here in town." He stirred the coals in the stove. "Macklin told Lilly he was dead, killed by the Piutes, but I've learned differently. I wrote Lilly he was alive, but she'd already died in that stage accident before my letter arrived. I suppose Annalee got my letter."

"She said she'd written you saying she was coming."

"I got a letter a week ago from Placerville, but I didn't take her seriously. Guess I don't know her as well as I thought I did."

"She's here to find her father and relocate out at the cabin he shared with Frank Harkin."

"She can't go there. Frank's brother rode into town today."

"I met him at the Bucket. Samuel, what do you know about that claim?"

"That's what I've been looking into. That, and those mining shares Jack gave to Lilly. But there's plenty of confusion about his own claim out at Gold Canyon. There's so many claims now on Sun Mountain, they overlap three and four deep. There's confusion in the recorder's office, you can believe.

"Jack denies claim jumping. But then, my little brother has a way of looking me straight in the eye and lying through his teeth."

Brett hesitated. He was liking this less and less. "When did you see him last?"

Samuel didn't blink an eye. "In Utah. Before Lilly died. Don't even know if Jack is aware she's gone, but he must be. Word would have gotten to him somehow. When he came into Utah, he told me the Piutes nearly got him. It was close. They were on his trail. That's when he told me about the claim at Gold Canyon and Harkin being killed."

"He must have his own idea as to who shot Frank in the back."

"Oh, sure. Said it was Hoadly. And that Macklin paid him."

Hoadly...it made sense. "Did Jack say why?"

"That's when he told me he was going to be a rich man some day. He gave me a tobacco-size pouch of gold dust. Said it was to go to his family if anything happened to him. That, and a few other things he had wrapped in a little packet.

"Anyway, I rode to Carson and gave that packet to Bill Stewart and had a talk about the legality of things."

"A good lawyer. The best."

"When I was returning from seeing Stewart, that's when I got hit."

"Got any ideas about who took that rifle shot at you?"

"Don't know if it was Harkin's brother or not. I got waylaid between Carson and Gold Hill."

Brett didn't think it was Dylan. He'd been fired up at the Bucket. But he only had Jack Halliday on his mind. A rifle shot at Samuel from behind some rocks didn't sound like the way Dylan worked. Instead, it pointed to one of Hoadly's hired guns. At Macklin's order?

Brett stood. "I need to find Jack before Dylan Harkin does."

Samuel wore a worried brow. "Jack will show himself. You can count on it."

Brett waited. Samuel sighed. "I've something he wants. Something I didn't take with me when I saw Stewart."

Samuel got to his feet, holding his shoulder, and motioned to a door in the back wall.

"There's forty feet of tunnel back there. I started to mine years ago between my travels. Here's where I keep a few important things, including Jack's gold dust. And something else he gave me to keep when I met him in Utah."

Brett followed him through the narrow wooden door into a dark tunnel.

Samuel lit a lantern that sat on a small crude table. His mining tools lay propped against the rock wall. On a ledge there was a small iron box. He took it and set it down on the table beside the lantern's glow.

Brett saw several small bags of gold dust taken in placer mining. There were some old photos, probably of Samuel's parents. Samuel lifted a soiled envelope and took out a wrinkled piece of ledger paper.

"With Frank shot in the back, Jack knew he needed to make a run for it. He just had time to tear this from the ledger before he lit out. Vigilantes were on his trail."

With Macklin Villiers in the lead? Probably. And Brett didn't doubt a moment that Macklin would have urged them to hang him then and there if they'd caught up in time. With Harkin dead, and Jack blamed for his murder, Macklin was free to seize the claim at Gold Canyon.

Except Jack wasn't dead, and Jack had heirs as well. Lillian Halliday, for one.

Slowly, Brett was seeing the pieces of the puzzle come together.

"Jack found me in Utah," Samuel was telling him. "He asked me to keep this for him." He handed the ledger paper to Brett.

"Doesn't look like much, does it? Yet men have died because of it. Men who weren't ready to enter eternity."

Brett read the names, dates, and location of the Halliday-Harkin claim in Gold Canyon.

Samuel shook his head. "Least it's written in ink. Some men just wrote their claims in that ledger in pencil. Heard names have been erased in the last year and other names written in."

"This piece was torn from the ledger," Brett said. He noticed Jack had deliberately zig zagged the tear that later could be proven to belong to the legal mining ledger.

"In '57 and '58, men were just going into the saloon where Nick kept the ledger and signing their claims," Samuel explained. "The ledger wasn't protected as far as I know. Anyone could walk in and make whatever amendments he wanted. So they settle disputes with guns. And the fastest draw wins. Bill Stewart says more land is taken up than Washoe can provide. Swindlers are happy. Says Washoe's in a mess. Arbitration is the thing."

"He's right. He's going to have his hands full. From the looks of this," Brett tapped the paper, "that's where it'll head. If Macklin did have Frank Harkin killed and the death blamed on your brother, he's looking for this. Jack was smart to hand it to you. It gives him something to bargain with if Macklin finds him. But it puts you in danger once it's known you have it."

And Annalee. She was Jack's daughter. Could this claim have been the reason Macklin first went to San Francisco to see Lillian? Maybe it wasn't the mining shares in the Pelly-Jessup he wanted. And when he found out she didn't have the claim, he had eliminated one more heir? Maybe...

Annalee's baggage.

Was Macklin growing anxious? He was taking no chances. If Lillian didn't have the claim, then maybe her daughter did. So he'd sent someone to trail her—Big Birdie? It was true he worked for Jang Li, but he was also the sort of character Macklin could use to do his cheap, dirty work.

"Whoever tried to shoot you last night might have worried after they saw you visiting Bill Stewart. What was in that packet you brought him, do you know?"

"It was sealed. Mining shares, is my guess."

"In the Pelly-Jessup?"

"I'm sure of it."

"Samuel, do you know if Jack's claim runs near the Jessup?"

"Looks to me like they rub noses. Jack will be wanting that packet of shares back, along with this proof of claim to his own mine at Gold Canyon."

Brett folded the torn sheet and placed it within the yellowed envelope. He tapped it against his palm thoughtfully.

Samuel noticed his concern.

"You do what the law says, lad. Jack will come back for it. If he knows you have it…"

That was exactly what Brett had in mind. He placed it carefully inside his jacket pocket. He now had the bait. But there was more than one stalking wolf. There was a pack of 'em.

Brett looked around, interested. "Quite a place you have."

"I did it all myself through the years. I've known there was gold and silver in this mountain same as Ol' Virginny. Let me show you my abode, lad. Solid rock, she is. Safe from the elements."

"The wind?"

"Washoe zephyrs, we call them. The miners are learning the hard way. Tried to warn them. In the middle of the night that wind comes ripping down the mountain, rending their canvas shelters to bits. After a few times of running like scared rabbits in search of some dirt hole in which to scamper, they're catching on fast."

Brett knew that many simply burrowed in the ground. Some scooped out tunnels to spend the winter. Others had rock dugouts like Samuel.

"We run our stovepipes through the rocky roof. In the winter you'd think the mountain was a regular smoking volcano. When the cold weather arrives, some miners are desperate enough to drive the coyotes out of their lairs.

"We look like a pack of lizards at times. It's not so bad here for me, but others get wet as the snow melts and drips."

Samuel had three small "rooms." The one nearest the opening was the kitchen. "This is my sleeping bunk. Comfortable as a baby in his cradle. And in here is my library."

Brett took in the incredible sight of books stacked and lined neatly in the wall.

"On Sundays I do my teaching here. Some of the boys gather around and we discuss the true riches of the Word. I tell them to lay up their treasure above where claim jumpers can't steal, where rust doesn't corrode, and where the wind can't take it away."

"Wise advice. If I'm around come Sunday, I'll stop by."

He walked back to the opening and Samuel followed him. "Thanks for taking the slug from my shoulder."

"You'll see to Annalee?"

"I will."

"I'd like to take a look at that mine out at Gold Canyon."

"There's a cabin there. Be as wily as a coyote, though. There's been a shoot-out on the mountain nearly every morning. Everyone's greedy and out of patience."

Brett shook Samuel's hand and then walked down to where he'd left his horse. After thanking the Arkansas brothers, he mounted and rode along the dirt street. Just ahead he saw Hoadly and the big boxer, Roc, walking to the Bucket of Blood saloon.

They also saw him. Roc stopped like a bull sniffing the air, but Hoadly wouldn't look toward him and continued on into the Bucket.

Brett turned his zebra dun to ride on. The last thing he wanted right now was to tangle with Roc. He was having dinner tonight with Annalee, and he didn't want to walk into the Vesey bloodied up.

He wished to avoid the boxer altogether, but that depended on Roc. He wasn't going to run from a big gorilla who had it in for him. What Roc didn't know was that he and Yancey had taken boxing lessons of their own.

Roc finally turned away and followed his master into the saloon.

Brett rode on to the livery stable and dismounted. His spoiled dun was already complaining that he wanted his lunch.

Before going into the livery, he stood on the street alone, with enemies all about him, and considered the present situation with care. He'd definitely kicked over the applecart coming into

Virginia Town with a commission as Downey's deputy marshal. No mistake about it, the news would be out by now, moving fast.

Hoadly would have reported to his boss—Macklin Villiers?—about what happened at Strawberry and that Brett was looking for Jack Halliday. If Macklin was the one in the murky background pulling the strings, one could be sure he was busy making inquiries.

Word, too, would have spread to the hired guns Hoadly had sent for. But until Brett went a step beyond looking for Halliday to whoever stood in the background calling the shots, he didn't think the hired guns would be given the order to turn on him.

Brett entered the livery stable. The old hostler in charge was half-dozing on a bench. He awoke, jumped to his feet, and took the horse's reins from Brett.

"Where's the headquarters around here for signing up a claim?"

"Down at Nick's tavern. Mining ledger's on the counter."

At Nick's, men lined the counter or were playing poker at the tables. No one paid much attention to Brett as he went over to the end of the barrel counter. There, against the wall, sat the beat-up old ledger.

Samuel had been right. Security was lax. No wonder Bill Stewart was talking arbitration.

He turned the pages until he found the bottom of a page that had been torn out.

Brett looked up. No one watched him. He casually removed from his jacket the piece he'd received from Samuel and placed it down into the book. Smoothing it out flat—it matched perfectly, completing the original page with Jack Halliday and Frank Harkin's name, date, and the location of their claim. He placed the legal evidence back inside his jacket.

He turned to the next page. There it was, written in ink, the name of Macklin Villiers, claiming the same section of land that bordered the Pelly-Jessup.

Brett closed the ledger and pushed it back into the corner. Turning, he walked out.

He stood on the boardwalk thinking. This pretty well cleared things up as far as he was concerned. Macklin was the big man in the shadows calling the shots. He'd probably hired Hoadly and his gunfighters. What Brett didn't have was proof that would convict Macklin in a court of law.

He decided to ride out to Gold Canyon and have a look at the Pelly-Jessup before returning to the Vesey Hotel. He'd also have a look at the Halliday-Harkin claim.

❧ ❧

The wind was blowing cold down the mountain slopes as Brett rode along Gold Canyon.

He'd already done his research on the Pelly-Jessup. The mine was a stock operation. The heaviest investors, three wealthy businessmen in San Francisco who'd first made their money in the California gold rush, had set claim to a hundred feet along the Comstock Lode, buying out two prospectors who'd been friends with Ol' Virginny and Pancake.

Macklin Villiers had bought fifteen percent stock in the operation early on by an arrangement with Colefax, the lawyer working with the San Francisco businessmen.

They'd sunk a shaft some seventy feet deep and from there had run a second drift at right angles to a shaft that produced a good showing of rich ore. The width of the silver vein had widened as they went still deeper, and soon the Pelly-Jessup was sending tons of high grade ore over the Sierras.

The bonanza had appeared as though it would never end, but Brett learned in California just how swiftly some of the best lodes were cleaned out, or how a rich vein would fail to continue and run into a dead end.

Such was the history of the short-lived Pelly-Jessup.

The mine had looked nearly deserted under the overcast sky of the oncoming winter as he rode up.

The few buildings were close together and might have been empty except for some mules and ore wagons out front. A few lone miners walked along carrying their picks and jacks as a dust devil stirred about them. The wind crooned a lonely, almost mournful, dirge.

He rode slowly into the yard and tied his horse to the wooden rail.

Ahead, there was a low building that looked as though it held more than one office. He walked there and saw the signs flapping in the wind: Assay Office, the Superintendent, the Business Office. Brett smiled to himself. Someone went in for long titles of importance. That, too, was like Macklin Villiers.

He walked around to the back and saw the hoisting engine house, the head frame, and the mine shaft collar. Two or three men loitered about and when they saw him they began to act busy, not knowing if he was connected in some way to the mine.

He glanced behind him. There was a blacksmith shop, a large toolshed, and large bins where the ore was dumped when hoisted.

Everything stood still. There was something a bit sad about a tired, worn-out mine. It had given its heart of silver and gold and now stood empty of its soul and forgotten.

Brett smiled at his sentiment and turned toward the shaft when he heard bootsteps coming toward him.

Just like the mine, the older man looked tired and sun-faded.

"Howdy. I'm Miller. Something I can do for you?"

Brett flashed his badge. "Deputy Marshal Wilder. Just thought I'd like to look around, if you don't mind."

Miller wore a worried face. "Er, ah, why no, Marshal. Where'd you like to tour?"

Brett smiled. "How about going into the mine?"

Miller glanced back over his shoulder toward the collar.

"Not too much to see now. Compared to the Hale and Norcross, the Savage, the Ophir, an' such like along the lode, we're small pickings."

"Heard those pickings have about run out."

"You heard right, Marshal. We're still hauling some ore, but not much, just enough to stay open for the rest of the year. Next spring when the Californians come in with the money and know-how, Mr. Villiers will probably close down. He says we need to go deeper, lay another shaft to work it proper, but he needs capital for that."

"What about the controlling stock interest in San Francisco? Don't they want to keep going?"

He shrugged. "They sold out some months ago. It's Mr. Villiers and Mr. Colefax who own the Pelly-Jessup now. Mr. Villiers has controlling interest."

That didn't surprise Brett. Macklin would always insist on being on top. Strange, though, that the two of them had bought up all that worthless stock floating around San Francisco.

Why would someone as shrewd as Macklin trouble about a dead mine when there were other possibilities still waiting to be discovered?

Many mines were opening up bonanza ore; the Gould & Curry, for instance. Close beside it, the Savage, the Yellow Jacket, and the Ophir were tremendously rich. He'd heard the Ophir alone had a vein sixty-five feet wide.

Why, then, the Pelly-Jessup unless Macklin and Colefax had plans that would yet make them rich?

Miller was waiting at the collar of the shaft when Brett joined him.

"Mr. Villiers know you're having a tour, Marshal?"

"I didn't think he'd mind," Brett said with an innocent smile.

Miller scowled but kept quiet. He watched as Brett lit his own lamp and, always careful, slipped extra candles in his coat pocket.

They descended by ladder into the dark.

Below, Miller stopped and sat down on a barrel, and Brett was aware of the foreman's nervous gaze following his every move. Brett walked along the drift, studying the rock formations. The timber work and the mining that had gone before appeared to be thorough and professionally done. But it wasn't the past work that interested him.

He lifted his lamp high so it would shine down on the rock walls. He certainly was no geologist, but he knew about mining from growing up around Sutter's. He and Yancey had enjoyed working for several summers at Jackson Hole during their school years.

The ore here looked to him to be low-grade quartz. He recognized what the professional miners had told him and Yancey was galena, and a little argentite, and even more sphalerite. The silver wasn't evident, but he knew it would have a fair showing when professionally mined.

Miller seemed to guess his conclusion. "Pretty bleak. All the blue stuff's been extracted."

Brett turned, and the light of his lamp shone for an instant onto the rock wall farther ahead. The rough arch of a Y-shaped crosscut was visible. *The right branch of the Y...where does the drift lead?*

He gestured. "Why is the crosscut sealed off?"

Brett's iron gaze met the foreman's in silence.

Miller shifted his eyes away. "It's bad ground for sure. The men are afraid of a cave-in. The roof's not shored up yet. And there's water leakage. You can tell from the black muck oozing from under the rock wall. If that roof goes, twenty or thirty feet would go with it. Pay ain't as good as it used to be, now that the mine has reached its end. The men won't risk it in there for low pay. Not when they can go to work at the Ophir or the Savage with safer conditions."

Brett walked over to the crosscut that opened the other drift. The area was barred, and he lifted his lamp.

Powder had been used recently and there was still some ore and rubble that hadn't been cleaned up.

Miller came up beside him.

"I'm no miner, but it looks to me like the major thrust of the lode drifts northeast, away from the Pelly-Jessup."

"Then you know more'n the best miners working here," Miller said a little stiffly. He wiped his brow. "Warm in here. A mite stuffy too. Maybe we ought to go back now."

"If it was safe, and you proceeded in this direction, where would that tunnel end up?"

"Pelly-Jessup can't go any farther, Marshal. That's the end of the claim."

Brett looked at him. "That drift would end up where?"

"Can't say, as a matter of fact."

"Try a guess."

"We'd drift into another man's claim."

"If my memory serves me right, the Halliday-Harkin claim lies beyond that wall. Looks to me as if the Pelly-Jessup's already crossed over, that you've drifted into another claim."

Miller shook his head. "Not me, Marshal. I wasn't even around here back then. I was working at the Ophir. You ask, a man named Hanks will tell you. I just started working for Mr. Villiers mebbe two months ago. The other foreman quit."

"Who's responsible for this drift?"

He was nervous now and talkative. "Had to be the other foreman. Don't remember his name. I think it was Carr. But Mr. Villiers would have given him orders. Mr. Villiers knows about mining. I was surprised he did, till one of the boys told me he was at California in '49. Yuba, too, and even the Fraser.

"I heard a man named Harkin was working around that area. Some of the boys said he'd some good showings too. Him and Jack Halliday. Heard they shipped a pack train of rich ore for milling two months before Harkin was killed by his partner over a squabble. But if them two fellers was working behind that wall, then they was claim jumpers. Because Mr. Villiers staked his claim on that section over a year ago, maybe longer, so I'm told."

Brett didn't tell him otherwise. As it was, Miller would soon be running to Macklin with the news that he'd been here asking questions. Macklin would know he was onto him.

Brett left the mine shaft and mounted his horse. He rode from the Pelly-Jessup toward the Halliday-Harkin claim.

Eighteen

*A*fter a long nap, Annalee spent the afternoon preparing for dinner with Brett below in the hotel dining room. She relished a soak in the fancy clawfooted tub and washed her hair. Most of her clothing was packed in the trunk that was over in Dayton with Callie, but she had the dress she'd worn on the stage to Strawberry. She took it out and sent it down to be cleaned and pressed.

She was pleased with her appearance and fussing with the set of curls at the back of her neck when there came a knock on her door.

Brett, so soon? Nervously she took a last look at herself and then rushed to the door and opened it.

"Uncle Samuel!" she recognized the burly man at once and broke into a happy smile.

He laughed his pleasure over seeing her and swept one hefty arm around her.

"Why, you've grown into a beautiful young lady, Annalee."

"Your arm! What happened, Uncle?"

"Nothing that won't heal. Just a stray bullet, is all."

She rather doubted that but let it go. He already knew about Callie and Jimmy staying in Dayton and told her he'd spoken to Brett that morning in his dugout on Sun Mountain.

Once the greetings were over, she could see by his expression that he'd come with dark news.

"Better sit down, lass. What I have to tell you is upsetting."

Annalee did as he asked and looked up warily into his rugged face.

"I'll get right out with it. You look like a sensible girl, one who respects the law. Your pa's alive, I talked with him in Utah before Lilly's death. But we've bad news…he's wanted for shooting a man."

"Uncle Samuel, I already know about Frank Harkin. Cousin Macklin came to San Francisco to tell Mother the news. But I don't believe a word of it. Not now. I don't trust Macklin and—"

"I'm not talking of Harkin. I think you're right. Jack didn't shoot him. But there was another shooting a few years back, and your pa's wanted in Sacramento for murder. It brings Wilder no pleasure, but there it is, girl, the truth."

For a moment she couldn't speak. Then, her voice weak and thready, "Are you saying Brett came to arrest my father for a murder in Sacramento?"

Samuel's voice was strained and unhappy. "I'm afraid he has, lass. When a man wears a badge, he has his duty."

Her mind kept darting back to that first night spent at Strawberry. Brett had behaved strangely when Callie mentioned that their name was Halliday. Now she knew why. He'd known even then who they were, that he'd come to arrest her father. And yet he'd kept it a secret, wishing to use her to trap her pa. *And all the while pretending to care about me when I was ill. Why, I'll wager he just didn't want to let me out of his watchful eye, is all.* The idea hurt more than she cared to admit. He'd behaved so kind, so thoughtful, and yet…Brett had used her like bait!

"He wants you to go back to Sacramento to see his father. He's an outstanding doctor, I've heard, now with a new dedication to discover treatments for your condition. I'm in total agreement you should go."

"Go with *him?*" she stood, hands in fists at her side. "Does Brett Wilder think I'll trust *him* again? He lied to me!"

"Now, girl, don't talk that way. Wilder's a good man; I can see it in him. He's a rarity. You'd be wise to cast your lot for him. He's interested in you as a woman, I can tell."

"Fiddlesticks. Gordon told me he's about to become engaged to a girl back home. He was just using me to get information, that's all." She sank again to the chair, swallowing the cramp in her throat that appeared whenever she thought of that pretty girl in

Grass Valley. Tears wet her eyes. "If he didn't lie to me, then what do you call his deliberate deceit?"

Samuel's gaze was without apology. "He didn't deceive you either. I'm a good judge of character, and I can see he's got plenty of it. If he didn't mention your pa's trouble with the law, then it was because he cared."

"Cared!" she scoffed, for it was what she had soothed herself into believing for some time. She now knew she'd been foolish. She had believed—dared to hope—he did care for her, just the way she'd foolishly thought Gordon had been in love with her those years growing up on Weda's farm. The first opportunity Gordon had to get something he thought better—a girl with a good family name and money—he'd walked away from her. It didn't matter that he was here in Gold Hill now. He hadn't come back because of her but to start his newspaper.

"Yes, he cares. He cared too much when he met you back at Berry's to add more burden to your shoulders."

She wiped her eyes with her handkerchief. It was too risky to believe, to even hope. She was finished with Gordon, and now she wouldn't even entertain the slightest notion that Brett had feelings for her. "I don't believe it, Uncle Samuel."

"Wilder waited to come straight to me. Just as he should have done."

She shook her head. "He treats me like a child, and I'm not. He should have told me the whole story, just as ugly as he claims it to be. And anyway," she argued, "what proof does he have that it was my father who shot the man in Sacramento? It's his word against Pa's."

"He has proof," Samuel stated quietly. "If there was no evidence Jack shot that card dealer aboard the *Golden Queen,* then the governor wouldn't have commissioned Wilder to arrest him."

She didn't want to hear it. She rose and walked over to the window. Standing there, she recalled the gunfight she'd seen just that morning. Even then, unaware that Brett was after her father, she'd feared he might be, that his quickness with a gun might lead to a horrible duel between them. It was too awful to contemplate. Her father, too, was quick on the draw. There was no guarantee Brett would win.

She turned to look at her uncle. "And this room! I won't stay here another moment while he pays my bills. I'm moving out to Pa's cabin, and I'll wait for Pa there. He's bound to come back. Sacramento is out of the question, and so is the notion of seeing Brett's father."

"You're making a mistake, Annalee."

Annalee paced. "I'll pay him back every penny he's spent on us." She stopped short. "Has Macklin contacted you about the shares in the Pelly-Jessup belonging to Mother?"

"No, he's been out of Virginia Town until a few days ago. Him and Colefax both. Now that he's come back, I'll pay him a visit."

"I'm going to speak to him too. I want to know about the stage accident. And when Pa does turn up, I'll believe him innocent until I have good reason not to. I'll get him the best lawyer anywhere around."

Samuel's brows lowered and he walked toward her. "Now you listen to me, girl. I know Jack better than you. When was the last time you saw him, eh? You couldn't have been much out of pigtails."

Annalee was ashamed to admit she hadn't seen her father in several years. She knew he had taken advantage of her mother and denied her loving support as husband and provider. Yet her mother had believed in him.

"I've a lifetime of experience with Jack. I know the kind of fellers he roams with. If he does come back because of that claim out at Gold Canyon, he's not likely to come alone."

Annalee felt the pain twisting her heart.

"He's still my father. I don't believe he shot that riverboat card dealer anymore than he shot Frank Harkin in the back."

"I wish I could say I believed the same about that night on the riverboat, but I can't. He was drunk on whiskey when he pulled his gun. A man who wouldn't harm a fly when he was sober can do evil things when his brain is sopped with tarantula juice."

Tarantula juice…where had she heard that strange expression before? The Indian girl when speaking to her father at Berry's Flat…

"I'm not making excuses, Uncle Samuel. Pa might do many things that are wrong, but kill a man over a card game? I can't believe it."

"Best not to put your morals on Jack. Don't say a man can't do this or that just because you wouldn't think that way. Lass, I've seen your pa come close to drawing his gun on a man over a card game a dozen times."

This was not what she wanted to learn, not the way things were supposed to be, not the way she wanted to remember her father, but the truth was staring her in the face. Facts so glaring that it was too painful to look at them for long. How could it have come to this? Why couldn't she have had a father like Dr. Wilder or Uncle Samuel? But if she began asking why, she would sink deeper and deeper into the dark muck of doubt, fear, and self-pity.

Brett had been right at Harry's cabin. God was to be trusted even in the dark.

"Sadly, Jack's been in trouble of one sort or another since he was a boy in knee pants. I worry about him. He's played lightly with sin. A conscience can become seared as if with a hot iron. Things that used to prick don't bother him like they did once. What seems a little wrong can become a habit with chains. A man never becomes an alcoholic by taking one drink, but if he hadn't fooled with the first—mark my words, lass, he'd be a sober man today. Just so with gamblin'. With most things that grow like an evil root in the heart."

Father God, help my pa...oh that it isn't true he killed a man...

"All this doesn't change the fact that Brett was using me to get information on Pa's whereabouts. He never cared a whit about us—"

"I think he cares more than even he knows right now."

"He's like Gordon," she breathed, showing her inner turmoil by pacing again.

"Gordon who?" Samuel's eyes squinted.

She glanced toward him. She really hadn't intended to speak about Gordon Barkly, but the disappointment she felt over Brett's betrayal had pulled the comparison from her.

"I once thought I was going to marry a man named Gordon Barkly. He's here now in Virginia Town to start a newspaper. Back in Sacramento my illness proved a stumbling block to our relationship." She looked at her uncle and saw compassion in his greenish eyes. "My illness showed me how weak I really am, how desperately I need God, but it also proved who my friends were and tested the depth of Gordon's commitment to me." A sigh escaped her. "His love withered like a frail blossom in the wind."

She turned away. In Brett she thought she may have found—no, she wouldn't go there.

Samuel walked up to his niece and laid a comforting hand on her shoulder. "I don't want to sound calloused, Annalee, but maybe it's good that Gordon's love was tested this way. A man can say most anything to a charming young girl with fresh blooms in her cheeks and a sparkle in her eye. But times and seasons change most things in this life. A lasting relationship between a man and a woman needs more than what's on the surface."

Annalee knew that now.

"I can also tell you that the kind of love you long for, one that's aways faithful, sure, and strong, is found only in your dear Savior. The Lord loves you, little lass, in all your weaknesses. He knows what He wants to do with your life. You just yield and let Him work. The divine Potter still loves His vessel of clay even when it passes through the fire."

She grew quiet. "You sound just like Brett."

"He's a man worth listening to."

"But, Uncle, maybe someone just thought they saw Pa on that Sacramento riverboat."

"You know down deep it isn't so. You've got to face the truth, honey, painful or not. You've got to get on with your tomorrows. Don't throw away the opportunity of going to Sacramento with Wilder to defend Jack. Not because he couldn't change, not because the Lord wouldn't turn his life around if he did, but because your pa doesn't want to give up his way of life. He didn't give it up for Lilly. He won't give it up for his children."

His words spoken about her mother penetrated her defenses. It was true. She knew that very well. Hadn't her mother been forced to work in the melodeons because her father refused to support them?

Yet…she wasn't quite ready to give up on him. "Maybe everything you say is true, Uncle. But then, maybe you've grown weary of trying. I come to Pa fresh and new, and I've only begun to try."

Samuel watched her a long moment, and then he smiled.

"Wilder told me you were a determined young woman. Looks as if he was right. So maybe I should just let you walk your extra mile and discover where it leads. I know one thing well; the grace of God is suffcient to save anyone who'd sincerely turn to the Savior. We'll keep praying for Jack."

"I suppose I must keep my civility close at hand each time I see the marshal."

"Brett's following his calling as much as I am mine. A lawman is a servant of God according to the Scriptures. It's not always easy, certainly not pleasant, but in a society where laws must abound for the good of its citizens, men must wear a gun to protect the innocent from men like murderous Sam Brown."

She didn't know who Sam Brown was, but he must have been in Virginia Town. She thought of Big Birdie.

"There are too many gunslingers too," Samuel said. "They come to steal away an honest man's claim by waving a pistol under his nose. Women must be protected from such ruthless men, and churches and schools must be built. Nevada isn't a U.S. territory yet, but with the silver bonanza I've a notion it will become one soon enough. Especially if there's a war with the Southern states. The president, whoever he turns out to be—either Douglas or Lincoln—will need the silver to finance the government.

"We need men like Brett Wilder, Annalee. I'm glad he's offered to stay on. He'll be down at Jack's cabin for a few weeks."

"Pa's cabin? But that's where I'm going with Jimmy and Callie."

"Thunderation, lass! It's dangerous as all get out in Gold Canyon right now. It might have been the younger Harkin who put a bullet in my shoulder. Dylan is as riled as a spitting cobra over what happened to his brother. Brett ran into him at the saloon this morning. The news has gone out that Jack killed Frank for that claim, and now Dylan's after him. That's another reason it's best Wilder finds Jack first. He'll get a fair shake at least."

She wondered. She wasn't as convinced as her uncle.

Annalee sank down on the bed. How could it have come to this?

"Honey, he wants you out of here. He's willing to work with Flint Harper to see you brought back to Sacramento to see Doc Wilder."

She shook her head no. "Uncle, I'm afraid I must disappoint you, but I'm staying. It's even more important to me now. I won't rest until these ugly matters are straightened out and Pa is cleared of murdering Frank Harkin. I'm of age now. Mother is with the Lord. Pa hasn't the time nor the ability to do anything for me, so I'll do it myself. Callie and I will care for Jimmy. And there's Pa's claim out in Gold Canyon to look into. What if he did find silver?"

Samuel's frown deepened at that, as though he knew more than he was telling her.

"You're looking at me with green eyes as stubborn as any Irish maiden," he said wryly.

She smiled suddenly. "Maybe I take after you, Uncle Samuel."

They stared at each other. Annalee, calm but resolute. Samuel, with brows thundering together. He looked about to put his boot down and threaten to haul her bodily off the Comstock Lode, but he must have decided it wouldn't solve the issue.

Unexpectedly, after several moments, his brows unfurrowed and the corner of his mouth turned. He laughed softly. "Maybe you do take after your ol' uncle. So be it then, lass, you win." His eyes narrowed deliberately. "For now, that is. You come to Virginny Town. You sketch all you want. Truth is, I could use help starting a Sunday Bible class for the few womenfolk in the camps." He surprised her by planting a kiss on her forehead. "There's a good girl. We'll see where the Lord takes us all."

In a moment she was in his bear hug.

"I'll do my best not to get in the way."

"Promise me one thing, Annalee." He looked down at her soberly. "Treat Brett Wilder fairly until you can prove he's as heartless as you say."

She folded her arms. "I'll try. But every time I look at him I'll know he's come to arrest Pa, and that won't make for good feelings between us."

"Until that time comes, lass, let's treat each other as Christians. Fair enough?"

"Fair enough, Uncle." She was uneasy, though, about the dinner she was expected to have with Brett. She tried to think of a satisfactory way to get out of it.

"Why not stay for supper tonight, Uncle? Brett will be here, and it would be...more pleasant if you ate with us."

His eyes seemed to laugh. "And play referee? Now, now, lass, it will be far better for you to speak with him alone."

She cocked a delicate brow. She had the notion Samuel thought this because he believed Brett would convince her he was right after all...well!

᠊ᡒᡅᡅᠱ᠊

The wind was blowing again, strong, cold, and rounding up rain clouds from the north. Brett lifted the collar of his buckskin jacket and pulled his hat lower as he rode along Gold Canyon. It would be a long cold winter. If he couldn't convince Annalee to leave soon, it would be too late until spring.

He'd left the Pelly-Jessup, but before he looked at the Halliday-Harkin, Brett wanted to check the map Samuel had made of Gold Canyon.

He veered from the dusty trail and rode toward some large whitish rocks where several creosote bushes grew, offering a wind break.

While his horse drank from the creek, he opened his saddlebag and removed the map of Gold Canyon. Resting a shoulder against a boulder out of the wind, he studied the map around the Pelly-Jessup and the disputed adjoining claim of Halliday-Harkin.

The four-mile-long Comstock Lode ran north and south in a fault line with dark granite-textured rock on the west and fine gray volcanic rock on the east. If Samuel's drawing was correct, Halliday's claim, the smallest on the Comstock—it appeared to be no larger than fifteen feet—was in a coveted position surrounded by established mines producing silver in an astonishing rate. The Halliday-Harkin claim held every possibility of hitting a bonanza.

He folded the map and straightened, his gaze squinting off into the distance. It was an accepted rule that once a miner made a claim, it had to be validated by serious work, making at least a hundred dollars. He was sure Jack had done better. Brett needed a piece of that ore for assessment. He aimed to take steps to ensure that whatever might happen to Jack Halliday, his half of the claim would not be stolen by Macklin and Colefax.

He mounted again and rode out to the claim. There wasn't a soul in sight when he arrived. A cold wind blew down the canyon, whipping up dust and throwing sand tinkling against the rocks. A few stubby sage bushes growing near the abandoned stone hut rippled in the wind. The hut was on the slope to the west, a mere fifteen feet above the claim. Brett tied his horse there and entered the tunnel.

He still had candles from the Pelly-Jessup in his coat pocket. He lit one.

The tunnel was not large. The drift where Halliday and Harkin had been working when the trouble started appeared to be of little strategic interest until Brett came to the face of the drift.

Here, he stopped. He held the candle higher as he studied the ground. He was no miner, but he knew enough to realize there should have been chipped or broken rock lying at the foot of the face, perhaps a good amount of it left there by the last powder blown by Harkin or Halliday.

Considering Frank Harkin was killed the morning he'd last worked here, and Jack Halliday had made a run for it to the Forty Mile to escape being lynched, the floor of the tunnel was puzzling, for it had been cleared of all debris so that only a few small pieces of blown rock and ore remained where they'd last worked.

Someone other than the two men had removed that rock and ore, and he could think of only one reason why. It must have shown they were nearing something important…and big.

He walked back a few feet and examined the tunnel wall once more, this time more carefully studying the thin vein of bluish ore.

After a moment he returned to the drift where they'd been working. There were a few smaller pieces of broken rock and chipped ore that remained after the bulk of it had been hauled away.

Brett stooped to look at the pieces under his flame. He tossed most aside, but a few specimens he dropped into his jacket pocket. He wanted an assayer to have a look. But he also knew the right man to take it to for a quick opinion—Ol' Virginny.

He stood, staring at the tunnel face. What prize might lie just beyond?

The vein of silver ore was thin, but perhaps its humbleness was deceiving.

He was willing to make a wild guess. If Halliday and Harkin would have had another day or two to blast their way farther into the mountain, they may have disclosed the silver heart of the lode—the heart that the Pelly-Jessup had fallen just short of owning.

Had Macklin guessed the same? If so, he would also know that it remained near his grasp. The drift he'd seen at the Jessup convinced him that someone else believed as he did. If the Pelly-Jessup could claim the Halliday-Harkin section on the lode as part of their original claim, they could blast through to that silver heart and own it all.

Someone had ordered Harkin killed and his murder blamed on Halliday.

But how to prove it? He needed more than mere conjecture to have it stand in a court of law. He needed proof that Macklin Villiers, when it came to a lust for wealth and power, was a cold-blooded killer.

Nineteen

Annalee paced the floor in her room, peeling off one white glove and then putting it back on. That she'd brought gloves surprised even her. Her skirts rustled over crinolines. For a moment she wished she had her mother's best theater dress, but then she lifted her chin in dismissal of her emotions. They had a tendency to run away with her good common sense. Brett Wilder was someone to beware of, not to charm. *He's here to arrest your father. Remember that.*

She ceased pacing and turned toward the door as a soft knock sounded. That would be him now. Her stomach fluttered.

She slid back the lock and opened the door wide.

Against her will her gaze fell over him. He'd exchanged his buckskins for black broadcloth and a white frilled shirt. He looked as handsome and in control of things as he might have in San Francisco. His gun belt left no doubt, however, that he was prepared for a recurrence of what had happened earlier across the street from the hotel. She wondered if she ought to bring it up or pretend she hadn't watched from her window. She flushed a little when she met his gaze. His eyes were clear and light and alive with energy as they took her in with one glance.

She could see he wondered if Samuel had given her the news, but she restrained herself now that she was in his presence.

He smiled. "After a day of unwashed miners and mules, you're a refreshing sight."

She moved her lips into a faint smile. "It doesn't take much to compete."

He laughed softly. "I think you'd do well anywhere." He glanced into the room, unsmiling again. "Did Samuel come to talk to you?"

She turned and gathered up her wrap and handbag. After hesitating briefly, she also brought the smaller portfolio of her sketches.

"Yes, Uncle Samuel was here. He went back to his dugout."

She walked past him as he held the door open. His quick gaze told her he realized she knew about her father.

No words passed between them as they went down the short hall to some steps leading to the dining room.

The hotel atmosphere was conducive to pleasurable dining and unhurried conversation. He talked quietly of matter-of-fact things, and she avoided directly looking at him. They both knew they would have to discuss her father, and they were reluctant to do so.

The table was covered with a fine cloth and shiny dishware and utensils. The light glowed beneath a pretty amber hobnail glass lamp. The meal was the best she'd eaten since some of Weda's Sunday cooking. Roast chicken, mashed potatoes and gravy, and peas. The coffee, too, was good. And the apple pie could compete with dessert from back home. For the first time in months she ate everything on her plate. When the dishes were cleared away and Brett had refilled their cups, she reached down beside her and brought up her small portfolio. She was still trying to avoid the unpleasant.

"I wanted to show you some of my work."

She sipped her coffee while Brett took his time leafing through the drawings she'd done over the last several years in Sacramento. He hesitated over one of the sketches, and she glanced to see which one. It was a riverboat on the Sacramento. *Now why hadn't I removed that one? I'd forgotten all about it.*

She tensed, waiting, but he showed nothing of what might be flashing through his mind, and then he merely went on to study the next sketch. It was one she'd done of Montgomery Street in San Francisco when she'd been attending Gilmore.

The minutes ticked by. She wondered what he thought, for he hadn't said a word. Maybe he thought they were amateurish.

"Well?" she asked when she couldn't stand it. "Do you like my work or don't you?"

"Excellent."

That took her breath away. "You mean that!"

He looked up with a lazy gleam in his eyes. "Of course I mean it. I don't flatter, not even to make you feel good. They're excellent. I like your style and your message."

Message. Then he had seen more in her work than her family had. No one else had caught the idea that she always had a message in her sketches.

"Then you understood I was saying something besides creating an attractive scene to be enjoyed."

"I saw it at once. Have you taken lessons?"

"I had hoped to go to art school…"

He needed no further explanation, and she appreciated that.

"I can see you haven't had professional training, but you have talent, a great deal of it." He looked at her again, a faint smile showing. "If you'll let Flint take you to Sacramento on his next drive, I'll arrange to have a friend of mine buy a few of these for his newspaper. I think he'll like them. He has contacts with a magazine in Chicago. He could arrange to show your work. They're hungry to know everything about the West."

Her heart tripped with excitement. "Then"—she lifted a brow. "You know how to bribe me, don't you?"

He smiled. "Flint's leaving with a load of ore in two or three days. A few good men will ride shotgun. We can try and come up with some way to arrange for a more comfortable journey for you, maybe a covered palanquin. That will keep you out of the weather."

It was hard to resist his concern. Was it genuine? Yes, to a degree. He felt sorry for her, that was all. Sorry for a girl who was ill and facing the sorrow of having Jack Halliday for a father. She must resist. She looked away.

"I can't go, Brett."

"Can't? Or won't?"

The moments slipped by in awkward silence.

"If you wait much longer it will be out of the question until the spring thaw. Samuel told you my father is opening a sanitarium for lung patients, didn't he? I want you to see him."

"Yes, he told me about…your generous offer, but—" she shook her head no, staring at the amber light glowing softly in the hobnail lamp. "I can't leave now. I want to stay. Uncle Samuel's already agreed to let me help him in his work. It's something I want to do until I open a business with Callie."

His gaze grew stormy. "Samuel said you could stay with him?" There was doubt and frustration in his voice. She realized then that he had already cooked it up with Samuel to get her to leave.

"For a while, yes. Then I'm moving into the cabin out by my father's claim. I know you think that's foolish, but that cabin and claim belong to us now. I must stay and see him."

It took all her determination to look back without flinching into those gray eyes. Coming up against Brett Wilder's will was like keeping her balance in an earthquake. She lifted her chin, refusing to be conquered.

He gave a short laugh. "I was right about you."

"About me?" she asked uneasily, narrowing her lashes.

"Yes. I told Flint there was iron beneath your silken exterior, and I was right. A whole lot of stubbornness too. But that's all right…for now."

Her lips parted in a show of surprise. "For now!"

"For now," he drawled with a smile. "I don't mind a good fuss before you decide to submit to what's good for you."

She leaned back stiffly against her chair and folded her arms, looking at him squarely. He showed not the faintest sign of apology.

"This brings me to what else I need to talk to you about."

She drew her brows together at the sound of his voice, knowing what was coming next.

"I'd rather not discuss my father."

"We must. Look, Annalee, we can't let this slide any longer. I don't like things between us dragging on like this. We've a few things to talk about and settle."

"Samuel told me everything. What else is there to say? You're here to arrest him, and you kept it from me until now. It's all very clear."

"There's a lot you don't understand. I didn't know who you were until Callie mentioned your last name. After you became ill I didn't want to add to your burdens. Believe me, I still don't."

She wanted to believe him, but...

"He may not even come back to the claim."

Even she didn't believe her own words.

"He'll come back," he said quietly, "to settle things with whoever killed Harkin and had it blamed on him."

"Then you don't think he shot Frank Harkin in the back?"

"No. Someone else did that. I have an idea who, but I can't prove it. There's going to be trouble, Annalee, and I won't be able to stop it until someone gets hurt badly. I'd rather it wasn't your father. I'd like to make an arrest and bring him into Sacramento for trial."

He told her about running into Frank Harkin's younger brother, Dylan. Without Brett saying so, she guessed he feared Dylan would try and kill her father. The napkin in her hand was balled into a tight knot as she listened, afraid and angry at the same time.

"Dylan wants that claim. I had a look at it today, and if I had to make a guess, I'd say there was a good showing of silver. That complicates matters, because Macklin may be involved in this. He's out to destroy any legal papers connecting your father to that claim."

"Macklin," she whispered. "Brett, my baggage. That must be the reason why it was searched on the trip from Strawberry. If Macklin thought I had proof of the claim, that would explain a lot of things, including some of his behavior toward my mother when he came to Aunt Weda's. He asked questions about any papers or mining shares my father may have sent her."

"Did he? Well, then, that just ties it all together for me. What Macklin didn't know was that your father entrusted proof of the claim to Samuel when he found him in Salt Lake."

"Samuel has it?"

His eyes glinted. "Not anymore. I have it. More than one man wants that claim, and they'll need to show themselves to get it."

She stared at him. "But that puts you in danger."

"I'll be riding over to see Bill Stewart soon. I'll turn it over to him. He's promised to arbitrate the matter, not that it will help your father any. Whatever happens out at Gold Canyon, Annalee, Jack Halliday is still wanted in California, but if half that claim is rightfully his, you, Callie, and Jimmy will inherit. So I'm bringing it before Stewart. Samuel is in total agreement."

She wondered if he thought she'd involve herself in anything tainted.

"The only interest I have now is in helping my father. I'll tell you the same thing I told Uncle Samuel. Until I know Pa is guilty of killing a man, I won't believe it. He's been falsely blamed for his partner's death, why not for what happened on the riverboat? I won't rush to be his judge and jury."

"He'll get a fair trial."

"Will he? You're sure of your own feelings? Because I'm not."

She saw a flicker of temper. It was one of the few times she'd seen a flaw in his armor.

"You think I'd enjoy seeing him hang? You're wrong. These past weeks have been some of my most difficult."

"Well! I'm glad to hear that, Marshal. Then what do you think it's been like for me? It's my *father* you're tracking like some poor, wounded wolf bleeding in the snow."

"Your father is more aptly portrayed as the wolf."

"I suppose you're the defenseless deer?"

"He'd send a bullet clean through me if he got the chance. Am I to throw justice aside because the man's your father? What kind of a father would leave you and your mother to struggle alone these years?"

"Words that speak truth shouldn't be hurled like daggers."

Pressured by their tightening circumstances, they stared unrelentingly at each other. Annalee was still squeezing the napkin. Unable to control herself any longer, she threw it down on the table and stood to leave. Brett stood, too, and took hold of her arm, his fingers firm but gentle.

"I'm sorry. I lost my temper."

Aware that heads turned in their direction, Annalee grew silent. She sank back into her chair and picked up her cup. The coffee was cold.

"You're right about my father not caring for us as he should have. We wondered a thousand times where he was when we needed him, when my mother needed him." She remembered the melodeons. "If we thought too long, it brought confusion and pain. Jimmy constantly asked where his pa was and talked about going to find him in the mining camps to help him dig for gold and silver. He thinks his father is everything you are. How do you expect me to tell him that he isn't? And that it's you who arrested him?"

He reached across the table and took her hand. Her first impulse was to pull away, but she found in the tender yet strong pressure of his fingers everything she needed and wanted. She wanted to believe he understood her tormented love for her father, her divided loyalties.

"I'll talk to Jimmy when the time comes. Samuel, too, will know what to say. I'm sure a deep bond will form between the boy and his uncle. But Annalee, I can't compromise what's right because of personal feelings. I took an oath before I came. I'm under the governor's authority."

In studying his face she could see that he was calm and resolute once more. If he was telling the truth now, then why not about everything else, including her father's guilt?

"I don't hate your father, Annalee."

"When you're convinced he shot *your* father?"

"I admit I did hate him at first. But that was some years back. I was younger then. A bit wild too. I had a passion to hunt him down. That's when I learned to use a gun. I was determined to be faster than anyone else. That night when I went aboard the riverboat and found my father bloodied and in pain because of some cheap card game—even though I knew better, I hated the gambler named Jack Halliday."

Uncertainty nudged her. "You...were there on the riverboat? You saw it?"

"I arrived afterward. Yancey and I were working at Sutter's for the summer. We heard what happened when one of the men rode in and told us. We dropped everything and went down to the river. It was all over by then. Everything except the anger, the dismay. I hated enough to strike back as hard as he had struck my father. I thank God he wasn't there then. I grew wiser with time."

Sorrow choked her heart. "I don't want to hear the details—"

"You must hear them. My father was a skilled surgeon. His steady hand under God's control had saved many lives. And when I saw his arm shot to pieces, his wrist splintered—"

Annalee lowered her head and shut her eyes. Her heart was thudding. The idea that her father could have done this to his made her feel sick.

Why my father? Why Brett's? Why did they ever have to meet in so horrid a way? Why hadn't this terrible moment in time happened to strangers who didn't love God? Why Brett? Why me?

The sensation of his thumb gently stroking the back of her hand comforted her and gave her the courage to raise her head and look at him. She owed him the courtesy of listening to his story.

Brett restrained his emotions with careful discipline. "I was bitter. That's when I left medical school. I couldn't keep my mind on the studies. I wanted out. To be free. To hunt Jack Halliday down and kill him."

Annalee shivered as she looked into those cool gray eyes. What had stopped him? She had little doubt he could have done it.

"Even though I was raised in a Christian home I hadn't come to terms with what my faith meant. I had a hot temper, and it never dawned on me that my quest for justice was personal vengeance. In my mind I was justified.

"I can't remember the exact moment when my thinking began to change. I was doing a good amount of Scripture reading at the time. Slowly, the anger driving me was ebbing away, as though some refreshing breeze from heaven had moved within my soul.

"I began to look at the situation with a new perspective. When I did, I understood the Lord had something in mind that I wasn't capable of understanding yet. My father's life wasn't left to mere chance. Life isn't governed like the gambling games in Virginia

Town, where both life and silver are thrown to chance. Win or lose, God's plans have reason to them. When I finally could accept that God was there that night, I could let go of my anger. He's with us this moment, and He knows your dilemma and mine."

Annalee couldn't speak. She was ashamed, yet thankful that neither Brett nor his father had been swallowed up by the bitterness of broken dreams and injustice.

She felt a stirring within. She must not succumb to that destroying bitterness that demanded the right to question everything allowed by God in her life.

"Something else. My father's abilities as a physician weren't taken away from him. He merely changed from surgery to the study of lung disease. And he's excited about it. He's into every piece of research he can find. He has exciting plans for that sanitarium I told you about. I would say the Lord's hand is evident in all our circumstances."

She studied him, his calm acceptance of things and then the disciplined decision to do something about it, if he could. She had once compared him to Gordon, but she'd been wrong. Gordon was not the man that Brett Wilder was.

"I don't think your father would wish to treat the daughter of the man you say destroyed his surgery hand."

"Never underestimate the grace of God. My father was depressed for a year, even longer. But he's snapped out of it. Dad doesn't sit around moaning over his loss, complaining that the Lord let him down. He's a man of faith. I want you to meet him, Annalee. I think he can help you."

She sat for several moments in silence, struggling with fiery emotions that were pulling her in all directions at once. When she could make no sense of them, she set them aside in confusion.

"Thank you for telling me your story," she said quietly. "I'll consider what you've said. But don't ask me to make a decision yet, Brett. I can't."

He didn't speak. He studied her for a long moment and then nodded. He squeezed her hand once more and let it go. "All right. We'll give it more time."

She said nothing and relaxed a little. There was some piano music coming from the other room, accompanied by the sound of voices and laughter.

"If you stay, be prepared to put up with hardship until spring."

She looked at him. "I understand, and I'm ready for that."

"I still have a job to do. There's that oath I mentioned."

Her mouth tightened. She would not relent on that, nor would she say she understood. She felt his gaze measuring her response, but she refused to look at him.

He stood and looked out the window.

"Looks like the storm's finally blowing in. I'll see you up to your room, and then I need to get back to talk to Samuel."

Annalee was quiet as he drew her chair back and escorted her from the dining room to the stairs. The piano music dimmed.

Brett turned to say something to her when she heard her named called from across the room.

"Annalee!"

Gordon, freshly bathed and well dressed, was smiling as he walked toward her, but his smile froze when he saw Brett. She remembered there had been trouble on the trail.

"Hello, Gordon. Are you staying here?" she asked.

"I've been here for about a week, but I'm moving to the Virginia House in the morning." He glanced at Brett, his amber eyes unfriendly. "Come to establish law and justice, Marshal?"

Brett turned to Annalee, ignoring Gordon. Gordon flushed angrily.

"Since Samuel's agreed he can use your help with the women, I suppose you'll be moving out to his dugout tomorrow?"

She was planning on staying at Samuel's until she moved out to her father's cabin, but she wouldn't bring that up again now. She was aware that Gordon was seething.

"Yes. Callie and Jimmy will be here in the morning. Flint is taking us over to Virginia Town."

"Callie may not be pleased with your plan."

She passed over his hint of a smile. Callie would definitely *not* be satisfied in their uncle's dugout, nor would she approve of their father's cabin at the Gold Canyon claim.

She looked down at him, holding the banister. "Thank you for dinner, Brett. Goodnight."

His gaze captured hers. Slowly she dragged her eyes from his and ran into the angry gaze of Gordon Barkly. He was not looking at her but at Brett.

"I asked you a question, Wilder," he gritted. "And you'd better listen up with some respect."

Annalee froze and looked from one man to the other; Gordon, angry, Brett appearing unruffled by the offense.

Gordon took a step toward him before she could throw herself between them. She expected Brett to lash out and was surprised when he did not.

"There's a lady present, Barkly. Or has that fact escaped you?" he turned to Annalee, nodded, and walked away.

Her lips were slightly parted as her eyes followed him across the room and out the door.

After a moment she ventured a glance at Gordon. He looked stunned. Then a white line showed around his mouth.

She avoided his eyes, knowing how foolish he must feel, and turned to go up the steps to her room. She covered a smile as she went up. Brett knew when to use force and when it was wiser to walk away. He was very attractive...

"That man is a fraud," Gordon said, coming up behind her.

"I thought he was a gentleman."

"Wilder?" he scoffed. "Just because his father's a respected physician? That man hiding behind his commission has ridden close to the line of breaking the law himself. There are all sorts of stories about him a few years back. He was close to being a gunfighter himself."

"Then you'd be wise not to provoke his temper."

Gordon shot her a surprised look. "He means nothing but trouble in Virginia Town. He's out for your father. Isn't that enough to show you what he's like under that composed facade of his?"

She unlocked her door, but before going inside she turned toward him. "Are you still planning to start a newspaper here?"

"Of course. I've already lined things up."

She noticed the shortness in his tone. He didn't appreciate her defense of Brett.

"And one of the first stories I plan to run is the truth about Wilder's ranch in Grass Valley."

Someday she would ask Brett about Gordon's charges against him.

"I don't appreciate journalists who have a personal vendetta and use the public press to vent their own dislike."

With that she walked into her room and closed the door, sliding the bolt into place.

She could imagine the surprise on Gordon's face as he stood in the hall. A few moments later she heard him walk away.

Twenty

~

Callie had noticed the handsome young man before. In fact, she'd seen him on several occasions since Flint Harper had brought her and Jimmy to Ma Higgins' place. He looked dangerous. She noticed him riding with a man someone had addressed as Hoadly. There'd been three of them. The young, good-looking one wearing a poncho, Hoadly, and a brute of a man who reminded her of a gorilla. He seemed to follow the one called Hoadly like a pup did its mama. Those two had ridden off together, but the young man in the poncho, who was now leaning against a post across the street by the livery stable, had been around Dayton for the last two days. Each morning when she came out, helping Ma Higgins with the chores, she'd seen him. If he wasn't already leaning against his post, he would appear soon after she did.

She was keenly aware of his appearance, even though he frightened her a little.

This morning Callie poured water into the drinking jug from the barrel Ma kept beside the house, and as she did she glanced sideways across the street. Her breath sucked in. The handsome stranger had straightened from the post and was walking in her direction.

Callie knew what Annalee would have done. She'd have turned her back and walked quickly inside. But she wasn't Annalee. Callie didn't like men who thought they could just take over a woman and tell her what to do straight off. No trouble-making bronco was going to frighten her into turning tail and running to Ma Higgins. Anyway, Flint was due back soon from the mule station. He would be taking her and Jimmy over to Gold

Hill this morning to meet Annalee at the Vesey Hotel, and then he would take them to Samuel in Virginia Town. It was the only thing she'd heard from Jimmy all morning: "We're going to see Uncle Samuel! We're going to see Indians and help him dig for silver."

Callie was aware of the stranger before he spoke. She pretended he wasn't there and went on pouring water, pausing to brush a curl from her throat that the cold, dry wind tossed.

"Where's your bodyguard hiding?"

That got her. She looked up, and in the flashing instant their eyes met across the water barrel she was left startled and confused. There was no effort on his part to mask the look in his dark earthy eyes. It was the look a man full of himself gives to a girl he intends to have.

Her breath caught, and she spilled some of the water before she set the jug down on the rough wooden table beside the barrel.

"Who's asking?" she managed with a dignified voice that sounded nothing like her own.

"Rick Delance." He gestured his dark head toward the back of Ma Higgins' house. "You tell Harper to take better care of what interests him. He's fallen asleep on the job."

"And just what do you mean by that?" His hair was not as dark as her own, but a sunlit brown. A thin mustache gave him an almost sinister look, though she'd need to be blind to deny his good looks. His clothes were rough, mostly leather, and she was very aware of his guns.

"Just what I said. If it wasn't for me keeping an eye on you and that boy of yours yonder," he gestured again with his head toward the back where Jimmy was playing with his cat, "you'd have been stolen away by now and working for Jang Li over in the Barbary Coast district."

How dare he? Who did he think he was speaking to her like this? She had a wish to slap his arrogant face, but those level dark eyes of his were as sober as death. Instead, she stood in silent amazement.

"That's Big Birdie yonder. He works for Jang Li."

Callie did not know who Jang Li was, and the name Big Birdie sounded both foolish and unheard of. Was this man who called himself Rick Delance playing her for a fool?

But she tore her eyes from his and glanced across the street. He was right—there was a man outside the saloon sitting on a barrel, whittling. She'd noticed him there for the last week. She'd thought he worked at the tavern. He was a brutish sort, one that made her skin crawl.

"You tell that bodyguard of yours to keep awake. I've things I need to do. I can't keep hanging around Dayton seeing you safe."

Again, his boldness took her aback, but then she considered. What if he were being truthful? She could at least thank him. He looked serious enough. He didn't wear the expression of a young man taunting her.

"Who told you to keep an eye on me?"

"It was my own idea," he said, smiling rakishly.

From over her shoulder she heard Jimmy call happily: "Hey, Callie! Flint's here! We're going to Virginny Town to Uncle Samuel's dugout!"

Just then Flint Harper came around the bend leading the pack mules with supplies. Callie could see the surprised look on Flint's face settle into a frown when he saw her talking to Rick Delance.

"I'll see you in Virginia Town," Delance said.

"I don't think so."

He smiled at her again but said nothing more, and then he strode away in the direction of the tavern where the odious man was still whittling.

Flint Harper came up and removed his coonskin cap. His fair hair shone pleasantly in the sunshine. He was not smiling as he looked after the young man in the poncho and high-heeled star boots with their California spurs.

"He giving you any trouble, Callie?"

"A brash man."

Flint's brows rushed together. "That's Rick Delance, a gun-fighter. He hangs with Hoadly's bunch. Delance is as dangerous as an angry rattler. You shouldn't have spoken to him."

"He forced it."

"Mebbe I'd better have a talk with him then."

She quickly laid a hand on his arm. "No, don't, Flint. If he's a gunfighter, he might cause real trouble. Let it go, please."

He looked at her with troubled eyes. "I wouldn't want any skunk thinkin' he can get sassy with you. You're a lady, an' you'll be treated like one long as I'm around."

She smiled, her hand still on his arm. "Thanks, Flint. But he wasn't rude. Actually, he warned me against that man over by the tavern. Said he's been looking out for me and Jimmy. I don't know how far to believe him, but that's what he said."

Flint looked across the street. "What man?"

Big Birdie was no longer sitting on the barrel. Instead, Rick Delance stood on the boardwalk. He didn't look their direction. Pulling his hat low, he mounted his horse with style, turned the reins, and rode out of Dayton.

"He called the man Big Birdie. Said Big Birdie plans to steal me away to someone called Jang Li."

Flint's gaze shot back to hers. "Burt! Why that louse-ridden galoot. I'll knock him for a loop for this."

"Flint, it probably wasn't even true. C'mon, I've had enough of Dayton. Take us to Gold Hill, will you? Annalee's probably wondering where we are."

"Are you packed?"

"All ready."

"Where's that trunk of Miss Annalee's?"

"Out on the porch. She'll be happy to have it at last. It has all her clothes and mementos. If she hadn't locked it I'd have borrowed some of her things. I tore my dress…" Callie looked down at her soiled and torn muslin dress with dissatisfaction. She hated old clothes. She wanted pretty things. Lots of silks and satins, lace and ribbons, slippers and silk stockings. *And… one day I'll have them. I'm going to work in the theater in Virginia Town soon as there's one built. Annalee's not going to stop me.*

Twenty-One

Two weeks had passed since Annalee left the Vesey Hotel in Gold Hill with Callie and Jimmy for Samuel's dugout on Sun Mountain. One of the first things Annalee had done was to open her trunk to make sure Big Birdie had not rifled through her things. Everything was just as she had packed it. She removed her mother's keepsake chest and found the letter her father had written to her mother in Sacramento. The cartoon drawing looked back. The drawing no longer brought happiness and hope, not even a smile. Her heart was sore.

She opened the envelope and read the letter. Her father spoke of the claim he had with Frank Harkin and that they were both sure they'd struck rich ore. There was nothing else important in the affectionate letter. Macklin was not even mentioned.

Disappointed in coming against a dead end, she had put the letter back and returned it to her trunk.

In the days following there was no word from her father, and nobody, including Samuel, knew where Jack Halliday was hiding. Would he return? Samuel believed he would, someday, sometime, but no one knew when. He couldn't very well come riding into Virginia Town when he was wanted for murder.

Annalee had heard that Dylan Harkin hadn't been seen around town for ten days, but Samuel wasn't convinced. Dylan was dangerous, and he wanted his brother's death avenged. He wanted the claim out at Gold Canyon too.

"There's probably nothing there anyway," Callie said. "Nothing but dust devils and trouble."

Annalee was the last one who'd try to convince her otherwise, though on the trip from Sacramento to Placerville Callie had played along with Jimmy's game of "striking it rich at Washoe."

Jimmy was impatient to be off to explore his pa's claim, but Samuel wisely kept him busy. Already a strong bond had formed between uncle and nephew, just as Brett had thought it would, and Annalee was grateful to God for making it so. Jimmy desperately needed good, strong men in his life to teach him what it meant to be a man of honor and faith in God.

In the days following their arrival at the dugout there was no word from either Brett or Macklin Villiers. Samuel had tried to contact Macklin at the Virginia Hotel but learned he'd ridden out toward Carson two days before and no one had seen him since. Annalee was disappointed. She must see him. He owed her an explanation, and she intended to have it. Callie wanted money and was growing impatient.

"I'm not staying in a dugout all winter, Annalee. Aunt Weda's money is as much mine as yours and Jimmy's. And what about the gold dust Pa left us? I want my share. I want to move into the Virginia House. I want to think about starting a business. We can't just keep house for Uncle."

"Give me a little more time, Callie, please. We need to move slowly. We don't dare invest that hundred and fifty dollars into something we'll be sorry for come spring. And we've got to send money to Aunt Weda to pay those back taxes."

Callie's determination convinced her more than ever that she must meet with Macklin soon. She decided she wouldn't wait for his return; who knew how long he'd be away? Or what he was even doing? She'd go see his lawyer, Mr. Colefax. Colefax should be able to tell her everything she wanted to know about the mining shares in the Pelly-Jessup. If her mother hadn't sold them before the stage accident, then she'd ask Mr. Colefax to sell now. There wouldn't be much, but they needed every penny.

Annalee was aware of the warning Brett had given about Macklin, but again, it was speculation. He could be wrong. Brett was staying out at the cabin in Gold Canyon. She knew why. He thought Jack might show up there secretly. Or maybe he felt inclined to guard the place from a move by Dylan Harkin to take over his brother's half of the partnership. Again, she was told by Samuel that Brett had seen the lawyer he trusted in Carson, Bill Stewart. Samuel, too, had spoken to Stewart.

Annalee soon discovered that Virginia Town was developing into more than one mining community. There was what was called the Divide, Gold Hill where she had stayed in the Vesey, Silver City, American Flat, Devil's Gate where the toll house was, and Dayton, all strung like Indian beads along Gold Canyon. There was even a Lousetown, which brought her a smile. Some miner, as the story went, had slept in the "hotel" and wrestled with bedbugs and fleas all night, so he warned others of "Lousetown." The unflattering name stuck. There was some horse racing and boxing there. The thought of boxing made her shudder. She had heard of the "Jawbreaker" named Roc who was fighting there, taking on any man who would step into the ring. Lots of money was made gambling on Roc winning. As far as she was concerned, only a poor fool would willingly step into the ring with him. She'd seen him once in town when Jimmy pointed him out, and once was quite enough. "Where do you learn all these wild tales?" she asked him with a pretended scowl.

"The miners. 'The Boys' from Arkansas, as everyone calls 'em."

" 'Them,' Jimmy. You're picking up Western slang."

He shrugged, undisturbed. "The Boys can fill your ear full of things," he boasted. "Arkie says there's only one who can beat 'Jawbreaker' Roc, and that's the marshal."

Annalee shuddered some more. Anything but that.

Gold Canyon was her destination this early chilly morning, but she didn't want to talk things over with Brett until she'd spoken to Mr. Colefax. Those plans changed, however, with the news Callie shared with her over pancakes and coffee.

Samuel had gone on one of his preaching trips to Silver City for a couple of days, taking Jimmy with him. Annalee and Callie sat in the snug little dwelling in the side of the mountain. Although the winds blew cold outside, they were warm inside. A fire glowed in the woodstove and the table was spread with their steaming breakfast.

"Macklin's back all right. Gordon told me so. He's staying at the Virginia Hotel."

"When did you see Gordon?"

Callie looked at her curiously. Although Annalee hadn't seen him since that evening at the Vesey with Brett, she'd heard the news that he'd opened his newspaper office and was waiting for spring, when his printing press would be hauled over the Sierras from Sacramento. Until then, he was writing one-page reports on the mines and handing them out free among the miners and storekeepers, hoping to earn their respect and friendship for when he actually started his newspaper.

"He rode by yesterday," Callie said over a mouthful of pancake and molasses. She made a face. "Aunt Weda's syrup is much better. This is strong enough to curl your hair."

"Gordon rode by yesterday?" Annalee asked.

"Yes, but you weren't here, so he just talked awhile and rode on. He's at the Virginia House too. Says it's as good as the Vesey, maybe a bit better. He says Macklin is back. He went to see a doctor in Carson."

"Doctor? What for?"

Callie shrugged. "Gordon says he was injured badly in the stage accident."

They said no more about it, but Annalee was relieved Macklin was back and anxious to talk to him. Were their suspicions of Macklin unfair? If he was seriously injured and recuperating, he had a reason for not contacting them. Annalee's conscience pricked her. It was only right to give Macklin the benefit of the doubt. After all, Lillian had believed in him.

I'll go see Macklin this afternoon, she decided.

❧ ❧

It wasn't until late afternoon that Annalee was able to slip away from the dugout unseen by Callie.

From outside she could look down the slope of Sun Mountain toward town. She took the footpath, passing near other dugouts, but she didn't encounter anyone.

The feel of winter was in the wind and a dusky blue twilight was falling over Virginia Town as she walked down C Street. The saloons were busy. Nothing new there. Piano music wafted on the wind. Passing open doors she heard the voices, the shuffle of cards, the roll of dice, the senseless laughter. Her eyes took in the signs along the street: Delta Saloon, Young American Saloon, Bucket of Blood Saloon....

Annalee walked on until she came to the Virginia House and entered the new hotel. She walked slowly past the beautifully appointed dining room. No wonder Callie wanted to move in here. She wouldn't mind herself, except it would cost plenty to stay indefinitely, and they couldn't afford to waste that kind of money without ending up penniless in two or three months.

"Mr. Macklin Villiers?" the clerk repeated when she walked up to the front desk and asked for his room number. He pushed his small spectacles up his button nose while glancing toward the stairs. "He has rooms in the back, number 7."

She went up the stairs and turned into the hall on his floor, her footsteps softened by a red rug. His door was closing, and she arrived there just as it shut. Muffled voices sounded.

She waited a few moments and then knocked. It grew silent behind the door. After a good minute had passed it opened, but the man wasn't Macklin.

The young man was remarkably good-looking in his own way. But the hard dark eyes and slashing brows across his deeply tanned face spoke trouble. He wore a poncho and heeled boots with spurs. His hand movement away from his hip was a gesture she was accustomed to now, having seen Brett's manner. She knew what it meant. The man in the poncho had relaxed.

"You're Miss Halliday," he stated.

She was uncomfortable that he knew. "Yes. I wish to speak to Mr. Macklin Villiers...my father's cousin."

Something glowed in those dark eyes. He slowly looked over his shoulder as though waiting to see someone's response.

"Send her in, Delance, by all means."

The young gunfighter—for that's what she took him for—stepped aside, and she walked into the room.

Delance went out, shutting the door after him. Even with the carpet in the hall she could hear the sure tread of his booted feet leaving. He was a ruthless, determined young wolf; she could sense it. There went a man who wanted something in life he did not yet have, and he was at conflict with everything around him, including, perhaps, himself. Why she would know that, she couldn't say, but she knew.

Annalee turned to face Macklin. She looked at him in blank astonishment.

Macklin wheeled his chair toward her and stopped a few feet away. There was a gray shawl over his knees and one hand rested under it. The other he held out toward her. A thin smile crossed his otherwise tanned face.

All at once her suspicions melted into doubts, then confusion.

"How good to see you, Annalee! You'll forgive me for not calling on you and your sister at Samuel's. But as you can see, the task of getting out and about takes a good deal of time and effort. I do get out once or twice a week, but not without my servant."

Delance? No, he wasn't a servant. Someone else then.

His hand was cool and moist and displayed no strength when she took it.

"I didn't know," she began, "I didn't realize…"

"No, naturally you wouldn't. I've been very ill for quite a long time. You'll forgive my procrastination in contacting you? It's only been the last month or so that I've been out of bed. This wheelchair is only a little better. A tragedy for someone of my outdoor background, but I'm lucky to be alive. I won't complain. The doctor says I may even walk again in due time, but it will be a long, slow recovery."

What could she say? She was thoroughly disarmed. She'd expected a showdown of sorts. She'd been prepared to argue, to protest, even accuse, and now…

"Won't you sit down? Can I have something sent up? Tea perhaps? Yes, amazingly they have tea. Next year by this time the Virginia House will match any hotel in San Francisco. The International is going up soon, and a theater is being built. Two, in fact." He sighed, as though mentioning the theater brought him sadness. Lillian?

She sat down very softly on a velvet upholstered chair, breathing shallowly.

"Thank you, nothing for me, Cousin Macklin."

"If you don't mind, my dear? Life has been very difficult of late," and he reached over to the low inlaid table and poured himself a small drink from a cut-glass decanter.

"I know what you've come about. We shall waste no time. You've waited too long already."

Macklin began telling her about the stage trip from Placerville, how the journey had been troubled from the beginning. They encountered a lot of snow on the trail, and the storm had worsened once they were in the Sierras. The driver was reckless; if ever found he should be brought to trial for endangering their lives. There was a sudden jolt, the horses had screamed, and the next thing he knew they were toppling from the trail over the side of a ridge.

It was a miracle anyone survived, but the driver had come out of it better than any of them. Lillian had been thrown clear from the stage and hit her head on a boulder and was unconscious. While the driver salvaged one of the unhurt horses and started for Placerville for help, Macklin carried Lillian to the stage and laid her on the seat. The other passenger was dead. If there was one blessing in this tragedy, it was that there'd been few passengers.

"I waited for the driver to return with help, but he never came. I did what I only could do under the circumstances, I started out on one of the injured horses for Carson. I thought the driver would come back soon and told Lillian so. She had a concussion and was not doing well at all. I promised her I'd do my best."

He'd gone only a few miles on the injured horse when the blizzard worsened. The horse gave way beneath him, and in mercy he'd shot the poor creature to put it out of its pain. He'd proceeded on foot, but his leg, partially crushed in the fall, was growing more and more painful. He took shelter in a hollow log and waited out the snowstorm before continuing his torturous journey to Carson. Except for the little food he'd shared with Lillian, he had nothing. He ate snow for water. He'd learned later that it was ten days before he'd staggered into Carson.

"You know the rest," he said, wiping his brow with a handkerchief as though the telling of his ordeal brought pain. "When help did arrive, it was too late. Lilly...was gone."

His head drooped. "I don't mind letting you know this now, Annalee. I was in love with your mother. Always had been. I'd intended to ask her to marry me when Cousin Jack came riding into Sutter's. Despite my best efforts to convince her otherwise, she fell in love with him and they were married. I drifted away...I couldn't bear to see them together. After a few years drifting from one camp to another, I was able to pick my life back up again. By then Jack was following the gold fever too. We met up on a few occasions and, generally speaking, found that time heals everything. I held no resentment toward him, but I was sorry for Lilly. He didn't treat her well, nor any of you."

Annalee could think of no reason to doubt him, but the uneasiness she always felt around him remained. Perhaps that was because her emotions were unable to respond to a man whose smile seemed forced, whose eyes left her feeling cold. It could just be his personality. Certainly her mother had trusted him.

"The driver never showed up in Placerville."

He shook his head with distaste. "I had no confidence in the man. If he'd been more careful, this entire episode could have been avoided."

"What happened to him, Cousin Macklin?"

"Froze to death, most likely. He was an inept sort of fellow."

"They never found his body, whereas they located Mother and the other passenger. If he'd frozen to death wouldn't they have found his body and the horse?"

He delicately poured another small drink.

"Wolves," he said.

"Wolves?"

He nodded. "There are lots of wolves in the mountains. I had to be careful myself when my leg was bleeding. A pack of 'em trailed me for a while. I had to shimmy up a tree once to sleep. Most painful struggle of my life getting up that tree." He laid a hand on his knee.

"But...even if the wolves came, it would seem the authorities from Placerville would have found some evidence—"

"That's where you're wrong. Wolves carry things off. An arm, a leg—"

She stopped him quickly. "I see, yes."

"The horse may have run off, who knows? An Indian or a trapper may have found it and kept it. A horse is worth plenty, you know. They wouldn't turn it in. At least Lilly was inside the stage. Nothing could get at her. I made sure. As sure as I could. The body of the other passenger I buried in a shallow grave. The man was located, I believe, and brought for proper burial to Sacramento. Lilly is buried at Carson. Did you stop to visit her grave?"

Annalee had to admit they did not. "I had planned to, but there was no time. Eventually I'll go there with Callie and Jimmy."

"You'll appreciate the lovely site I picked out for her. Under a pepper tree. I had an angel carved into her headstone. A fitting tribute."

Annalee silently sat there, thinking about her mother. After a moment he said, "You'll also want to know about those mining shares. They've been sold according to her wishes. Unfortunately, the Pelly-Jessup has reached near bottom in the mining business. The shares sold cheaply. Most unfortunate."

"Then there's nothing?"

"I wouldn't say that." He looked at her closely. "Lilly gave me fifteen shares to turn over to Mr. Colefax to sell. Her last words to me were puzzling. Perhaps you can settle the issue for me?"

"If I can. What is so puzzling?"

"Lilly told me there were ten more shares. She left them, she said, with you."

"She did? How odd."

"Is it so odd? She seemed certain she left them with you. Are you saying she didn't?"

"No, of course not. I have no shares in the Pelly-Jessup. We have very little money, Cousin Macklin. It was one of the reasons we came here. Aunt Weda's about to lose the farm on account of back taxes owed. If I'd had ten shares of my own, I'd have sold them immediately."

"Then you have no more shares?"

She wondered at the flat, almost suddenly unpleasant tone of his voice.

"You are certain?"

Annalee took offense at his continued questioning.

"I *told* you I did not."

"Yes, yes, you would know. Very well, then."

He was thoughtful. Then he looked at her. He smiled. "You must bear with me, my dear Annalee. I am not the man I used to be. Any request your mother made of me before her death is important to me. You can understand that."

"Yes, I understand. But I have told you what I know."

"Yes. Well, then." He slapped a hand on the arm of his wheelchair. "That's that, isn't it?"

"Yes, I suppose it is." She stood, looking down at him. "If there's nothing from the fifteen shares she turned over to you and Mr. Colefax, then Callie and I will proceed as best we can."

"No, no, my dear Annalee. I won't hear of that. In the sweet memory of Lilly I wish to give her three children a gift." He smiled.

Puzzled, she wondered. "What kind of gift?"

"Five hundred dollars apiece. That will be fifteen hundred dollars altogether. You'll probably wish to see Jimmy's invested for his education as he grows older. I'll have it for you in the spring. By the time the trail is open, you'll all have a little nest egg to fall back on."

Stunned, she stared at him. Five hundred dollars apiece—in gold. She found her voice. "Oh, but you owe us nothing. It's too much to ask. I…we couldn't."

"Now, now. I'll not hear any protestations, my dear. It is a gift from your cousin. I'm sure Callie will not wish to decline." He smiled, but his eyes remained unreadable. She began to think it was the color of his eyes that made him seem so emotionless and cold. Surely she was wrong about him.

"You're very generous, Cousin Macklin."

"I understand Callie's interested in the theater?"

Annalee answered cautiously. "Mother wanted her to be a teacher."

"Callie is a beautiful young woman, as are you. I doubt if she would be content in a classroom. I noticed a restless spirit in her in Sacramento. How her eyes brightened at the mention of the theater. She may take after Lilly in that regard."

Annalee studiously avoided agreeing. What was on his mind? Was he going to offer Callie an opportunity to try her acting talents in the theater he said he was going to open?

"I'll be opening a theater next year," he said, as though reading her thoughts. "By next year Virginia Town will become Virginia City. We'll have people pouring into here from California. This is the place where a man can get rich, my dear. A woman could too."

He looked at her for a long moment. She didn't know why he made her uncomfortable. She was quickly ashamed. *Five hundred dollars for each of us!*

There was no cause to doubt Cousin Macklin. None at all. He had explained things to her satisfaction, and now it was time to put the past to sleep.

She smiled and picked up her wrap from the back of the chair. "I can't tell you how grateful we are."

"It's the least I can do for family. Come and see me often. You must stay and have dinner next time, and bring Callie."

She thanked him again and stepped out into the hall. She went downstairs and out into the cold evening. The sky wore a lavender hue, and one sparkling star glimmered above Sun Mountain.

So he had loved her mother. She'd been right about that. But wrong about him.

She must talk to Brett about Macklin. Brett was wrong. Perhaps he was wrong, too, about her father.

Tomorrow I'm going to get a horse somewhere and ride out to Gold Canyon.

❧ ❧

Callie was waiting impatiently for her when she returned.

"Why didn't you tell me you'd gone out? I was looking all over for you."

Annalee took off her wrap. She tried to keep her excitement from showing too much.

"I went to see Macklin."

Callie walked toward her, her blue eyes alert. "Well, what'd he say?"

"He explained about the stage accident and why he hadn't been in touch. Goodness, Callie, he's in a wheelchair. I think he's telling the truth. He said he was in love with Mama."

Callie looked as surprised as Annalee had been back in Macklin's room.

"A wheelchair..."

Annalee nodded. "Sit down and I'll tell you everything."

When Annalee finished the tale, her sister sat musing, chin in hand, elbows on the table. "So he loved Mama. Well, I'm not surprised. Looks like we were wrong, doesn't it? About Macklin's motives."

Annalee agreed, but, afraid Callie would take her five hundred dollars and her share of the money Weda had given them and go into business for herself, she kept back the promise Macklin had made. He'd said it would take until spring when the Sierra trail reopened. She'd wait till then.

"What about the mining shares? Is there any money coming to us?"

"The shares were almost worthless."

Callie sighed and stood up from the chair. "Just as I thought."

Twenty-Two

~

The next morning Annalee took her art satchel and walked down the mountain slope to the spot where Elmo was digging for silver. The old man looked up from his mucking and saw her standing there, looking down.

"Find anything yet?" she asked lightly.

"Now you be pullin' my whiskers, Miss Annalee."

Annalee took a good look at his mule. Jenny seemed healthier and stronger than when she'd first seen her at Strawberry Flat.

"Elmo? Would you lend me Jenny for the day? I'll buy you something from Lar's bakery for her use."

"You can borrow my little Jenny-girl anytime you want. No need to buy me nuthin', but if you be hankering to, I'll take one of them doughnuts."

She then proceeded to the Norwegian's bakery, a tent-shop with a big woodstove out back. A whiff of fresh goods whetted her appetite.

The big blond Norwegian smiled. "You're up early this morning, Miss Annalee."

"I'm going out to see some things."

"When's Samuel coming back?"

"Tomorrow."

She bought two doughnuts, one for herself and the other for Elmo, and then she walked back to his diggings.

She wanted to see the claim her father owned half of, but besides talking to Brett, she wanted to do a sketch of the cabin and claim to send to Weda when the mail opened up again in the spring. She tied her satchel on the back of Jenny and mounted, reins in hand.

"You know where you be going?"

"Gold Canyon. My father has a claim out near the Pelly-Jessup, and I want to have a look at it."

He leaned on his shovel. "There's more'n one mine out there. Along the base of the mountain you'll find Williams' Station, Steam Boat, Dutch Nick's, and Sutro's holdings." He squinted at her. "Samuel know you're goin'?"

"He's still in Silver City. I'm an artist. I'm going to spend the day doing some sketching out there."

"You be careful now," Elmo called as she rode off. "You tell ever'one you're Samuel's niece. They all know him."

"I will. Thanks."

The morning was gray with clouds, and the constant winds blew down the canyon, washing it clean. The miners who knew Washoe were all saying it was going to be a bad winter. The snows had already come to the Sierras and heavier storms were due, just as Flint Harper had warned.

She remembered how Brett had warned her about leaving. She'd need serious shelter from the elements. Without her father's cabin, Annalee had no idea where they would stay through the cold, harsh winter. They couldn't continue sleeping in Samuel's tiny stone dugout unless another room was added. And adding another room appeared to her to be impossible unless they hacked through the rock wall, but Samuel said it could be done if he had a little help. Annalee preferred the cabin at the mine. Callie was nursing several different dreams, not the least of which was that word would arrive in the spring from their mother's aunt in New Orleans.

Relentless questions pecked at her brain. Who had killed Frank Harkin? Even Brett didn't think her father was the guilty one. Where was Frank's brother, Dylan? She'd not seen or heard anything about him since arriving at Samuel's. Was he even in the area? Maybe he had left to trail her father into Utah. Was her father still there? Maybe he'd crossed into Colorado. But it was likely he'd return sometime. He wouldn't give up his half of that claim as long as he believed there was rich ore there. Brett seemed to think there was. She hadn't told Callie that, either.

What if her father returned but not alone? And if he brought hired guns with him, how could she talk sense to him?

The sound of Jenny's hooves clattering across the rocks harmonized with the melody of the wind crooning down the canyon. Boulders lifted steeply in some places, and the pungent odor of sage was on the wind blowing against her. Annalee watched a dust devil swirling ahead until it played itself out. She found the unique aspects of the high desert a treat for her senses.

When she came within sight of a stone hut, she climbed down from the mule and looked about her. There was a natural amphitheater in the hills, a little creek barely flowing over pebbles, and, not far off, what looked to her like a prospect hole. She didn't see Brett's horse. Could he have gone?

She led Jenny to the little creek and tied her to a shrub within reach of the scraggly grass growing there. She bent down to wash the dust from her hands in the cold water, eying the rocks with a bluish cast to them.

She picked up a rock from alongside the creek and stood to examine it in the weak sunlight. A hissing zing from a bullet glanced off the side of the boulders above her head. What—

"Get down!" Brett said from behind her. She dropped to her knees and turned her head to see where he was. He crouched behind a bigger boulder to her left. She began crawling toward him. Another bullet smashed into the boulder, spraying gravel.

He picked up a rock and threw it. A bullet struck where it landed. Then he was beside her, drawing her down and firing his .45. Another bullet cracked the silence. Annalee spat gritty dirt from her mouth and huddled there, feeling the weight of his arm across her back, keeping her down.

For a few minutes they didn't move. Annalee raised her face.

"Keep your head down."

"Who's firing at us?"

"Somebody who doesn't want us here."

Annalee buried her face in her arm. After a minute or two there was no sound except the wind stirring among the rocks and rustling sage.

"Maybe he's gone," she said.

"Maybe, but we're not taking any chances with a rifle. Between here and the cabin is open ground. I asked you not to come, remember?"

The tone of his voice held such certainty that she turned her head to look at him.

"It's my father's cabin," she said, smiling, "and his claim."

He glanced back up at the ridge. "I think he's gone now, but stay put until I make sure." He took his arm away and crawled off into the boulders. How could he know? Yet he'd seemed sure of himself. It was one of the characteristics about him she most admired.

She waited, keeping her head down until she saw him returning from another direction. He must have circled around, checking the area. He was walking, so she knew it was safe. She sat up, brushing off the front of her dress. She stood and waited for him.

"We'll go to the cabin now."

He was shaking something in his closed hand.

"Find anything?" she asked.

He opened his hand and showed her a few empty shell casings.

"I found them in those rocks up behind the cabin. There's a good view of the canyon from there, and I caught a glimpse of a lone man riding back toward town. I've seen that gray gelding before. I can't say for sure, but I think it belongs to Dylan Harkin."

"You think he was just trying to scare me off?"

"You're Jack Halliday's daughter. He's not popular around here at the moment."

"Many of those men who knew my father think he's Jack Dawson. I'm looked upon as Samuel's niece."

"I wish it were that easy. By now Dylan knows Dawson is Halliday. That makes you and the others unwanted company, perhaps even Samuel."

Annalee considered, showing no undue alarm. She accepted the ugly situation to be as inevitable as her illness.

She caught him looking at her.

"A lot of women would be in a tizzy by now. You've got a cool head."

She looked away, refusing to blush at the compliment, but she was pleased.

"That is, most of the time," he added.

She looked at him. He smiled.

"If the claim holds up and something happens to your father, you're an heiress. Your sister too."

Heiress to a silver mine. She could hardly imagine it. She deliberately showed no excitement.

The wind was bitter cold, and he took hold of her arm. "Let's go inside."

They walked toward the stone cabin.

"Looks like snow," he commented. "We're in for a long winter this year."

"Which is the reason I've come to take possession of my father's cabin. That means you move out. We can't stay permanently with Samuel. Callie's already complaining about space and privacy."

"You're a reasonable woman, Annalee. You saw what just happened. Do you really want Jimmy running around out here?"

She admitted the rifle incident cast things in a different color.

"Why did you come?"

"To see the mine, the cabin. To sketch—"

"Sketch?"

"Yes, I brought my art supplies with me. I'm doing something for Aunt Weda."

She watched him put water on the woodstove to boil for coffee. She glanced him over. He looked incredibly capable. He was also quite appealing in the buckskin shirt, his dark hair windblown. He burned his finger on a match and winced. She smiled. He could face down a handful of gunfighters and look calm, but he winced when he burned his finger.

"Are you all right?" she asked innocently.

He looked at her and then grinned.

She moved slowly about the cabin. "If there were another room for a bedroom, this would do us nicely." She turned around, hands behind her back. He'd gotten the coffee going and was putting out two mugs.

"They're clean. I scrubbed them myself last night."

"I'm curious about the mine. Do you really think my father and Frank Harkin discovered silver?"

He reached into a leather saddlebag, took out some pieces of ore, and laid them on the roughly hewed table.

"I first took this ore sample to a miner whose opinion I respect. He agrees it's good stuff. Then I took it to the assayer in Carson. I got word back yesterday. It looks like bonanza ore."

She picked up one of the samples and turned it around in her fingers. "I have to admit my ignorance. It looks just like an ordinary rock to me. But I'll take their word for it, and yours." She looked up. "Then that means my father and Harkin really *did* find treasure. Do you think that's why Frank was killed? You said you didn't think it was my father."

He poured the coffee and handed her a cup. "That's true. I don't."

"But who did it? What would anyone gain by his death? The claim still belongs to my father and Harkin's heir."

"There's plenty to gain if Jack's blamed for Harkin's death. Harkin was liked in Virginia Town. It wouldn't have taken much to provoke a few hotheads to form a lynch mob. That would have settled things fast. And with both of them gone, it would have been easy for the Pelly-Jessup owners to take over the Halliday-Harkin claim, insisting it belonged to them. It would have too, if the Jessup hadn't run into a 'horse.'"

"A horse?"

He pulled out a chair for her and she sat down.

"It's a stretch of barren rock between rich mineralized areas. When miners come up against barren rock, the mine owners sometimes decide to quit drilling, thinking that's all there is. The other option is to spend more money and keep going, hoping to hit rich ore again. The Pelly-Jessup called it quits. But that decision cost them the rich lode waiting just beyond the horse."

Brett sat down across the table from her. He took out a drawing and pushed it toward her. With a pen he showed her the area he was talking about.

"This small section here connects with the horse from the Jessup. It lay unclaimed until your father and Harkin staked it. After a few weeks of work it became apparent to them that they were into something big. Harkin begin bragging in the saloons that he and Jack would soon hit a bonanza.

"Someone in the Jessup caught wind of it and ordered a few miners willing to do illegal work to drift into the Halliday-Harkin claim. It was then they realized the size of the lode just past that horse."

"In my father and Frank Harkin's claim," she breathed, amazed.

"Someone in the Pelly-Jessup decided to amend their blunder anyway they could. I can't prove it, but I believe someone approached Harkin with an offer he refused. He was then killed, and you know the rest."

"But who in the Pelly-Jessup would do such a thing?"

Brett's eyes flickered. "Macklin, of course."

She stared at him and then drew back against her chair, shaking her head. "No, Brett, you're wrong."

His dark brow lifted.

"That's another reason I rode out here," she insisted. "The most important reason. I wanted to talk to you about Macklin. I went to the Virginia House to see him yesterday. He's in a wheelchair with an injured leg. He's been telling the truth all along about the stage accident. He was in love with my mother. He admitted it. Even though his leg was hurt, he went for help and traveled in the snow for several days until arriving too late, exhausted and suffering from weakness and exposure."

She went on, explaining everything Macklin had told her, including the gift of five hundred dollars for each of them.

"So you see," she concluded, "he wouldn't have done such an evil thing. It couldn't be him. My mother trusted him too. She told me so, but I doubted her then."

"And now you've changed your mind about him."

"I don't see how I can possibly question his good intentions now."

Brett was quiet and thoughtful. So thoughtful she assumed he now believed as she.

"He's in a wheelchair, Brett. I believe he's a broken man."

"Macklin Villiers will never be a broken man. When your father fled from town, he tore this out of the mining ledger book at the saloon."

She watched, curious, as he took a piece of paper from his pocket and put it on the table.

"Why is it torn like that?"

"Jack knew what Macklin had in mind. Your father tore this out of the mining ledger. It is a perfect match to the missing part of the page in dispute. Macklin's name is written in ink on the next page of the ledger. Macklin's claiming that piece of ground for the Pelly-Jessup."

She stood, restless, puzzled, confused.

"I don't know...I'm not convinced, Brett. I think Macklin was honest with me."

"I've heard from Bill Stewart. He tells me Colefax is saying Halliday and Harkin jumped the Jessup claim. Bill Stewart has already said he'll represent you, Callie, and Jimmy."

"I don't want any of the mine if it means somebody has to die over it."

"I know you well enough to understand that. But, Annalee, somebody has already died. It's not your response to all this I'm concerned about; it's the others. Do you think Dylan Harkin and your father will choose to negotiate a settlement with Stewart? Each will want it all for himself. That includes Macklin. I've found out Macklin and Colefax have bought up all available shares in the Pelly-Jessup. They each own half, even though a few shares are still unavailable. I don't know yet what they have in mind, but I think it spells trouble."

"Do you think my father and Frank Harkin *could* have jumped claim on the Pelly-Jessup? That Mr. Colefax is right?"

"With this?" he held up the paper her father had torn from the ledger. "This claim by Halliday and Harkin is on an earlier page than Macklin's claim. They must have made their claim first."

She watched as he carefully folded it and placed it back inside his pocket.

He stood and walked over to her. For a moment he looked down at her soberly. "Annalee, there's one man who can set all this straight. Your father. He knows what happened. He knows who killed Harkin. He'll come back for this proof of his claim. When he does, I don't think he'll come alone. He'll come in strength against Macklin. That's why Macklin's hired a killer like Hoadly to bring in a half dozen gunfighters. He's waiting for Jack Halliday. That's why I've got to contact your father first." He took hold of her shoulders. "If I can get him to trust me, to talk under oath before a judge, I'll do everything I can to help him."

She sucked in her breath. "Brett…will you really?"

"You can count on it. That's why I'm leaving Virginia Town in a few days. I'm going into Utah to find Jack Halliday."

Her eyes searched his. Could this be true? Was he really interested in helping her father, the man who'd destroyed his father's medical profession? She remembered what he'd told her at the Vesey over dinner. As she looked into those eyes so full of vitality, she knew she did believe him.

"Oh, Brett, you mean it. You're willing to risk yourself to help me…to help all of us. I…"

He drew her closer. Her heart raced.

"I'm not going alone," he said quietly. "Someone has come to me and offered his help. A man I believe I can trust, and he's a man with a reputation for a gun. His name's Rick Delance."

She blinked. "Delance? I saw him in Macklin's room at the Virginia House yesterday. He was just leaving. Brett! Are you sure you can trust him, a gunfighter?"

He was thoughtful. "I think I can. I'm going to take the risk." Smiling then, he let her go and walked to the door. Opening it, he stepped out with her into a cold, bitter wind. Dark clouds were roiling in the sky.

"Winter's definitely going to be hard this year. Snow's coming. Harper says only Snowshoe can get through the pass." He looked down at her, the wind ruffling his dark hair. "There's one thing I need to do before I leave. I want to build you a cabin. I can get Harper to help me and a few others as well. With all of us working, it won't take long. We can get something up in a week if we go at it hard enough. But it must be in Virginia Town, close to Samuel. Not out here."

"You'd do that for me—for all of us?"

He turned her to face him, the wind against them.

"Do you need to ask, Annalee?"

His soft, intense question caused her heart to pound. She was enveloped again in the warmth that glimmered in his eyes. She turned away.

The wind felt good against her face.

"We'd better go back to Virginia Town." His voice was quiet. "We've work to do before the snow comes."

They walked to where Jenny waited by the creek. His horse was not far off. After mounting, they rode together down Gold Canyon to Sun Mountain.

Twenty-Three

❧

S un Mountain stood gray beneath gathering clouds when Annalee and Brett returned from Gold Canyon.

They dismounted and stood for a moment in the chill wind. She was the first to speak. "Uncle Samuel won't be back from Silver City until tomorrow."

Brett nodded as he looked about, hands on hips. Then he pointed. "Over there's a fair spot for the cabin, if it's not already claimed."

Annalee shaded her eyes and looked. "I don't see anything but rocks."

"Where's your creativity?"

She glanced at him. He smiled.

"I'm a realist," she stated. "Rocks are rocks, and they're gray."

"And rocks, gray or otherwise, are exactly what we need, Miss Halliday."

"I suppose...but Brett? Are you sure you want to go through all this trouble? I mean, after all, it's so much to ask, and I haven't yet paid you back for all the other things you've done."

His eyes flickered over her. "I'll put it on your account as a debt to be collected at the appropriate time."

She wisely kept silent.

He looked up toward the clouds. "Seriously, Annalee, you need appropriate shelter. Let's not bicker over trifles." He nodded toward Jenny. "I'll take the mule back to Elmo. You go in the dugout and get some rest."

She felt her lips turn in a smile. "Yes, Doctor."

"Good! I'm happy you see things my way at last." He caught up the mule's reins and led her toward Elmo's diggings.

Annalee paused for a moment, looking after him and trying to understand his behavior and her feelings. Finally she gave up and went inside.

In the next few days, the building process was underway. To her utter amazement, Brett, with the help of a dozen men willing to lend a hand, was able to put together the foundation, frame, and roof of a small three-room cabin in just a few days.

During this time she watched him working with Samuel, Flint, Gordon, and some miners, including old Elmo. Brett, while working hard, seemed not to mind at all. She wrestled her emotions. *Don't you dare fall in love with Brett Wilder. Remember that girl in Grass Valley? You'd better remember, because he does. He's only being kind and helpful. He's a man who lives out his Christian values, that's all.*

Callie went out of her way to let all the hardworking men know how delighted she was. She was never more in her splendor than when carrying-on with compliments and dimpled smiles before a passel of handsome men. Annalee glared at her a few times, but Callie merely lifted a brow and redoubled her efforts.

One morning Annalee thought she was deliberately trying to capture Brett's attention. Annalee was perplexed by a feeling of jealousy. She frowned to herself and went in to make coffee for the men.

Callie came into the dugout a few minutes later, whistling.

Annalee looked at her over her shoulder, scowling. "Don't you remember what Mama told us? 'A crowing rooster and a whistling hen always come to some bad end.'"

Callie burst into laughter. "You're impossible, Annalee. You've got it bad for Brett, that's all. You might as well admit it. You turn green whenever you see him smile at me."

"That's not true. What is true is that you are embarrassing me. You might as well just blow a trumpet and say, 'Here I am, men! Aren't I sweet and pretty?'"

Callie dimpled, refusing to get angry, and changed her whistling to humming as she smoothed her dark hair into place and gathered together the tin cups the men had brought from their dugouts. "I'll be waitress," she announced.

"You go right ahead." Annalee poured the hot coffee. "You seem to forget Brett is a deputy marshal out to arrest Pa."

"I haven't forgotten. He's my father too, remember?" She added, serious for the first time, "Pa or not—maybe it's best he does."

Annalee paused, coffeepot in hand. "Callie!"

"I mean it. Suppose Pa kills someone else with a temper he can't control? What then?"

Annalee stared, unable to answer. She'd been turning those ugly thoughts over in her heart for weeks.

"Unlike you, Annalee, I've no quarrel with a man over his duty to uphold the law. If Pa didn't kill that card dealer aboard the *Golden Queen,* then a God-fearing jury will acquit him."

Annalee merely tightened her lips and finished her task.

A few days later, several of the men moved Annalee's and Callie's belongings into the cabin. A woodstove had been donated by one of the miners. Others offered various services, everything from making sure they had wood to burn to keeping a watchful eye on the girls' cabin at night—though the only danger seemed to be the threatening weather.

Samuel gave the prayer of thanksgiving and asked the Lord's blessing on the work of their hands, committing all things to Him.

"Amen," Jimmy said loudly. "Now even Keeper can stay warm and safe."

"Barrels will make fine chairs," Samuel was saying, "if we can get Elmo to fix a few." He turned to the old miner. "You're good with your hands, Elmo. This is better than mucking. Maybe you can come up with a table as well."

"For some of Miss Annalee's biscuits and stew, I'll make her and Miss Callie a whole room o' furniture."

Annalee smiled, pleased her cooking was appreciated. It was something she did better than Callie, who often burned things.

"If my biscuits are worthy of your carpentry, Elmo, the credit goes to our Aunt Weda. She taught me how to cook just about anything."

"Pa will be back soon and like your biscuits too, Annalee," Jimmy said happily. "We'll bring a mule load of silver from Pa's mine over to Carson."

Annalee's eyes passed from Jimmy to Brett. His expression was unreadable.

Samuel gestured toward the door. "Looks like we just made it, Brett."

The smooth change of subject caught Jimmy's attention, and he went to the door. Annalee came up beside him. Raindrops were pelting the soil.

"Snow's in the wind too."

She heard Brett from just behind her. He stood so near that her shoulder brushed against his buckskin jacket.

Jimmy grinned as he looked up at him. "We can build a snowman, Marshal!"

"I thought you got your fill of snow on the Sierras." Brett said, ruffling Jimmy's brown hair.

"This'll be different. I wanna use silver for his eyes and nose— and maybe silver buttons too."

Annalee's eyes met Brett's. They smiled and turned as Samuel came up.

"With them passes over the mountains blocked earlier than usual, food supplies will pose a problem."

Annalee went to sit on a barrel, trying to mask the weariness that stole away her strength. As they talked in low tones, she watched raindrops drumming a heavy torrent. They hadn't built a fire in the stove yet, and she felt chilled. She glanced up to see Gordon walking toward her. He'd been generous enough to lend a hand these last few days. Despite their coolness toward each other after their little episode in the Vesey Hotel, he appeared more friendly, though she couldn't recall him exchanging a single word with Brett since showing up at the cabin. He'd spent most of his time around Callie.

"You should have let me put you and Callie up at the Virginia House. Jimmy could have stayed with your uncle. This place isn't really adequate for ladies."

Annalee didn't think he was making a genuine offer as much as he was trying to outdo Brett, even though there'd been no trouble between them.

"I wouldn't hear of such a thing, Gordon. The cabin will do just fine." She added, seeing his jaw stiffen, "But thank you so much for your help these past two days. I know you're not the sort who normally enjoys physical labor."

His head lifted. "Now what do you mean by that?"

"Why, nothing really. It's just that—"

"I suppose the 'Marshal' has been impressing you with his brawn. Has he mentioned his boxing skills recently?"

Annoyed, she stood from the barrel and kept her voice low, "What are you talking about?" Thankfully, Brett was with Samuel and Flint, and he hadn't been listening.

"Just what I said. Roc the boxer is out to take him on. Is Brett going to sneak away?"

"Gordon, *what's* gotten into you? I don't recall you ever being like this—or is it just that I never really knew you before? And I would certainly hope the marshal does get away!"

She walked over to the stove, where Elmo was building a fire. She smiled down at the old man. "Thanks, Elmo. You've been a true friend."

He chuckled. "Me and Jenny, we don't fergit old kindnesses, miss."

She watched Gordon leave the cabin, and then she heard Brett talking.

"There'll be a scramble for the supplies on hand once the snow deepens. Right, Flint? Those mules have made their last crossing over the pass this year."

"For sure. You'd better get over to my warehouse in Carson soon's you're able."

"Brett and me'll ride back there with you," said Samuel.

"We need all the food we can get," Jimmy piped up. "After Uncle Samuel preaches for two hours on Sunday, we'll be starved."

They all laughed. Samuel caught the little boy and swung him up on his broad shoulders. "Just for that, lad, you're coming to Carson with us."

"That's what he wanted you to say," Callie said. She followed Samuel, who was still hauling Jimmy on his back, out the door with Flint just behind her.

Annalee was still with Elmo by the stove. She became aware of Brett, who was leaning his shoulder against the wall, watching her.

She walked over to him, finding that his clear gray eyes warmed her even more than the wood fire.

She smiled. "Thank you again, Brett."

There was an awkward moment when she wanted to emphasize her thanks by putting her hand on his arm, but she dared not. The faceless form of the undoubtedly lovely girl awaiting his return to Grass Valley was in the back of her mind.

Brett didn't appear the least troubled as he met her gaze. He studied her face and the way her hair fell down her shoulder.

"Anything I can get you while we're in Carson?"

"Hmm? Oh…yes…"

She hesitated briefly before taking her grocery list from her pocket and handing it to him along with a handkerchief with some gold pieces. She'd finally dipped into the money Weda had given them. There was no choice. She felt embarrassed handing him the list, but a smile loitered around his mouth.

"What's this?" he tossed the handkerchief of gold coins in his hand. He raised it to smell the faint odor of perfume. She could feel the heat pink her cheeks.

"Money," she stated. "For our winter supplies."

"Better keep it for that business you and Callie intend to open." He took her hand, opening her fingers and setting the knotted handkerchief on her palm.

"But—"

He brushed her chin with his finger. "See you later."

She walked with him as far as the door and then watched him join the others. Callie was in conversation with Gordon Barkly. Flint did not look pleased as he turned and walked away.

Annalee liked Flint Harper. For all his Western ways and lack of precise English, she thought him a man of honor and stability. As for Gordon…she wondered what she had ever seen in him.

A while later, after Elmo had gone back to his diggings and it was quiet on Sun Mountain, Annalee walked into her private little bedroom. She stood there counting her blessings as she listened to the rain drumming on the cabin roof. She looked up, half expecting to see rainwater beginning to leak through, but it was dry. She offered up a prayer of thanks to her heavenly Father, not only for their shelter, but for the friends they'd discovered among the miners.

❧ ❧

Annalee was aiding Samuel by helping to research his sermon topics. She'd also begun her own Sunday class with some success. One afternoon, as she was preparing for her class in her uncle's "library" in the dugout, she heard Brett talking to Samuel in the front area by the stove. She hadn't meant to eavesdrop, especially with her Bible in front of her! But Samuel's voice was quite loud.

"There you are, Wilder. I was hoping you'd show up. I'm going to be meeting with Winnemuca in the Forty Mile. I've an open door from the Lord to preach the gospel to him and some of his young braves."

"That's rough territory, but I don't need to tell you that."

"I know that area well around the Humboldt River. The trips are rough, but I've a friend in the tribe. Saved his life once. Found him bitten by a rattler near the river. I nursed him through and let him go. He's not forgotten that. He's arranged this meeting with Winnemuca. This is something I've worked long and hard for."

Ooh! What a sketch his meeting with the Indian chief would make! Annalee stood. *I know I could sell it to an Eastern paper. I've got to have it!*

Brett's voice darkened. "My grandfather had an Apache 'friend.' He ended up filling him with arrows and taking his hair."

Annalee shuddered. But she said nothing about the incident as she went to pour Brett coffee and offer him the plate of sweet cakes she'd baked that morning.

Samuel scowled and ran his bronzed fingers through his dark hair. "I'm not looking forward to losing mine just yet. So your grandfather was a preacher, was he?"

"Yes. You remind me of him. A good man. My grandmother was quite a woman too. She rode beside him all the way."

"Indians get her too?"

"They did."

Brett was leaning against the wall in his buckskin jacket. A disarming smile appeared on his handsome face when he saw Annalee. His eyes flickered to her as he took one of the cakes and the cup of coffee.

"Thanks." There was a teasing gleam in his eyes. "My favorite. You must have made them just for me."

Her eyes teased back. "After all that grocery shopping in Carson? Why, of course, Marshal."

She turned and looked at her uncle. "Did I hear you say you were meeting Chief Winnemuca?"

"That I did, lass."

Brett must have read her thoughts, for when she glanced back at him his eyes narrowed.

"Going along with Samuel would be dangerous," he warned. "You heard what I just told him about my grandparents."

Annalee's eyes deliberately dropped to the Colt barely showing under his jacket.

"Not with you along, Marshal Wilder." She offered one of Callie's dimpled smiles.

Brett paused.

Annalee set the plate down on the table and went to the library for the research notes for Sunday's message. She returned and handed them to her uncle. "What do you think?"

Samuel leafed through them. "Ah! Good work, lass."

Annalee looked over at Brett.

"How's the prospect of starting that church?" Brett asked Samuel.

"This summer should be a good time for building. Thanks to you, Brett, I've now got funds to buy the materials we need, and Flint's offered to haul them over the pass for free."

Brett gave Uncle the money he needs to build the church? Annalee glanced him over thoughtfully. She was impressed, to say the least.

Brett turned to her. "I noticed the Indian girl who carries that Winchester wherever she goes was in your Sunday class. That was quite a feat. You must have impressed her to get her to show up, considering her father."

Annalee smiled. "The Lord brought it all together. Her name's Della. Her father is a friend of Ol' Virginny."

Samuel snorted. "And staggers in his walk just like Ol' Virginny too. I'm pleased Della's taken to you. She wouldn't have anything to do with me. Garth glowers whenever he sees me." He soaked his cake with black coffee and swallowed it in one bite.

"When are you leaving to meet Winnemuca?" Brett asked.

"After the service tomorrow. Thought I'd travel by night. Safer." He touched his shoulder where the bullet wound was healing. His face sobered. "Any news about Jack?"

At once Annalee lost her pleasant mood. A sense of gloom pervaded. Alert, she watched Brett, but he showed nothing.

"Spafford just told me that three men stopped at his station out on the Forty Mile about two weeks ago. One of them fits your brother's description. They were asking questions about the mine and Macklin Villiers."

Annalee stood silent and still.

Samuel frowned. "You think Jack has hired gunfighters out of Utah?"

"I'm thinking he did. Jack would have heard about the men hanging around Virginia Town. He'd take steps of his own." Brett looked over at Annalee. "I'm sorry to have to tell you that."

She said nothing. Her eyes searched his and then Samuel's, who sat with a troubled scowl. She turned and brushed past Brett on the way out the door.

❧ ❧

After she'd gone, Samuel sighed. "Think you should have said anything in front of her?"

"She's asked me to be truthful with her."

"You're right, of course. It's hard for her, though. Worse than for Callie, I think."

"Annalee would be more disillusioned if I kept the facts from her. The showdown will come. When it does, I want her prepared."

"You think it's coming then?"

"I do. The question is whether Macklin is behind Hoadly and his gunmen. I'm risking the idea Rick Delance may come through with the information I need."

"I'd not put much confidence in Delance."

"Without him I'm up against a small battalion. I can count on Flint, maybe a few of the miners, but only Flint can use a gun. That's why I'm figuring on Delance."

Samuel was looking down at his worn Bible. "If it's possible, Brett, I want to see Jack first."

"That's why I'm here…."

Samuel gave him a measured look. "Then you did find him?"

"No, but one of the men with him goes to Spafford for supplies. Spafford says he'll pass on my message that I want to meet with Jack."

"He'll want that proof of claim from the ledger, all right."

"Jack will want to get rid of me. I think he'll pretend he wants to talk."

"I'd like to be with you when he does."

"If you're willing to risk it, I've no reason to try and stop you. He's your brother. If you can talk Jack into coming with me, we can slip away quietly to California."

"I've no doubt you'll do your best, lad. When he contacts you, I'll ride along and try to talk sense to him."

"Now this is something I'd rather Annalee didn't know about. She'd want to come with you."

Samuel nodded his agreement and pushed his cup away, appetite gone.

❧ ❧

When Sunday arrived there were only a few men gathered before Samuel's door. Callie stood with Flint Harper, and Gordon Barkly showed up as well. Flint had begun riding from Dayton to

Virginia Town on Saturday to stay with Samuel in order to attend the service, and he would stay for supper and ride back at dawn on Monday. Annalee was hoping that Callie would fall for Flint, but her sister appeared to be inclined toward Gordon.

Samuel preached from the book of Proverbs. The difference between the foolish man and the wise man was stamped indelibly upon Annalee's heart. She ached for her father and continued her prayers for him.

When the service ended, she escaped to the cabin, changed into riding clothes, and carried her art satchel out back to where Jenny was waiting. She'd already arranged with Elmo to use her again.

When Samuel arrived for the ride to meet Winnemuca, he saw that she was already mounted on the mule with her art satchel.

She smiled cheerfully. "That was mighty good preaching, Uncle."

"You trying to butter me up?" he asked with a pretended scowl.

"Now, Uncle, I'm going with you to meet Chief Winnemuca. This is the painting of a lifetime, and I simply must have it."

His scowl was genuine now. He shook his head as he crammed on his dusty old hat. "You heard Brett. It's too dangerous."

"I'll keep a safe distance from your powwow, I promise. All I need is about fifteen minutes to sketch the scene. I'll fill in the details later. Brett promised to show my work to an editor he knows in San Francisco. A sketch of Preacher Samuel Halliday with Chief Winnemuca is a risk I'm willing to take."

"Hah! But not your ol' uncle. I won't hear of it, Annalee. There's talk of trouble with the Piutes. It may come to some fighting. I hope to soothe Winnemuca, but it could go wrong. Brett, too, will be waiting for me near the meeting. One eyeful of you on ol' Jenny, an' it'll be more than Piutes I'll need to be worrying about riling."

"Uncle Samuel, please, I've *got* to get that sketch! It means so much to me.'"

He scowled again, his eyes quizzing hers for the validity of her request.

"Lass, you don't know what you're asking me."

"I certainly do. I came to Virginia Town with the idea of sketching a Piute. What could possibly be better than this? You know as well as I that I may not live to be a grandmother, not with this illness. So let me spend my remaining years doing what I feel zealous about."

"What's this, talking like a woman with a last request? A young girl hardly out of her teens?"

"Uncle," she said wearily, "I've been out of my teens for years. I'm nearly twenty-two. Brett treats me like a child too. But I'm nearly his age, even though he insists on treating me like Jimmy."

"A mere fledgling," said Samuel. "And Wilder's a man with plenty of experience with trouble."

"A fledgling who wishes to spread her wings."

"But why over Piute country?"

"Uncle Samuel, I've set my heart on going. You wouldn't turn me down now, would you?"

"It's bad territory, Annalee. The dust wouldn't be good for you."

"I've brought a bandanna. Please, Uncle Samuel!"

He scowled. "Wilder's not going to like this."

"Well, he'll just have to accept the idea that I'm going to get my sketch. He can't tell me what to do."

"How is it, lass, you manage to get your way with me?"

She smiled down into his bearded face. "Maybe we've got more in common than you realize."

"All right, you win, but don't say I didn't warn you."

✤ ✤

They rode toward Spafford Hall's Station on the Carson River. Samuel was right about the alkali dust of Twelve Mile Canyon. Even though it had rained, the area had dried quickly. Out of caution to please her uncle, Annalee wore a bandanna around her nose and mouth. The wind scuffed up the whitish dust. The hills were rugged and mostly bare, but the distant mountains of Utah lifted up a contrast of indigo and rust. Some fluffy clouds floated lazily across the gray-blue sky.

Samuel rode a short distance ahead of her. When they neared the gray river, he drew rein and called over his shoulder. "Wilder's ahead, lass. Wait here until I explain. He's going to be blistering mad at me for bringing you."

Annalee stopped her mule and waited, removing the bandanna. Just what gave Brett the right to decide what she could do? She reminded herself, though, that she ought to be pleased and flattered. If a man didn't care what a woman did, it usually meant he had no vested interest in what happened to her.

She watched Brett ride up from the river to meet Samuel. She could see them talking, but the wind kept their voices from her hearing. She smiled to herself. He would know soon enough that she was not a "little girl" but an adult, a woman who knew what she wanted.

She watched Brett ride his long-legged zebra dun toward her. His dark jacket was dusted with whitish alkali, and his hat was pulled low. Even so, she could sense his displeasure.

"Trying to prove something, Annalee?"

His quiet voice, devoid of challenge, disarmed her.

"Yes, that I can get the best sketch that San Francisco newspaper will see in years. I want a drawing of Winnemuca meeting with Uncle Samuel."

"The worst part of our journey is ahead. The Humboldt River and the Forty Mile Desert."

"Is it as bad as it sounds?" she asked innocently.

"Worse in the summer. Men have died crossing it from Utah."

"Yes, but as you said, that was in the summer, and I've heard many of those deaths took place in the 1840s, when people tried to cross and the poor oxen had no water. Besides, Uncle Samuel said we weren't going that far. And after the rain we've had, it won't be as bad. He expects to meet Winnemuca just a few miles from here."

"Even so, wind gusts can come in the fall too. On the Forty Mile they can sweep you right off your mule. The wasteland is still littered with bleached bones and old wagons." He tilted his dark hat. "Now, I suppose, you'll want to sketch that too."

She smiled sweetly. "Maybe another time?"

"So you'll settle for Winnemuca."

"Brett, I want that sketch. I aim to get it."

"I'll describe everything to you when I get back."

"That's not good enough, and you know it. To catch the flavor I've got to see it, smell it, taste it."

"Honey," Brett drawled flatly, "you're going back."

She stiffened. "Now look here, Marshal Wilder—"

"Don't start that 'Marshal Wilder.' "

"Didn't you tell me to exercise the gifts the Lord gave me?"

"You can exercise them in a nice, safe environment. I'm not risking you to a meeting with the Piutes."

Suddenly she saw that he was sincere in his concern, that he wasn't just trying to order her about. She recalled that he'd lost both his grandparents to the Indians when he was a boy. A wave of understanding swept over her, and she said softly, "I appreciate your concern for my safety, Brett, but nothing will happen to me. We're too close to Spafford's Station. I understand what you must have gone through with your grandparents, but this is different."

His eyes glinted a little.

"I'll never get another opportunity like this one. I've just got to have that painting! I can't go back now. This is a chance of a lifetime. Please. I need you to help me."

A slight smile formed. "If you put it that way. Now I know what Samuel was up against." His gaze swept over her. "It really means that much to you?"

"I wouldn't ask you and Uncle Samuel if it wasn't important to me. I'm not resisting just to nettle you. Callie might, but…"

His smile deepened. "Never mind, Callie. It's you I'm thinking of."

She knew what he meant, but the way it came out sounded to her as though he may have meant even more than concern for her safety. She felt a warm prickle. *Do you really think of me, Brett?* She caught herself just in time from saying it aloud as Callie might have done.

He sat quietly for a moment, and she noticed he was watching the wind tossing her auburn hair. His eyes were anything but indifferent.

"If it means so much, Annalee, then I'll see you get your sketch."

She was about to speak when he turned in his saddle and looked toward Spafford's Station. Annalee, too, turned to follow his gaze.

She saw little except some whitish dust kicked up by a gust of wind. Moments later two riders appeared on horses, looking like a dark mirage. They rode toward them.

Brett put his horse in front of her, shielding her. She saw him push his jacket aside and his hand moved within easy reach of his gun belt. Her heart began to beat faster.

Samuel rode up beside Brett. His knee-length coat was flapping in the wind, and a ring of white alkali had collected around the rim of his tall dark preacher's hat. He and Brett watched as the two men neared, slowing cautiously.

Was one of them her father?

Annalee could see their faces now. She didn't recognize them. They were dusty and soiled, wearing unkempt beards and carrying rifles beside their pistols. The horses snorted and shook their manes.

"Afternoon. Name's Samuel Halliday, servant of the Lord. Who be you gents?"

The cold, bloodshot eyes of the two men slid past Samuel to glimpse Annalee before fixing on Brett. For a moment all was silent as they measured one another.

"Name's Smith," the blunt-featured man said with sarcasm.

"Jones," said the other, grinning and stroking his rifle.

Annalee tensed as a sensation of something sinister reached out in the wind to brush against her skin.

Brett ignored their responses. Annalee noted how he'd edged his horse slightly to one side to make sure Samuel was not in the way of his range. Her palms turned sweaty.

"What do you want, boys?" Samuel asked flatly.

"Just thought to be neighborly," the man named Smith said. "Wanted to warn you of trouble ahead. Piutes be putting on war paint."

"How do you know this?" Samuel asked.

Annalee was aware that the men's eyes kept shifting toward Brett's gun hand. He, too, had a Winchester lying across his saddle casually pointed in their direction. Noticing this, their expressions changed. The spokesman spat his tobacco juice in the dust, ignoring Samuel, even though he was doing the talking.

"Saw a man die passing through there a few weeks ago. Piutes got him. Scalped him. Left him naked and punched through with arrows."

"Sure it was Piutes?" Samuel asked with a trace of scorn.

"Reckon it weren't nobody else, Preacher. If'n I was you, especially with a woman, I wouldn't be crossin' that route. The man's buried out yonder. Didn't have much time to make him a decent marker, did we, Jones?"

Jones chuckled. "Makes ya' wanna' cry. No good words spoken over him and all."

"Seems to me," Brett said easily, "that a man would be a whole lot wiser if he did his hearing of those words when still breathing. You never know how long you're going to live."

They looked at his gun hand again. The blunt-face man lost his smile. Jones said, "Looks like we got us two preachers. Only one sports a Colt and a Winchester."

"And a badge." Brett moved his jacket aside, revealing glinting metal. "You don't seem surprised."

"No reason to be. Ol' Spafford told us a lawman's been nosing about. You lookin' for silver or a scalp to hang on your belt?"

There came the chilling click of a gun.

"Don't try it," Brett warned Jones. "Not long ago a man was gunned down in Gold Hill for something as foolish. Maybe you know him?"

"Why should I know him?" came the surly response.

"Coyle Hardy sound familiar? He rode in from Utah, hired for trouble. Just thought you might have something in common with him."

Jones glared, started to say something, and then looked at Smith, who calmly spat again.

"Never heard of him. We just came in from Salt Lake and buried that there fella the Injuns got. His name was Halliday. Say! No relation to you is he, Preacher?"

Annalee gasped. She gripped the reins and sat still, aware Brett couldn't take his eyes off the men.

"Jack was my brother," Samuel said. "And she's his daughter."

"Now ain't this wretched news. And to think we went and busted it on you careless like. Please accept our apologies. It so happens before he died, he gave us this here token. But seein' how you're his brother and all, he would've wanted you to have it." His eyes shifted to Brett. "I'm gonna' reach into my pocket, if it's all right with you, Marshal."

"Nice and easy."

The blunt-faced man calling himself Smith produced a little black book and held it up so Brett could see it.

"Hand it to me," Samuel said hoarsely.

Annalee bit her lip. It was her father's Bible. She'd seen it several times before.

"If you folks intend to go on toward Piute country, remember our neighborly warnin'." He tipped his hat. "Afternoon."

They rode off in the direction of Spafford's Station.

"This is Jack's Bible, but they're lying," Samuel said.

Brett turned his horse to face him and Annalee. "They're paid to lie."

"They're hoping you'll give up the search," Annalee said.

"She's right. If Jack's dead, you'll have no reason to stay in Virginia Town. That would leave him free to carry on at Gold Canyon."

"Once he settles accounts with Macklin Villiers," Brett said.

Annalee said sadly, "He doesn't even care if Jimmy and his daughters believe he's been killed."

Brett looked at her. "Not necessarily. He may not have known you're here. He must think Samuel can handle it well enough."

"Well, he'll know I'm here now."

"I don't think we need to go look for any marker," Samuel said.

Annalee noticed Brett gazing out across the desert toward the outer rim of the Utah mountains.

"Doesn't appear as if Winnemuca is very interested in your powwow, Samuel."

Samuel also looked into the hazy distance. Not far away, Annalee saw an Indian sitting immobile on the back of a pony, watching them.

"Looks like Redbird. I'll ride ahead and see what's up."

Annalee watched him go. "Maybe you're right about my father, Brett. Maybe he did shoot that man in San Francisco."

"Don't think about it now. You've come to get that sketch, and I intend to see you get it. Maybe not Winnemuca," he said with a smile, "but a Piute, just the same."

Samuel returned a few minutes later, his face sober.

"Trouble?"

"Some man died out there, all right, but it wasn't Jack. It was a Piute. His pony went lame and he was on foot. Redbird swears those men killed him."

"Let me talk to Redbird. Maybe I can convince him the white man's law will bring them to justice. If not, there'll be trouble for sure."

They rode toward the lone Piute, and when they were a hundred feet away, Brett and Samuel left her to ride ahead. Annalee watched uneasily as they talked. She looked behind her. There was nothing to see for miles except white, dusty desert.

When Brett rode back to Annalee, she could see he was troubled. "Things didn't go well?"

"No. They've had experience with the white man's justice before. But he remains our friend. That speaks well for your uncle."

Samuel rode back. Brett turned toward him. "I say that Redbird, seated on his pony, is every inch as worthy of Annalee's sketching pad as Ol' Winnemuca. What do you say, Samuel? Think you can get him to pose with you?"

Annalee believed Brett was trying to cheer her up. Samuel, too, seemed to take the hint as his gaze met Brett's. Samuel rubbed his chin and sniffed. "What do you have to pay him with?"

She made a vain attempt to sort through her satchel. Of course, she had nothing, and she knew it. Brett produced a gold coin. "I'm sure the sketch will be worth every penny of this," he said to Samuel.

In a few minutes her easel was set up and Samuel and his Indian friend faced each other astride their horses, Samuel using Brett's tall dun. Samuel had a Bible in his hand and was reading as his stalwart friend listened, arms folded across his broad chest covered with deer hide.

Annalee was frowning. "This isn't exactly what I had in mind, Brett."

Brett was sprawled comfortably across some rocks, his hat pulled low to keep the sun and wind out of his eyes, sometimes watching her sketch, yet also keeping an eye out for unwanted company from the direction of Spafford's trading station.

"Did Gordon ever tell you he was in love with you?"

Surprised by the unexpected question, she stammered, "G-Gordon?"

"You do remember the man who devastated your life?"

"Oh. Him." She ignored the veiled sarcasm. "As a matter of fact, no, he didn't."

"That fits him. My guess is that he's sorry now. That's why he can't stand me. I would think Gordon should have had enough sense to tell you he loved you deeply."

Deeply. Annalee liked the way the word sounded in Brett's voice. Her breath paused. Her heart contemplated not Gordon Barkly loving her deeply, but what it would be like to have Brett love her that way. She glanced sideways at him through her lashes. Anything he said now would tell her what kind of a romantic Brett Wilder could be. Now was an opportunity to ask about the woman in Grass Valley, but she must play it carefully so as not to give her feelings away.

Her voice was deliberately nonchalant. "Oh? Why would you think so? About Gordon, I mean?"

"I can think of several reasons. You're a beautiful woman. You're a woman who loves the Lord. You're a woman who is virtuous and worthy of a man's devotion."

Annalee dare not look at him. She pretended to be busy sketching, but her heart was pounding, and she felt her skin growing warm.

She was surprised how calmly her voice came. "We sort of took our relationship for granted."

"I've heard of couples taking love for granted after twenty years of marriage, but before you even say your vows before God?"

Annalee didn't know how to respond. She couldn't think of an answer that would satisfy him.

She nudged him on with a deliberate question. "Why do you want to know?"

"Curious."

That was too vague. She wanted more of what he thought. "Strange. I never thought of you as a curious man."

After a few moments of silence, he said, "Callie told me she didn't think you were in love with Gordon."

Annalee was enjoying herself. "That was nice of Callie."

"Seems like when a man and woman are in love, they ought to know it."

Now was her chance! "Seems like they should. I imagine that woman in Grass Valley is probably worried about you out here in Virginia Town while she stays home not knowing what's happening."

He pushed his hat back and leaned on an elbow, looking up at her. "What woman in Grass Valley is worrying over me?"

She raised her brows. "You don't even remember the name of your intended fiancée?"

He was quiet. Then, "I see. Gordon Barkly again. It's not his first lie about me. He must be getting desperate."

She looked at him, happiness filling her heart. He wore a smile and looked positively dashing with the wind tossing his dark hair.

"Then...you're not engaged?"

"If I were, I wouldn't be sitting here admiring you, would I?"

"I should hope not." She looked quickly away, mulling over his words again. Admiring her...she felt suddenly joyful and carefree. Brett wasn't engaged, but...

"Somehow I thought a half dozen women would have their eyes on you."

"Sure, plenty, but none that interest me."

It sounded as though there were more women after him than a dog could shake his tail at.

"Sounds to me like you're hard to please, Marshal," she said, a little miffed.

"Oh, I'm extremely hard to please."

Extremely hard to please…he would certainly have no interest in a frail young thing in Washoe who was losing weight. But he had said he thought her pretty—no, he'd said "beautiful." He was exaggerating, of course.

"You see, I happen to be very particular about the one woman I want."

Her hand tightened too much on the pencil. The line came stiff and hard. She erased it.

"Am I disturbing you?"

"Not at all. Why should you?" Airily she tossed her auburn hair from her shoulder.

"No reason I suppose. Just thought I might be," came his lazy drawl.

"Well, I hope you find the *particular* specimen you're looking for, Marshal. Someday I'll sketch her for you."

"That would be nice. What do you think she'd be like?"

"She would be healthy, of course," Annalee stated, wondering at herself for being so blunt, even feeling irritated. "Strong, capable, mature, a woman of fine Christian character who knows how to handle any situation that comes up."

"A strong, robust woman has always been my first priority." She gritted her teeth.

"The reason is plain," he continued. "She'll be expected to do a lot of hard labor on the ranch. Up before dawn both winter and summer to get the fire going. She'll need to chop the wood too. I don't care to fool with such things. Fix my breakfast, rub my horse down, do the laundry. Then there's strays to round up, and sometimes the cows need help birthing. 'Course, any money she makes selling the butter she churns will be turned over to me. She might decide to spend it on something foolish—like fancy dresses."

Her eyes came to his. She knew he was teasing, but the conversation hadn't gone the way she intended.

"Maybe you can make a deal with the Piutes. I hear Indians treat their wives like slaves too."

"Do you think Samuel's friend might be interested? Let's see," and he pretended to go through his pockets. "I have several more gold coins. You don't think my expectations are unrealistic?"

She smothered her smile. That scamp.

"Oh no, not at all." She abruptly finished the sketch and called, "I'm done, Uncle."

Annalee stood and gathered her things together, each gesture one of irritation.

He reached to carry her satchel.

"I'll carry it myself, thank you."

At the mule she glanced back over her shoulder. He was smiling to himself as he walked up to his horse, taking the reins from Samuel.

Redbird had ridden away, and Samuel was mounting his mule. Annalee was already in the saddle when Brett rode up.

"Brett, I've been thinking…"

"Yes?"

"A Piute might not be tolerated well in Grass Valley. So, I've just the woman for you."

"I'm pleased to hear that. Is she strong and robust?"

"Very, far as I can tell. You know Eilley Orrum? You know how she does a good deal of the miners' washing and cooking?"

"Heard about her." He wore an amused smile.

"She's as sturdy as a mule. I think I heard she even crossed the Forty Mile with her first husband—or was it her second? Either way, I'm sure she'll meet all your expectations."

"Ah, but does she have green eyes? Won't even consider it unless she does. I forgot to mention that. Green eyes are a must."

She felt a hot flush steal up her cheeks. A thrill of excitement tickled her senses. "That will narrow your list considerably."

"So it does."

Twenty-Four

❧

*T*he weeks passed. Unexpected illness broke out among the miners. Annalee found herself too busy nursing the dying and aiding Samuel to think of Brett or her father.

Samuel shook his head. "It's the water. Some seasons it seems to get worse. They just won't listen about using snow from the higher elevations."

Arsenic as well as heavy traces of gold and silver were in the Washoe water. Large quantities taken at one time doubled a man over with hideous cramps and intestinal disorders. Most folks were now using melted snow boiled and set aside in containers.

Back in November a Dr. McMannis had arrived in Virginia Town from Downeyville just before the snow had sealed off the mountain passes. His presence comforted everyone, especially Annalee. When the sickness broke out, she and a few other women in the surrounding areas volunteered as nurses. He had asked some of the men to help him put up a canvas shelter for a makeshift clinic so the worst could be brought there. The weather, however, was so severe it was difficult to keep the ill men warm. Some brought in their own blankets and Flint Harper brought in more supplies from his warehouse. Thanks to the doctor, the outbreak wasn't as deadly as it would otherwise have been.

When Annalee wasn't nursing the sick or helping Callie at cauldrons of hot broth or rice, she was at Samuel's elbow. Her uncle was everywhere among the men, day and night, offering prayer and encouragement from the Scriptures.

Late one afternoon Annalee wearily joined her sister, who was stirring a huge cauldron of rice.

"So far a hundred men have died."

Callie sighed, pausing to push her hair away. "Buried amid the sage. Not much of a eulogy. I suppose they have families. We'll all need to take turns writing them in the spring."

"Samuel's collecting their addresses now. But if there is a war between the States, some letters will not get through. Their loved ones may not know for years."

So many were sick that Dr. McMannis continued to need their help. Annalee worked as long as she could until she was forced to return to the cabin sapped of strength.

Annalee was in the canvas shelter with Dr. McMannis when Della pressed her way through the sick and came toward her. Since Annalee had begun her Sunday class, Della had surprised her by showing up and attending every week. Annalee had tried to talk with her before, but she never stayed long enough to say hello once the hour was over.

Della came to Annalee and firmly took hold of her arm. Her dark eyes were intense and her long black hair framed her grave face.

"It's my pa," she whispered, her voice stern but shaking. "He's gone and got himself real sick."

"Oh, I'm sorry. Wait a moment and I'll ask Dr. McMannis about medicine. Where is your father now?"

"He won't leave the claim. He's in the dugout, but it's not from the water; it's whiskey. The cheap stuff they make around here. He's been drinking it almost straight for the last week."

Annalee could see the despair in Della's eyes. Her heart went out to her. The girl couldn't be much over eighteen, yet she'd seen so much of the ugly side of life. Her face showed none of the youthful innocence of the girls Annalee had known at Gilmore.

What could she do? If it wasn't the water but the liquor—

"I'll tell Dr. McMannis," she repeated.

"I already did that. Said there's nothing he can do for him with medicine. I want you to talk to him."

Annalee hesitated. She was pleased that Della thought her words held the answer, but would her father even understand in the state he was in?

"If he's been drinking too much, it wouldn't do any good to speak to him now," Annalee said as kindly as she could.

The girl's black eyes turned hard. "You said your God was love. Yet you won't come!"

Annalee saw the fear in her eyes and it struck her heart. She must do something. Della would be wounded by her apparent lack of concern if she did not. Thinking more of Della than her father, Annalee laid a hand on her shoulder. Then she grabbed her hooded cloak from a hook in the tent room.

"Let's go find Samuel—"

"You know my father don't like him."

"He won't listen to me either, Della."

"You gotta try!"

"All right, I'll come at once. Let me just tell my sister where I'm going."

Annalee stepped carefully over the ill until she came to Callie.

Callie looked tired and cross. This was not the kind of work she cared for. She'd been coerced into helping Dr. McMannis because there wasn't anyone else and he had stared her down.

"It's Della's father, Garth. He's mighty sick on liquor. She's come to ask me to see him. Let Uncle Samuel know where I've gone."

Callie looked horrified. "You can't go off with that Indian—"

"Hush, Callie, she'll hear you."

"And that old goat, he'll be too drunk to understand anything you say, and—"

"I know all that. I'm doing this for her. She won't admit it, but I can tell she really does love her father. If I show compassion now, even though Garth won't understand, she will. I'm trying to reach her. This is the opportunity I've been praying for, I'm sure of it."

"Well, I'm not. Uncle Samuel won't like this either, Annalee."

"Don't you see? This will show her that Jesus cares for those whom even the church cringes from. Just tell Uncle Samuel where I've gone. I doubt if I make it back till late."

Not waiting to argue further, Annalee hurried after Della.

❧ ❧

Callie watched her sister leave the tent with the Indian girl. Annalee's decision hadn't surprised her. She knew her sister had a heart to please the Lord, which often made Callie feel defensive and sometimes even rebellious. *I just can't be like her,* she sighed. She untied her smock and tossed it down on a barrel. She had no idea where her uncle was at this hour. He could be anywhere among the camp of sick men, for not all had wished to come to the clinic tent. Many had refused to leave the dugouts and tents by their claims.

She told Dr. McMannis she'd be away for a short time and went out to find Flint. She couldn't see him anywhere about C Street, but as she turned away she saw the young man she'd met at Dayton. She stopped short. Her defenses sprang into order.

He had come out of the...saloon. He noticed her and stood, watching. She turned away, intending to go the other direction, but that horrid boxer, Roc the "Jawbreaker," was striding up the wooden walkway.

She preferred the young man with the gunfighter reputation to Roc. She turned back, drew in a breath, and walked up the street as though she knew exactly where she was going.

Rick Delance stepped toward the middle of the walkway, making it difficult for her to pass.

"Looking for Harper?"

She ignored the amusement stirring in his dark eyes.

"Yes, have you seen him?"

"He's gone off somewhere. Didn't look like he was coming back soon."

She glanced away, folding her arms against the wind coming down from Sun Mountain.

"What did you want?"

His direct question took away her guard.

"Have you seen Mr. Wilder around?"

"Not today. Why?"

She didn't want to tell him Annalee was alone at Garth's. She had no reason to trust him, even though he'd claimed to have protected her from Big Birdie.

"Wilder?" said a bearded man from the street, unloading his mule. "Saw the marshal over at Lyman Jones' not more'an an hour ago."

"Lyman Jones?" Callie repeated. A tavern, no doubt.

"I'll talk to him," Rick Delance told her casually. "What's the message?"

She'd better explain. "My sister's gone with Della to see her father, Garth. He's bad off. But my sister isn't well either. She's been working ceaselessly to help Doc McMannis back at the clinic, and, well, I'm worried about her."

"I was just goin' to Lyman's place. I'll tell the lawman what you said."

She looked away from his troubling eyes. "Thank you." She picked up her skirts and hurried back toward the clinic, not looking back. Somehow she knew he would do just as he said. Who was Rick Delance? And why did he seem friendly toward her? He was a man to stay clear of, to be sure.

✤ ✤

Annalee ducked under the canvas flap and entered the small dugout cave, which reeked of stale whiskey. There was an Indian blanket on the dirt floor, and in one corner, a large mound of pine needles covered with blankets for her father's bed. Garth was mumbling in restless sleep.

She could see Della had tried to keep things clean. There were other Indian artifacts about, and Annalee wondered where she had gotten them.

"My mother was a Piute," Della announced proudly, following Annalee's glance.

"Your mother—?"

"Dead."

"Garth's your only family?"

"Mother had a brother. He's with the tribe."

"An uncle. Do you ever see him?"

Della's black eyes narrowed slightly, as though she were combing Annalee's interest for sincerity.

"Don't suppose it matters now to say. Pa don't know, but I ride out there often. My mother's people don't accept me, but my uncle does, and so do his wife and daughter. The scowls from the others ain't so bad as they used to be. Now they expect to see me. If something happens to him, I'm going back to my people."

Annalee could hardly protest. The girl was undoubtedly better off with the Piutes than with gamblers and drinkers in Virginia Town, especially with no one taking an interest in her. Annalee had never seen Della talking with a man or out walking the streets. She was mostly in Garth's shadow, watching, picking him up, and doing the washing and cooking.

"I think you should, Della. There's nothing for you here, unless you hope to marry one of the men. But good men are hard to find."

"I've listened to your words in the Sunday meeting. I think about them." Della gestured toward her mumbling father. "He won't do it. I keep asking him to listen. He keeps telling me to shut up."

"You must keep praying. As long as he lives there is hope."

Della nodded. "Your pa is like mine. They both face a dark passage that narrows."

Annalee was silent. A dark passage that narrows…and when they came to its end? What would they do after having shunned the only Light?

For a moment Annalee was so distraught with thoughts of her own father that she hardly noticed Garth.

"Your pa's wanted for killing Frank Harkin, isn't he?"

Annalee looked at her. "Jack Halliday did *not* kill his partner. Someone else did. Even the marshal believes that."

Della looked back with fathomless black eyes. "The marshal is right. I know who killed Frank Harkin."

Somehow Annalee kept her surprise from boiling over. She waited silently as the wind cried eerily around the entrance to the dugout.

"It was Hoadly. I heard Pa say so."

"Then you must tell this to the marshal, Della. He—"

Garth let out a cry and begin to flail about as if fighting off some assailant. He was sweating profusely, and the odor coming from his unwashed body made Annalee wish she could open a window.

Between the two of them they wiped him with rags. Annalee tried to soothe him, but even in his condition he was too strong for her. It took Della's firm grasp to hold him down.

"Pa! Be still! I've brought the Christian girl who teaches about God to talk to you. You listen to her. You do just what she tells you."

"It's after me again! Get it off me!"

Annalee looked down to his blanket to see what could be disturbing him, but when Della held the lamp closer his eyes were glassy and transfixed.

"He sees bad spirits," Della explained. "Things like spiders and snakes."

"He's hallucinating. It's the effect of the liquor. I fear he's drunk too much this time. I wish there was something I could do."

"He just pours that juice down him. I tried a hundred times to get rid of it. When he wants it, he wants it. Ain't nothing can stop him but himself."

Annalee laid a hand on his shoulder and leaned toward him, reeling under the smell of whiskey. Surely he wouldn't understand a word she was saying. But she had come to show Della that God cared about her and Garth. Even if he didn't understand, Della would.

"Garth?" Annalee whispered. She wondered that her voice sounded so weak. "Garth, the love of God reaches out to you in this moment through His Son, Jesus. Jesus has the power to set you free from the chains of sin. He's the only one who can. God's Spirit, by the atoning sacrifice of Jesus, can break through the darkness that binds you.

"Listen to me, Garth. You've turned your back on Him, but He would prefer to show you mercy. He takes no pleasure in the death of those who reject Him. He can forgive you now, if you'll really turn to Him. He came not to condemn men but to forgive, to pay the debt of sin each of us owes a holy God."

A moaning noise gurgling in his throat turned to a wail that made her spine tingle.

"Garth? Can you hear me? You're not ready to face eternity without getting right with God. Even now you can call upon Jesus Christ, trusting that He can save you from your sins. You can come to Him like the dying thief on the cross. He was forgiven and taken to paradise."

Garth shuddered and grumbled, shaking all over, and his eyes rolled.

Annalee blinked hard with exhaustion. The ceaseless work of recent weeks had already drained her. She wasn't thinking only of the pitiable man before her on the mat of pine needles, but of her own father, in many ways as bad off as Garth.

And who would be willing to help my father?

She knew it is never so dark that God cannot deliver, never so late that He cannot save, but what about the human will? Was there a point when a soul that had long rejected God's forgiveness could no longer reach out?

As though the Lord reminded her, she remembered the four friends who brought the crippled man on a stretcher to see Jesus. When they arrived at the house Jesus was teaching in, it was so crowded they couldn't get through the door, but they did not give up. Instead, they tore away parts of the roof to lower the helpless man with ropes into the presence of Jesus. *We must continue to believe and pray for our loved ones, helpless as they are.*

Garth groaned loudly and began flailing his arms. "Help! Get it off me! It wants to kill me! It's laughing at me—"

Annalee tried to control her own trembling caused by weakness and Garth's hysteria. Outside the cold wind moaned. Della held the oil lamp toward her shaking father. Annalee swallowed and went on, quoting Isaiah 1:18, "Come now, and let us reason together, saith the LORD: though your sins be as scarlet, they shall be as white as snow; though they be red like crimson, they shall be as wool."

Della's young face echoed those who sorrowed with no hope.

The certainty of death without the Savior gripped Annalee as it had never before. When a man's last breath is taken, all dreams and schemes are left behind, even though he had struck the greatest silver bonanza in Virginia Town.

If a soul meets the Creator having rejected the only means of redemption, whether a hopeless drunk or a powerful silver king, he still passes through the gates of death. Apart from Jesus Christ, there would be no hope or joy for either.

"Does he hear?" Della whispered.

Annalee didn't know, and she wondered why the girl's frantic voice seemed so far away. At the moment she felt too ill herself to go on.

"Pray for him," Della urged.

Annalee felt the girl's strong fingers digging into her arm, shaking her, as though Annalee's very prayers could bring about the miracle she sought.

Garth shouted loudly, his voice reminding Annalee of a wounded animal. His arms suddenly struck out and smashed the oil lamp from Della's hand.

"Be gone, snake!"

The cabin sank into dark shadows, except for a glowing wick. Della was wrestling to hold her father down.

Overcome with dizziness, Annalee's brain was reeling as she tried to gather her wits together. She smelled something smoldering.

"Della," she cried weakly.

A bright flame flared up from the brittle dry leaves and pine needles.

Garth was delirious, yelling at Della, his hand clutching a fistful of her dark hair and refusing to let go.

Annalee struggled to beat out the flames, but her movements seemed slow and clumsy. "Della—"

The pine needles and branches—like a dry Christmas tree—seemed anxious to ignite. The smoke burned Annalee's lungs. A deep breath of the irritating fumes brought her to her knees in a coughing spasm. In desperation, Della struck her father and broke free. Grabbing the Indian blanket from the floor, she beat the fire, smothering the flames but generating dense smoke. Annalee bent over on the floor, choking.

Della ran to the door and flung it wide. Then she caught Annalee under her arms and pulled her toward the opening where the rain beat in.

"I'm sorry, Annalee. So sorry…." There were tears on Della's cheeks as she watched Annalee's terrible struggle to breathe.

Garth was thrashing wildly on his mat again. Della covered Annalee with another blanket before going back to her delirious father.

"Pa! Wake up, Pa!"

Twenty-Five

*T*he wind was picking up in bitter blasts as Rick Delance walked down to Lyman Jones' place, a tent-tavern and eatery. He had other news to tell Wilder besides what Callie Halliday had asked him to relay.

December had arrived blustery and cold. The busy mountainside was changing with the seasons. Many of the thousands who had first joined the Washoe silver rush had grown discouraged and gone back to California before the snow closed the Sierras.

He entered Lyman Jones' wood-frame structure—forty by twenty-five feet covered with canvas. There was a sheet-iron stove where some of the men were gathered discussing the future.

"Mark my words," a grizzled miner was boasting. "There's less'n a few hundred here now, but you jes' wait till the thaw. It'll be more crowded 'round here than a yellow jacket nest. If'n you're goin' to buy a claim, now's the time to do it. Yessir. Folks is anxious to sell out now. A man who knows what he's doin' might git himself a real good bargain. Them rich boys from Frisco will flock in here buying everything they can get their hands on. Jes' bought me a claim over near Union Street. Looks promisin'."

"You stayin' then?"

"You bet I am. Been waiting all summer fer ever'one to scoot so I can buy up. All ya need is some cash."

They looked up and saw Delance. He felt their uneasy stares and then their heads turned away. He shrugged. He was accustomed to being shunned by everyone except men with reputations.

"Anyone seen Wilder?"

Arkansas turned and looked at him in silence. His eyes dropped to Delance's gun belt.

They think I want to draw on Wilder. The notion elicited one of Delance's rare smiles. "Samuel's niece is looking for him. Seems Miss Annalee could use some help out at Garth's diggings."

That brought the response he wanted. Arkansas looked back at Delance.

"He and Harper are talkin' to Lyman 'round back."

Delance walked toward the cooking area, the spurs jangling on his boots. Lyman looked up from his cookstove. Wilder, sitting on a barrel, eyed him calmly. Flint Harper sized him up cautiously.

Delance helped himself to coffee.

Flint gestured out the window. "Don't like the looks of the weather. Seen too many snowstorms on the Sierras to take it lightly. There are some miners that want to sell out and leave before all the passes close. If a man had a mind to it, he could pick up a decent claim, Brett."

"Thinking of doing so?"

"Don't know. Ralston's wanting to sell his claim. He's had enough. Took a look at the shaft. Not bad. How about it, Brett? Come in with me, and we'll make it a straight fifty-fifty."

"I'd prefer the Savage or the Gould and Curry. The Yellow Jacket looks good too. I think they might make it."

"I'd be interested in going in with you," Delance said.

Brett looked at him thoughtfully, but Flint didn't. It grew too quiet.

Rick Delance smiled to himself again. He drank his coffee.

Flint reached for the pot behind the makeshift counter and spied half of a pie.

"This pie any good, Lyman?"

Lyman grinned at him from across the stove. "Should be. One of Samuel's nieces baked it. Don't know which one. Jimmy sold it to me yesterday. I've ordered a half dozen more."

"Sold it to you? Now that's what I call a smart boy."

Flint turned to Brett. "Winter's going to be rough on them."

"They should have left a month ago," Brett stated.

"You staying?" Flint asked Delance.

"Looks that way."

A Washoe zephyr sent the canvas walls groaning. The men looked up, half expecting to see the roof fly off. They were used to the sudden winds, and their expressions showed no alarm.

The wind brought in rolling clouds that darkened the tavern. Lyman went about lighting his lamps.

Flint was enjoying his pie.

Brett left his money on the counter and turned to leave. "See you later, Flint." He grabbed his duster and hat and put them on. He looked at Rick Delance.

Delance gestured his head outside. He set his empty cup down and dropped a coin on the table.

They left Lyman's together, heads turning slowly to watch. They stepped out onto the wooden walkway.

"I've been looking for you," Delance said. "Thought you'd appreciate knowin' two men from Utah are waiting for you down the street. There may be three."

Utah? The men he and Samuel had run into near Spafford's?

"Where's Hoadly?" Brett asked him.

"Haven't seen him in a few days. The two I saw aren't with Hoadly."

"Who do you work for, Delance?"

"Told you at Strawberry. Myself."

"No one's contacted you? Offered you money?"

"Heard more talk, is all. Big money, Hoadly promises, but he doesn't have it yet."

Brett considered. Why wouldn't the man who hired Hoadly and his killers have the money yet?

Brett glanced down the street and his gaze fixed on the Virginia Town Bank. Macklin's San Francisco business contacts had opened the bank, but Macklin owned shares in it. What had Macklin told Annalee about giving her and her siblings fifteen hundred dollars? He didn't have the money yet, she had told him out at the Gold Canyon cabin. Macklin said he'd have the money in the spring when the mountain pass was open into California.

Macklin, again. Brett was sure Macklin was the one paying Hoadly.

He turned to look at Delance. "Samuel's niece said she saw you come out of Macklin's room at the Virginia House."

Delance looked back evenly. "He called for me. Wanted me to ride shotgun out at the Pelly-Jessup. Told him I wasn't a guard. If you're thinkin' he's the chief behind Hoadly, you may be right. But he didn't mention Hoadly."

Brett felt he was telling the truth. Besides Delance had come to warn him. That was something.

"Thanks," Brett said. He started to walk away.

"Something else, Wilder. Speaking of that niece of Samuel's, the pretty auburn-haired girl. She's over at Garth's. The Indian girl brought her there. Her sister, the brunette, seems to think there could be some trouble."

Brett was just about to reply when from the corner of his eye he saw a man step from the shadows near the Delta gambling den. He wasn't either of the men Brett and Samuel met near Spafford's. This must be the third gunfighter Delance had warned him about. Brett tried to place him. Then he remembered. It was a man with a boasted reputation. Lazaro had killed thirteen men who'd taken him on.

Lazaro wore a gray duster and hat. His boots came up to his knees, and his long hair was pulled back and tied. He stepped into the street, his hands flexing as he moved to the center.

Across the street a second man stepped down from the boardwalk and casually cupped his hands to light a smoke. Brett recognized him as the one who'd called himself Smith. That meant the other was nearby too. Up in one of those rooms above the tavern?

"Wilder!" Lazaro called.

Brett moved toward the dusty street. "Who sent you, Laz?"

"Where's the ledger page Halliday gave to the old preacher? Hand it over!"

"Tell Halliday he'll have to come and get it himself."

At once the street began to clear.

Where was the other gunman? Smith was still lighting that smoke.

Lazaro walked slowly toward Brett. His hand moved into position.

Just then, Brett's eye caught movement on the roof across the street. An ambush...

A blast of bullets sprayed in several directions—

Lazarro went for his gun and fired—

Brett beat him by a hair, striking him through the heart.

Smith fired into the ground as Delance's Colt .45 nailed him. He was slumped against the post, his cigarette still dangling from his mouth.

Brett fired twice and Jones twisted back against the store wall, slowly releasing his gun as he sank to his knees and fell off the roof to the street.

Brett smelled the acrid odor of powder smoke.

Hideously unconcerned, the empty piano music started up again. There was laughter, the shuffle of a deck, and the slosh of a bottle. The moment went as unheeded as a yawn, and backs turned. Three more souls had stepped into eternity unprepared.

Brett was sure Jack Halliday had hired them to go after Hoadly and his crowd, but when Jack heard the news at Spafford's that he had proof of the mining claim, Halliday had turned his hired guns on him instead.

Flint Harper and Arkansas had come running at the first sound of bullets, and now they stood there outside Lyman's. Flint looked over at Rick Delance.

Brett holstered his gun and walked over to Delance. "Thanks."

"I figured three against one wasn't playing it fair. They were sent by Halliday."

That meant Halliday might be alone out near Spafford's. He'd ride there now and see if he could find him, but there was Annalee...

He turned to Flint. "See they're taken to Boot Hill, will you?"

"I'll git a wagon, Marshal," Arkansas spoke up. He sauntered down the street toward the livery stables.

There was friendliness in Flint's eyes when he turned to Delance. "Say, how's about some coffee? Come inside."

They walked into Lyman Jones' together.

❧ ❧

Della heard the shout coming from outside the dugout. She hurried out into the wind, feeling the snow blowing against her face.

She saw the marshal leading his horse by its reins and ran to him. "There's been fire and smoke. It's Annalee! It done her sick. Don't know what to do for her—"

Brett went past her into the mouth of the dugout. He saw Annalee lying on a blanket and covered. In another corner Garth appeared to be unconscious. Brett scooped Annalee up into his arms and carried her in the blanket to his horse. The snow was covering everything in white. He had to get her home to her own bed. It was freezing, and the gusts were strong.

"You got everything you need for a few days, Della?" he called back toward her.

She nodded in silence. Then she went in and shut the canvas flap.

⇒ ⇐

Annalee hovered in and out of consciousness. Somehow she was sitting on the saddle with Brett, and they were riding uphill into a flurry of white flakes. The blowing snow flitted against her face, causing her to catch her breath. Brett's strong arm was close around her as she leaned back into his chest. Her eyes closed again...

⇒ ⇐

Snow continued falling throughout the following day and night, and the Washoe zephyrs howled like angry tyrants buffeting the cabin.

Jimmy, more frightened than ever, spent the next two days in the shadow of Samuel. Death hovered over the cabin. Jimmy was sure of that. The fact that Callie wouldn't deny it only made matters more frightening. Each time he tiptoed into the shadowed room to gaze upon his sister, Annalee looked worse.

Brett insisted he stay out of the room, and he wondered why no one could go in unless they wore a cloth over their nose and mouth. It was Mr. Wilder who had told them this. And when Annalee helplessly coughed herself into a faint several times, it was Mr. Wilder who attended her, holding a cloth for her to cough into. He seemed to know just what to do, and he didn't look scared or bothered by it. Jimmy decided the marshal must have a hankering for Annalee.

It was most frightening when Marshal Wilder wasn't at the cabin. Annalee looked pale and thin. Jimmy found Callie by the stove crying once. The sight of both his sisters in a bad way made him plain scared. He found a private spot in Samuel's dugout and prayed out loud.

"This is worse than Sacramento, Lord Jesus. I ain't never seen Annalee look so bad. Even Dr. McMannis told Marshal Wilder there was nothing he could do for her. Please, Lord, You can do everything. Ain't nothing too hard for You. Please don't let her die like Mama died. Amen."

In the following days only the quiet confidence of Brett or the strong squeeze of Samuel's hand on his shoulder told Jimmy that God was still in control.

"You keep praying and trusting, Jimmy boy. We both will," Samuel said. "He has the right answer to every one of our problems."

But Callie didn't seem to think so, least Jimmy didn't think she did, because every time he saw her when she thought she was alone, she was crying. And when either Flint Harper or Gordon Barkly stopped by, she spent most of the time with them telling them her troubles and fears.

Jimmy went to bed with the verse that his uncle had written out for him. Sometimes in the middle of the night when he heard Annalee coughing in the next room he would light a candle, and picking up Keeper, he would unfold the piece of paper and read the words again until he had them memorized.

"God is our refuge and strength, a very present help in trouble."

Annalee reeled under new bouts of coughing that Jimmy was sure would deliver her to the gates of death. Dr. McMannis took

Brett and Samuel aside, talking to them in a low voice Jimmy couldn't hear. The doctor shook his head and went out the door, letting in a flurry of snow.

The look on Brett's face made him real scared for the first time. Annalee was going to die. The emotion he'd felt when his mother died swept over him in a cold, withering blast. He burst into tears.

Samuel caught him up into his arms and held him against his broad chest as he walked the floor. Jimmy wrapped his arms tightly around his neck.

❧ ❧

From the bedroom, Annalee could barely hear voices. They echoed in her ears like distant calls. Her eyes were blurred and the room was unsteady each time she tried to sit up. Her feverish mind groped for answers through the night watches as a small yellow light burned on the barrel beside her bed.

Where was she? Home...yes, Sacramento. "Mama?" Where was she? Why didn't she come the way she always did...

Why couldn't she concentrate...too tired. Her lungs burned, yet she felt no fear. Peace wrapped about her like a soft, cozy blanket.

There were arms holding her, but they were not her mother's. It was Brett's voice speaking into her ear. He was holding her with hands that didn't shake. His touch assured her, and she clutched him weakly, hearing his reassuring voice. This time she didn't faint. She was awake, and he was still holding her. She couldn't make out what he was saying, but she didn't need to. In that desperate moment, they were united in spirit, and her wordless prayer ascended with his to the throne of grace.

Rest ebbed through her soul, and slowly her body was growing less rigid with pain and anxiety. Feeling his nearness, comforted by his hand soothing her damp hair, a heavy sleep closed her eyes and the darkness was welcomed.

When Annalee awoke it was morning, and Callie was trying to get her to drink hot broth. The next time she awoke it was dark, and the yellow light burned low beside her bed. She was too tired to think or talk. On and off through uncertain passage of time, she would hear her uncle praying beside her bed or sense Jimmy's quiet presence hovering over her until someone scolded him for being in the room. But Brett was there too. And it was his presence she would wordlessly seek, and when she felt it she slept well. She would reach a hand to find him, and he would take hold, giving her a squeeze to show he was there.

Sometimes at night she would glimpse him standing near the window looking out, and she thought he was only a shadow or that she was dreaming until her weak murmur of his name brought his immediate response. Brett Wilder was not a shadow but a strong consolation, though he rarely spoke. His presence, and his hand holding hers through the long nights, spoke clearly, and she would not awaken again until morning light.

A vision of a warm, sunny morning in Sacramento flooded her mind. She was all dressed up in green satin, and she and Brett were going to church. They were laughing and talking of marriage. Then suddenly she was lost in a blinding snowstorm and stumbling into a gully where she lay shuddering. Brett wasn't there…he was out hunting for her father to arrest him…

❧ ❧

The snow continued to fall through the night and into the dawn. By morning it was over four feet deep. Brett and Samuel had gone to help shovel out two men trapped in a tunnel. Jimmy had gone with them. They were trying to keep him busy and optimistic. Callie opened the door and looked out. Sun Mountain stood white and still in the early dawn, the sky a misty gold.

Flint had told her they were all confined for months. That thought didn't frighten her. The only thing that brought fear to her heart was the image of a life without Annalee in it.

I should have been kinder to her. I should have tried to help her more.

The miners had abandoned the tents for any hole or covered hovel they could find. Those that had anything to burn held their hands and feet to a fire to keep away frostbite. The saloons were filled with those seeking shelter from the cold. News arrived that some of the tunnel lodges were overcome by avalanches, and some men were unaccounted for in an avalanche up at Six Mile Canyon. They hadn't heard a word from Macklin and Rody. She'd heard Brett tell Samuel he believed something was astir. What could he have meant?

Callie worried on. It was at times like this that thoughts of Flint Harper or Gordon Barkly offered her no consolation. Her longing, empty heart ached for something more.

✄ ✄

Annalee's eyes fluttered open to face the bright light streaming through the bedroom window. Fully awake, she lay very still, her eyes glancing about the room. She was alone.

Reality came in with a rush.

How many days had she been in bed? A week? A month? She touched her face and found her hair in two thick braids across her shoulders. Dazed, she felt her body beneath the blankets. Thin! Terribly so! She must look a fright. A start of despair came when she remembered that Brett was seeing her in this wretched condition. Surely any thought of romance was dead.

She groaned, feeling humiliated. What was the Lord doing with her? Why was her life so fully open to the one man she had wanted to impress with her qualities? And what a burden she was to everyone!

She tried to rally her faith, to rebuke the waves of self-pity that welled up inside, but deep depression settled in.

Slowly, with difficulty, she raised herself to an elbow and turned toward her barrel dressing table. Gritting her teeth, expecting the worst, she managed to pick up her small hand mirror. As her eyes beheld the thin face looking back at her, a choked sob died in her throat and she fell back.

She turned her face from the doorway, closing her eyes as tears ran down her cheek and wet her pillow. She stiffened as she heard footsteps cross the room. She tried to pretend she was asleep. She knew it was Brett without even turning. She had come to sense his presence before he spoke. Quickly she tried to hide the evidence of tears, but nothing seemed to escape him where she was concerned. She didn't know quite how to take it.

"May I sit down?"

"I want to be alone," she murmured, trying to wipe her eyes, but he sat down anyway and reached for her hand. She clutched it weakly. With his other hand, he gently dried her cheeks with his handkerchief.

She said nothing and swallowed the lump in her throat. It wasn't right to enjoy his touch and attention this much. But she was sure his attitude was merely that of a doctor. Hadn't he attended medical school for a few years?

"Is—Garth?" she asked weakly.

"He died in his sleep."

"He died lost?"

"No one knows that except God. He never gained consciousness for very long. Yet, Garth had time to turn to the Lord had he wanted. Della said you told him everything he needed to know. She asked me to thank you."

"How's she handling it?"

"You know Della. It's hard to know how she feels. She conceals herself behind her sober face. She left a few weeks ago to live with her mother's family among the Piutes."

A few weeks ago. "How long have I been ill like this?"

He was quiet a moment. "Almost four weeks," he said gently. Her eyes closed. No wonder she was skin and bones.

"Did she say anything else? Was there a message for me?"

"If you're asking if she believes in Christ, I don't know. She didn't mention it. I started to talk to her about it, but she ran off."

The wind crooned mournfully around the cabin roof. Tears pricked her eyes again.

"My health is gone...what else is there?"

He squeezed her hand. "Christ. You have Him."

"Yes, but I'll never be able to teach His Word the way I wanted to. I'm hindered from doing *anything* worthwhile."

"You're wrong, Annalee. Many opportunities will open to you in the future. You have friends who'll do all they can to see that those doors open, including me. That invitation to stay with my father for treatment remains open as well. As for serving the Lord actively, it's not your strength or your ability to do something important or great that makes you valuable. It's *you* He wants."

Her heart warmed with comfort. Despite her desire to remain awake, her eyes grew heavy and closed again. *God loves me and wants me, weak and helpless as I am...*

Within a few moments she was asleep once more.

When she awoke she saw an envelope addressed to her sitting on her dressing table. She sat up, feeling a little stronger. She opened it and read:

Dear Cousin Annalee,

> *I've been worried about you. I've heard from Gordon Barkly, who has a room here in the Virginia House, that you are very ill. If there is anything I can do, please don't hesitate to call upon me.*

> *Your faithful cousin,*
> *Macklin Villiers*

Twenty-Six

❧

*C*hristmas Day found Annalee sitting up in bed and Jimmy obediently holding her small hand mirror as she brushed and worked her curls into a semblance of feminine grace. She scowled. Why was it that sickness took the shine from hair? Well, it was the best she could do. She sighed and stared at her green eyes and thick lashes. At least they were the same! She pinched her cheeks, trying to put color into them. She heard Jimmy smother a laugh.

"Come on, Annalee, hurry. The marshal don't care what you look like."

"Who said I'm trying to look nice for him?"

"You don't need to say it. I know. Besides, he's seen you at your worst and still comes 'round. No use worrying none."

She couldn't help laugh. It was true and also comforting. Brett Wilder had definitely seen her at her very worst.

"He's here now." Jimmy dropped the mirror on the bed and ran out, leaving her door open.

Brett's and Flint Harper's voices mingled with Samuel's as they entered, stamping snow off their feet. Callie joined them, and for a moment she heard the rise and fall of voices and laughter as the shout of "Merry Christmas" rang out.

Things were hard in Washoe, but Annalee was alive, and it looked as if she would live until spring when she was expected to leave for Sacramento to visit Dr. James Wilder.

"Look! A present, wrapped in paper, even!" cried Jimmy. "With my name! Thanks, Marshal!"

"When are you going to start calling me Brett?"

"Yessir."

Everyone laughed.

"Brett, how on earth did you come up with wrapping paper?" Callie was asking.

"You can ask Flint about that."

Hearing their voices, Annalee settled herself as nicely as she could against the back of the bed, and touched her hair again as she heard steps. She looked up and smiled as Brett came through the doorway. He was the image of masculine strength, and her heart gave an odd little lurch at seeing him again. He had been gone for over a week.

"Merry Christmas, Brett," she murmured.

He smiled at her. "It is now."

He walked up and she made room on the edge of her bed for him to sit. "I'm sorry I don't have a present for you. Especially after all you've done for me the last six weeks."

"Emerald eyes and auburn hair, what more could a man ask for on Christmas morning?"

"You're kind to say so. I can see you've been raised as a gentleman. I look terrible and we both know it. I've lost so much weight."

His steady eyes contradicted her words. He handed her a package. She opened it and discovered a warm, fur-lined hooded cloak. "Oh, Brett! How did you ever manage?"

"Flint brought it over on his last trip. It's not exactly the style I have in mind for such an attractive young lady, but it will keep you warm. We'll save the high fashion for San Francisco."

She held the soft fur to her cheek. "I think it's beautiful!"

He reached into his jacket and handed her an envelope.

"More?" She smiled and opened it, removing the short message. He'd drawn a Christmas tree. It was dated December 25, and signed. She read the promise he had written. Her eyes met his, and they sparkled like emeralds.

"*Anything* I want in San Francisco?" she teased cautiously. "Aren't you afraid I'll take advantage of you?"

"Anything. And you can take advantage of me whenever you wish."

To cover her embarrassment she said, "I shall have the finest dinner on the wharf, and then a carriage ride along the bay."

"It's probably best if we don't talk San Francisco cuisine just now," he said with a sigh. "Looks like salted mule is going to be the staple of Washoe until spring."

"Thank you, no. Is it really that bad, Brett?"

"It is. Not that I want to dishearten you, but I've always thought a woman ought to know what she's in for. Besides, I think you can handle it."

"Salted mule?" she grimaced. "You give me more credit than I deserve." Seriously, she pondered the thought of more trouble to come. She knew food and wood were scarce; Callie had told her that, but she hadn't thought it was that desperate.

"How bad is it?"

"Sugar sold out last week. No more chocolates." He smiled slightly and his eyes teased her.

"I'll manage," she said smiling back at him and thinking of the boxes he had regularly bought her.

"How about eighty dollars a sack for vermin-infested flour?"

She gasped. Eighty dollars!

"Not that there's much flour to buy."

Annalee remembered with trepidation the precarious pass they had traveled over back in October. Now it was far worse. It would take months before the prairie schooners could get through.

"I hope no one panics and starts out thinking he can make it back to Placerville," she said.

"They already have. Some are trapped up there freezing to death. There's nothing any of us can do about it. Rescue teams started out but had to turn back. Drifts are sixty feet high in places, and there's no letup in the storms."

She remembered her mother…

"How many are still here besides us?"

"Several hundred, probably. It wouldn't be so bad if we could hunt game, but birds and mammals know better than to get trapped on the peaks in winter with nothing to eat."

Della, what about her? Would the Indians starve before spring? "How are the Piutes? Do you think there's going to be trouble?"

"I hope to have you out of here by then. The animosity they feel toward the mining settlement is worsening. Their children are weakened from hunger; some will likely die. It won't take much to start a skirmish this summer." He stood. "Enough gloomy talk. It's Christmas, and Flint and I managed to get a nice fat bird for Callie to cook. I'll carry you into the kitchen to see this marvelous sight."

She saw the hint of humor and at once grew suspicious. "What *kind* of Christmas bird?"

"Oh…a real plump fellow."

Brett walked to the door. "Samuel, do you have that Christmas goose plucked yet?"

"He's still trying to get the feathers off," came Flint's innocent reply.

Annalee leaned forward. "Still *trying?* You mean they don't want to come off?"

"Stubborn goose."

"What is it, Brett? It couldn't be a—dare I say the word? A buzzard?"

"Annalee, I'm disappointed in your lack of confidence in Flint and me. You couldn't find two better buzzard hunters in all Washoe."

She smiled in spite of herself. "If things are as bad as you say, and going to get worse, then Callie and I had better show more appreciation."

"I'm glad you see it that way. No objections?"

"No. You know what they say about looking a gift horse in the mouth."

He laughed and walked back to the bed. "It's time you sat by the fire. Feel up to it?"

"I feel wonderful."

"No, don't get up. I'll carry you."

✒ ✑

Later that night when Annalee awoke from a sound sleep, she realized something that took her by surprise. They had all spent a wonderful Christmas Day together, and neither she nor anyone else had asked Brett about Jack Halliday. No one had heard from him, and indeed, her father had not even crossed her mind. She prayed for him and for Brett before letting sleep claim her again.

The long wintry nights through January 1860 passed in flickering candlelight.

"The situation in Virginia Town is growing worse," Callie told her. "We're indebted to the abilities of Brett and Uncle Samuel in providing food and wood. Gordon said meals at the Virginia House are down to weak coffee and pancakes without butter."

"That's better than most are getting. You're right about the men. If it weren't for Brett, Uncle Samuel, and Flint, I don't know what we'd do."

Along Six Mile Canyon, folks strained their ears for the familiar tinkle of the bells of a mule train, but only the icy wind greeted them. Sadly, to stave off starvation, some of the prospectors were resorting to butchering their ponies or mules for food and burying their carcasses in the snow to preserve them for the weeks and even months ahead.

"I'll starve first befer I do in ol' Jenny," Elmo assured Annalee. "Don't you worry none. Jenny's kept inside the dugout with me."

Washoe, covered with white, was silent and abandoned for the winter. Now food, warmth, and staying alive filled the minds of those trapped.

What would tomorrow hold for them? For each of them?

❧ ❧

One day in March when Annalee was feeling much stronger, Jimmy came tearing into the cabin. "Mule train!"

"Hear that?" Callie cried, slapping her palms together. "Hurry, Annalee."

Annalee snatched her fur-lined cloak from the peg and followed after Callie and Jimmy. Men were coming from everywhere like ants. The word spread by mouth, "Mule train!"

There was not a sweeter sound to any ear than the clattering hoofs and the tinkle of the bells. "Mule train!"

The men were hollering with delight, tossing their battered hats into the air.

This mule train was driven by a man they'd never seen before. He was one of the first who'd made it over the Sierras in the new rush from California.

Annalee saw the mules heavily loaded with barrels and packs. Men hauled down the first barrel and opened it with shouts, fully expecting mouthwatering bacon or flour, but their cries of joy soon turned to groans of despair.

"Why, this here ain't nothing but whiskey!"

The owner, a man from San Francisco, scowled. "Why, just yesterday I turned down eight thousand dollars cash for this load!"

The miners went to the next mule and opened the barrel, and the next, and the next...

The men looked at each other. Nothing but seventy gallons of assorted alcohol! One old man sat down and wept.

Annalee, moved with compassion, returned to the cabin and brought him a loaf of bread and a little honey. His eyes brightened and he hurried off with it as though it were a bag of silver.

Groaning, the men begin to tear at the other barrels. Tobacco, pretty drinking glasses, shiny plates—

"What's the matter with you? What'd ya take us fer up here, a bunch o' drinkin' scum?"

The driver, intending to go into business for himself, was speechless.

One man stepped out of the hungry crowd to grab him and vent his frustration, but others stopped him.

The driver watched them slink away, their stomachs growling with disappointment.

Jimmy's mouth was open as he looked up at Annalee, who'd watched in silence. Finally, she drew him away, and with a grave-faced Callie, they started walking slowly back up Sun Mountain.

"Hey miss, isn't this Virginia Town?" the driver called after them.

Callie turned. "It is, mister. But that's the only thing you got right."

It wasn't long, however, before a second train arrived with a load of flour, and the spirits of the miners picked up.

"They held an auction," Annalee told Callie. "A man paid five dollars a pound for it."

"Then I saw him mixing it with snow and eating it right there!" Jimmy said.

"We need to be very thankful to God that He's helped us stay alive," Annalee said.

As spring approached the snow around the cabin was melting. With the arrival of food and the promise of a prosperous summer, Sun Mountain was emerging from its winter cocoon and humming with activity. It didn't take long before the men forgot the lessons they had learned in hardship. The taverns filled, the cards shuffled, the dice rolled, and bullets flew. It was Virginia Town once again.

One bright morning Annalee felt the cabin shake and rumble. She left the stove and went to the front door. Opening it, she saw Flint, Brett, and Uncle Samuel come walking up for breakfast.

"What was that noise?" Annalee called.

"Nothing but a little dynamite, lass."

"Dynamite?"

"The mining shafts of the Ophir and the Gould and Curry were emptied of winter water."

"Mining's resumed," Jimmy said brightly, taking a seat at the table. "Maybe now we'll get to visit our mine in Gold Canyon."

"The deeper they go in the mines, the richer the silver sulphurets," Flint said. "We'll have ourselves some millionaires before summer's out, is my guess." He rubbed his hands together as he saw Annalee coming out with a huge platter of hotcakes. "Ah! Now *that's* worth getting excited about!"

"We're celebrating with BIG pancakes," Annalee told them cheerfully. "I went to the little store yesterday and saw barrels stacked to the roof with food supplies."

As weeks passed, a steady stream of new "silver seekers" wound their way over the pass. Gold Canyon was once again in touch with the States.

The trail over the Sierras had been widened, and now the Overland Stage was rumbling down Gold Canyon once or twice a week. The grapeline, the telegraph line strung from tree to tree, was also in operation.

"I don't know if it's worth it," Callie stated. "It's not dependable. Gordon says the people flocking in over the mountains have been cutting the wire and taking it."

The silver rush continued. Flint was back at work with his mule train. Jimmy was breathless with news. "Down at Wells Fargo I saw 'em loading bullion, flat, square bars—big ones, like this!" He exaggerated, showing their shape with his hands.

"Jimmy? How big?" Annalee asked.

"Well, at least like this."

"That's better."

"Wells Fargo's Express is bringing them all the way to San Francisco. Do you think Brett will ride with Fargo to keep bandits from holding them up?"

"No. He doesn't work for Wells Fargo. They'll be hiring private guards to ride shotgun."

"Well, they'll have to be plenty good if they're going to reach San Francisco alive, I heard say. Delance may hire on. He's the best. Well, maybe him and Brett are tied."

"Who is Delance?" Annalee asked.

"A friend of Brett—and Flint too."

Callie turned and looked at Jimmy. "How do you know that? About being their friend?"

"I heard Uncle Samuel say so."

"Rick Delance is a gunfighter, nothing more," said Callie.

Annalee looked at her sister, noting the coolness in her voice. "You've met him?"

"Once or twice," she murmured. She turned back around and went on drying dishes.

Annalee raised her brows. "What's been going on while I've been sick and out of things?"

"Plenty," Jimmy said, misunderstanding. "Uncle Samuel said we're no longer called Virginia Town but Virginia City, and we need law and order. Maybe Brett will stay," he said hopefully, "or maybe Delance will take the job."

Callie tossed her dark curls from her shoulder. "They'd better watch the silver shipments if he does."

Annalee looked over at her again, this time thoughtfully. *Rick Delance...*

❦ ❦

Callie stood staring at two letters in her hand one beautiful May morning. One had been delivered to her by the Pony Express, the other was addressed to both her and Annalee.

"What is it?" Annalee came up beside her sister and tensed. One of the letters was from Macklin Villiers at the Virginia House. The money he'd promised them?

"I don't believe it," said Callie. "It's finally come. A letter from Aunt Lorena in New Orleans."

"Open it. I'll open Macklin's—"

Callie held the envelopes back. She opened Lorena's. She read silently to herself for a few moments, and then she looked at Annalee, shocked. "It seems she wants us to come and live with her after all. All three of us."

"Well," said Annalee, slowly, "then it's settled. This is what you've been waiting for."

Callie shook her head. "I've changed my mind. I'm staying here in Virginia City." She drew in a breath. "I didn't tell you sooner, Annalee, not with the uncertainty about you and Pa and everything, but," she lifted her chin. "I'm going to start performing as Callie O'Day this summer. There's a theater going up. I walked down to where they were building it a few weeks ago and met the manager, Mr. Hill. He says he knows Mr. Maguire too. And Mr. Hill also knows Macklin. After I told him who I was, the daughter of the great Lillian O'Day, he got all excited! Said I could try out for a part this summer when the theater's up. If I'm any good, he's going to let me work there."

Annalee was stunned. "Well, you sure kept that a secret."

Callie ignored the scolding tone in her voice. "You were sick. I didn't want to worry you."

"Have you talked about it with Uncle Samuel?"

"Not yet. He won't like it, but I'll be of age soon. I've my own life to live, Annalee, and my own dreams."

Annalee knew that, but she wasn't happy about the direction her sister was going.

Callie stuffed Lorena's letter back into its envelope.

"I'll write her and explain that my circumstances have changed and that you'll be going to Sacramento soon with Brett to see his father."

"I haven't said I was going just yet. I don't even know where Brett is." He had been away for several weeks. Even Samuel said he didn't know "exactly" where Brett was.

"I don't wanna go either," Jimmy stated firmly. "I'm staying with Uncle Samuel. I'm going to learn to be a preacher."

Callie didn't appear to be listening. "Gordon says Virginia City is going to grow richer and more glamorous in the next couple of years. There's going to be great silver discoveries besides what's already been found. They're all saying so. We'll all make money if we play our cards right."

"Callie, please don't talk like that," Annalee's voice was quiet.

Callie looked away and then shrugged. "Sorry, I wasn't thinking. It's easy to pick up slang here. Even Jimmy's talking like Arkansas."

"Arkansas says 'hep' a lot and 'durn mule'," Jimmy said.

"You're going to school back East when you reach twelve," Annalee stated.

"Can't do anything if war comes." He scooped up Keeper and left the cabin in search of adventures.

"Well, what'd you know. A letter from Macklin."

"Let's see that, Callie—"

Callie tore it open and read. Annalee watched her expression change to one of shock and then amazement. "Five hundred dollars apiece—" she sucked in her breath and looked at her. "He's giving us money to compensate for Mother's old shares in the Pelly-Jessup."

Annalee sat down on the chair. "Yes, I know. He told me."

"And you never mentioned it?"

Annalee didn't answer.

"The money's in the bank for us now—just waiting! And we each have our own private account! Except Jimmy's is being drawn up separately to claim when he's of age." She turned, her face flushed with excitement. Her blue eyes gleamed and the smile on her face convinced Annalee that her fears for Callie were justified.

"You know what this means?" Callie cried. "We've no more reason to wear our old clothes and stay here. We can move into the Virginia House, dine with style, and meet people important in the silver business! And this money's come just in time too. I'll be all set with a new wardrobe this summer for my first acting part. Wait until I tell Gordon. He'll be so happy for me—I mean, us."

Callie ripped off her calico apron and ran into her small room.

Annalee was on her feet, hurrying after her.

"No, Callie. Please don't go to the Virginia House."

"Don't be silly. We've money now, you goose. We can do anything we want." She touched her hair. "I want that sweet little hat I saw at the store, the one with the rhinestones that shine."

"Then, you're leaving the cabin?"

Callie looked at her. She smiled suddenly, reached over, and hugged her. "I'm going to call on Gordon right away. He can get us set up at the hotel this afternoon."

"I'm not going, Callie. I'm staying here in the cabin."

"Well if you're going to be stuffy about it, then go ahead and stay. I'm leaving. And no one's going to stop me. Not you, nor Uncle Samuel."

Annalee sank to the bed. "I'm not going to try and stop you. Knowing Uncle, he won't either. I just wish you wouldn't leave. Save the money and—"

"Look, Annalee. You've been lecturing about saving *our* money since before we left Aunt Weda's. This time *I'm* doing as *I* please. I'm going to work in the theater. And I want to get settled in a decent life at the hotel *now*. By the way," she turned from her trunk where she was already tossing her things inside. "I want my share of the gold pieces Aunt Weda gave us."

Annalee stood quietly. She already knew she couldn't stop her sister. "All right. I'll go divide it up."

"Keep Jimmy's portion, of course. You're the one who looks after him. I won't have time anyway. And don't forget my part of the gold dust Uncle Samuel has for us. I want that too."

"You'll have to see him about that. He's been keeping it in hopes of sending us back East to finish college."

"I've had all the learning I need. I'm ready to *live.* All right, I'll tell Uncle I want my gold dust. Just go get the gold pieces from Aunt Weda."

Annalee did so. Later, Callie counted them out, her cheeks flushed. She wrapped them up in her handkerchief and stuffed them in her trunk. She put on her hat and grabbed her cloak.

"Soon I'll be able to throw these old things away." She left her room and went toward the front door. She paused to look back. A happy smile touched her fair face. "I'm going to see Gordon about having my things moved to the Virginia House. I'll need to go to the bank too. And sis, don't look so troubled. I'll make you mighty proud of me this summer. You'll see." Callie smiled again and walked out.

The door closed behind her.

Annalee stood there. She walked over to a barrel chair and sank down. *Oh Callie…*

Twenty-Seven

%

*A*nnalee set her Bible aside and rose from her bed as Jimmy came in, looking glum.

"I never thought Callie would walk out on us."

So he already knew.

"I saw her down by the Virginia House with Mr. Barkly. He was taking her across the street to the bank. I heard her say she's moving into the hotel."

"Yes, she told me. She's moving out of the cabin to work in the theater this summer, like Mama did in San Francisco."

"And she's not coming back here?"

Annalee tried not to show sadness or alarm, though she felt both emotions.

"No, she's going her own way. We have to let her go. She'll come to see us," she added quickly. "Maybe we'll go see her at the theater. When the play has a nice story I can take you."

He said nothing for a long studious moment. "I don't like that Mr. Barkly none, not even when he used to come see you at Aunt Weda's. And his hair's parted in the middle, all sleek. I don't know what Callie likes about him. I like Flint a lot more." He sighed and then said, "Annalee? Pa's in trouble, isn't he? Big trouble?"

At the change in the conversation she looked more closely at him and wondered how he knew. Recently their father hadn't entered their conversations at the cabin. If he knew enough to ask, it was time to be truthful.

"I'm afraid he is. Did Uncle tell you about Pa?"

"I heard Uncle and Brett talking. The marshal's gone to arrest Pa. He knows where he's at now."

She felt stunned by his announcement. "Jimmy! Whatever do you mean!"

"Last night I was with Uncle Samuel and Brett. It was late, and I was supposed to be sleeping, when a man rode in from Williams' Station."

Williams' Station. That must be another supply store she hadn't heard about. Since she'd ridden out toward Spafford's Station with Samuel and Brett several months ago, she'd heard of a gunfight in town during the time she'd been so ill. Two men who'd called themselves Smith and Jones were dead. There'd been another man too. Someone named Lazaro who'd been sent to kill Brett. Samuel had hinted that Jack may have sent the three gunfighters, but she feared to consider that. Were there more men out at Williams' waiting for Brett? Or could her father be there?

"Tell me, Jimmy, what did you hear?"

"The man gave Brett a message. It was from Pa."

"You're sure?"

"I heard Brett say Pa wanted to see them both. After that, Brett went into town."

So that was why she hadn't seen him recently. He had been sure he'd get that message once her father learned the men he'd sent were dead. It was the only way to get that ledger sheet back. To see Brett Wilder face-to-face. But her father wouldn't permit himself to be brought back to Sacramento, she was almost sure of that—unless Samuel could talk him into it.

Why hadn't Brett and Samuel told her? Anything might happen. Did Brett still think she wouldn't understand?

"I've decided I'm going to like Brett anyway. What about you, Annalee? You'll still like him too, won't you? Even if he arrests Pa?"

"Has Uncle Samuel left yet?"

"He was saddling the mule a few minutes ago."

"Stay here, Jimmy."

Annalee left the cabin and hurried toward the dugout situated a little farther up Sun Mountain.

Samuel was already leading the mule down the pathway when he saw her and stopped. She picked up her skirts and ran toward him.

"Uncle Samuel, I've learned about the message. Can you trust it? Suppose it's a trap? There may be someone else waiting to kill Brett!"

"I'm not sure of anything, neither is Wilder. But Jack's there, and he wants to talk, so Brett's willing to meet with him."

Annalee felt a stab of guilt. "This is my fault, Uncle, I've forced him into risking his life. Oh, why didn't he tell me before he left?"

"What was he to say, lass? He's been waiting, expecting Jack to send that message since before we rode out to try and meet with Winnemuca. Is Brett supposed to tell you he's riding off to arrest your father? As for risk, he knows. He doesn't do anything he doesn't want to." He looked tired and worn, and his eyes were troubled. "You do some praying. Not just for your pa, but for Brett. It's one thing for me to ride knowingly into a possible trap to give Jack another chance. It's another thing for a deputy marshal." He laid a sturdy hand on her shoulder. "He's doing it for you, Annalee. You understand that, don't you?"

She could find no words. Fear and guilt seized her. She reached and grabbed his arm, and Samuel leaned forward. Annalee kissed his bearded cheek and watched him ride off.

Her wounded heart turned toward heaven.

❧ ❧

The sun felt warm, and it was one of those days in early May when even the Washoe zephyrs were silent. After spending some time in prayer for Brett, Samuel, and Jack, Annalee took advantage of the sunshine and left the cabin with her art satchel. She walked up to a spot that overlooked C Street. Virginia City was growing by leaps and bounds. She seated herself on a smooth rock and began to sketch the town. She hadn't gotten far along when she saw Jimmy running up the hill toward her, holding onto his hat.

"You should see Callie! She's all dressed up mighty fine. Never seen her look so pretty. Delance was in town gettin' supplies, and he saw her too. She dropped something and he picked it up for her, but she just walked away without so much as a thank you. I like Delance—I heard he sure can shoot!"

"You be careful about that. Let Uncle Samuel be your hero. He doesn't often carry a gun."

"Sure he does—sometimes. Brett's a hero too, and he carries one. Think how bad things would be if there weren't deputy marshals like Brett Wilder who can shoot faster than them snakes in town."

Annalee could only shake her head.

"Guess what! I counted thirty-eight general stores," he told her breathlessly. "And guess what else! Ten places to eat, thirty saloons—"

"And," Annalee said with a twinkle in her eye, "one little school. Uncle agrees with me that you're going to enroll soon."

Jimmy's face fell. He crawled up on the rock and looped his thumbs under his suspenders as he stared at the sprawling town. "I'd just as soon not have to think about things like arithmetic and spelling." He pushed his hat back away from his forehead. "I've never seen Arkansas and Elmo so excited."

"Hmm…about what? Silver, I suppose." She went on with her sketch.

"Yep. I heard them talkin' down near the barbershop. They say silver's being extracted from the mines faster than anyone thought. Arkansas thinks he might of struck something big."

"Gordon should hire you as his reporter," she said with a smile. "You have more information than his newspaper." She wondered why Gordon hadn't published that promised threat to muddy Brett Wilder's name about California land. He might know it wasn't true and decided against it. Perhaps it was because of Callie. He was getting on well enough with her that he might not want to upset her. Whatever the reason, she was pleased there seemed to be no more trouble between him and Brett.

"There's something about a lot of trading in mining stocks on the San Francisco market—what's that mean?"

"It means people in San Francisco have gone rather mad," she said dryly. "People are buying into the mines, and many shares are sold for more than they're worth. Some mines will have no value at all."

Jimmy thought about that. "That doesn't seem right."

"It's not. It's risky and often dishonest." She thought of the Pelly-Jessup, where work had ceased. And the Halliday-Harkin mine was inaccessible due to the ownership resolution struggle.

He scooped a fistful of pebbles and begin to toss them down the slope. "Flint says milling is going to become big business in Washoe soon. Since the road over the Sierras is good now, he's switching from all mules to wagons." Jimmy squinted up at her. "What about us, Annalee? Do you suppose Pa's claim has rich ore? Maybe we ought to go out there and start working it—"

"Bill Stewart's still working on legal details. Don't go getting silver fever. It can poison your blood."

"Is it wrong to get rich on silver?"

"No. But like many things in life, it's the way you go about it. If you cheat, steal, kill, and lie, then it's wrong. But if you honestly work hard and hit rich ore, then a miner has the right to celebrate."

"Brett's bought into the Gould and Curry, the Ophir, and the Mexican. He also changed his mind and went and staked that claim with Flint and Delance. That's how come Delance was in town. He was getting things he needed. They ain't struck anything yet, but Brett thinks they will."

She was astounded.

Jimmy grinned at her response. "Brett came flat out and told Uncle Samuel. Uncle said he did the right thing in taking a risk on Delance too. Said Brett would be rich someday. Even Uncle bought a percent or two in Brett's mine."

He tossed his last pebble and slid off the rock.

"He did not."

"Did so! He's already drawing plans for stained-glass windows in that church he's going to build. He's starting it this summer. Me, I'm going to help him. There's going to be a rug and some good furniture. Pews, he called 'em."

"Where did you learn all this?"

"From the company I keep," Jimmy said, settling his hat. His expression was that of a person of sound judgment. "I gotta go down the hill now. The Pony's due. Pony Bob was supposed to arrive two days ago. The men are hanging about the streets waiting for all the important news from the States. Say, maybe I'll be a newspaper man when I grow up. I met a man down at the *Territorial Enterprise*. He can be real funny. Name's Mark Twain. But he said he uses other names too."

"I thought you were going to be a preacher like Uncle Samuel," she said with a slight smile.

"Oh, I am. Maybe I'll be both, plus do a little mining on the side."

"Well, you'll sure have enough to keep you busy. And just what is this important news the men are all waiting for?"

"Other than mining? Why, the Heenan-Sayers championship fight!"

"Oh." She turned back to her sketch, bored. How folk could get so excited about two men knocking each other out in a ring, she could never understand. She thought of the boxer named Roc.

As if reading her mind, Jimmy said, "Did you hear about Roc the Jawbreaker?"

"I'm not sure I care to hear."

"I bet you will. Elmo told me the whole story. Roc was waitin' for the marshal two weeks ago down by the livery. He challenged Brett to a fight. Called him a yellow-bellied chicken. All the folks gathered round to watch. It…it was bad. They was both all bloodied, but Brett beat him good. Roc's left Virginia City. Elmo said a man named Hoadly was sure mad when Brett won."

So he won! And that's probably why he hasn't come around for a few weeks. He's letting his bruises heal.

"A man named Terry wants to seize the Comstock for the South. He keeps saying, 'As the South goes, so goes the Lode.' His secesh friends already call him 'Governor Terry.' Why, even Governor Downey and the man who runs the military are Rebs." He cupped his hands to his mouth and yelled, "As the South goes, so goes Californie and Virginny City!"

"Shh, Jimmy. I don't believe it!"

"But really there's more Union folks here, like that Bill Stewart. Uncle Samuel says Stewart wants to be our governor too, maybe someday a senator."

"I think you've been listening to gossip. I want you to stay away from the men milling about the gambling rooms."

"I didn't hear any of this near the saloons, but by the *Territorial Enterprise* office and Wells Fargo. Barbershop too. I gotta go now, Annalee. Pony Bob's bound to come in today—unless something bad happened."

Annalee watched him run down the hill toward town. She thought over their conversation. So Brett, Flint Harper, and Rick Delance were partners in their own claim.

❧ ❧

The May morning was quiet and lazy with the murmur from the Carson River and the wind sweeping softly through the willows. It was too quiet, Brett decided. He had ridden into a stand of trees not far from Williams' Station with Samuel. There was no sign of Jack.

Brett turned in his saddle and peered up at a vulture circling in the clear sky. "Something's dead."

He had been uneasy since leaving Virginia City. He looked at Samuel from under his hat. Samuel's bushy dark brows were hunched in agreement. Brett touched his Colt, easing it slightly.

"Let me ride in first," Samuel urged. "If this is all wrong, I'll know it straight off. You get yourself out of here fast."

Brett gestured his head toward Williams'. The barn door stood ajar. He studied the situation.

"That buzzard's mighty interested in what's on the other side of that slope. I'll circle around and have a look. You'd better stay out of sight. Keep an eye on that barn."

Brett rode unseen through the trees back to where a bend in the canyon led up into some split rocks. The zebra dun took the climb like the good mountain horse it was.

There was an entrance to an old abandoned mine located farther up. He leaned to the side of his horse. There were footprints. Some were smaller, and he judged them to belong to a woman. Perhaps two.

He studied the entrance. It was blocked. Was there someone inside?

He left the horse behind a boulder and edged his way closer toward the path. He saw what had interested the vulture. A Piute lay face down in the dirt with several bullet wounds.

"Hello, Wilder."

Brett turned slowly.

A man stepped from behind some rocks. He was in his forties, slim, handsome, with a shock of dark wavy hair and green eyes that were all too familiar. He was dressed well, with a white shirt and sleeve garters. Brett would know a gambler anywhere.

"Halliday." Brett glanced at the Winchester aimed at his chest.

"Easy, Marshal. Nice and gentleman like, unbuckle your gun belt. One move toward that Colt and you'll force me to kill you."

Jack Halliday flashed a smile. It was so much like Annalee's that Brett felt a prick of pain.

"I know your reputation, Wilder. You'd have to be fast if you beat Laz."

"Did you send him?"

"I had to. There's something I've got to take care of in Virginny Town. I only hired them to get rid of Hoadly and his gunmen—but then your arrival made things messy."

Brett moved his hands toward his belt. He might be able to shoot, but Halliday's rifle couldn't miss at this range. They'd both be dead when Samuel found them.

"Easy," Jack breathed again. "Don't try anything."

Brett loosened his belt.

"Set it down slow like...that's it. Now, step aside and move toward the mine, hands behind your head."

"They say you shot Frank Harkin in the back."

"I didn't kill Frank."

"Who did?"

"Hoadly. Under orders from Cousin Macklin."

"So it was Macklin. I thought it might be him all along. He's paying Hoadly, then?"

"Yes. To kill me. He failed the first time. He hoped to have a lynching, but luck was on my side. I got proof of my claim from the ledger and lit out fast. They chased me for a while, but when he neared the Forty Mile, Mac turned back. He always was a coward. Uses money to pay killers to do his work."

"Are you any different?"

"I was never a killer. That night on the *Golden Queen* went bad, is all. I didn't intend to kill the dealer, but I'd had too much to drink. Things went from bad to ugly. I didn't know that other man who got shot was a doctor—or your father. I told him to get back from the dealer and he wouldn't. I wanted my money in the dealer's pocket. I took a shot, intending to scare the doc away, but it hit his arm."

"And this man lying here?"

"What makes you think I did it? It might have been Jessie or Ernie. They're with me. Right now they're keeping an eye on the Piutes. They're heading this way."

Brett didn't know who Jessie and Ernie were. Just more hired guns.

"Why would Piutes be headed for Williams'?"

"You can ask them, Marshal. I don't like doing this, but I've no choice now. It's too late to turn back. And like I said, there's something I must do. I'm afraid you and Samuel will be here to greet the Piutes."

And before the Indians arrived, of course, Halliday would be headed for Virginia City.

"So you intend to use Samuel again for your selfish purposes?"

"How righteous you sound, Wilder. A pity…too bad you can't be tempted. Think what we might share together. Why, with your gun you could take them all, and then together we could run the place. I'd run the gambling, and you'd run the town. We'd be sleeping in silver-encrusted beds and have them all eating from our hand."

"I never cared for cowards eating from my hand, and silver beds bore me."

"I see. Well, I guess it ends here."

"Like him, in the back? You're a brave man, Halliday. I hope Jimmy never knows just how brave."

A muscle in his cheek twitched. "Leave my boy out of this. I'm doing this for him and for my daughters. That claim's half mine and theirs. No one's taking it from me. Hand over the claim paper, Wilder. If you don't, I'll need to kill you here and now."

"I don't have it on me."

His green eyes darkened. "You're lying."

"I'm a careful man, Halliday. It was getting a little too crowded in Virginia City for my liking. One lucky shot in the back, and Macklin could have had it in his hand."

"So you know about Mac."

"Who else could be calling the shots from the shadows? I've known about him since his younger days in New Orleans. He sent for his nephew Rody. Macklin's just waiting for the right moment to kill you. You ride back to town, and Rody and the other hired guns will move on you. You don't stand a chance, Halliday. Let me take you back to Sacramento."

"And hang? I'll go down fighting. You're right about Mac and Rody. They're both killers. Rody's proud about his reputation. Mac has the cold blood of a reptile. He won't draw lest he's forced. All right, Wilder, you've made your pitch. Who'd you give that claim paper to?"

"The best lawyer in these parts, Bill Stewart."

"Stewart's all right. I've heard of him."

"Ownership will be decided by arbitration. No matter what happens to you, if your claim proves legal it'll be left to your children. Give yourself up. For Jimmy and your daughters."

"I'm not interested in that!"

"Of course you're not. Responsibility demands unselfishness—and some honor too."

"Keep jabbing at me and I won't wait for the Piutes to take your scalp. Did Samuel come with you?"

"Did you think he wouldn't?"

He shook his head sadly. "Poor Sammy...I haven't been fair, using him like this. But that's the way it has to be. I had my doubts, actually. Not about him, but you. I thought you might see through the message. But I figured Sammy would come. He can't help it. It's the preacher in him. He wants to convert me so bad he'd cross the Forty Mile on foot to do it."

"You'll sacrifice anyone who gets in your way, won't you, even Samuel and your kids. Your wife too—"

"Never mind her." His face looked pale and his green eyes glittered. "She's the reason I'm going to Virginny City."

"She's not there. She's dead."

"If you know so much, Wilder, you weren't very smart in showing up."

"I came because of Annalee."

Brett saw his jaw muscles work. For a moment there was silence.

"She's in Virginia City. So are Callie and Jimmy. Annalee believes in you. She's asked me to give you a chance to turn yourself in peaceably."

Jack stared at him and then his hard green eyes swept Brett with a soft laugh.

"Well, well. Between my beautiful daughter and Preacher Samuel you've allowed yourself to get backed into a corner, Wilder. I almost feel sorry for you. It's the same pressure I feel when Sammy gets going on me with those words of his. So you got tender feelings for Annalee, do you?"

"I don't suppose her trust does anything to soften you up?"

"If things hadn't already gone past all that, I'd think about it. If I gave myself up now, I'd hang."

"At least let Samuel live."

"I've no intention of shooting Sammy. What do you take me for?"

"Why would the Piutes attack Williams'?"

Jack Halliday gestured toward the mine. "Two Piute Indian squaws are in there. No, I had nothing to do with it. It was the Williams brothers. The fools lured them here." He glanced up toward the sun. "In about an hour from now the braves will sweep down on the station. I didn't plan this, Wilder. It just worked out for me. Gambler's luck, I call it. I won't need to do anything but leave you here for the Indians."

"You've got to warn Williams' Station."

He gestured to the cave. "Get in there."

When Brett remained where he was, Jack raised the rifle. "If you cooperate, the Piutes will come and find those two Indian girls alive. You wouldn't like to see them hurt, would you? I didn't think so. One of them says she knows you. Her name is Della."

Brett said nothing.

"You see?" Jack said with a smile. "I can always trust a Christian to do what's right. I knew Samuel would come. And I know you're not going to force me to shoot you. So let's not waste anymore time. I've no intention of getting caught here when those Indians come."

"For Jimmy's sake, spare Samuel. Get him out of here."

"Move."

"What about Annalee?"

Jack measured him. "You're real interested in my daughter, aren't you?"

"She's ill. She came close to dying last winter."

The green eyes mellowed. "I know she needs medical attention. That claim out at Gold Canyon has some of the best ore I've ever seen. I'm going to hit a real bonanza, Wilder. And when I do, Annalee will be well taken care of. Callie and Jimmy too."

"You'll have trouble convincing the younger Harkin brother. Dylan's riled over Frank's death. I'd say he won't rest until you're dead."

"I'm not worried about Dylan. It was Hoadly who shot Frank in the back. An' Dylan will get Frank's share in the mine. Mac's the slimy snake trying to claim jump. But he won't win."

"If you let the Piutes raid Williams' Station without warning them, you're guilty of murder."

"If two stupid brothers manhandle a couple of squaws, is that my fault? The braves are up in arms, and there's no stopping them. It just worked out this way. Get moving, Wilder."

The tunnel was dark. Brett couldn't see how far into the rock it went. Jack kept a safe distance back, knowing he might jump him. He reminded Brett of a wily coyote.

Two Indian women were ahead, huddled in a corner with a glowing lantern above their heads. One was very young, and glared daggers at him. Della let out a breath. "Marshal Wilder!"

"Far enough, Wilder," Halliday ordered. "This is the end of your road."

Brett felt a sharp blow to the back of his skull. He staggered to one knee, struggling against the darkness, trying to turn toward Halliday when a second blow sent him to the ground.

❧ ❧

The Piutes came with a strange, eerie yelp that sent the blood running cold in those who heard it.

Inside the station, people knocked over their chairs trying to get to their feet. A dog barked frantically and a woman screamed. An Indian swinging his tomahawk came galloping toward a man running for his horse. The Piutes charged, yapping like coyotes. Swiftly the wooden structure was encircled as arrows whizzed. Within minutes the station was blazing.

Not far away, two gunmen, Jessie and Ernie, made a desperate break toward the Carson River, whipping their horses. Several braves headed them off. An Indian fell from Jessie's bullet. Two Piutes waited behind cottonwood trees as they approached, their bow strings taut. Their arrows, dipped in rattlesnake venom, found their mark with deadly accuracy. Jessie fell from his saddle, and Ernie looked back. "That sneakin' Halliday betrayed—" his voice halted when an arrow struck him, and he struggled to ride on as the venom did its gradual but certain work.

The Piutes soon rounded up the horses, and one brave reached for a scalping knife.

❧ ❧

A gust of wind whipped down from the hills, making a moaning sound in the mine. Brett raised himself to an elbow, his skull throbbing. There was a movement outside the entrance. He squinted toward the shaft of sunlight to see the shadow of a woman standing there. She bent low and came toward him.

"Water?" Della knelt before him and handed him a pitcher. "Others are all dead at the station. Burned to the ground. Preacher Samuel is in a bad way. There was rattlesnake poison on the arrow tip."

Brett tried to silence his groan as he thought helplessly of Samuel.

"He's dead?"

"Unconscious. I got most of the snake poison out."

Brett emptied the jug of water, splashing some of it on his face to clear his brain. He pushed himself up from the floor, and leaned against the tunnel wall until the dizziness ebbed.

It dawned on him that the other Indian girl was gone, and that the Piutes had spared him.

"What happened?"

"I told them who you and Samuel were. By then Samuel had already been hit, but they left him alone after that. They understood he was a man of God, that he knows Redbird, that you, too, are a friend. They let you live."

"The other girl?"

"Gone back with them. I told them I would nurse Samuel first. There will be war now. The Pony Express went through here, and the rider saw what happened. They attacked him too. I think he was hit. Soon, all Washoe will be up in arms. They will come against my people. We cannot win. We will have to go back to the mountains of Utah."

War with the Indians…he couldn't think about that now. He felt for his holster. Della noticed and went to a dark corner and brought his gun belt.

"I owe you, Della."

She shook her head firmly. "Friends do not owe."

He looked down at her. "I'm sorry for what happened here with the Williams boys."

"They didn't get me. Only afterward they found me in the rocks, hiding. The other two they treated badly."

"There was only one Indian woman here with you. What happened to the other?"

"She got away later. You must tell Annalee I have done what she said. I believe in Jesus as my Savior and God. He is my Master now. He used me to save you and Samuel. Annalee must know her words to me and my pa were not dead words."

"I'll tell her. She'll be as pleased as I am. Can you take me to Samuel now?"

"He's resting by a tree. He was too heavy for me to move."

Brett picked up his hat and winced as he put it on. He felt the hair at the back of his head. It was matted with dried blood. He followed her from the mine, trying to walk without weaving. He squinted as the afternoon sunlight hurt his eyes.

Della led the way across the hill. Smoke still clung to the air as they neared the charred structure that had been Williams' Station. The wind picked up a man's hat and sent it tumbling through the dust.

"I found five dead. I couldn't stop the raiding party from taking your horses, but they left me a mustang to ride back. You can take him to carry Samuel. You go. The Lord has helped me so far. If the braves come back without Redbird, they will not let you and Samuel go again."

"Come back with us, Della. Annalee would be happy to have you."

She shook her head. "I'll try to teach my people. They should know that Pah-Ah is not God. But the Mighty Christ can do everything good."

"Can you read?"

"Yes."

"Remind me to have Samuel give you his Bible before we go. Annalee's going to be happy you've become a missionary to the Piutes. It was something she wanted to do, but the Lord has called you instead."

Della smiled for the first time, making her pretty. "I am Annalee's spiritual child. Do you think Samuel will give me his Bible?"

"He will. Where did you leave him?"

"Over there." She took him to the tree where she had hidden him with brush. Samuel was now conscious and leaning against the tree trunk. His rugged face brightened when he saw Brett.

"Praise God. Got an arrow in me, but Della's patched me up pretty good. I'll make it."

Brett wasted no time. He checked the wound and saw that she'd done a decent job.

"Della told me what happened with Jack. Sorry, lad. I should've known better." His voice grew husky. "I had hoped he was going to change."

"We're still alive," Brett said with a smile. "What do we have to complain about? But we won't be, if we don't get out of here."

"It's going to be ugly. More will die before it's over. Virginia City's full of hotheads. They'll be screaming for vengeance before they even know the reason behind the raid."

"The Piutes are meeting to form a war party," Della said. "There was talk of an ambush. They'll lure the men from town into the desert near the mouth of the Truckee. There's a narrow, rocky ledge leading to a valley. Tell them to be on guard."

"Close to Pyramid Lake," Samuel said. "Right place for an ambush if that's what they're planning."

"Can you ride?" Brett asked him.

"Just help me up in the saddle."

When Samuel was astride the mustang, Brett looked at Della. "I don't feel comfortable leaving you on foot like this."

"You are on foot too."

"I'll make it."

She smiled. "So will I. I have a feeling a friend will be waiting for me on the way."

They both looked at her.

Again, she smiled. "Redbird's son, a buck…" Her head turned toward the hills, the wind moving her long black hair. "I think he's watching us now."

Brett's eyes scanned the hills. Just then a man on an Indian pony rode into view leading another horse. The horse raised its head, nostrils sniffing the breeze. It neighed. The buck released it. The long-legged zebra dun came galloping toward its master.

The horse nuzzled against Brett, who mounted quickly. He raised a hand toward Redbird's son. The Indian raised a salute in return.

"Let us part with a prayer," Samuel urged.

Della lowered her head as Samuel committed her to the safe-keeping of Christ and to a fruitful life.

Brett turned in the saddle. "Your Bible, Samuel. A parting gift among true friends."

Samuel glanced down at Della. Her dark eyes shone. He smiled and reached into his old frock coat and produced the small black Book.

"To Della. Soon to be daughter-in-law of Redbird. May you use the words herein wisely, lead many to our Savior, and be the godly mother of ten braves who serve the true God."

Della smiled, bowed her head, and took the Bible. She held it against her heart and then looked toward the young man who patiently waited astride his pony on the windblown hill.

"Tell Annalee her name is written on my heart."

Brett and Samuel watched her run ahead as lightly as a doe to the man she loved. Together they disappeared into the barren Nevada hills.

Twenty-Eight

&

The front door flew open. "Annalee!"

Jimmy ran in from outdoors flushed and breathless. His brown eyes were wide and glistening.

"Pa's—Pa's here!" he stammered. "Our Pa is home!"

She sucked in her breath.

"He's in Uncle Samuel's dugout. Hurry! Come on!" Jimmy ran back out, leaving the door wide open.

Annalee rallied from her daze. He was here in Virginia City! Impossible...or was it?

A terrible suspicion ruined the moment. Where were Brett and Samuel?

Annalee rushed out of the cabin into the twilight, purple above Sun Mountain.

Jimmy was running ahead, beckoning her to hurry up. Where was Callie? Did she know?

Annalee entered the dugout and paused. Her father was waiting for her.

"Pa! I brought her," Jimmy cried. "Pa, here's Annalee."

Jack Halliday walked up to her.

Jimmy looked on with eyes shining, waiting.

Annalee stood there. An endless moment passed before she could form the words. Surprisingly, they sounded calm.

"Hello, Father."

His lashes blinked nervously, and then a smile formed on his mouth. His strong, lean fingers took hold of her shoulders giving her a little shake. "Annalee?"

She swallowed and nodded, smiling.

"Well, I'll be!"

How he had changed! Older, thinner, sadder—much sadder. He was still as tan as leather, but now crags showed in his cheeks. He remained a handsome man. His eyes were the same, like hers, tinted jade. A reminiscent smile tugged at his mouth. "By golly, daughter, you're a beautiful young lady. How proud Lilly must've been of you. You make me proud too.

"Pa—"

She was in his arms. He held her tightly, his face buried in her hair, his shoulders shaking. She sobbed as well.

Jimmy sat down on the rug and dropped his head into his trembling palms and covered his face. Soon his hands were wet with warm, salty tears and his nose was running.

She didn't know how many moments had passed before she heard her father murmuring over and over, "What am I going to do…what am I going to do…"

"Pa, did you meet with Brett Wilder and Uncle Samuel at Williams' Station?"

No answer.

"Pa! Word just came of a Piute raid—"

She felt his body tense. He let her go and turned away, digging into his pocket for tobacco and paper. His fingers trembled as he made a smoke, a sight very familiar to her from childhood.

He shook his dark head, a shoulder toward her as he lit the end of his makings. "Nothing I could do, honey, nothing. It was a smoking ruin when I got there. Them Piutes killed everyone. I don't know if Samuel and Wilder were there or not. I was supposed to meet them. But when I saw the smoke, I beat it out of there fast."

Annalee felt faint. She sank into a chair, looking up at him.

He drew quickly on the cigarette. Pacing, he mumbled, "There's something I've got to do. No time to waste." He went over to the peg and put on his leather jacket and hat. His gun belt was already strapped on. He dropped the cigarette and ground it out. He looked up, first at Annalee and then at Jimmy. His jaw set.

"Wait here."

He walked toward the door. She jumped to her feet, as did Jimmy.

"But, Pa!" Jimmy cried.

He looked back. "Too late, son. You stay here."

"But Mama's dead," Jimmy said. "She froze on the Sierras."

His eyes hardened like green stone. "I know. I know, son."

He walked out.

Annalee rushed after him, but he was already mounted and turning to ride down the hillside.

"Where did Pa go?"

Annalee didn't turn at the sound of Jimmy's disappointment. She couldn't bear the pain that would be in his eyes.

"He had to go away for a while, Jimmy."

"Again? But he just came home!"

Something in his voice made her turn sharply and look at him. What she saw pierced her heart. "Oh, Jimmy…" She reached for him, the tears on his face cutting her.

He jerked away, his eyes wide and unexpectedly angry.

"I hate him! I hate Pa!"

"Jimmy—"

"I'll never forgive him, not this time. Never—"

He turned and ran up the hill.

"Come back, Jimmy!"

She tried to go after him, but the way was too steep and he was too fast for her. He ran on until he disappeared into the indigo shadows draping Sun Mountain like a mourning robe. Annalee stood alone, the wind tugging against her, stinging her tearful eyes.

⁓ ⁓

Macklin Villiers was worried as he sat at his desk in the Virginia House. Things weren't going as he'd planned when he'd sent for Hoadly. Naturally he hadn't wanted Hoadly to know who hired him, so Macklin insisted Colefax do it. Colefax could get by with it, he'd told him. "You're a lawyer. No one will ever suspect you. Offer Hoadly big money. I want the best gunfighters he can dig up."

Hoadly had done his job, but he'd made mistakes too. Rick Delance had taken a shine to Callie and was bent on turning a new leaf. He'd never make it, but that wasn't what bothered Macklin now. It was Wilder. He'd outsmarted him by finding that claim paper.

Macklin sat staring coldly at the desk in front of him. To think that missing claim record was with Samuel all that time. He could have had him killed as soon as he'd found out Lilly didn't have it on her when they'd taken the stage from Placerville. All that wasted effort! Sending that blundering fool Big Birdie to search Annalee's baggage was all for nothing. Samuel had it, had given it to Wilder, and Wilder had taken it to Bill Stewart.

There had to be another way to get control of that section of mine Halliday and Harkin had claimed.

Macklin balled his fist and pounded the desktop. He *must* have that silver lode. If he could just get Callie to marry Rody…maybe. There was no use even trying with Annalee. She was taken with Wilder.

Something had to be done about that too. It would be too dangerous having Wilder married to Annalee. He was too smart.

He wrote a brief message to Rody.

"Wilder must be eliminated soon. No later than the next day or two."

He stood and walked briskly from his office into the main room of his suite. He'd reached the door when he remembered, stopping short. That wretched wheelchair was a nuisance. He was sorry now he'd ever decided to appear injured. It had, however, given him a plausible excuse to stay out of sight while still calling the shots.

Those fools, Lazaro and the two other hired guns. Even the three of them together had bungled it! Thanks to Delance. Delance must be gotten rid of eventually. As soon as Wilder was out of the way. A mine explosion could do it. Delance was too quick for Hoadly, and Macklin didn't want to risk Rody. He'd need his nephew in the future to marry Callie.

It would work. It must.

He pulled the cord for a messenger boy and then seated himself in the wheelchair. Within a minute the boy had run up and he'd given him a sealed envelope for Rody. Macklin then returned to his office.

And there was Dylan Harkin too. It didn't fit Macklin's plans to lose control of half the mine to a hothead like Harkin. He'd leave him to Rody. Rody could handle him. Where was Dylan?

Macklin thought of Lilly. It was unfortunate, but she just wouldn't cooperate. She'd caught on to his plans during the stage trip from Placerville. He'd made a mistake by asking too many questions about Jack's papers. He'd tried to make it look as though it were the Pelly-Jessup shares he was interested in.

Macklin moved uneasily in the chair. He looked at himself in the mirror above the desk. He looked worried. He smoothed back his ash blond hair with one palm and straightened his silk cravat.

She had looked him straight in the eye, her face grave.

"You're after Jack's claim, aren't you, Macklin?"

He had insisted she needed to tell him where the official record was, but by then she knew too much. She was the type who wouldn't leave things alone. He hadn't wanted her to die, but she'd left him little choice. He'd hired his own man to drive the stage, a gunfighter he'd known in New Orleans. His man had taken care of the driver working for the Overland Stage back in Placerville as well as arranged Lilly's death to look like a stage accident, then had disappeared on his own, two thousand dollars richer. By now he was in New Orleans again. The blizzard had been luck. Very good luck. He'd faked his injury, rode the horse down the mountain, and then turned it loose. The rest had been easy. He'd staggered into Dayton a sick and delirious man sharing his tale of sorrow and woe.

Then he'd gone into hiding, keeping to his wheelchair. They'd all believed him, even Annalee. He looked into the mirror and saw his rueful smile. She'd been moved by his tale of unrequited love for Lilly. But he had never really loved any woman. He loved power. Money gave him power, and power gave him respect. He was going to become a very respected gentleman in Virginia City.

He picked up his writing pen to send a letter to Bill Stewart contesting the Halliday-Harkin mine claim. He was continuing to insist that it was Pelly-Jessup land that they'd claim jumped.

Stewart was already meeting with Colefax to talk the matter over. Yes, things were going to work out.

As he started to write he heard a noise in the other room. He turned his head. Had he locked the door? Was the messenger boy back? The upstart! He dared to walk in on Macklin Villiers?

❧ ❧

In the cabin Annalee paced, hearing the wind blowing rock granules across the roof. It was dark, and her father hadn't returned yet.

Jimmy came quietly through the door, refusing to look at her. He tried to steal past her, but she took his arm gently.

"I understand why you're hurting, Jimmy. I'm sorry."

"It's okay. I'm okay now."

"Keeper's been looking for you. I think she's hungry. Why don't you feed her something? She needs you, you know. So do I, Jimmy."

He nodded, but he said nothing and went into the next room. A few minutes later he came back holding Keeper in his arms.

"Uncle Samuel once said I can stay for as long as I want. Even until I grow up."

"Yes, sure you can. He loves you. We all do." She changed the subject. "I made your favorite cornbread with bacon pieces. It's still warm on the stove. Hungry?"

"I don't know..." he put a small hand against his tummy. "Maybe, once I start eating. It's like that sometimes. When are Uncle Samuel and Brett coming back?"

Annalee's anxiety increased, but she held it in. "Maybe tomorrow. I'll get your supper. Then I think I'll go into town and look around a little. Maybe I'll see Callie. I'll tell her Pa's back."

He said nothing and sat down to nibble at his meal. While he did, she found her cape, and putting it around her shoulders stepped outside into the windy night.

Brett should come walking up the hill now. It would be perfect...she would run to him. He would enfold her in his arms.

Nothing moved on the slope but a gust of wind stirring the dust. She turned her face and held her breath until it passed. She remembered the many times he'd come to her aid. Always strong, his calm acceptance of danger balanced with unmovable trust in the Scriptures.

At this moment, when the night seemed restless with the threat of danger, she had a tremendous longing for Brett. His strength and faith always helped feed her own.

A partial moon was rising like a sliver of silver above the mountain. On the slope, campfires glowed like candles near the dugouts. The lights of Virginia City shone from hundreds of yellow lanterns. She walked down the footpath along the slope that brought her to C Street.

She wandered up and down the boardwalk but didn't see her father. Then she went down B Street. He must have ridden out to Gold Canyon to the mine and cabin.

She walked back to C Street and stood outside the Delta Saloon glancing through the door. It was filled with men drinking and gambling. Her eyes sought her father's face, but in the press she couldn't pick him out.

"Lookin' for somebody, miss?" She looked into the face of a gnarled man who rolled his cigar to the other side of his mouth.

"My father," she said calmly.

"What's his name?"

Each time she told someone Jack Halliday was back, she was doubling the chances the news might reach Dylan Harkin.

"Jack Halliday."

The big man stepped inside and his voice boomed, "Anyone seen Halliday?"

"Who's askin?"

"His daughter."

"He left."

The gnarled man turned back to look at her. "You heard. He's taken off."

"Thank you."

She turned away and walked down the boardwalk. As she did so, another man stepped out of the Delta Saloon and looked after her. Hoadly's cold shrewd eyes followed her before he turned away and walked quickly in the other direction.

Annalee looked back in time to see him enter the Bucket.

She couldn't go wandering through thirty saloons asking for Jack Halliday. She may have already made a mistake. She'd better find Callie at the Virginia House and tell her their father was in town.

At the hotel, the clerk told her Callie had gone out earlier in a carriage with Mr. Barkly, but that both were expected back for their dinner reservation at eight. Was there a message?

"I'll call again later, thank you."

Outside Virginia House she stood, uncertain, thinking. The lights of Virginia City burned brightly. The piano music carried, echoing on the wind.

She climbed up the slope to the rock where she often went to sit and sketch. She sat down to rest and pray.

Her eyes scanned the flickering campfires around the mining areas, and while she could see little, her mind visualized a hundred Indian fires on the hills, sending out war signals as a chant danced through the night.

She bowed her head and closed her eyes, the wind ruffling her auburn hair. The Lord was sovereign. He knew the end from the beginning. "Trust in the LORD with all thine heart; and lean not unto thine own understanding."

She would not listen to disturbing fears that were pressing upon her mind and demanding entrance. Instead, she prayed for wisdom and strength.

❧ ❧

"Annalee!"

An hour must have slipped by. She turned her head to look toward her uncle's dugout. Jimmy came running.

He stopped, cupped his mouth, and hollered, "They're back! Uncle Samuel and Brett! They rode in a few minutes ago. I've been looking for you."

She rose quickly, her heart leaping, and hurried toward him. They were safe! *Thank You, God.*

"Uncle Samuel's been wounded, but he's all right. Brett went into town. Said he'd be back."

"Wounded!" she quickened her pace beside Jimmy.

"By a Piute! They were at Williams' Station by the Carson River when the attack happened. It was an Indian raiding party. Wait till Uncle Samuel tells us all about it!"

When she reached Samuel inside the dugout, he was in bed drinking hot broth with some of his notorious dried herbs sprinkled on top. "Strong enough to chase even a rattler's venom away."

"Uncle Samuel!" She dropped beside him. "Thank God you're back safe. I've been so worried."

His strong arm hugging her shoulder was comforting. "Take's more than an arrow to do me in, lass."

"Did Jimmy tell you and Brett? Pa headed toward town."

"I know." He sighed. "I'm afraid he's still got plans to lay hold of that mine."

"We've got to stop him. I thought I might have seen Dylan Harkin in town an hour ago. There was another man too. He left the Delta and went to the Bucket. Uncle, I'm afraid. Brett can't face them all down. I've got to see him."

"You stay put, lass. When Brett means to find you again, he will. Jack won't listen to sensible truth, and I don't see him changing. We've got to understand that."

"You saw him, then? You talked to him?"

"Well…" His eyes were troubled. He sipped his steaming broth.

She searched his face. What was he hiding?

"But Pa said he hadn't seen either of you."

"Jack has a smooth tongue when it suits him. He was waiting for us at Williams' Station with two gunslingers from Salt Lake."

"Then…it was an ambush? Oh, Uncle Samuel, no!"

"It was a trap, just like Wilder thought it might be. I almost got us both killed by insisting on going there. We walked right into it."

"I don't understand. I thought the Piutes attacked the station."

"They did, and that attack fit well into Jack's plans. He didn't need to do anything but leave us there and hope the Indians scalped us both."

The idea her father could do such a thing left her reeling with confusion.

"He's a bitter man, Jack. Worse than I remember. I think Lilly's death hit him hard." She listened as he told her what happened when they arrived at the station.

The one gleam of light in the otherwise dark saga was Della. "You say she's safe now? She's not hurt?"

"She's more than all right. We have blessings to thank our Lord for too, don't we? All's not loss. He sends us sunshine along with clouds. She's accepted the Savior."

Annalee felt an ember of warmth come to life in her otherwise cold heart. Della had come to believe.

"Frail and sick as you were, Annalee, God used you to do what I couldn't all these past years. You see? God can use any vessel that's yielded to Him. His strength is perfected in our weaknesses."

He smiled at her and patted her hand. "Why, she's even got my Bible and intends to be a missionary to her own people. I'm sure the Lord has good plans for Della."

The news brought some comfort. Like the hundreds of campfires on Sun Mountain, hope bloomed in the darkest of times.

"There's something else you should know, Uncle Samuel. Jimmy loves you like a father. So do I, and I know Callie loves you. I thank God for you." She leaned over and kissed his cheek. "Thank you for choosing to be a godly man. You brought us to the Lord. Mama too. I have the Bible you gave her at Sutter's Mill so long ago. She was anxious to see you again. Before she left Sacramento, she said she would be one of your most loyal members at church.

"Jimmy wants to stay with you when I go away for medical treatment. I've decided to go. That is, if Brett hasn't changed his mind."

"He hasn't." His eyes twinkled. "And I wasn't about to let that little boy slip through my fingers. Don't you think I'm wise enough to see a future preacher when the lad stands before me?"

"Then it's settled? No matter what happens?"

He squeezed her hand. "No matter what happens."

She smiled and stood. "You'd best get some sleep now."

"First, get me Jimmy. He and I need to do some talking about a lot of things."

"Yes. I'll call him."

Twenty-Nine

$\mathscr{A}$nnalee was back in the cabin—alone. Jimmy was staying the night with Samuel, and she was missing Callie. The cabin wasn't the same since she'd left it. She went to the mirror again and checked her sweep of curls. Then she smoothed her green organdy dress with the princess collar.

Why didn't Brett come? Had he ridden out to the mine? Her father might be there…and what about Dylan Harkin?

Who was that man she'd seen leaving the Delta Saloon earlier?

She could ride out to the Gold Canyon cabin to see if her father and Brett were there, hoping to stop any showdown between them, but she didn't dare, not with the Indian scare.

The news about the attack on Williams' Station had alarmed most everyone in town. There was talk of forming a company and riding out to fight the Piutes. Samuel had said that Brett was informing the leaders in town of a possible trap waiting for them at Pyramid Lake. Whether they would pay any heed was another matter. There were plenty of hotheads demanding swift action.

She went outside to look toward town, and then she saw Elmo coming up the slope leading Jenny. It appeared as though he'd been out of town. She walked partway down the footpath to meet him.

"Evening, Elmo."

"Miss Annalee. I heard 'bout Samuel. How is he?"

"Better. I think Della got most of that snake poison out of his wound, but he's weak. He's asleep now. Jimmy's staying with him."

He tugged at his beard and glanced back over his shoulder down the hill. "Heard Jack Halliday rode in earlier today. Seen your pa?"

339

She found herself tensing. "Not since he left Samuel's dugout. Why? Have you seen him tonight?"

"Can't say as I have. But them fellers in pay to Hoadly who've been keeping to themselves recently have all shown up in town sudden like. Seen Hoadly, the younger Harkin, and that fancy fella, Rody Villiers. There's one or two other mean ones too. They're keeping mighty quiet in the shadows. Ain't a one of 'em drinkin', not even Hoadly. That tells me big trouble's expected soon. Don't like it at all. I jes' got back from the diggings belongin' to Wilder, Harper, an' Delance. Harper's away with his mule train, but I tol' Delance how Wilder's alone in town. Think I'll bring my Winchester and mosey on along just to see what I can see."

Annalee's heart was racing. "Where's Mr. Wilder now, do you know?"

"At the new hotel down the street from the Virginia House. Fancy new place."

"Thanks, Elmo." She gathered up her skirts and went past him.

"You be careful," he called. "Wilder's not goin' to like you bein' there tonight."

↝ ℘↜

Night fell across Virginia City. Brett stepped from the hotel. His gaze missed nothing as he surveyed the street. He studied the Virginia House.

He'd heard that Hoadly and his hired guns were looking for him as well as Jack Halliday. Word traveled quickly. Dylan, too, was looking for Halliday. Brett had no doubts about the younger Harkin. He was nervous and hot tempered like so many of the infamous gunfighters of the day. They used fists and guns first, and reason last. He would need to stop Dylan, if he could. Then he must arrest Jack Halliday.

Arrest him. He was kidding himself, and he knew it. He kept putting off the thought that he may need to use his gun. How could he become the man who fired upon Annalee's father, deputized or not? He could understand how she felt. No matter what, he was still her father. He'd thought many times that this was the worse job he'd ever taken. There'd been moments when he'd almost wired Governor Downey to send someone else.

He stood on the street thinking, feeling the wind in his hair. Down the street near the Delta saloon a brawl had broken out. Not even the threat of the Piutes had sobered many of them for long. News had been sent him from a friendly tavern keeper that Hoadly was staying away from whiskey. The meaning was clear.

He put his hat on and automatically moved his jacket aside to try his belt and gun position.

Someone came hurrying down the boardwalk from the direction of Sun Mountain. He looked up to see Annalee, who paused and then continued toward him.

She was like a delicate fresh breeze on a summer morning upon the veranda of a fine Southern mansion. Her dress, the set of auburn hair—beautiful. He didn't need words from her to interpret the way she looked at him, thinking she showed nothing of her feelings when all the time he could read her as easily as print.

The timing couldn't be worse.

Brett's jaw set. He stopped.

❧ ❧

Annalee paused again when she saw the steady gaze of his clear gray eyes. She lifted her chin and walked straight toward him.

"What are you doing here now?"

She felt no inclination to pretend. She walked up, meeting his gaze directly.

"I grew impatient waiting for you to show up."

His gaze drifted over her. "This isn't exactly a night to sit in the moonlight and hold hands."

"I don't recall ever sitting in the moonlight holding your hand."

"No…because when we do, I intend to get straight to the point of what moonlight is all about. No use playing games until you intend to win or know you really want to."

He'd not only accepted her challenge, but doubled it.

"I'm sorry I had to make you wait, Annalee, but we can't talk now. What I want to say to you has to come later. There's something I must do."

Annalee noticed that he kept glancing about. He looked calm, almost careless, but she sensed he was alert. She knew what he had to do, and that knowledge made her shaky in the knees. "Brett, you can't face down three or four gunfighters! Elmo says they're all here in town waiting for you."

"Honey, wait in my room," he said quietly.

"What?" she breathed.

"My room. You'll be comfortable there."

Her brow lifted. "People will talk."

Brett, with another glance down the street toward the Delta and Bucket of Blood, took her arm and drew her into the hotel lobby.

"Everyone in Virginia City knows you and Samuel. There'll be no talk." He walked with her across the soft red carpet toward a fine stairway with a polished banister.

When she still hesitated as they went up the stairs, he looked at her with a faint smile.

"Fear not, fair damsel, your reputation is perfectly safe. I can't stay. Besides, if I lock you in, I won't need to worry about you showing up where you shouldn't for the next few hours. Maybe I'll take another room and leave you there till morning."

She stopped midway up the stairs and looked at him indignantly. "You wouldn't dare."

"I'll let you decide that," he said silkily. "I'm looking forward to taking you up on your dares."

Somehow Annalee found herself standing in the open doorway of a very fine room with a carpet, a plate-glass mirror, and rich crockery, all hauled over the Sierras in mule-drawn freighters. It was enough to take her breath away.

"Like it?"

Her eyes met his reluctantly in the mirror and saw them teasing her, but his voice was serious.

"Sometimes I think you're a tempter."

"Because I want to do something nice for you?"

What could she say to that? Her eyes went to the bed. Goose down! What a night's sleep—

She turned and started out. "I must help Uncle Samuel—"

He blocked her way. She stared at his chest. "Don't you know better than to fib? Jimmy's staying with him. I keep up with details, dear."

He took her shoulders, gently guided her back into the room, and then he shut the door behind him.

Their eyes met. He wasn't smiling any longer and there was no familiar teasing glint in his gaze. She tried to ignore the heady feeling his nearness gave her.

"I've heard from my father. He's at my place in Grass Valley. He'll be staying for the summer. Your presence is requested at the Wilder Ranch. I think you'll like it."

His ranch. Requested? What was he saying?

"You'll fit in 'mighty well,' as they say. My father will compliment my good taste when we show up together."

Her heart slowed and then raced. His meaning was growing more obvious.

"I want to buy you some beautiful dresses with bonnets to match, and one with one of those preposterous feathers sticking out. I can't wait to see you looking like a princess. And when my father opens up that sanitarium in the desert, we'll go there and stay until you're strong again. You can paint and sketch all you want."

She shook her head, bewildered, thinking she understood what he meant and hoping she was right, but she was afraid she'd misread his intent.

"Brett...what are you saying?"

"Honey, you know what I'm saying. I just don't have time to say it the way I want to."

Annalee wanted to melt under that gaze.

Then he said slowly, "All right, I'd better say it now. If anything goes wrong tonight I don't want you to ever wonder if you'd misunderstood me."

"Nothing must go wrong!" She took a step toward him.

"This is a terrible moment—but I intend to marry you, Annalee. That is, I'm asking you to marry me."

There they were…some of the most cherished words in the world, and Brett Wilder was speaking them to her with a depth to his voice that took her breath away.

"You must know by now how much I love you," he said. "Do you think I'd have stayed with you all these months since Strawberry if I didn't? Fact is, I can't concentrate on much else." He smiled ruefully. "And that's a dangerous situation for me to be in, especially tonight."

She held back the desire to throw her arms around him. Brett was actually going to belong to her. Her eyes swept his formidable figure, handsome, poised, and perfectly confident in the Lord. She almost laughed at the gift dropped into her lap from heaven. And she had thought the Lord had forgotten her. She had thought the Lord deemed her unworthy of Gordon Barkly—

Gordon. She knew she'd never loved him. She hadn't even known what true love was until recently. There'd been an attraction to Gordon, but even that had been for a man who hadn't really existed. The real Gordon Barkly left her cold. But Brett Wilder…he lit a thousand candles in her soul.

Her heart sprouted wings, and for a moment she thought they would bear her away into giddy delight. Brett was in love with her.

He folded his arms and sighed. "Well, I can see we're going to be very casual about this whole thing. This is a great night, Annalee. I'm in the middle of stopping a gunfight, arresting your father, and asking you to marry me. It's all coming together very nicely, isn't it? After all, it's not every night I'm privileged to ask a beautiful woman to be my wife and still make sure my gun comes out of the holster like silk." He tested it. "Works fine." He smiled and glanced down at her. "I don't suppose you could ease my frustration just a little and say yes or I'll think about it, or even a flat out no?"

"I don't think this moment is a bit funny."

"I don't either."

"I always dreamed of being proposed to in moonlight, with blossoms, and nothing to disturb the enchantment."

"Just say yes, honey, and I'll make it up to you later."

"Yes! Oh, yes!"

He swept her into his strong embrace. Her heart thundered in her ears. "I love you," he whispered.

He bent toward her, but she reluctantly stopped him. "My illness. You can't kiss me, Brett. I'm not well yet—"

"I'll be the doctor, and I know what's best for my patient." He bent toward her again, and their lips met and clung together. His arms tightened around her longingly, protectively.

The roaring in her ears made her dizzy. Her eyes came back to his. "I couldn't love anyone else the way I do you." She melted into his arms.

"Gordon?"

"Don't remember him…"

"The name's Brett. I want it branded on your heart the way Annalee has already been branded on mine."

"That happened a long time ago, when you introduced yourself outside Berry's Flat—"

His lips touched hers again. She clung to him as though she had entered an exhilarating new world. He came away, steadied her, and then backed toward the door, unbolting it. He glanced down the hall. "I've still got lots to say."

She was still thinking of his kiss.

"I'll see you in the morning."

"Morning. Wait—"

His smile was disarming. She rushed to reach the door before he shut it, but she wasn't quick enough. She heard the outside key turn in the lock.

"Brett!" Annalee rattled the ornate knob. Locked!

"Brett Wilder! Let me out of here!"

She heard his steps fade away down the hall. Exasperated, she sank against the door.

Thirty

*B*rett walked slowly down C Street. He heard a voice call his name. Alert, he stepped to the side. Hoadly?

It was Rick Delance.

The handsome young man had taken off his mining clothes and was dressed in his poncho and leather jerkins. His six-shooters were tied down.

"Thought you might be feeling a little lonely tonight and could use some company."

Now it was two against—how many? There could be five, even six. So much depended on going after the brains behind the hired gunfighters. That meant Macklin. Hoadly would be next. The others might slip away into the night once they saw that their paymaster was soon to be buried on Boot Hill. But Jack Halliday was a different matter, as was Dylan Harkin.

"Delance, raise your right hand."

The dark eyes narrowed. "What's that?"

"Raise your right hand and repeat after me. I'm going to deputize you."

Delance stared at him, looking stunned. Brett knew the trust he'd placed in him since that first meeting at Berry's Flat had made an impression on Delance for good. Delance had a long way to go, but he was on the right path.

Rick Delance raised his right hand and repeated the simple but profound words. Then he said, "Dylan's promising vengeance. He's at the Delta now. He isn't helping himself any. He's been gambling all evening, boastin' about a silver bonanza out at Gold Canyon. He's got the place worked up. Word has it Halliday's on his way aimin' to fill him full of lead."

346

"That could be a ruse. I don't think Halliday's looking for Dylan. He mentioned trying to make peace with him."

"Hoadly's pushing a story trying to turn them against each other so he and his guns can fix on you and Halliday."

"I've a feeling—call it what you will—but I'm not buying all this about the Delta." Brett looked farther down the street toward Lynch's Tavern. "I think Hoadly's hanging out down there just waiting for me and Halliday to go to the Delta."

"Could be. I ran into Elmo. That old codger is mighty good with a Winchester. He's across the street on the roof of Wells Fargo."

Brett looked across the narrow street and above the building. He couldn't see Elmo, but he was sure he was there.

"I'll go to Lynch's alone, Delance. This one's between me and Hoadly. I've been tracking him a long time. Besides shooting Frank in the back, there's that ugly business at Sutter's gold field."

Delance nodded and stepped back into the shadows out of sight. He kept his eyes open while Brett walked toward Lynch's.

❧ ❧

Inside Lynch's Tavern, Hoadly waited. He had a man out watching the hotel where Wilder was staying. He'd already gotten the word that he'd left the hotel and was walking toward the Delta as Hoadly planned. He knew Dylan was fired up on whiskey and temper, so he'd call Wilder out if he walked inside.

Hoadly was chuckling to himself. Wilder was too fast for Frank's kid brother, which meant he would be buried tonight on Boot Hill right next to Frank. Nice sentimental touch. Dylan would never learn it wasn't Halliday who killed his brother, but Hoadly himself.

Once Dylan was dead, Hoadly intended to make his own move on Wilder, but not fair 'n' square. He wouldn't win that way, and a man had to win anyway he could. So he had a man with a rifle on the roof across from Lynch's. All Hoadly needed to do was play along. He'd step into the street and face Wilder. It would happen so quickly it would look as if he'd out gunned him. In the dark nobody would much notice. An' once Wilder dropped, it wouldn't matter what anybody thought. They'd keep quiet or wish they had.

His chuckle died. Delance was the snake in his garden, and that no-good snake had turned on him. Told him to keep his blood money and keep outta his way. Then he'd turned his back on him to team up with Flint Harper. Wilder, Harper, and Delance had themselves a claim somewhere nearby.

Delance. Hoadly worried about Delance. He should never have sent for that sidewinder. Shoulda left him in Tombstone.

Hoadly was craving a drink, but he wasn't crazy. Afterward. After that two-bit Wilder was full of lead, then he'd have him a whole bottle to celebrate.

Someone entered Lynch's. Hoadly looked cautiously to the door. It was that sleek kid Hoadly didn't take to, Rody Villiers.

Young Villiers brushed past the tables crowded with poker players and came up to Hoadly's table in the back. He pulled out a chair and sat down. His lean fingers flexed nervously.

Hoadly didn't think much of him, but he was fast. He looked like his uncle, Macklin Villiers. Hoadly knew now it was Macklin he worked for.

There was a mocking look in Villiers' eyes. A smirk on his lips. Hoadly knew the dislike was mutual.

"It's Wilder. Delance is with him."

Hoadly glanced toward the window beside his table. It was dark out there, and he couldn't see too much, but he could see the Delta's lights.

"Delance," Rody breathed. "I knew that Yankee couldn't be trusted. I don't like him at all. Makes me mighty uneasy."

"Delance is yours. Take him."

"That's what I was hoping you'd say, 'Boss.'" Villiers' cold eyes flickered with scorn. "But you're in a mite of trouble yourself. You might need me here. Wilder isn't headed for the Delta to face down Dylan. Somebody told him you was here. Wonder who?" Rody Villiers' icy gaze swept the room. "Things ain't goin' as you planned, Hoadly."

"You think I'm scared or something?" Hoadly stood, pushing back his chair. "Then it'll be now. I don't need you here. You get out there on the street and take down Delance."

Rody Villiers stood, still wearing that nasty little smile. "Sure, Boss. You all be careful now. When this here is all over and done, you and me are going to have a little confab with Uncle Macklin."

Hoadly guessed that Macklin would give his nephew what he wanted. He'd turn the running of things over to Rody. Macklin was going to turn respectable. Macklin would want someone sleek 'n' fancy for the future. It all had to do with Halliday's daughter, the feisty one with the dark hair and blue eyes. He intended Rody to marry her and gain more of the mine.

The other daughter was another matter. She belonged to Wilder. Everyone knew that. But Wilder would be taken away from her tonight. His friends would be carrying the dept'y marshal out to Boot Hill. He chuckled with anticipation.

❧ ❦ ❧

Brett Wilder waited on the boardwalk directly across from Lynch's. Hoadly came through the saloon door and paused on the walk. Then he stepped down.

"Well, Wilder? What d'ya waitin' for?" He stood feet apart, arms slightly extended beside his holsters.

Brett's gaze moved up to the roof. He hoped old Elmo had a steady hand tonight beneath the silver moonlight.

Brett stepped from the shadows across the street and down from the boardwalk. He walked a few feet forward and stopped.

"You're under arrest, Hoadly, for the murder of Frank Harkin. It didn't take much courage to shoot him in the back, did it?"

"You want'a take me, Marshal? You just try it."

A single rifle shot split the night. A rifle slid down the roof across from Lynch's Saloon and fell to the street.

Hoadly froze. He sent a nervous glance toward the roof from where the rifle had fallen and then quickly fixed his eyes on Wilder.

"You're under arrest, Hoadly. Don't draw or you're dead."

Hoadly went for his pistol.

Brett palmed his .45, firing.

Hoadly jerked back, his gun slipping from his hand. He slumped to his knees and then clawed for his pistol. He clutched it, hand shaking, and raised his head, hate scrawled across his face.

Brett kicked his hand and the pistol spun out of reach.

"Should have listened to me, Hoadly."

"Go to…" his eyes widened in unexpected terror. He slumped forward onto the street.

Brett glanced toward Lynch's, but no one came out. He looked soberly at Hoadly.

Up on the roof Elmo peered over, Winchester in both hands. He shook his grizzled head sadly.

"Ne'r seen it end much different, Marshal," he called down. "Them snakes will curse God an' man to their last dyin' breath."

⚘ 9 ⚘

In the Virginia House, Macklin Villiers had just finished addressing his letter to Bill Stewart when he heard a door open softly.

He waited a moment. If it were the messenger boy he'd have spoken by now.

Suddenly he was pleased he was seated in the wheelchair with the cover over his knees. He reached under the blanket and felt for his .36 caliber Remington. It was there. He always kept one out of sight. He held it on his lap, ready.

"Who's there?"

Footsteps walked across the floor, but no one answered.

Macklin wheeled into the main room and glanced about slowly. The red drape moved and someone stepped away from the window facing C Street.

Jack Halliday was smiling, his green eyes glittering. "Hello, Cousin Macklin."

Halliday!

Jack smiled again, an unpleasant look in his eyes. "Why, I must have startled you. You look a little pale." He came slowly out from behind the divan in front of the window. "Aren't you glad to see me, cousin?"

Macklin recovered. *What is he doing here? How did he get past Rody? Rody is supposed to be guarding the lobby.*

Macklin forced a smile. "Yes…yes, by all means, Jack. Glad to see you. Sorry about that ridiculous misunderstanding about Frank. It was Colefax, you know. Colefax got some of the men riled up, and before I could talk sense to them they resorted to mob rule."

"Sure, Mac, I understand. I understand everything now."

What does he mean? He can't know about Lilly—

"Have a drink, Jack. Help yourself. Good scotch sent over from San Francisco. When did you get into Virginia City?"

"No drinking now, Mac. Surprised to see me, huh? I thought you would be. All the action's happening down on the street. Seems everyone forgot about you up here all alone."

Macklin was sweating now. That smile…

"What's the matter, Mac? Not feeling too good? Why don't you get up outta that wheelchair and stretch your legs? Make you feel better. Surprised your pals didn't warn ya? Hoadly and the rest of those scummy pals of yours? They're mighty busy right now facing down Wilder and Delance. No one suspected I'd come straight here. They thought I'd be down at the Delta drinking and gambling. You thought Hoadly or that cold-blooded nephew of yours would kill me in the street while you hid. It's not going to work that way, Mac."

Macklin's eyes saw the gun in Jack's hand for the first time. His mouth went dry. Even if he raised the .38 on his lap and shot through the cover, Jack might still be able to shoot point-blank. He had to get out of this alive, some way—

"Jack! There's no need for this, no need at all. The money! The mine, it's yours! We can make a deal."

"You think it's the mine and Frank Harkin that brought me here? Oh, I'll admit it was that at first. You had Hoadly kill Frank and then hoped to have me lynched. But it's much more than the mine now, Mac. Much more." Jack Halliday's eyes narrowed into slits of green fire. "I'm here because of Lilly. What you did to her—

a woman too good for either of us. You killed her. You left her to freeze to silence her. Oh, I know you, Mac."

"No, it was an accident. Just ask Annalee, she believes me, she'll tell you. Listen, Jack, this is all a mistake."

"Annalee believed you 'cause she's a good girl. She's so innocent she wouldn't think you're such a cold-blooded killer. As for the mine, you'll never have it. And you'll die because of Lilly!"

"Jack—wait—"

Jack lifted his Colt .45, determination in his eyes.

Macklin jerked his hand and fired his .38, striking Jack. With bared teeth Jack squeezed off a shot that struck Macklin. Jack fired again before slipping to the floor.

They were both dead when the door burst open and people rushed into the room.

One of those who'd heard the gunshots was Callie. She was leaving her room to go downstairs to meet Gordon for dinner. Realizing the shots had come down the hall from Macklin's room, she'd shouted for help along with others. She came with the hotel clerk and Gordon as they rushed into the room.

Her hands flew to her mouth as she stood in the open doorway. Macklin was dead, slumped over in the wheelchair. Another dead man was on the floor—her father. As the confusion mounted, she walked numbly to where Jack Halliday lay and dropped slowly to her knees, her new blue satin skirts rustling over crisp crinolines. Dazed, she stared down at him, sick of heart.

Seeing him again for the first time in several years didn't lessen the shock or grief of looking upon the man who'd been her father.

Tears spilled from her eyes and coursed down her cheeks. Her fingers shook as they rested on his shoulder. Hesitantly she smoothed his dark hair into place.

I'm sorry, Pa...so very, very sorry it turned out this way...so sorry....

⤞ ⤝

Rick Delance heard the shooting at the Virginia House and, guessing what may have happened, ran in that direction. He arrived to see a small group gathered outside the hotel. Callie Halliday was with Gordon Barkly. It looked as if Barkly were trying to lead her off to a buggy, but someone barged between them, demanding answers.

Delance stopped in the middle of the street, listening. It was Rody Villiers.

"I *said* I want to know what happened up there. You'll tell me—" he pushed Gordon Barkly aside contemptuously and took firm hold of Callie's arm, giving her an impatient shake. She drew back and slapped him. Rody slapped her back, hard.

"Villiers!"

Rody, eyes blazing wildly, jerked around. He knew that voice. He saw Rick Delance standing in the street.

Delance called, "I hear you're looking for me, Rody. Well, here I am. I'm not one to disappoint a man who brags about his reputation with a gun and who's cowardly enough to strike a lady."

Rody pushed away from the carriage and entered the street. "I'm going to kill you, Yankee."

"Sorry. I got big plans ahead. No cheating gambler from New Orleans is going to ruin them."

Rody palmed his gun—

Delance got off two shots, firing at Rody's gun hand.

Rody dropped his pistol and spun, grabbing his hand. He began to holler and stamp his feet like a child having a tantrum.

Delance walked up. His dark eyes were fixed on Rody. Delance grabbed the front of Rody's ruffled white shirt and slapped him hard across the face several times. When he'd finished he hauled Rody over to a watering trough and pushed him in.

"You need a little cooling off, Rody boy. Need some growing up, some manners to learn."

Sputtering, cursing, and crying in his humiliation, Rody sat in the water, and looked at his smashed gun hand. "It's ruined. I'll never use it again."

"Good. Now you can learn a new trade. Stay out of my sight, Rody. Next time I won't be as generous."

All was quiet and then a few bystanders chuckled.

Delance picked up Rody's pistol from the dirt and shoved it in the back of his belt. He turned away, starting to leave, and then he looked over at Callie.

She was staring at him.

"You all right?" he called.

She touched her cut lip and then nodded.

Delance looked meaningfully at the sullen Gordon Barkly, who turned his shoulder toward him.

"I keep tellin' you, Miss Halliday, you need a better bodyguard."

Delance turned away and walked back down the street to where his horse waited. He mounted easily, held the reins, and circled in the street back toward the buggy. Gordon had helped Callie into the seat. Delance looked down at her.

She tore her eyes from his and straightened her hat, tied beneath her dimpled chin. She glanced sideways at him as Gordon flipped the buggy whip and the horse lurched forward.

Delance wore a smile as he caught her side glance. He tipped his hat before riding out of town toward his diggings.

~≈ ≈~

Brett had heard about the showdown between Jack Halliday and Macklin Villiers. Rody Villiers was seeking medical care for his shattered wrist. His pride, too, had been busted. He'd be anxious to get out of Virginia City now that Macklin was dead and his reputation was in shreds.

That left Dylan Harkin. But when Brett had walked down to the Delta, Dylan was gone.

"He took off like a fire were lit under his breeches, Marshal, once he heard how things turned out," said the bartender. "Don't think you'll be seein' him for a long while. Maybe by then he'll cool down enough to know it was Hoadly who killed Frank."

Brett hoped so. He wanted no further trouble with Dylan. Once the legal matters were finally worked out by Bill Stewart, half of the mine would belong to him. Maybe he'd wise up enough to realize he could settle down as a wealthy young man and straighten his life out. It was a thought.

Brett left the Delta and walked back to the hotel where Annalee waited. He removed his black flat-crowned hat and ran his fingers through his hair. He glanced up at the sky. Gleaming stars sprinkled the blackness. Behind Sun Mountain the silvery moon was climbing higher.

From up the street he heard piano music.

He entered the hotel and walked to the desk.

"Good evening, Marshal," the clerk said. "Happy to see you looking well."

"So am I. I'd like a second room for the night."

"Sir?"

"Miss Halliday is asleep in my room. I don't want to awaken her. She's not well."

"Oh. Yes, I see, of course."

Brett paid. "Have some coffee sent up, will you?"

"Sure thing, Marshal."

Brett took the stairs slowly to his new room.

He sank into a chair and begin to think about the future. With God's help, his father would know how to treat Annalee. She would get well. Jimmy could come and visit the ranch at Grass Valley anytime he wanted, and he would work with Samuel to see that the boy had good schooling, so he could be all God intended. As for Annalee's younger sister, he'd bet Callie had some hard lessons to learn in the future.

She had a heart for the stage, and no one was going to change her mind. It would take someone stronger than even Samuel to tame that girl.

He got up from the chair and walked to the open window, moving the curtain aside to look down on the town. Let Virginia City take care of the Piutes, its business with mining ore, and fighting over claims. He was through with his commission for Governor Downey and was going back to ranching. It was time for him and Annalee to move on, to walk to the beat of a different drummer. He was leaving Virginia City as soon as possible…and he was taking his future bride with him.

He drank a cup of coffee, and then he decided that Annalee probably wasn't asleep either. Even if she was, he had to awaken her. He couldn't bear being alone without her. He wanted to talk and plan and make her happy. She'd had enough sorrow in life.

He set his cup down. What was the matter with him? He opened the door and went out into the hall.

A moment later he stood in front of her room and listened. There was no sound. He took the key out of his pocket—did he dare?

He dared. The door opened.

The light was on.

Annalee was by the window. She turned at once, her heart in her eyes, but also her dismay. He sighed to himself. He had to tell her about her father and Macklin.

He stepped in and shut the door. He walked toward her and she rushed into his arms.

⪦ ⪧

Annalee held him, and by Brett's sober expression she knew, and she waited.

They looked at each other for a long moment and then she said, "It's over, Brett?"

"It's over, honey."

She swallowed. "You?"

"No. Macklin."

"Macklin!"

"Jack went to the Virginia House to confront him. They're both gone."

She leaned her head against his chest, eyes closed. He held her, comforting her. Her tears were for the Jack Halliday she remembered as a child.

"Honey, everything's going to be all right now. It's time to forget the past and move on. We're leaving Virginia City. We're going home to the ranch."

Annalee looked up at him, her tears quieted now.

"I'd like to leave in the morning if that suits you."

"You're sure your father won't mind a Halliday for a daughter-in-law?"

"One glimpse of those green eyes and he'll fall head over heels in love. I think you'll love him too. He's a special kind of man, Annalee. One God has used. A man He will yet use. You'll soon have the best opportunity of getting well."

Her eyes searched his. "Do you think so, Brett? Will it turn out well? Our life, our marriage?"

He smiled. "When two people are committed to Him and to each other, they have everything going for them."

"I think I'm going to love you too much."

"You can never love me too much," he drew her closely to him. "I won't be satisfied with anything less than all your love."

She rested her cheek against his chest. "Brett?" her voice was quiet. "Suppose I don't get well?"

He, too, was quiet for a moment.

"Whatever happens, Annalee, I could never love you less than I do now. We're going to be happy, you and I. We're going to live out each day to its fullest, for however long God gives us."

"And leave our future to Him," she agreed. "He knows the end from the beginning. I read a wonderful verse earlier tonight. I was praying about everything, including about you and me. I wanted to share it with you."

He released her, and she crossed the room to where his Bible rested on the table. She opened it to Jeremiah 29:11 and read, "For I know the thoughts that I think toward you, saith the LORD, thoughts of peace, and not of evil, to give you an expected end."

Her eyes met his, and she smiled.

He slipped his arm around her and looked down at the verse she was showing him. "I underlined it," she said.

He planted a kiss on her forehead and then a longer one on her lips.

"Our life verse, Annalee. We'll face our tomorrows with confidence, unafraid."

Analee smiled again as he held her. Morning couldn't come quickly enough. She could hardly wait for the next epoch of her life to begin.

Harvest House Publishers
For the Best in Inspirational Fiction

❧

Linda Chaikin
Desert Rose
A DAY TO REMEMBER
Monday's Child
Wednesday's Child
Thursday's Child
Friday's Child

Mindy Starns Clark
THE MILLION DOLLAR
MYSTERIES
A Penny for Your Thoughts
Don't Take Any Wooden Nickels
A Dime a Dozen

Sally John
THE OTHER WAY HOME
A Journey by Chance
After All These Years
Just to See You Smile
The Winding Road Home

Roxanne Henke
COMING HOME TO BREWSTER
After Anne
Finding Ruth

Craig Parshall
CHAMBERS OF JUSTICE
The Resurrection File
Custody of the State
The Accused

Debra White Smith
Second Chances
The Awakening
A Shelter in the Storm
To Rome with Love
For Your Heart Only
This Time Around
Let's Begin Again

Lori Wick
THE YELLOW ROSE TRILOGY
Every Little Thing About You
A Texas Sky
City Girl

CONTEMPORARY FICTION
Sophie's Heart
Beyond the Picket Fence
Pretense
The Princess
Bamboo & Lace

THE ENGLISH GARDEN
The Proposal
The Rescue
The Visitor
The Pursuit

❧